P9-EDM-217

The

Countess

The
Countess

Catherine Coulter

COUNTY LIBRARY
DISCARD
TILLAMOOK, ORE.

DOUBLEDAY DIRECT LARGE PRINT EDITION

A SIGNET BOOK

This Large Print Edition, prepared especially for Doubleday Direct, Inc., contains the complete unabridged text of the original Publisher's Edition.

SIGNET
Published by New American Library, a division of Penguin Putnam Inc., 375 Hudson Street, New York, New York 10014, U.S.A.
Penguin Books Ltd, 27 Wrights Lane, London W8 5TZ, England
Penguin Books Australia Ltd, Ringwood, Victoria, Australia
Penguin Books Canada Ltd, 10 Alcorn Avenue, Toronto, Ontario, Canada M4V 3B2
Penguin Books (N.Z.) Ltd, 182–190 Wairau Road, Auckland 10, New Zealand

Penguin Books Ltd, Registered Offices: Harmondsworth, Middlesex, England

First published by Signet, an imprint of New American Library, a division of Penguin Putnam Inc.
Originally published in a somewhat different version by Signet under the title *The Autumn Countess*.

Copyright © Catherine Coulter, 1999

Excerpt from *White Knight*, copyright © Jaclyn Reding, 1999

All rights reserved

ISBN 0-7394-0572-1

 REGISTERED TRADEMARK—MARCA REGISTRADA

Printed in the United States of America

Without limiting the rights under copyright reserved above, no part of this publication may be reproduced, stored in or introduced into a retrieval system, or transmitted, in any form, or by any means (electronic, mechanical, photocopying, recording, or otherwise), without the prior written permission of both the copyright owner and the above publisher of this book.

**This Large Print Book carries the
Seal of Approval of N.A.V.H.**

CSABA—A Real Winner

Chapter One

Of course I didn't know who he was the first time I saw him. Nor did I really care who he was—not at first. It was only three weeks after I'd buried my grandfather. My cousin Peter, who had miraculously survived Waterloo unscathed, except for his soul, he wrote me, had been unable to come home from Paris until the French, who, he always said, lived in a constant state of overwrought emotion, had accepted Louis XVIII, their rightful, albeit idiot, of a king.

At the moment, unlike the French, I didn't feel much of anything.

Until I saw him.

I was in the park walking George—my Dandie Dinmont terrier, whom some people believed to be ugly as a devil's familiar on a bad day—oblivious of all the beautifully dressed people driving around in their landaus, riding their prime horseflesh, or simply walking, as I was. George and I were both silent, George out of habit, as there had been little else but silence since Grandfather had died. He was silent even when I picked up a small tree branch and threw it a good twenty feet away for him to fetch, an activity that usually sent him barking hysterically, leaping and bounding about until he clamped his jaws around the wild prey he'd captured and wrestled it to the ground. He was silent in his chase. He managed to get the branch, but it was at a cost.

The man beat him to it, picking up the branch, eyeing George, then giving my dog a blinding smile even as he threw it a good thirty feet. He stood there, hands on hips, watching George, again silent, run so fast his runty legs were a blur. Instead of bringing his beloved mistress—namely me—the branch, George trotted back to the man, tail high and wagging as steady as a metronome, and deposited the branch at his booted feet.

"George," I said, too loudly, "come away now. You know that you are the king of dogs. You have the silkiest topknot in creation. God looks down upon you daily and is very pleased. Come along. I don't want anyone to steal you."

"It's true he is a magnificent animal," the man called out, and I knew sarcasm when it punched me in the nose. "Yes, he is blessed with an amazing presence, but I swear I am not thinking of his abduction for a possible ransom. You know, though, there may be some people, dolts naturally, who just might say that with all that mustard and red hair, someone would steal him in order to blind an enemy."

"He doesn't have mustard and red hair. Mustard on a dog is ridiculous. It's more a fawn and a lovely reddish-brown sort of color." I walked to where the man stood with my terrier. I thought George's colors, particularly the fawn, even though one could perhaps call it, unkindly, sickly yellow, was splendid. At least there wasn't all that much of it, since George wasn't even twelve inches high and weighed only a bit over a stone. I frowned as I looked at him. His coat, a crispy mixture of both hard and soft hairs, needed a good brushing. I hadn't groomed him for nearly a week. I'd been sunk too deep inside myself. I felt guilty for ignoring him.

As for George, the little traitor looked besotted. I came down on my knees and patted his large domed head, peeled back his silky hair, and looked him straight in his very large and intelligent eyes. "Listen to me, you miniature ingrate. I'm the one who feeds you, who walks you, who puts up with your snoring when you've eaten too much of Cook's rabbit stew at night. I am going to walk away now, and I want you to come with me. Do you understand, George?"

George cocked his head at me, then turned to the man who had come down on his knees beside me, his damned eyes all fluid and adoring. The man said, as he tried for a disarming shrug, "Try not to be upset. You see, animals adore me. I was born with this gift, a sort of power, if you will. If I'm not careful, when I merely go for a walk on Bond Street all the frivolous little dogs the grand ladies are carrying about leap from their arms and chase after me. Dogs all over Piccadilly hunt me down. I try to ignore them. I always return them to their owners, but it just doesn't stop. What am I to do?"

Humor, I thought, something that hadn't been in my life for more weeks than I could now easily remember, hit me between the eyes. I smiled, unable not to. He smiled back at me, a beautiful white-toothed smile, took my hand, and helped me to my feet. He was big, too big, and too tall. Most of all, he was too young. He wasn't just there—he overwhelmed. Immediately I took a step back, then another.

"George," I said, growing more uncomfortable by the minute, "it's time to see what Mrs. Dooley has made for our lunch. You know that on Tuesdays, she does something very special with bacon for you. Yes, bacon, fried down to its core, cooked so stiff you can bang it on the floor several times before it crumbles. Come along, now. You will ignore this gentleman. He may be nice to you here, where there's an audience who can see how talented he is with you, but he doesn't want you to catch his coattails in your teeth and pursue him home. Come along."

I turned then and walked away, praying

that George wouldn't stay with the man, wagging his tail and cocking his very homely large head in that cute way he had, his ears at half-mast, that clearly said, "Do you really think she has bacon for my dinner?"

"Wait," the man called after me, coming after me, his hand raised. "I don't know who you are." But I didn't wait. I didn't want him to know my name. Besides, why would he care? Didn't he see that I was wearing deep mourning? Didn't he know that being three feet away from him was too close? I even quickened my step. He was big and tall, and he was too young, too strong. No, I thought, he couldn't do anything here, in the middle of the park, with all these people about. I merely shook my head, but didn't turn around. I nearly shouted with relief when I looked down to see George trotting beside me, his tongue lolling, carrying that branch in his mouth, his topknot flopping up and down. I did turn once I reached the corner.

The man wasn't there.

Well, what did I expect? That he would unfold a pair of wings and fly after me? Snatch up both me and George and haul us off to a derelict old castle? No, he wasn't a monster, he wasn't bent on no good, but he was a man, I thought, too young, and too sure of himself. He was capable of things I couldn't bear to think about. But he'd made me laugh. Imagine.

We went home, George to eat not bacon, but rabbit stew for dinner and snore all night, and I to read some soul-wrenching poetry by Coleridge—*The death-fires danced at night*—and wonder if he had written that line inside a cloud of opium.

I forgot the man.

The second time I saw him, I didn't know who he was then either.

I was still swathed in black, and this time I even wore a black veil that half covered my face. When I came out of Hookham's bookshop, he was just standing there holding an open umbrella, for it had begun to drizzle. He wore a smile on his tanned face, aimed at me.

I stopped in my tracks. I wanted to ask him what in heaven's name he was doing here, beaming that brilliant smile at me, but what came out of my mouth was "How can you be so tanned when there hasn't been a hint of sun in over two days?"

The smile smoothed out, but it was still

there, lurking, waiting to become a laugh. I knew it. "At least this time you've looked at my face, something you refused to do that first day we met in the park. I have some Spanish blood in me, something my father abhorred, but he fell in love with my mother, Isabella Maria, you see, and so I was born. I wonder what he would think of me now, so unlike a pure-blooded Englishman, all pale and pink-cheeked, were he still alive."

"Well, that does explain it," I said, nodded to him, and added, "Good day," and walked away. I wasn't really surprised when the rain suddenly came down thick and hard, because, after all, it was England. What I hadn't realized was that he was just behind me, the umbrella now held over my head.

Well, no hope for it. I turned again to face him. "Thank you for keeping me dry. What are you doing here?"

"I saw you buying a book inside. It's raining. You don't have an umbrella. I plan to protect you from the harsh elements, see you to wherever you wish to go, and thus earn your undying gratitude."

"Excuse me," I said, looking up at that iron-gray sky. "Harsh elements? Are you mad? This is England."

And he threw back his head and laughed. He'd laughed at what I'd said. I tried to frown at him. He took a step closer, but I wasn't worried. There were at least a dozen people either hurrying through the rain or setting their umbrellas over their heads.

"Where may I escort you, Miss—?"

I prepared to walk away again. He lightly touched his hand to my arm. I stopped dead, didn't move, just stood there, waiting to see what he'd do.

"Very well," he said slowly, eyeing me, and I knew he wanted to pull the veil off my face and stare me hard in the eyes. But, of course, he couldn't. He said, "I had hoped that George would prove a suitable chaperon and acquaintance to vouch for me that first time in the park. But he wasn't then, and he isn't, unfortunately, here now. If not a dog, then I must find a human acquaintance to introduce us properly. You are obviously a lady of rigid social code. Do you see anyone you know and trust walking by who would perhaps pause to introduce us properly?"

The urge to laugh was strong, too strong. It was wrong to want to laugh now, very wrong. Grandfather had been dead only a month. No, no laughter.

I stared at his beautifully fashioned cravat, then worked my way up to his chin. He had a dimple in that stubborn-looking chin of his, and he was still smiling down at me, all white teeth and good humor. Since the rain was coming down at a fine clip now, I didn't step away from him. I didn't trust him an inch, nor that winsome smile of his, but I wasn't stupid. I didn't want to get soaked. "What do you want?"

"I want to know who you are so that I may meet your parents and all your siblings and the rest of your pets, and assure them that I'm not some devil-may-care rogue bent on ravishing their fair relative. I'd like take you for an ice at Gunthers. I'd like to take you riding. I'd like to make you laugh again."

All that, I thought, and knew it was impossible. "I have only one sibling—actually he's my cousin—and he's in Paris. He would shoot your head off if he saw you bothering me like this."

The man stopped smiling. "You mean bothering you as in keeping you from getting soaked down to your lovely slippers?"

"Well, not exactly."

"That's a beginning. Now, you're in mourning, deep mourning. Does that mean that everyone you chance to meet must be long in the mouth and sigh and prepare to hand you a handkerchief?"

He was hard with muscle, just like Peter. I recognized that even though he was dressed elegantly in riding clothes, which meant, of course, tight buckskins, a frilled white shirt, a jacket no man could get into without a lot of help, and highly polished black boots that came to his knees. A fine figure of a man, my grandfather would have said. "I don't want a handkerchief from you. As for you being long in the mouth, I don't think you have it in you. Your mouth is too busy laughing."

"Thank you."

"I hadn't really meant that as a compliment, it simply came out that way, by accident."

"I know."

"I am merely going about my business, not whining or begging for sympathy, or quivering my lips, and you just turn up like—"

"Please don't make me a bad penny."

"Very well. You just turn up like mad Uncle

Albert, whom we keep locked in the third-floor attic, but who periodically bribes the tweeney and escapes."

He laughed. He had a wonderful laugh, full and rich and heady. I hadn't heard a laugh like that in far too long, truth be told. Not since the first time I saw him in the park. Had I inadvertently been funny? I hadn't meant to be. Truly, there wasn't any more humor in my life. When I had thrown the first clods of earth on Grandfather's grave, I decided that twenty-one years of smiles and laughter were enough to grant any human being—more than enough. Grandfather had been in my life since I was ten, when my mother had died, my father had left the country, and Peter was at Eton. And Grandfather had loved to laugh. To my utter embarrassment, tears leaked out of my eyes and slid down my face.

They stuck to the wretched net veil. I pulled the veil back and wiped the back of my hand over my eyes. The tears kept coming. It was humiliating.

"I'm sorry," the man said. "Very sorry. Whom did you lose?"

"My grandfather."

"I lost mine five years ago. It was difficult.

Actually, though, to be honest about it, it is my grandmother I miss the most of all of them. She loved me more than the sunsets in Ireland, she'd tell me. She was from Galway, you know, where she said the sunsets were the most beautiful in the world. Then, she said, she loved my grandfather so much, she willingly said good-bye to the sunsets, married him, and came to England. I never heard of her speak of the sunsets in Yorkshire."

For a moment I thought he was going to cry. I didn't want him to be nice, perhaps even to have an inkling about what I was feeling. I wanted him to be a man, and act like a man. That way I would know what he was without having to bother with his name. My tears dried up.

Then he offered me his left hand, since his right hand was still holding the umbrella over both of us. It was raining so hard it was as if we were enclosed in a small gray world, completely alone. I didn't like that, but I did like the umbrella. I wasn't even damp.

"No," I said, looking at his hand, which didn't even have a glove on it. Like his face, that hand was tanned. I wasn't about to touch that hand. It was large, the fingers blunt and strong. "No," I said again. "I don't want to meet you. I live with my companion, Miss Crislock, and we have no visitors, since we're in mourning."

"How long do you anticipate this blacking out of life?"

"Blacking out of life? I'm doing no such thing. I loved my grandfather. I miss him. I am respecting his memory. Also, truth be told, I am rather angry at him for dying and leaving me here alone, to go on without him, to have no one anymore for me. He shouldn't have died and left me. He was old, but he wasn't ill. Everything was fine until he went riding and his horse slipped in a patch of mud. He shot off his horse's back, hit his head against an oak tree, and fell unconscious. He never woke up. I protected him from the doctor, who wanted to bleed him every day, the idiot. I pleaded with Grandfather, I promised to let him eat all of Cook's apple tarts he wanted, I begged him not to leave me, to open his eyes and smile at me—even curse at me, something he enjoyed as much as laughter—but he didn't. I don't wish to be reminded just yet that life simply goes swimmingly on its way despite the fact that I have lost the single most important person in my life through an idiotic accident, and no one else cares."

"How can someone care if he can't even find out your name?"

"Good day, sir."

This time he didn't follow me. I was soaked within seconds. The veil stuck to my face like a second skin, and itched like sticking plaster. *Blacking out of life.* What a ridiculous thing to say.

And cruel. He'd said it because I'd refused to tell him who I was. Men were hurtful. They thought only of themselves; the important things to them were those things that only they wanted and desired.

My grandfather had died. I was grieving. Who would not with a grandfather like him? I was not blacking out my life.

The third time I saw him I still had no idea who he was. He was speaking with a friend of my grandfather's, Theodore, Lord Anston, a gentleman who still covered his bald head with a thick curling coal-black wig, wore knee breeches everywhere—and not just to Almack's on Wednesday nights. He rode with his hounds in Hyde Park, chasing not foxes, but pretty ladies and their maids. My grandfather had once told me, laughing softly behind his hand, that Theo had even worn black satin knee breeches to a mill held out on Hounslow Heath. One of the fighters had been so startled at the sight that he'd dropped his hands for a moment and stared. His opponent had knocked him flat.

Lord Anston grinned to display his own surprisingly perfect teeth, patted the man's shoulder, and thwacked his lion-headed cane on the flagstone. He was wearing black satin shoes with large silver buckles. He strolled, I thought, very gracefully for a man walking two inches off the ground.

If I'd moved more quickly, the man wouldn't have seen me, but I was looking at those shoes of Lord Anston's, wondering how they'd look on me; then I stared at a mud puddle not three feet away, mesmerized, because I knew he was going to step into it, and thus I didn't move in time. He was on me in the next two seconds, smiling that white-toothed smile of his as he said, "What? No George? Poor fellow, he'll grow fat with lack of exercise."

"George suffers from an ague right now. He's improving, but it is still too soon to bring him out into the elements." There weren't really any elements to speak of, it being a bright sunny day, but the man merely nodded. He said, as would a wise man pontificating, "The ague is always a tricky business. I would keep George close until he's able to stick his tail up straight and lick your hand at the same time."

I smiled, damn him, seeing George and that flagpole tail of his at breakfast, wagging wildly when Mrs. Dooley had hand-fed him a good dozen salmon balls, all small and hand-rolled.

"I've got you now," he said, and I took a step back before I realized it wasn't at all necessary. He cocked his head to one side, in question, but I wasn't about to tell him that I didn't trust him or any other man any further than I could spit in that mud puddle some three feet away from me.

"Don't be afraid," he said finally, and he was frowning, perplexed, his head still cocked. "What I meant was if a man can make a woman laugh, she's his."

I was shaking my head when he added, smiling again now, "That was a jest, but not really. Lord Anston told me who you were. I told him not to scare you off by calling out to you. And he said, 'Eh, what, John? Scare off that Jameson girl? Ha! Not a scared bone in that melodious little body of hers. She sings, you know, which makes for a melodious throat. Perhaps the melodiousness extends to the rest of her, but I don't really know anything else about her body. Maybe it's sweet, who knows?' Yes, that's exactly what Lord Anston said. He also said he'd known you since you were puking up milk on his shirt collar."

"It's possible," I said. "But I don't remember doing that. Lord Anston was a lifelong friend of my grandfather's. I play the pianoforte much better than I sing. My fingers are melodious, not my throat."

"He told me who you were. I must admit that it surprised me. How small the world shows itself sometimes. You're Peter Wilton's cousin. I've known Peter since we were boys at Eton. You're Andrea. Peter has spoken of you countless times."

"No," I said. "I'm not Andrea. You've made a dreadful, yet perfectly understandable, mistake. Mistakes happen. You will not dwell upon it. You will forget it by tomorrow. Good-bye. I wish you a good day."

I looked back when I reached the corner. He was standing there, just looking after me, his head still cocked in question. He raised his hand to me, then slowly lowered his arm and turned away.

It was the third time I'd seen him, and I still didn't know who he was. Just his first name: *John*. A common, ordinary name, but I knew he wasn't either of those things.

Knowing his first name was fine. I wouldn't ever know anything more about him. I knew to the soles of my slippers that he was dangerous.

Any man who wore laughter like a well-loved shirt was dangerous.

Chapter Two

I was lying on one of Grandfather's beautiful Axminster carpets, my feet propped up on his big leather chair, reading about my hero, Lord Nelson. If only I had been aboard the *Victory* with him, to guard his back, I know that he would still be alive today. At least he had known he'd won the battle before he died. Now he was only a beloved memory, a part of history, a hero for the ages and the pages of books. But I'd wager anytime that he'd rather be here, with me, telling me his adventures, particularly the amorous ones involving Mrs. Hamilton. Ah, what wickedness, Grandfather would say. Not that I approved, but that was the way things were. I'd learned that at a very young age. It was infuriating, and it was despicable, but it was the way things were.

"A man's man he was," Grandfather had told me more times than I could remember. "He didn't cater to incompetence, deplored the madness of the king, fought the ministry to get enough money, ships, and men to fight those damnable French, and he remained true to his country. I knew him well. I will never know another man with more guts and courage."

And, sometimes, when Grandfather was feeling a bit of the devil's encouragement, he would tell me how Lady Hamilton had wanted him, not Lord Nelson, but Grandfather had been married, more's the pity, and so she'd had to accept Lord Nelson. "He was short, you know, Andy. Dreadfully short, but he made up for it with brains. Sometimes his brains didn't help him, though. He couldn't seem to figure out how to keep the ladies happy, despite all those brains he had. Not to say that ladies are stupid— they're not. Just look at your grandmother; now, there was a lady who kept me at half-mast, her tongue and her brain worked so well together. Well-oiled, both tongue and brain.

"No, what I mean is that Lord Nelson was always coming up with excellent new strategies, and never one of them involved how to make a lady happy."

I wanted to ask him where he got that precious theory. I wanted to tell him that men only wanted to make themselves happy. Once they had a woman in their power, why would they care?

"Andy, where the devil are you?"

I looked up at my cousin, Peter.

"Peter." I had to look a long way up to get to his face. "Goodness, you're in Paris. But now you're not. You're here."

"And you're lying there on the floor with your feet up and a book pressed to your nose. I've pictured you in my mind that way more times than you can imagine."

I leapt from the floor and hurled myself at him. Luckily for me, he did raise his arms in time to catch me. I kissed his face thoroughly, even his earlobes. "You're home," I said in his ear and kept kissing him and hugging him.

He was laughing as he hugged me back. Finally, he set me on my feet and held me back from him. "You're looking well," he said at last, and I knew a lie when I heard it. I looked white and thin and had eyes that were so shadowed they could scare children away from the door on a sunny day.

I kept rubbing my hands up and down his arms, wanting to reassure myself that he was really here, with me. "Why are you here? I didn't expect you. Oh, goodness, is something wrong?"

Peter dropped his arms. "I won't be here long," he said over his shoulder as he walked to the sideboard and poured himself a brandy. "I must return to Paris soon." He held up the decanter, and I nodded. He poured me a bit in one of grandmother's magnificent crystal snifters.

We clicked our glasses together and drank. I realized then that he was angry. How very odd to see his movements so measured, to see how he was holding himself in. I stepped back and waited. I hadn't seen him for six months. He hadn't changed, save he was perhaps more handsome now than when he'd left England the previous May to go to Brussels. I'd never prayed so often or so rigorously in my life as in those weeks before the fateful Battle of Waterloo. Peter was Grandfather's heir, son of Rockford Wilton, who had died, his wife with him, when Peter had been only five years old. He'd been nominally raised in my parents' household until Grandfather deemed Peter ready to go to Eton. I remember that Peter had been fond of my mother. I had no idea what he had thought of my father.

Peter reminded me of that man, John, a man I still didn't know even if I had seen him on three different occasions.

That last time had been three months ago. Time had dragged. It was now in November, cold and damp, not a glimmer of sun to be seen for days at a time. I hated it. The air was thick with smoke from too many coal fires. White wasn't the color to wear during a cold London autumn and winter.

I wanted to go to the country, where the air was clean and fresh, but Miss Crislock wasn't well. I couldn't very well demand that she travel for four days—at least not now.

Grandfather's study was warm, the draperies drawn against the cold gray late afternoon. "Sit down, Peter," I said at last, still drinking in the sight of him, "and tell me why you're angry."

"I'm not angry," he said in an amazingly clipped, hard voice that could shatter the glass I was holding.

I realized then that Mrs. Pringe, my grandfather's housekeeper for many years longer than I had been on this earth, was standing in the open doorway, watching us, one of her thick black eyebrows arched upward a good inch.

"I should like some tea, Mrs. Pringe," I said, nodding to her. Mrs. Pringe was a large lady, larger than Grandfather had been, and she always wore heavy bombazine violet gowns. I could tell she didn't want to leave, bless her. She'd known both of us forever. She wanted to know what was going on. She wanted to fix whatever was wrong. And she'd always scented when something was out of kilter. I, naturally, had a very good idea why Peter was here and why he was angry, but still, I figured I had the right of first hearing, without Mrs. Pringe hovering with pursed lips and patting hands.

But Peter just stood there, staring at me as if I were a soldier in his unit and I had sent my bayonet through a friend rather than a foe. Too handsome for his own good, Grandfather had always said. Too much hair, more than a young man needs or deserves, he would howl. There was no justice in life, none at all. Grandfather had lost most of his hair six months shy of his fortieth year.

Peter could have looked like an angel or a monster, it wouldn't have mattered to me. I wasn't afraid of Peter. I'd trusted him implicitly since I'd been three years old and he'd pulled me out of a sinking mud hole by a pond that was dragging me under. I had worshiped him ever since, much to his disgust and chagrin, since he'd been a strapping boy at Eton and had occasionally brought his friends home, only to have his little cousin staring up at him with naked adoration, her skinny arms held wide for him to pick her up.

"Tell me that it isn't true," he said at last.

"Is this why you came here? Is this why you're angry?"

"Naturally. I knew nothing of this. I had to learn about it from Major Henchly, who read it in a letter from his wife. You didn't even have the nerve to write me and tell me yourself what you planned to do. Tell me it's a mistake, a bit of unappetizing gossip, nothing more. Tell me."

"I'm twenty-one years old. I am my own

woman. I don't need anyone's permission to do anything. You are not my guardian, Peter."

"You're wrong there. Not only am I the seventh Duke of Broughton, I am also your guardian. You may be a grown woman, but you're still a woman and that means that as long as there is a male relative, it is his responsibility to see that you come to no harm."

"We're not talking about protecting me from harm here, Peter, we're talking marriage, a simple, straightforward marriage."

"Nothing in your life to date has been simple or straightforward. You have a Machiavellian mind, Andy. Grandfather always told me you did. He marveled at the way your mind worked, wrote me endlessly about how you would solve this puzzle, come up with three options for the resolution of another problem, and dance until dawn, all at the same time. He said you thirsted after conundrums.

"In my opinion, your mind is a woman's mind, twisted and brilliant, all of it mixed together, and many times you don't realize which one is which."

"Have you just insulted me?"

"No. You'll know it well enough when I insult you. Like now. Prepare yourself." But he didn't give me more than a second for any preparation. He shouted right in my face, "You're an idiot, Andy, if this nonsense is true. A blithering idiot who needs to be locked away, something I might well consider."

"You're a man when it comes down to it," I shouted back, and I heard my own deep anger, the miserable bitterness lacing through my words. "I wouldn't be surprised at how low even you would stoop, if it pleased you."

He backed up a step, reined himself in, and said more quietly, "I apologize for yelling at you. No, we are not going to leap for each other's throats or say things that will do irreparable damage. I'm going to be calm about this. I am your senior by nearly six years. I am a man filled with reason, overflowing with common sense. I am now the Duke of Broughton. You are my responsibility now. I love you. But now it's time for you to tell me the truth."

I watched, holding my tongue, fascinated at the fury I saw building up in him. He drew in a deep breath, held it, then it burst out, and he shouted again at the top of his lungs, "What the devil has gotten into you, you damnable twit? And don't try to sidetrack the issue, as you do so well. Tell me what the hell is in that twisted mind of yours."

I took another sip of my brandy, still silent. That caught his attention. He frowned, then proceeded to sidetrack himself. "I gave it to you, damn me. You shouldn't drink that stuff. Only men drink brandy. Grandfather gave you the taste for it. Curse *him* for not realizing you were just a thirteen-year-old girl when he gave you your first snifter. Damnation, speak to me, Andy, and don't you dare tell me why you must needs drink brandy."

"I've done what I deemed right and proper for me," I said, and nothing more. I waited. There were usually after explosions, smaller outbursts, after the great initial one or two. But not this time. This time Peter pointed to a lovely brocade wing chair. "Sit and listen to me."

I sat.

"I've come from Grandfather's advocate, Craigsdale. I'd been putting it off. You are a very rich young lady, but you already know that, don't you?"

"Yes. Very rich, that's me."

"I went to see Craigsdale before coming to see you because I needed time to think about all this. Naturally he brought it up, so I guess it's the truth, even though I'm praying that you've broken it off. Don't do it, Andy. Don't."

"I will do it," I said. "I'm sorry that you disapprove, Peter, but when you peel things right down to the core of the apple, it's my life, my choice, not yours, not anyone else's. You may be my guardian, but you are not my jailer. I shall do what I believe is best for me. Do you think I am so stupid, so unthinking, that I would agree to something that could harm me?"

"Andrea," Peter said, and his use of my full name nearly brought me to my knees. He hadn't called me Andrea since I had been fifteen and crammed my mare over a fence too high for my abilities and nearly broke both my legs. He'd been furious, which at the time I hadn't understood, since I was hurting so badly I wanted to die. But then I did understand, later. Now I was Andrea again. He was very upset with me.

He said, "I happen to know that the Earl of Devbridge is in his fifties, if not older, a widower, and has two nephews, one of whom is my age, who is his heir. In short, he is an old man, much too old a man to wed a girl who is barely twenty-one years old. Tell me that Henchly's wife and Craigsdale are wrong. Tell me you have retracted this, or that it was all malicious gossip in the first place, or tell me you have come to your senses and sent the earl about his damned business." He paused a moment, and eyed me. "Dammit, you're white as my cravat. What the hell is wrong with you? You did it, didn't you? Damnation, you've said you would marry this wretched old man."

I had the horrible urge to beg his forgiveness in the face of his absolute disgust and disbelief, but I didn't. I just sat there, watching my cousin, realizing fully now the depths of his shock, of his incredulity. But it wasn't ridiculous. There were many spring-winter marriages, and no one said anything about those decisions. Surely Lawrence wasn't beyond autumn in his years. He still had all his own teeth. He wasn't stooped over or didn't need to keep his foot swathed in covers and propped up on a stool because of the gout.

"I would have informed you," I said. "I

would have written you a letter. I didn't intend for you to come to the ceremony, for it will be a very small one, and you didn't come to Grandfather's funeral, did you? And so why would you come to my wedding? Yes, I would have written to you tomorrow."

He jumped up from the settee and paced the long narrow room. Then he came up to me, leaned over, and cupped my chin in his hand. He forced my face up. "Damn you, look at me."

"I'm looking."

"Yes, you are, but are you seeing? See me, Andy, see your cousin who loves you, who thinks of you as he would a beloved sister. All right, I've yelled enough. Yelling never does anything except to another man. With another man, yelling unplugs the sink and lets everything erupt, mainly curses to blue the air and a fist here or there, ending up with reasonable words.

"With women, it brings either tears or mutiny. But it doesn't bring wisdom or reason. No, listen to me, now, as well as look at me. I won't yell at you anymore. All I ask is that you tell me why you've agreed to marry a man who is nearly three times your age."

What could I say that sounded logical and

reasonable? That it was done all the time and what was his problem? No, that would make him froth at the mouth. He was still staring down at me, still holding my chin against his palm. I had to say something that would make sense to him. Instead, what came out of my mouth was "The earl isn't that old."

He cursed, let my chin go, and resumed his pacing. At the far end of the library, he called out, "You can't be marrying him for social position, and certainly not for money. For God's sake, you're rich and you are the granddaughter of a duke. You can look as high as you wish for a husband, and that includes a man who still has his own teeth, has his feet planted firmly in this century and not in the last, a modicum of energy, some muscle, and a flat belly." He paused for a moment and took a deep breath. "Oh, the devil. Listen, Andy, I know it has been diffi-cult without Grandfather. And I wasn't here to help you. But I had responsibilities, and you told me you understood. Ah, curse me. That doesn't really say much of anything, does it? Look, I'm sorry I chose to remain in Paris rather than come back to London to be with you. I'm sorry. You're not marrying this man because you're punishing me, are you?"

Men, I thought, did they honestly believe that everything revolved around them? That all of a person's decisions and actions had to, perforce, put them in the very center?

I felt tears sting my eyes. Grandfather had always been in the center of things, and I had never minded, never even thought about it. Dear God, how I missed him. The memories sometimes overwhelmed me. They did now, and I just couldn't stem them. I knuckled away the ridiculous tears. Grandfather had disapproved of tears, actually hated them. I think now it was because my grandmother had cried very seldom, and when she did, it always brought him to his knees. If they were arguing, she could cry without saying a word, and he'd curse in a whisper, fold up, and unconditionally surrender.

"I'm sorry, love," Peter said, coming down on his knees next to my chair. "I'm so sorry." And he pulled me into his arms.

I laid my head on his shoulder. There weren't any more tears, but the feel of him, the strong beat of his heart against my chest, the smell of him—musk and lemon—

it was all so very familiar, so beloved, it all filled my memories with belonging, with acceptance, with unconditional love.

"Come, tell me about it," he said as he lightly stroked his big hands over my back.

I stayed where I was, leaning into my cousin's shoulder. I didn't want to tell him anything. I just wanted to stay where I was, and have him be silent. Just hold me, I wanted to tell him. Don't demand anything of me.

Of course he did. "Tell me, Andy. Tell me."

Chapter Three

There was no hope for it.

I said at last, my voice dry now because the tears had faded into the old pain, "When Grandfather died, I had no one to help me. Miss Crislock is a distant cousin, and she has been with me forever, but she always viewed Grandfather with a mixture of fear and anxiety. She had no wonderful memories of him like I did, just autocratic ones. I would say something to her about when he did this or that, and she would just stare at me and say, 'now, now, my dear child.' I suppose I just stopped talking since there was no one else."

His big hands continued rubbing my back. "You could have written to me. You could have told me to get my selfish hind end home."

"No, it was impossible. I did try to write to you, several times, but the words just wouldn't come. I felt stupid and helpless. And very alone. Then I met this man, no, not met. I just happened to see him on three different occasions. He wanted to meet me, but I wouldn't allow it. He found out from Lord Anston who I was. He said he knew you."

"What is his name?"

"I don't know. Well, his first name is John. He made me laugh, and he laughed at things that came out of my mouth. He was marvelous with George."

"I know at least half a dozen Johns. No hint of a last name? Or anything about his family?"

I shook my head.

"All right, get on with it, Andy. It won't get easier with waiting. Spill it."

"All right. About two months ago, the earl came to the house. He told me that his father had been one of Grandfather's dearest friends, that he himself had admired and respected Grandfather for nearly all his life. He was kind to me, always sincere and direct. He was never cloying or oozing that false sympathy that drives me to the brandy bottle."

I paused a moment and smiled when I felt him chuckle. "He made me feel that he understood the sudden emptiness, the god-awful pain of it all. But he didn't treat me like a helpless female in need of a man's care.

"We talked of Grandfather, for even though Grandfather had been his father's close friend and not his, still, he told me, he and Grandfather had been friends. He said that Grandfather had made his entry into the *ton* easier by sponsoring him at White's and the Four Horsemen's Club."

Peter frowned. "I never heard Grandfather mention the Earl of Devbridge before, either the former or the current earl. The Devbridge family name is Lyndhurst. Lawrence Lyndhurst. I've heard his name mentioned in passing, but I've never met him, never heard talk of him. Doesn't that seem rather strange to you, Andy?"

I nodded. "Yes, it did, and so I asked the earl why we had never met before. He said that after Grandfather married and retired to

Yorkshire that he and Lawrence's father had lost track of each other. Then Lawrence met Grandfather when he was a young man here in London."

"It's strange," Peter said. He must have felt me tense because he patted my back. "It's all right. We'll work this all out. Tell me more."

"He asked me to marry him three weeks ago. Listen, Peter, I'm not right out of the schoolroom. I'm twenty-one years old, a woman grown. I've given this a lot of thought. Grandfather believed I had a good brain. Please, you must try to understand. I'm not being silly or flighty or pathetic, none of those things. I've given it a great deal of thought. I know that Lawrence can offer me the kind of life I want and need."

Peter pulled away from me. He rose, towering over me, a method of intimidation I'd learned that men used whenever they were losing ground, particularly to a woman. "That is no answer," he said. "Dammit, Andy, what do you want and need—another grandfather?"

I jumped to my feet, then climbed up onto Grandfather's leather chair. It made me at least a foot taller than Peter. "That was uncalled for," I said, leaning toward him, my nose nearly touching his. "What do you know of my wants and needs? You only see me as the little twit who worships you, but you don't know me as a person, Peter, as a woman, a grown woman."

"That's absurd, and you know it."

"Ha," I said. "You're a man. You're free. You decided you wanted to fight Napoleon. Even as Grandfather's heir, you hared off, putting yourself in harm's way, not worrying that anyone would criticize you or condemn you for pleasing yourself.

"Can you even begin to imagine what would happen to me if I decided that I wanted to travel, say, with just a companion? Goodness, I would be locked away in Bedlam or utterly condemned by friends and foes alike. It isn't fair. Just look at you. You're appalled that I could even say such a thing, much less want it." I stopped and sucked in a deep breath.

This was going nowhere. I said, "Forgive me, I've let fly things that don't rightfully belong in this conversation. Wipe that repelled look off your face. No, don't say anything. I'm talking right now."

But he just couldn't help himself. He

shouted, "What do you want? To be like that Stanhope woman and not bathe for months at a time and share your meals with desert rodents and evil-smelling Bedouins? That's bloody idiocy, and well you know it."

I stepped down from the chair and walked away from him. When I turned, we stared at each other across the room. It was a long silence. I said finally, "Well, then, since I'm not going to eat my breakfast with the villains in the desert, then it would appear that I am in full agreement with you. I will marry, just as I'm expected to. I will be a wife, just as I'm expected to be. I will oversee a household, a responsibility that seems to be attached to women alone. No idiocy at all. Nothing at all to be disapproved by society.

"So, Peter, the only problem seems to be in years. You believe the earl is too old for me, and I wouldn't care if he were a hundred."

"Why?"

"Why what? That I don't care about his age?"

"Yes."

"His years are irrelevant to me. As I told you, he is kind. He offers me what I want. I expect no more because there isn't any more. All there is, and I know this all too well, is a good deal less. I will take the earl as my husband and count myself pleased at my bargain."

"Are you telling me that you have fallen in love with this man?"

"No, certainly not. There is no such thing. There are other things, certainly, but with luck and a modicum of honor on his part, I will never have to deal with them."

He walked to the bowed windows, pulled back one of the draperies, and looked out onto the park across the road. He said finally in a meditative voice, as if he were speaking to himself, "Devbridge, from what Craigsdale said, is a rich man. Thus, I don't have to worry that he is in need of your fortune."

"No, he doesn't even require a dowry."

"Very well. You don't love him. He gives you what you say you need and want. Thus, I am forced to conclude what I originally said—you, Andy, need and want another aged mentor. Can it be that the earl in any way resembles our martinet of a grandpapa? Do you really see him as a substitute?"

"Ah, that was quite low, Peter, but I am not going to shout at you. You're just trying to shake me, rile me, make me say things that I don't want to say. Are you quite through now?"

"In your long line of things you were doing, you said marriage, wife, housekeeper. However, you said nothing about presenting the earl with an heir. As I told you, he has a nephew who is currently his heir. That is not the same thing as having your own son as your heir. Doesn't he want to breed one off you, his new, ripe, not to mention very young and quite appetizing, bride?"

It was out of my mouth before I could bite down on those damnable words. "No, there will be none of that, do you hear me? None. Ever."

He cocked his head at me. "Why? Is he too old to perform his husbandly duties? I thought a man had to be on his deathbed before he was incapable of taking a woman."

"Shut up." I shook my fist at him and shouted, "I won't listen to this. You're like all the others, aren't you, Peter? Well, married to the earl I will not have to worry about my husband parading mistresses in front of my nose or bedding the servants. I shall be spared the humiliation of watching my husband indiscriminately spread his favors among all my friends. The earl swore to me that he would not touch me, that he didn't want any children. He swore to me that he has a mistress nicely tucked away to see to his needs. She will never intrude on our life. He swore that he would never hurt me or humiliate me in any way."

Peter looked at me for one long moment and whistled to himself. "I've often wondered how much you knew of your illustrious sire's, ah, amorous exploits. I had hoped that your mother would have had the good sense and intelligence to keep her bitterness and disappointment to herself. But I see that she did not."

"If you would know the truth of it, at the age of ten, I believe I knew more about men's dishonor than any female child alive." I looked at him and then added, no fury at all because I meant it, and it was clear and cold in my mind, "Had I been my mother, I would have killed him."

"Perhaps you would," he said slowly. "Still, you were only ten years old when she died. So young and yet you knew?"

"Yes, I knew. I can still hear my mother's

sobs, still see her white face when he told her of his other women."

"That dratted woman," Peter said, frowning down at the carpet. "I have always pitied her until this moment. After all, she took me in after my parents died, treated me quite well. But now, now I see that she was a selfish woman without an ounce of sense. She poured her misery into your ears, a little girl, not a wise or clever thing to do."

"Don't you dare talk about my mother like that. You don't know, you cannot know what she suffered. You were away at school most of the time. Well, I was there, all of the time. I saw what she suffered. My bastard of a father killed her. Don't you know? She could bear no more humiliation, and—"

"And," Peter finished for me, "she caught a chill and died only a week after reaching Grandfather. Ancient history, my dear, it has nothing to do with you or me. We can curse your father, even feel sorry for your mother, but they have been out of your life for more than ten years now. I repeat, their mistakes, their selfishness, all the tragedies, none of it has anything to do with you."

"I really mean it, Peter, had I been my mother, I would not have run away. I would have taken up a pistol and I would have shot him, and I would have rejoiced when he lay dead at my feet."

He didn't leap on that, and I suppose I was grateful, until he said, "So you are marrying a man you won't have to murder?"

"That is not bloody funny. My father deserved to die for what he did, for what he was, which was a philandering dishonorable bastard. And if you think I would ever take a chance of that happening to me, well, I would rather die first or die trying to take my vengeance on him."

"Jesus," Peter said very quietly. He walked to me and pulled me against him. He didn't say anything for the longest time, just held me. Finally, he said quietly, right next to my ear, "You cannot let your parents' blunders ruin your life. You think to escape your mother's humiliation by marrying a man too old to have desires, or unable. Yes, he has told you he has a mistress. Perhaps it is true. Perhaps he doesn't even want you in his bed. I find that very hard to believe, however. What makes you think you can trust him? You are young enough to be his daughter. Why, my dear, why the hell does he want to marry you? Do you know? Has he told you why?"

"I believe," I said, "that the earl much admires me, as our grandfather's child. He is very fond of me. He enjoys my company. I amuse him. He enjoys pleasing me. He is lonely. He knows I will run his household to perfection. He knows he can count on me. He knows I will not interfere with his private comings and goings. He knows he can trust me. He knows I would never betray him, since I want none of that, ever."

"And if he has lied to you? If he changes his mind and tells you he wants you in his bed?"

"I won't do it. I have told him so. He will not cross that line. Unlike the tolerant attitude of most men when a woman is adamant about something, when I am resolute, he knows it. He believes me."

Peter didn't say anything for the longest time. He walked away from me. He stroked his chin, a habit of long-standing. "Oh, my God," he said, turning back to me. "I wondered why you turned down young Viscount Barresford, an excellent man and sincerely attached to you. And Oliver Trever—another very nice man who worshiped you—you went driving with him once, Grandfather told me, then you refused to see him again.

"You believe to avoid all unhappiness by running from life? By shackling yourself to an old man who swears he won't touch you as a man touches a woman?"

Blacking out of life, that was what John had said. I shook my head. I was silent, there was nothing more to be said, but Peter didn't realize that. "Andy, listen to me. Not all men are like your father. I never heard that my father was unfaithful to my mother. Believe me, Andy, I am not like your father. When I take a wife, I will be faithful to her. Many more men are like me rather than like your father."

Silence lay deeply between us.

He shook his head, and there was such sadness in his voice I wanted to cry. "No, I can see that you refuse to believe that."

I said, then, for there was nothing else to say to reconcile him, "The wedding is Tuesday next. We leave immediately for Devbridge Manor. You are, of course, welcome to come if you wish."

"This is dreadfully wrong, Andy," he said, "and it breaks my heart."

I did not reply, for my throat was choked with tears.

I heard him stride quickly from the library, the doors banging behind him. Through the windows I saw Williams, the groom, bringing around Peter's horse, Champion. He swung a leg over the saddle and was gone.

I curled up in the window seat and stared out at the gathering fog. Peter's final words rang in my head. "This is dreadfully wrong, Andy." *Dreadfully wrong.*

Was he right? Was I escaping life, afraid of repeating my parents' failure? Was I blacking out life? I dashed my hand across my eyes, trying to rub away the tears. And he had said that it broke his heart. But men didn't have hearts that broke, even Peter, though I had little doubt that he believed what he had said. I had no doubt either that he did truly love me. But he hadn't come home when Grandfather had died because he'd had other, more important things to do. And no one had thought very much of it. No one blamed him—no one except me.

No, men took and took and did just as they pleased. They were to be tolerated, perhaps even loved, but never trusted. Even cousins who were so close they were like brothers, and you loved them and they loved you. I would never find myself with child and thus dependent upon a husband.

Grandfather had been different. I prayed that my future husband would be as well.

There was a light tap on the door. Skinny Lord Thorpe, a name Peter had given Thorpe the butler ten years earlier, entered the library, stood straight and proud as any aristocrat in front of me, and announced the arrival of the Earl of Devbridge. I blinked in rapid succession to make the tears recede. Rising from the window seat, I quickly smoothed my gown and my hair.

"Andrea," he said in his smooth, beautifully modulated voice. "Andrea."

I jumped, startled, and looked quickly around me. I wasn't in Grandfather's library in Cavendish Square, but rather sitting across from my new husband in a gently swaying chaise.

Chapter Four

"Andrea," he said yet again, smiling at me, "have you been bored to death, my dear? Or mayhap dreaming a bit yourself? I do believe that I nodded off for a moment. Do forgive me."

"I was just thinking of Peter," I said, refusing to think more about what Peter had said and what I had said in return. Lawrence leaned over and patted my gloved hands. "I know it is difficult for you. I, too, was very disappointed when your cousin refused our invitation. Ah, well, he will grow reconciled once he sees how very happy and content you are with me. He will also be impressed when he sees how your funds continue to accumulate, since my man of business needs but look at a guinea and it leaps to become two guineas."

I laughed. My husband made me laugh, just as John had. I frowned at myself. That man had appeared only three times in my life. He was long gone. He was nothing and no one. It was time to forget him.

"Do you think you can call me Andy, my lord? I have never cared for Andrea. Grandfather only called me by my full name when he was irked at me for some misdeed."

"Andy? A boy's name?"

"I answer to it easily, sir. It's like a very comfortable shoe."

"Very well. It is odd, but I will try. I wish you had mentioned this to me before, then I would have been accustomed to it by now."

"I didn't know if you would approve. I didn't wish to take the chance that you would flee if I told you about my unfeminine name before we were wed."

He smiled at me, truly a charming smile. He really didn't look his age. Since he was tall and quite lean, there were no jowls to add years. His nose wasn't veined and red from too much drinking. His eyes were a dazzling dark blue, and one had but to look at him, listen to him converse for but a few minutes, to realize he was an educated man, a man of sensibility and refinement, whatever those two things meant. I had heard them so very often growing up, that I suppose they were important, and was thus as certain as I could be that he was fully endowed with both of them.

He was dark, his eyebrows full over his eyes. His hair was still thick, and thin streaks of white threaded through the darker brown hair. He was fine-looking, my husband.

Had he been my father, perhaps things would have been different.

And then he said, "Your upbringing was unusual, what with only your grandfather to see you after your mother died. There is much in it that is both charming and disconcerting. We will see."

Whatever that meant, I thought. I watched my husband settle again against the comfortable upholstered cushions and stretch his legs diagonally away from me. He folded his arms gracefully across his chest and tilted his head slightly to one side, resting his chin lightly on his cravat. He seemed peaceful, calm. I was unused to a man who wasn't a volcano, as Grandfather had been. Always quick to rage and equally as quick to laughter.

I said, "Peter told me that you have two nephews who live with you. One of them is his age, Peter said, and he is also your heir."

"Yes," the earl said, "the older boy is my heir. We have, unfortunately, been somewhat estranged over the past years, but he is home, at least I pray he is, by now."

"What happened?"

An eyebrow shot up immediately. He looked ready to blast me, and I suppose it made some sense since my question was on the impertinent side, but I was, after all, his wife now. Then he just nodded, as if to himself, making a decision, drew a deep breath, and gave me a smile that was as shallow as a mud puddle after a light rain. Still, he said easily, "It is just that he is too much like his father. He was greatly distressed when his parents were killed by bandits in the Lowlands of Scotland. He and his brother were only twelve and ten years old when it happened. I was their uncle; my wife had died without children. I had no desire to remarry. Thus they both came to me, and I groomed them to be the sons of the house.

Thomas, the youngest, settled in quite admirably, unlike his brother, John, who fought me from the very first day he arrived at Devbridge Manor."

He saw the question forming on my lips, and added, "He blamed me, I believe, for being alive whilst his father had died. He didn't believe it was fair."

I hadn't meant that at all. "You said his name is John," I said, a catch in my voice. Surely, I thought, surely it couldn't be the same John. There were dozens of Johns hanging about, showing their names everywhere, bunches of Johns coating the countryside, too many to even consider such a coincidence. I said, "I ask because I met a man whose name is John shortly after Grandfather died. All in all, he seemed a pleasant enough man."

"What was his family name?"

"I don't know," I said, and knew I sounded like an idiot. "He was just someone I saw on three different occasions. He enjoyed laughing. He also liked George. As for George, I believe he would have preferred staying with the man, if he could have been certain he would have been fed as well as I feed him."

"Well, then, he can't be my nephew. I

have never heard John laugh. He is a silent, somewhat sullen young man, not at all charming or at all remarkable when it comes to either dealing with me or dealing with estate matters. I have never even seen him with an animal to be able to estimate his charms in that arena. He is, however, something of a war hero, so perhaps he will improve with time.

"To be fair, he hasn't been home very often to have learned much. Yes, time will tell."

"And Thomas?"

"Ah, my sweet, self-absorbed Thomas, who has never given me a moment's concern since he was ten years old. No, he isn't at all selfish, I don't mean that. It is just that he is concerned with every ache and pain he ever feels. The truth is, he quacks himself. Whenever he hurts a finger or bangs an elbow, he must needs read and study every booklet he can find on possible cures. His wife, Amelia, deals well with him. I believe she has an entire closet filled with potions and herbal remedies to treat everything from hairy warts to belly cramps. Whenever the gypsies come around, she is off buying every restorative they possess.

She is the daughter of Viscount Waverleigh, a vastly unusual gentleman. She is quite lovely, and something of a snob—a good thing in most situations, I've found.

"And now, perhaps, John is home to stay."

He grew quiet again, and I looked out the carriage window, surprised at the sudden darkness of the afternoon. It began to drizzle, and I pulled the warm rug snugly about my legs. The chaise was well sprung and quite luxurious, I thought, as I fingered the pale blue satin upholstery. I removed a lemon kid glove so that I could touch the soft fabric, and in doing so, revealed the Devbridge family ring that covered my finger to the knuckle. I gazed at the massive emerald surrounded by diamonds, and realized with a start that I was now the Countess of Devbridge. Had Lawrence's first wife worn it? Had they taken it from her finger when she was dead? Now, that was a gruesome thought. And I wondered how George was faring with Miss Crislock. They quite liked each other, and she had insisted that it was only right that I be alone with my new husband, and not sitting there talking constantly to George.

Not an hour later we arrived in Repford,

where Lawrence had arranged accommodations for us at the Gray Goose Inn. No sooner had we pulled into the inn yard than several boys came running to hold the horses and open the chaise door.

We were greeted at the door with a very low bow from our landlord, who had not a single strand of hair on his shining head, a fact easily ascertained since he was very short. When he bowed, the top of his head was right under my nose.

"Good day, Pratt," Lawrence said. "Your establishment looks prosperous."

"Aye, my lord," Pratt said, wiping his hands on his very clean apron. "I took the advice of yer business feller and am making meself a tidy profit."

Lawrence just nodded. "I trust our rooms are ready? Her ladyship," he added, smiling at me, "is quite fatigued."

I wondered why it was always ladies who were fatigued and never gentlemen.

"Yes, indeed, my lord, if yer lordship and ladyship will jest come with me, I will show ye to yer private parlor."

"Let me get Miss Crislock and George settled," I said. "Then I will join you."

"Surely Miss Crislock can settle herself.

She and Flynt can see to each other. Indeed, Flynt can see to George's needs. I don't wish you to trouble yourself now that you are a married woman."

I didn't particularly like Lawrence's valet, Flynt. He looked too much and said too little. "Miss Crislock is a nervous sort, my lord, unused to change or strange places. Also she was ill. I wish to make sure that she is feeling all right."

"The Gray Goose ain't at all strange," I heard Mr. Pratt say under his breath. "It's common, but not strange."

"Indeed, Mr. Pratt," I said. "Even though I am now a married lady, I don't feel that it's any particular trouble. I will join you shortly, Lawrence." Before he could say anything else I didn't agree with, I was back outside. Flynt, as was his wont, just stood there, silent, watching, doing not a single thing that was helpful. I waited as the coachman assisted her to alight from the carriage. As for George, no sooner had Miss Crislock's feet touched the ground than he leapt into my arms, his tail wagging faster than a windmill in a high wind. I fastened his collar and let him down to the ground. "I'll be back, Milly. Just ask Mr. Pratt to see you to your room."

I just looked at Flynt, who was studying his thumbnail, then laughed when George leapt up a good three feet to grab the stout lead out of my hand. "Oh, no you don't, George. You just trot on ahead. I'm right here."

And so George and I walked and ran and leapt in the dying sunlight in the lovely countryside. He had more energy than I did. It was a good hour before he was content to go to Miss Crislock and settle down to his dinner and to bed.

The Gray Goose parlor was a cozy, wood-paneled room, with a brightly burning fire, smells of roast beef, and a thin veil of smoke that filled the air. I tossed my muff and pelisse on a chair, walked over to the bright fire, and fanned my hands toward the heat. Lawrence, who had been reading a newspaper, now gave orders to Pratt for our supper. When Pratt had bowed himself out, Lawrence joined me by the fire.

"Flynt should have walked George," he said. "It isn't the duty of a married lady."

Was there a list of specific duties a married lady was and wasn't to perform? I sincerely prayed that there wasn't. If there was, I would probably shortly find myself in deep trouble. I said, "Flynt doesn't know George.

Moreover, Flynt doesn't wish to do anything for anyone who isn't you, namely, his master. What's more, George doesn't like him. He missed me and danced around me until he keeled over he was finally so tired."

I thought my husband would say something more, but he didn't.

When Pratt came again into the parlor, he was followed by a large bosomy girl with a lovely wide smile, whose name, we were informed, was Betty.

Lawrence turned to me. "Would half an hour suit you, Andrea, er, Andy, before we dine?"

"Suit me for what? Oh, but I don't need to change." I didn't want to move away from the heady smell of butter-drenched roasted potatoes seeping from beneath one of the silver-domed platters. "I will wash my hands, all right? They do smell rather like dog. Yes, I'll be back in five minutes, no more. Don't eat all that delicious roasted meat yourself, my lord," I called out over my shoulder as I dashed from the parlor. Once in my room, I quickly washed my hands, petted George, and thus had to wash my hands again, kissed Miss Crislock even though her mouth was full of her own dinner and she couldn't kiss me back, then ran lightly back down the stairs.

I paused by a long, narrow mirror that was on the closest wall at the bottom of the stairs. I looked at the pale girl and frowned. I had no reason to be pale. I'd been dashing about in the outdoors for nearly a full hour. What was wrong with me? I looked at the girl again. She looked very alone, very pathetic, really. But that was equally silly, I thought. I was used to being my own mistress and being alone. Now I was still my own mistress, but I was no longer alone. No, now I had a very fine husband. I remembered what Lady Fremont had said behind her hand to me when she'd come to visit the day after our engagement had been announced in the *Gazette.* "What a sly chit you are, Andrea Jameson." Then she'd actually tapped her fan on my arm. It had stung, and I realized she had meant it to. "Here you have trapped one of the most eligible gentlemen about, and you refuse to tell anyone how you did it. But surely, my dear, it is too soon for you to wed? Your dear grandfather only passed from his mortal coil not six months ago? Isn't that right? Shame on you. But I suppose since you have no mama to tell you what is right and what is impulsive—"

The spiteful old bitch. But unlike Peter, no one had seemed to see anything amiss with my marrying Lawrence. Except that we had married too soon. But I simply couldn't bear London any longer. I couldn't. And it wasn't as if I planned to go to Almack's, or dance away the soles of my slippers at balls and wear low-necked gowns.

No, we were going to the country, and there we would remain. My dear Miss Crislock had developed a nasty cough in London that still hadn't gone away. It was doubtless from all the burning coal smoke. The country was the best place for both of us. And my husband, too, of course.

Lawrence sat again by the fire, still reading the *Gazette.* Pratt was busy crowding our table with roasted beef, potatoes, stewed turnips, and peas. Goodness, there was even a brace of partridge tottering toward the edge of the table, and more side dishes than I cared to count.

My stomach growled, loudly.

Lawrence looked up and gave me a pleasant smile.

"I'm glad you only took the time to wash

your hands, Andrea, no, it's Andy. Elsewise you might have collapsed in your bath from hunger."

That good-natured speech didn't sound like he was overly concerned about my consequence. Everything would be all right. I'd married well. My decision was sound.

Every dish was delicious. I couldn't remember when I'd eaten so much. I didn't talk, just ate and ate. I tucked away some of the delicious roasted beef into a napkin for George. I had a mouthful of some sort of partridge when I glanced up at Lawrence. He was looking in some astonishment at my refilled plate. I stopped, my spoon in midair. "Oh, goodness, I am eating more than you ever imagined a young lady eating, aren't I? Do you believe me to be a glutton? I really don't blame you for thinking that. It's just that everything tastes so wonderful, and riding all day, with nothing at all to do, hollows out my stomach—"

Lawrence raised an elegant hand to shut me down, which I did, instantly. "I don't mean to embarrass you by staring, Andrea— no, it's Andy. I'd just forgotten the extraordinary appetites of the young. As one grows older, one either seems to expand or re-tract."

"I'm very relieved that you chose to re-tract," I stopped dead, disbelieving what I had said. I clamped my hands over my still-open mouth, dropped my fork, and stared at my husband, so horrified and embarrassed I wanted to take George's roasted beef pieces and slink away. To add more sticks to the fire, I very nearly said that I was feel-ing matronly now that I'd married him, and hoped I wouldn't expand, but at the last min-ute I realized how precariously close to in-sulting that was, and so managed to keep my mouth shut.

He stiffened up. I saw that clearly enough. I hadn't meant an insult, I hadn't. I had not meant to slight his age. I began shaking my head wondering how I could get out of the hole I'd just dug beneath my feet.

He rescued me. The splendid man actu-ally lifted me out of the hole and cut me free. "My dear Andrea, no, Andy, don't apologize. No harm done. You speak what is on your mind, and for the most part, that is a charm-ing thing. Not always, to be sure, but some-times. Perhaps moderation is not a bad thing to consider, occasionally. Now, would you care for one of Pratt's delicious pear tarts?"

Naturally I was too full now for the pear tart, and so shook my head.

When Pratt showed himself again with the bosomy Betty to remove the dinner remains, he bowed low again, then poured Lawrence a glass of rich red port. Lawrence raised the glass to his lips, rolled the wine around in the crystal glass as I'd seen Grandfather do, then nodded his approval. Unthinking, without a pause, I held up my own glass.

Chapter Five

Pratt looked like he had just been pinned down by a hunter with a very big gun. He didn't move a muscle. I doubted he even breathed. He stared at my glass, still held toward him, and that bottle of port, like it was a serpent to bite him. He sent an agonized look toward my husband.

I realized in that instant that I had done something a lady would never do, not even on her dying day. I waited, for there was nothing else I could do. Lawrence looked at me and saw that I was perfectly serious. He started to open his mouth, to blast me, I figured.

But then he surprised me. He merely nodded that Pratt fill my glass. He didn't think I was a trollop or whatever you would call a lady who enjoyed drinking port and brandy. I smiled to myself as Pratt, not meeting my eyes, gave me approximately three skinny dollops.

I remembered my distaste when Grandfather had first poured me a bit of his port. He'd looked down his long nose at me when I had dared to make a disgusted noise. "What is this? You turn up your nose at my excellent port, Missy? My excellent port that has journeyed all the way from the Douro region of northern Portugal?"

"Perhaps it spoiled on the long trip?"

"Enough. It is the most excellent port in the world. Port, since you are so ignorant, is named for the town of Oporto. Listen to me, Miss Prude with no taste buds worth speaking of, this is part of your education, a very important part. You will develop a sophisticated palate. I will never watch you drink that nauseating ratafia that some idiot deemed proper for ladies to drink the good Lord knows how long ago. Drink up and don't you dare frown or make noises again."

I'd drunk up. I now quite liked a bit of port

after my dinner, but it had taken a good three months to train my poor sensitive palate.

For nearly eight years I had been admitted to that male tradition of good drinking and men's talk after dinner. Would it continue?

I waited.

When Pratt and Betty had left the parlor, loaded down with platters and silverware and dishes, my husband sat back, his glass of port gracefully held between slender fingers, and regarded me from beneath those thick dark brows. I wanted to tell him that Grandfather approved and he'd been even older than Lawrence, perhaps another whole generation away. No, better to keep my mouth shut if that was all I could think of to say to justify my drinking. I knew he wouldn't let this go. I waited. The reproach wasn't long in coming. However, it wasn't a screaming condemnation, as I was used to. No, when he spoke, his voice was cold and precise. "I presume the duke is responsible for your unusual taste in drink?"

"It certainly wasn't my idea at the beginning," I said, hoping perhaps to disarm him with candor. "I found it revolting when I was thirteen. At fourteen, Grandfather informed me he was pleased that he had educated my palate. Now it is merely a habit of long-standing. I trust it doesn't offend you."

It wasn't a bad defense, I thought. What made it better was that I hadn't lied. I was beginning to wonder if perhaps a lie would have served me better when my husband said in a very calm voice that didn't fool me for an instant, "It is entirely inappropriate for a lady to drink port. It smacks of commonness, of trollops in alehouses. I have always detested commonness."

"I believe that excellent port is far too expensive for the mouths of trollops, my lord. Oh, goodness, don't blast me. My mouth is amazingly fast, isn't it? My brain is somewhere off in the corner, just watching. Do forgive me." I decided not to mention my love of brandy, from Armagnac, in the Gers region of France, as every educated person knew.

He stared at me as if I was an amazing sort of creature he had never seen before.

"My grandfather," I said, slowly, ready to do battle, because I wasn't all that different from any other young lady. I stopped, cleared my throat, and began again. "My grandfather wasn't ever common, not even for an instant in his entire life. If he approved of something, then anyone who dared to question it would be regarded as the common one, not him."

I thought he would stand up and dump the table over on me, but he didn't. He drew a deep breath. "I should know by now that one must accustom oneself to the habits of one's spouse. I have the experience. You do not. You are very young. I don't wish to break your spirit, Andrea, no, Andy, but I cannot allow you to continue this habit when we will be in company. No, don't argue with me. I offer you a compromise. Your port drinking will be between the two of us. Isn't that fair?"

"I never drank port in company," I said. "It was always just between Grandfather and me."

"Then we have no argument." He raised his glass and clinked it lightly against mine. "To my beautiful new wife. May she not ever believe that she has married a stodgy old man."

"Hear, hear," I said, and grinned at him like a sinner who'd escaped punishment. I sipped the port. It wasn't nearly as good as the port from Grandfather's cellar. If I'd been drinking it with Grandfather, I would have made a rude noise and dumped it. I kept sipping. He was certainly fair, but life sometimes wasn't. I believe some people would say that I'd been hoisted on my own petard.

"You are perhaps strong-willed?"

"Not at all," I said, blinking a couple of times. I looked down at my napkin. I'd spread it, then folded and refolded it. "If I do anything to displease you, you must tell me. As you said, when married, one must learn compromise. One must bend. Perhaps one must even be in the wrong upon occasion."

"Do I understand that you've just given me permission to correct you if I happen to feel strongly about something?"

I hadn't said that at all, but he was being quite indulgent, something I'd heard older husbands many times were toward young wives. I was struck again how kind he was, and so I said easily, "That's right. You are a gentleman, Lawrence, just as Grandfather was a gentleman." The moment the words were out of my mouth, I stalled. I just stared at him. To my absolute horror, I started crying.

I swear I don't know where those blasted tears came from, but they just seeped out of my eyes and trickled down my cheeks to drip off my chin. "Oh, goodness, I'm sorry."

When he helped me to my feet and pulled me against his chest, I didn't hesitate. No one had held me after Grandfather's death, no one until Peter had come. I relaxed against him. He was tall. He was comfortable. I cried and cried.

His breath was soft and warm against my hair. "It's all right. It has been a difficult time for you. That's all right, Andrea, no, Andy. Just cry, my dear. That's right."

I would have given up my port had he asked it of me, willingly. But he had chosen to indulge me. He was offering me companionship and friendship. He was giving me comfort. I was very lucky that he had come to see me, and had found me acceptable.

I sobbed and hiccuped, then raised my face. "If you really don't like it, I will stop drinking."

He laughed a bit and hugged me again. "No, a countess and her port shouldn't be separated."

I would have killed for him at that moment. I smiled up at him through a veil of tears. "If you have any skeletons at all in your family closet, I swear upon my honor to keep quiet about them."

He paused for just the smallest moment, then said easily, "I would expect no less of you. Your grandfather raised you well. I hope you won't be disappointed, but my ancestors have been a fairly staid lot, one succeeding the other without much fanfare, much scandal, much treachery. Well, perhaps a bit, but not all that much. But I appreciate your vow.

"Now, my dear Andy, you have held up very well. I hope your new home, the new people you will meet, will help lessen your grief. But you know, my dear, grief is important. Eventually your memories of your grandfather will settle about you like a comfortable old cloak. They will comfort you, make you smile, perhaps even laugh, at the oddest moments.

"My shoulder will always be near should you desire to use it again."

"God made you a very good man, sir," I said, sniffed, and blew my nose on the handkerchief he handed me. "There are skeletons in my family, some quite scandalous ones actually, but none of them are old enough to be romantic."

"Between us, we will contrive to come up with one excellent horrifying tale of the past to entertain us on cold winter evenings."

"We must hurry, since winter is nearly upon us."

"I will check my history again to see what offensive lout I can dig up."

He walked me to my bedchamber, smiled down at me silently for a moment, and gave me a gentle pat on the cheek. "Pleasant dreams, my dearest Andy."

I watched him walk down the dimly lit corridor. He gave me a small wave before opening the door to his bedchamber. I wondered where his valet Flynt was sleeping. I personally wouldn't want Flynt sleeping anywhere near me.

I went inside to hear the delicate sleeping sighs of Miss Crislock, and George's loud snores. I remembered the steak bits I'd put aside for George. I'd left them wrapped in my napkin on the table. The thought of George's delight in the morning when I presented him a bite of steak made me finally pick up a candle and make my way back downstairs. Perhaps the bosomy Betty hadn't yet cleared everything away.

"She is very young."

I stopped instantly, my hand outstretched to turn the knob on the parlor door. It was a man's voice, and I didn't recognize it. It was coming from inside the parlor where Lawrence and I had shared our dinner, where I had cried for Grandfather and he had held me.

Who was the man speaking to?

"No woman is ever young," said Lawrence, and that stalled me. Of course I was young. There was a good deal of scorn in his voice that set me frowning. He had certainly gotten back downstairs very quickly.

"We will see," my husband continued. "Go on ahead. We will arrive at Devbridge Manor by dinnertime the day after tomorrow, barring any nasty weather. All goes well. Don't worry."

I ran back up the stairs, George's steak forgotten. Who was he talking to? Why?

Perhaps his man of business. I didn't plan to forget his voice. I was sure to meet him soon.

Because I was young and healthy, my stomach full, I fell asleep quickly. I slept throughout the night, deeply, even George's snores close to my ear, never breaking through my dreams.

Betty's knock on our bedchamber door came at promptly seven o'clock the next morning.

Miss Crislock shook my shoulder. "Andy, my dear, you must wake up now. If I don't take George for a walk this very minute, I fear there will be a mess that neither of us wish to face."

"Poor George," I said, stretching. "He never got his steak."

"He doesn't need any steak. Now, I will take George for a walk. You have your bath, Andy. I'll be back in a little while."

"Thank you, Milly. I am in your debt as is my fine beautiful George." At that moment I would have killed for Miss Crislock, as well as for my husband. I prayed that neither Miss Crislock nor Lawrence had any particular enemies, else I'd be hung for sure.

After a light breakfast, we came out of the inn to find a gray damp day. George growled. I kissed his head. "Now, George, at least the sky is gray because of the weather and not because of the ghastly pollution in the city. Don't whine."

Lawrence allowed George to ride with us part of the day. George, not a stupid animal, licked his hand. "You have no shame," I told him. My husband smiled.

It was a pleasant day, passed comfortably. We spent the night at the Hangman's Inn in Collingford.

"Just one more day," Lawrence said when he left me at my bedchamber door that evening. "We'll arrive home in time for dinner."

That was what he had said to the unknown man the previous night.

"Tomorrow," he said after I'd yawned, "I'll tell you about Hugo, my only ancestor of somewhat interesting gruesome parts. He even wrote a diary so all succeeding generations would know of his obsession with the cursed heretics. Sleep well, Andy."

And so I found out the next day that Hugo Lyndhurst, then Viscount Lyndhurst, was raised in 1584 to the earldom of Devbridge by Good Queen Bess.

"His diary still exists?" I asked. "You weren't joking with me?"

"Parts of it. The pages that remain are under glass in the Old Hall. I will show them to you. He built Devbridge Manor, completing it in 1590. After he obtained his earldom, he became less enthusiastic about butchering

Catholics in large groups. He contented himself with an occasional *auto-da-fé* for a random Catholic who happened to wander onto his land. He died of old age in his bed at the age of seventy-four, surrounded by his seven children."

I thought about Hugo Lyndhurst. "He sounds villainous enough, Lawrence, but he isn't the least bit romantic. Haven't you anything better to offer?"

He looked thoughtful for a moment. "After Hugo, there were no particular earls of interest. We did flourish under the Stuarts, being stout royalists. Unfortunately, this proved to be our undoing. Cromwell and his Roundheads took the manor when James Lyndhurst, then Earl of Devbridge, was hosting a very nice dinner for a regiment of royalist troops. Most of the manor was destroyed during the fighting, and only the Old Hall remains intact today."

"Now James Lyndhurst sounds more promising. What happened to him?"

"He followed the king and went to the executioner's block. I am forced to admit that your ancestors, who managed to skirt trouble with Cromwell, were more wily than mine. A good thing for the Devbridge line that the Stuarts came back quickly. From then until now, we have flourished. My most immediate ancestors managed to please their most Germanic highnesses and have been duly rewarded. And that, my dear, brings us to today."

"And the manor itself, when was it rebuilt, Lawrence?"

"As I said, the Old Hall remains from Tudor times. Every Devbridge since then has added on with his own particular artistic notions, and the manor today is a somewhat ungainly mixture of architectural styles."

I laughed. "It is just the same at Deerfield Hall. I first arrived when I was ten years old. I'll never forget getting lost at least once a day for a good three months."

"It will take you awhile to learn your way around Devbridge as well. I've closed off the north wing, so there will be fewer dark, musty corridors for you to worry about."

I have always loved Yorkshire. You know you're in a special part of England when you can see and smell the moors that seem to stretch on to Heaven. My husband's ancestral lands weren't more than twenty miles southwest of York, one of my very favorite cities. We spent nearly a half an hour in among rolling green hills with thick wide forests of oak trees. Better yet, Devbridge Manor was only fifteen miles from Deerfield Hall. I felt like I was coming home. Only Grandfather wouldn't be there.

When we rounded the last bend in the immensely long carriage drive, it was to see Devbridge Manor still glistening beneath the dying rays of bright sunlight. It was as my husband had said, a motley assortment of architectural styles, but all of them blended beautifully together, from the single crenellated tower to the lovely Palladian arches.

I was in love before we even stopped in front of the huge front doors. They were flung open by Moses. I will swear to my dying day that the Biblical Moses couldn't have appeared more impressive than the Devbridge butler, Brantley, with his flowing white hair, his stark black costume, his pale eyes surely alight with prophecies.

He snapped his fingers, and two footmen magically appeared, garbed in dark blue and white livery. One of them opened the carriage door and the other set a stool to step out upon.

Lawrence called, "Brantley, this, of course, is your new mistress."

I expected a commandment to issue out of Brantley's mouth, but when he spoke no hillocks shook and no bushes burst into flames. He said in a rich voice as smooth as brandy, "Welcome home, my lord, my lady. All the family is inside waiting for you."

I walked beside my husband into an ancient old hall that was dismal and smelled faintly of lemon wax and decaying wood.

Brantley preceded us to a beautiful set of walnut doors off to the right. He opened the doors, flinging his arms wide, and said, "The Earl and Countess of Devbridge."

The drawing room was long and narrow with a high-vaulted ceiling. Dark red hangings and heavy mahogany furnishings dominated the room. There were three lovely Turkey carpets dividing up the room, and the floor, showing between the carpets, shone with a dark, rich patina. Everything glowed in the soft light of at least fifty candles set all about the room in large ornate branches.

I saw three people in the room. They looked from Lawrence to me and back again.

They didn't look very happy.

Chapter Six

"Into the ogre's den," my husband said near my ear, and then he chuckled and squeezed my arm.

I tried to laugh, but it was difficult. I pulled myself together and swallowed hard as I looked over at the three people who were still staring. They hadn't moved an inch toward us, but just stood there. I cleared my throat, and walked forward.

Then I stopped cold. No, it simply wasn't possible. It just couldn't be him, it just couldn't. But it was. The man stepped out of the shadows at the far end of the fireplace. It was John, the John George had adored, the John who had wanted to meet me on three different occasions.

He was my husband's nephew and heir. The sullen one, the one who did not deal well with my husband, the one who was now home from the wars. To stay.

My step-nephew.

I decided then and there that I hated coincidences with all my heart.

Suddenly, without warning, I heard George's mad barking behind me. He must have spotted John, recognized him from the park, and broken free of dear Miss Crislock's arms. I didn't know he had such acute eyesight.

George came dashing in, his tail waving so wildly that it was hard to see. He barked and yipped and jumped as he ran full tilt at John, who quickly knelt down and gathered him up, laughing at he hugged him. George was well on his way to licking his face off, and John was still laughing. He was trying in vain to duck away from George's wildly licking tongue.

Lawrence said slowly, "What is this, John? You know this dog?"

John was laughing one moment, but at the sound of his uncle's voice, he stopped.

He tucked George under his left arm, but didn't stop pulling on his ears and stroking his fingers through his soft topknot.

"Yes," he said slowly, not moving an inch, "I know this dog. His name is George. I met him a while back in Hyde Park. His owner was with him. However, I never met her."

Lawrence turned to look at me. "I don't suppose this is the John you spoke of?"

I was surprised he remembered. I still didn't want to believe this was possible, even with the proof right in front of me, holding and petting my extremely happy dog. "Yes, that's the John. If you remember I also told you he was magic with animals, at least that is what he claimed. He certainly stole George's affections."

"Well, then," Lawrence said, "this makes things a bit easier. Major John Lyndhurst is my nephew and heir. John, this is Andrea Jameson Lyndhurst, my wife, the Countess of Devbridge. She mentioned meeting you, but all she knew was your first name."

John continued to stroke George's head. My terrier's eyes fluttered in ecstasy. He pushed his head against John's fingers. "Yes, I know who she is, Uncle. She is Peter Wilton's cousin. I am, however, surprised that she even remembered me, much less mentioned me to you."

I couldn't believe I'd done it, either. He was still too big, even at a distance of twenty feet. "I believe I mentioned you because your uncle spoke of you as being his nephew and heir. You had the same name. It was a coincidence, that's all."

I could tell nothing at all from his expression. He said finally, his fingers now lightly rubbing George's left ear, "Was Peter at your wedding? Is he well?"

"Yes, he is quite well. He stayed in London only briefly, then he had to return to Paris." It was none of his business that Peter hadn't come to our wedding. I realized that I couldn't put it off any longer. I had to face it and accept it and deal with it. I pinned a dazzling smile on my mouth. "It is certainly a pleasure to meet you, John. I suppose it is a relief that we are now related, since you have quite captivated my dog. George, do have some dignity. Stop licking his fingers."

John laughed, which was a relief, and set George down on the floor—only George didn't move. He just sat there at John's feet, his tail wagging, his tongue out. He waved his paw at John.

"George," I called out. "That is quite enough. You will come here to me, where you belong. I am your mistress, the only one in the world you can really count on for your next meal."

George whined, then, after about ten indecisive seconds, came trotting back to me. At the very least, George had broken the stiff-necked scene we had walked in on. Lawrence said as I scooped George up in my arms, "Now, my dear, this is Thomas and his wife, Amelia."

I walked to them and stuck out my free hand. "How do you do. Your uncle has told me all about you. I am very pleased to meet you both."

Thomas kissed my hand, and Amelia lightly touched her fingertips to mine.

"This is quite a surprise for us, madam," Amelia said, a beautifully arched black eyebrow hiked up at least one incredulous inch.

Madam? I beamed all my good will up at her. She was a good six inches taller than I was and very effectively looked down her nose at me. I said in a voice so oozing with affability that it would make even a vicar suspicious, "Do call me Andy. Even

Lawrence does now. It is ever so much more friendly, don't you agree?"

"Oh, yes, I do agree."

"Why are you surprised?" I turned to cock my head to my husband as I spoke.

"We didn't know that Uncle Lawrence was getting married until a messenger arrived yesterday," Thomas said. "That was our first surprise. I suppose we were all expecting a motherly lady, not someone so very young and beautiful."

"I suspect I'll become quite motherly in the years to come, Thomas."

"What? Are you already breeding?" This was from John, his tone low and quite vicious. He pushed away from the mantelpiece and took two long steps toward us.

My tongue was dead wood in my mouth.

"No, John," my husband said easily, taking my free hand in his, "what she means is that she'll become quite comfortable with all of you in the years to come."

I said nothing, just let all my new relatives look me over to their hearts' content. What did they see other than a girl who was on the small side with curling reddish-brown hair? I wasn't plain, but I doubted that I could lay claim to the "beautiful" that Thomas had just used to describe me. I knew I had nice blue eyes, "all summery," my grandfather had said, but the three of them were too far away to be able to admire them, if they so chose.

Why hadn't Lawrence told them he was marrying me? What was going on here?

Lawrence said to Amelia, "My dear, has Brantley told you when we can expect dinner? Andy here has a healthy appetite. I believe her stomach began complaining some ten miles distant from Devbridge."

My stomach had growled, but not loudly.

I gave him a sunny smile. "Perhaps a pheasant or two, nicely baked, mind you, would suit me just fine."

He lightly touched his fingers to my cheek, caressing me. I froze. I knew he felt me withdraw, even though I didn't move or twitch or anything at all. And I knew it, too. His smile never slipped.

"I'll ring for Brantley and see about your pheasant."

"Thank you, Lawrence." He hadn't meant anything. He was just showing me affection. I had to accustom myself to that sort of thing from a man. From my husband. It meant nothing. He was simply fond of me. I could deal well enough with that.

Amelia had sat down again on a lovely mahogany chair with scrolled arms from the last century and arranged her dark blue silk skirt. She was perhaps three years my senior, no more. And lovely, what with hair as dark as a sinner's dreams, as my grandfather had said upon occasion, all done up atop her head in a knot of loose curls.

I asked, "You don't ride, Amelia?"

George barked because John was walking toward us. He strained against my arms.

"Why ever would you think that I don't ride? John, don't encourage that dog."

"You are so very white," I said. "I can't imagine the sun ever touching you. You look like one of the statues of the goddess Diana I saw in the British Museum. George, maintain a modicum of decorum, if you please."

"Too white, I tell her," said Thomas. He was standing behind her, his hand resting lightly on her shoulder. "Perhaps even dead-white in the winter, and that's just around the corner now. I don't like death or anything to do with it. My constitution, you know, isn't what it should be."

"I don't like freckles," Amelia said. "The instant a single sun's ray gets to my face, I grow freckles." She smiled, and I was struck that the white skin on her face had flushed a bit.

"Freckles have always reminded me of age spots," Thomas said. "Age spots arrive just before death. No, I don't like freckles, either. Amelia, my dearest, I prefer the dead-white skin to freckles. The more I think about it, the more I believe I like all your white flesh. Yes, I now count myself content."

John, who was staring at his brother, a look of bafflement on his face, said then, "Thomas, what is all this talk about death? I see nothing at all wrong with you. You are healthy as a stoat. You will outlive us all."

"That is nice of you to say, John, but you haven't been around enough in recent years to see just how very precarious my health really is. Why, I coughed just this morning. It wasn't even seven-thirty in the morning yet, and there came this cough, very deep into my chest, perhaps just a bit on the liquid side. I immediately feared a congestion of the lung. I'll tell you that Amelia was right on it. Poured a potion right down my throat and wrapped a hot towel around my neck. Because of my careful darling, I have escaped something that could have put a period to my existence. Yes, it could have been a close thing. I say, Andy, that dog wants John very badly."

"Each day that God allots to Thomas is a gift to be treasured," Lawrence said to no one in particular, no expression at all on his face. Did I scent a hint of sarcasm? Just a bit of loving contempt? I couldn't be sure. Like John, Lawrence seemed to keep his thoughts close to his shirt pockets. "Yes, John, move away or take the wretched dog. He is creating a scene."

I looked beyond Thomas to John and held tightly to George. He had still not come forward, but now his eyes met his uncle's. I began humming softly to George, one of his favorite tunes, the one about the dog catching the rabbit and chewing on its ear.

"Well, John, I am glad to see you. You're home to stay this time?"

"I had believed so," John said slowly, looking at me now, or at George, I couldn't be sure.

"What, you're changing your mind again? You wish to be in peacetime Paris?"

"No, that isn't it at all."

"Dinner is served, my lord."

"Ah, Brantley, your timing is perfect. My dear, would you like to do something with George?"

"Let me carry him upstairs to Milly. She will take a tray in her chamber, you know. Did she already ask you, Brantley?"

"Yes, indeed, my lady. Mrs. Redbreast, our housekeeper, is taking fine care of your Miss Crislock. She simply told me to inform you that she would be delighted to meet everyone in the morning, when she is rested. Shall I remove the dog, my lady?"

I looked at George. "Would you trust a man who looks like Moses to take you to Miss Crislock?"

George leaned toward Brantley and sniffed at those long white fingers of his.

I'll say this about Brantley. He might look like a Biblical figure ready to hurl tablets to the ground, but he had a sense of humor and a good deal of kindness. He slowly eased his hand in George's little face and let George sniff for all his worth. Finally, George wuffed.

"Excellent," I said, and handed him over. "Thank you, Brantley."

"Now, my dear," Lawrence said, "let's see to your stomach."

We ate in the large formal dining room, the four of us seated around a table that could easily seat sixteen. I was gently placed in the chair at the foot of the table, or the bottom of the table, as my grandfather referred to as the lady's place, by a footman Brantley called Jasper.

John sat in the middle of the table, between his uncle and me. Thomas and Amelia sat on the other side opposite John. It was in that moment that I got my first really good look at Thomas. He was surrounded by candlelight.

I think I probably gasped out loud. Oh, goodness, I tried not to stare, but it was very difficult not to. Thomas was the most beautiful man I had ever seen in my life. He was rather slight of build, fair—unlike his Spanish mother or his brother—and his features were so perfectly formed, going together so flawlessly, that surely Michelangelo would have been mad to sculpt him. While his older brother, John, looked dark, dangerous, hard, and meaner than a mad hound, Thomas looked like an angel. He had thick waving blond hair and summer-blue eyes, nearly the same shade as mine.

He was simply beautiful, no other way to say it. Finally I saw something that saved him, barely. He had a very stubborn chin, but even that chin of his, tilted at just the right angle, made one want to run one's fingers over his face and just stare at him. It was disconcerting. I happened to look over at John to see that he'd raised an eyebrow at me.

"Sorry," I said. "I can't help it."

"Most ladies can't," John said. "Try to contain yourself."

"I will try."

Brantley returned then to direct the serving of the dinner. It was a very formal ritual, one obviously performed many times, much more formal than the one Grandfather and I had always observed. Miss Crislock would doubtless be pleased at this ruthless ceremony. She was the one who kept Grandfather and me to a reasonable dining schedule. She had always insisted that we dress for dinner, something Grandfather and I grumbled about, but did because it was important to her.

I watched the two footmen, Jasper and

Timothy, move silently about the table, making no unnecessary noise at all. They were also so well trained that they easily pretended they weren't listening when the earl spoke easily of the weather, the state of the grass in the east lawn, or even when he slipped into a more controversial area—the damned Whigs, a never-ending misery to be endured, since they couldn't be lined up and summarily shot.

It wasn't until Brantley nodded the footmen to the far side of the dining room and stood himself against the closed door, that Lawrence turned to John, who had just raised a fork with turkey and chestnut pastry on it, and said, "I had thought you planned to remain at Devbridge. Is there some chance that you will not remain here and begin to learn our estate management?"

John frowned at his turkey and pastry, ate it, saying nothing until he'd swallowed. He leaned back in his chair, crossed his arms over his chest, and said very deliberately, "You have just married a young lady, Uncle, a very young lady. She appears immensely healthy. It seems obvious that there will be an heir in the not-too-distant future. I can now see no reason for me to learn how to manage the estates. You will raise your future son just as an heir should be raised. The lad will doubtless know all the estate management he needs to know by the time he is twelve. There will be no need for me to hang about, cluttering up the dining table."

Lawrence raised his wineglass to me and silently shook his head. He said to John, his voice as cold as a late winter wind howling over the Yorkshire moors, "I have said this before, and I will say it again. You, John, are my heir. You will remain my heir. Therefore, you must prepare yourself to someday take my place. There is nothing more to be said."

"But, Uncle Lawrence," Thomas said, waving one slender, beautifully shaped hand toward me, "John is right. She is very young. Why else would you marry except to get yourself an heir?"

"Man cannot live by heirs alone," I said.

Dead silence.

Why hadn't I kept my mouth shut?

Chapter Seven

Amelia choked out the sip of wine she'd taken.

John choked on a bite of baked trout, then loudly cleared his throat.

Thomas was banging his fist against his wife's back.

Lawrence looked as if he would like to throw me through the dining room window, but he didn't. Thank goodness for his restraint. Indeed, on second look, I thought perhaps he was trying not to laugh. He wasn't angry at me, a blessed relief. But I still wanted to ask why bloody men believed that a wife's only purpose was to produce a boy child. I suppose I was surprised that both John and Thomas viewed Lawrence's marriage to me in that light only, and I shouldn't have been. I was a well-bred mare whose function was to produce a boy child—nothing more.

"Perhaps," I said, knowing I should keep chewing my own turkey and chestnuts, instead of diving into such muddy waters, "your uncle found me quite to his liking, and that is why he married me. After all, George likes me very well, and usually he is an excellent judge of character."

"I don't understand," Amelia said, her cheeks flushed from her bout of laughter, "Uncle Lawrence isn't a dog. What are you talking about, Andy?"

"An attempt at a jest, no more," I said. Of course I had known that this would have to come up and have to be dealt with. I just hadn't realized that it would be this soon and discussed right in front of everyone, Brantley included. I sighed into my plate and kept my head down.

"Andy has an excellent sense of humor," my husband said, but he wasn't smiling at all. Then he added, "We will see." And that was all my husband of three days had to say. He returned to his own turkey. Of course, he had really said nothing at all. I looked over at John. He was staring at me, and there was something in those dark eyes of his that I didn't understand. Then I did. It was violence. Then, just as suddenly, that something was gone.

Face facts, I told myself. So John had wanted to meet me. Perhaps he had felt a bit of interest in me, but for the life of me I couldn't figure out why. I had been dressed in deep mourning. I had barely been civil. Regardless, that was three months ago. Now I was married, and separated from him as far as could be. If he felt any disappointment, which would amaze me if he had, he would simply have to get a grip on himself.

At least Lawrence's words had stilled the family. I wanted to tell them all that we wouldn't be seeing anything at all, but I realized that Lawrence was protecting me. The last thing he would want to say was that ours was a marriage of mutual convenience, mutual respect, and mutual liking with nothing else cluttering it up, like a naked man humiliating a naked woman, namely me.

I looked again at John. He appeared to be staring into his wineglass. Why, I wondered, had he wanted to meet me? Well, it didn't matter now. Still, for a moment I didn't look away from him.

He was still too big and too dark in his black evening clothes. He appeared even larger now than he had the last time I'd seen him three months before. I could sense the danger in him, the cold control of an autocrat used to obedience, and he was surely too young for such control, I thought again. His face was still tanned from his years of campaigning and from his mother's Spanish blood, and his hair, like Amelia's, was raven-black. His eyes were so dark that they appeared black in the soft lighting, and his brows were thick and slightly arched.

"How were you married?"

John's cold voice, so formal and thick with indifference, had me wanting to smack the rudeness out of him, but Lawrence said easily enough, "By Special License, of course. Bishop Costain is a friend of mine. He also knew your father, John. He was pleased to perform the ceremony."

Of course I couldn't keep my mouth shut. I looked right at John and asked, "Did you think this was all a sham? Some sort of charade your uncle planned to entertain you?"

John sat back in his chair, his wineglass held between his long fingers. "I have heard of men bringing their current mistresses into their homes and passing them off as their new wives. Naturally, such a pretense could never last very long."

"No, I can't imagine that such a charade would long fool anyone," Lawrence said. "I remember all the gossip about Lord Pontly, an old roué of the last century, who brought five different brides home to his beleaguered family, only to be found out very quickly each time. The sixth time he tried it, his family refused to allow the supposed wife into the house. There was a huge ruckus."

Lawrence smiled at each of us around the table. "Naturally, number six really was the wife, the ceremony even performed by the local vicar."

"I've never heard of such a thing," I said. "You're not making that up, sir? A man really did that to his family? Five times? Why didn't a member of his family just shoot him?"

"I would think that there would be the temptation, but Lord Pontly died of just plain old age in his bed, his sixth wife, only a third his age, holding his hand when he passed, a peaceful look on his face, to the hereafter."

"I wonder," Thomas said, and I thought even his voice was beautiful, so filled with unconscious charm even the blackest sinner would be tempted to repent, "if perhaps Lord Pontly was on to something, sir."

"What do you mean, Thomas?"

"Well, if he died of old age, not some vile illness, then perhaps having all the sham wives kept him healthy. It must have added to his vigor, improved his outlook on his lot in life."

"At least a sham wife could be tossed out the window when the man tired of her," John said. "That would certainly go a long way to improve a man's contentment."

Amelia threw her buttered roll at him, which he handily ducked. "What a dreadful thing to say. You will take it back, John, right this minute, or I will think of something dreadful to do to you."

John raised his hands, splaying his fingers. "Acquit me, Amelia. Consider it unsaid. I apologize if you mistook my words."

"There was nothing at all to be mistook," I said. "If I had a roll I would be tempted to throw it at you, except that if I had one, I probably would eat it."

Thomas laughed, a delightful tolling of human bells, utterly charming to the ear. Did nothing the man do grate on one's nerves?

John said, "You must admit, Amelia, that occasionally women are fickle. Maybe more than occasionally."

I looked down to see that a roll had appeared on the edge of my plate. I looked to see Brantley removing himself once again to the dining room door. I picked up the roll and waved it at him, grinning. He had no expression whatsoever on his face. What was he thinking about all of us? Had he given me a roll so that I could throw it at John? Was he amused?

"I have never met a fickle woman in my life," Amelia said. "And your apology, John, rang as false as a sinner's third promise to reform. No, I believe it is you men who are the fickle ones."

"The reason Lord Pontly lived so long," Lawrence said easily before Amelia could throw another roll at John, "is because he was such a dreadful man the devil didn't want him. Finally, though, so many years had passed that even the devil had no choice but to fetch him home to bask at the devil's own hearth."

"That was quite clever," I said, and lifted

my wineglass to toast my husband. He just shook his head at me, as if to say, *Young men, what is one to do with them?*

I knew the answer to that. One shot them.

Thomas said, "Amelia, my dearest, you were fickle. Think back, and you will have to admit it." He turned to say to me, "She was charmingly fickle, however. I saw it as a challenge and worked to overcome her adorable capriciousness, although it did take me the better part of six months. I wrote poems to her, my very best titled 'Without You I Am Done For.' I believe it was that poem that made her place her hand in mine."

Amelia patted her husband's arm. "No, Thomas, it wasn't that poem, although it evoked startling images in my mind, it was the song you sang beneath my bedchamber window that quite won me over." She looked over at me. "Perhaps, if his lungs are properly pumped up and healthy, Thomas will consent to sing his song at your window, Andrea."

"It's Andy," I said. "I would like that, Thomas. Perhaps you can tell me the theme of your song?"

He frowned a moment over a spoonful of

peas. "It was one of my better efforts," he said finally, a slight flush on his lean cheeks. Then he opened his beautiful mouth and sang in a lovely tenor voice:

Wring my withers
You saucy wench.

Whisper you love me
But not in French.

Tell me you'll wed me and make it soon
Else I'll grow feathers and fly to the stars.

I was laughing so hard I couldn't breathe. My eyes teared. My husband rose, quickly walked to my end of the table, and slapped his palm between my shoulder blades.

"I will have to have Brantley take the leaves out of this table," he said. "I cannot be expected to rise every few minutes to thump your back."

"That is an excellent idea," I said when I caught my breath. "Then we can thump each other's backs."

I saw that John had utterly lost control as well. He was gulping down water and choking. To my astonishment, I looked over to see Brantley with his fist stuffed in his mouth.

"It did wring her withers," Thomas said gravely seemingly oblivious of the collapse he had caused. He leaned over and lightly kissed his wife's cheek.

"I was won over picturing him glued over with white feathers," Amelia said. "He drew me in with those feathers, even though I was forced to critique his effort, just a bit, you understand. I tried to tell him that *stars* didn't rhyme with *soon,* that one expected to hear *Else I'll grow feathers and fly to the moon,* but he just gave me that archangel's smile of his and told me, no, he never wanted to do the expected. That was boring. No perfect rhymes for him. He never wanted to bore me. And, of course, he hasn't."

Lawrence was just shaking his head. As for Brantley, he stood stiff as a fireplace poker now, all contained again. I looked at the two footmen, who were not, obviously, as well trained as Moses. Both their heads were averted. I could only see their profiles.

"Sir," Amelia said to Lawrence, "I hate to bring this delightful dinner to a close, but I have to be honest here. I believe your poor wife is nearly ready to fall asleep in her gooseberry foole."

I was tired, but how could she tell? I had laughed as hard as everyone else. But it was true. I was flying at only half-mast.

"You're right, Amelia," Lawrence said to me, that deep kind voice of his all filled with warm concern. "My dear, the gentlemen will be along shortly. I, myself, am ready for some relaxation. We will come into the drawing room with you and Amelia for a little while, then it's off to bed with you."

"Oh, all right," I said, and then had to catch myself on a yawn. "If you wish. It has been a long day. Besides, I'll need to walk George, and I never know how long he will wish to sniff around." I leaned over toward Thomas. "Would you really come to my bedchamber window and sing me a marvelous song like the one you wrote for Amelia?"

"I shall have to think of something like 'Ode to a Laughing Girl.' Hmmm. I shall work on this, Andy."

Amelia motioned to one of the footmen. He reached her side in but a moment to assist her out of her chair. She stopped, still halfway standing. "Oh, goodness, it isn't up to me now, Andy, you're the new mistress.

When you wish us to leave the table, you must give the signal and do the rising."

I put my fingers in my mouth and let out a light whistle. "There, the signal is given," I said, and pushed back my own chair. Brantley was beside me in an instant. "My lady," he said, and that level, very formal tone of voice chastened me immediately.

My husband wasn't pleased, either, but I refused to leave the dining table like a ponderous matron wearing a purple turban on her head.

"I see that you and Brantley will have to perfect a signal," Lawrence said. "Whistling will do to call a horse but not to call the other ladies to attention."

The three gentlemen rose, waiting until we were out of the dining room before they resumed their seats and enjoyed their port. I could almost taste the port, but it wasn't to be.

As I walked beside Amelia back to the drawing room, I said, "The house is really quite lovely. Lawrence told me about old Hugo's diary, filled with rantings about heretics and such."

"Yes, it's in a small room just yon, beneath those rusted old suits of armor that the maids don't like to dust. They think the knights are still inside, at least their bones and their ghosts are, just waiting to pinch them if they're not wary. I heard one maid tell another that she wasn't to get too close to any of them because one of the knights just might grab her and pull her into the armor and she would be imprisoned forever." Amelia laughed then. "This house sometimes makes me wonder if there aren't more ghosts than Thomas ever admitted to before we were married. It's the feel of it, you see, nothing overt or blatantly menacing, like sliding chains and creaking floor planks."

"You asked for a ghost reckoning before you were willing to wed Thomas?"

"Well, you see, my father is a renowned scholar on the delineation of otherworldly manifestations. He believes that there are probably many spirits and other spectral phenomena that reside here at Devbridge Manor, although no one likes to admit to them. He believes that most of them probably date from the sixteenth and seventeenth centuries when very violent things happened here, and, of course, everywhere else as well. He was the one who wanted every ghost produced and discussed until he was satisfied that none would harm me. Truth be told, I think my father is more interested in actually bringing to light the most infamous of the ghosts that is said to reside in the Black Chamber, so he could lord it over his colleagues.

"Unfortunately, Thomas couldn't even produce one ghost, and he promised me he had walked each of the long corridors at least twice at midnight, but none of them deigned to confront him. As I said, there is simply this feeling here. Soon perhaps I will ask my father to come and conduct some of his scientific spectral experiments. Perhaps he will feel something malignant in the Black Chamber. I never have felt anything in there."

"I should like to meet your father and observe him," I said, and then thought I must be a fool. Who wanted to come face-to-face with an unhappy spirit? Who wanted a ghost hanging around, clanking chains or moaning up and down the octaves in one's ear? What had happened in the Black Chamber?

"Goodness, I never considered ghosts when I agreed to Lawrence's marriage proposal."

I heard Lawrence's voice as he came out

of the dining room and said quickly to Amelia, "I want to hear more about any resident specters, Amelia. I want to visit this Black Chamber tomorrow morning."

I knew, just knew, that my new husband would hear the word ghost out of my mouth and regard me from that moment on as a complete fool. Better to keep some things to myself.

"Of course." She paused, studied her thumbnail for a moment, and added, "There are other rooms as well that are supposedly visited, but I have never seen or heard anything, and I confess, I have visited them often. But there are stories, particularly about one of them. You are wise to keep this between the two of us. Uncle Lawrence has no patience at all with ghosts."

What room?

"Amelia, my dear," Lawrence said, coming into the drawing room. "Andy will be in The Blue Room. Do you mind seeing her there?"

Amelia stared at him. She was silent as one of those suits of armor with the knights' ghosts inside.

I turned and stared at him as well.

Thomas cleared his throat. "The thing is, sir, perhaps you've forgotten that The Blue

Room is perhaps better suited to an elderly relative who is rather hard of hearing and perhaps has dimmed vision?"

"Yes, Uncle," John said, "a relative with very dulled sensibilities."

What was going on here? Was this the particular room Amelia had just mentioned?

Chapter Eight

Lawrence laughed. "The lot of you are incredibly gullible. Don't listen to them, Andy. The Blue Room is a lovely bed chamber with a comfortable adjoining sitting room that you will find charming. It is filled with light, and from the wide windows you have a beautiful prospect toward the east lawn and the home wood. This talk of ghosts is just that—talk. It whiles away the hours on a cold winter's night. Now, my dear Andy, go with Amelia. Miss Crislock is just down the hall from you, in The Dimwimple Room."

"Ah, yes," John said from where he was standing next to the fireplace. "She was an heiress of the last century who saved the Devbridge fortunes during a scoundrel's tenure as earl. I don't believe she's still hanging about, is she, Uncle?"

"Alice Dimwimple was a very happy old bird, I was told by my father, who knew her when he was a very young boy. She choked to death at a very advanced age on an excellent glass of brandy, and doubtless ascended to heaven to claim her just rewards."

"Unlike many of the males of the family," Thomas said, "who left so many bastards that pregnant females were always presenting themselves here at Devbridge Manor."

John said, "I understand that my great-uncle—the last of the major scoundrels—had his steward handle the poor females. The steward was a very religious man. The records show that he adopted three of the pregnant women and raised his lordship's bastards as his own."

"Grandfather never told me any stories like that," I said, and my husband patted my hand to ease my obvious disappointment. "That is quite amazing. I should like to hear more."

"Not tonight." Lawrence walked to me, lightly kissed my cheek, and said next to my ear, "The Blue Room will suit you very well. I will see you in the morning, my dear. Now, I must speak more closely with John. I believe it necessary to clarify some issues with him."

Issues that included John remaining my husband's heir, since there wouldn't be any children born of our union?

Excellent, I thought, get it out of the way now. I wanted no unpleasantness about that sort of thing with my step-nephew, ever again.

"Goodness," I said, looking over at that dark face, "you are my step-nephew."

"Indeed, dear Auntie," he said, and gave me a deep, mocking bow. There was that look in his dark eyes again, that flash of violence, then it was gone.

I turned back to my husband. "Is there an equally charming history for The Blue Room? An heiress who came into the family whose name was perhaps Miss Blue?"

He laughed, a full, deep, rich laugh. I loved that laugh of his. It was comforting and warm. I certainly preferred it to any show of disapproval.

"Go along with you, my dear. I shall try to

come up with something to amuse you on the morrow."

"Good night, sir, Thomas, John."

I walked with Amelia back into the central entrance hall. It was a huge area, the floor was stone, so old that it was uneven from all the thousands of feet that had tread upon it.

Amelia paused a moment, waving a graceful hand. "This is the Old Hall, surviving from the first structure built by Old Hugo in the 1580s."

It was magnificent, the tall wooden-beamed, smoke-blackened ceiling barely visible in the dim light cast by the wall flambeaux. The suits of armor, at least a dozen of them, none of them missing any armor parts, appeared to span the centuries, looked vaguely menacing in that dull shadowy light.

The staircase, all shining oak, wide enough to accommodate at least six people side by side, curved down into the center of the Old Hall. It could not have been older than two centuries, perhaps two and a half centuries at the most.

One wall was dominated by a gigantic fireplace that resembled a great blackened cavern in the half-light. The old stone floor was bare and echoed as Amelia's shoes click-clacked on her way to the staircase. There was no carpeting on the stairs, just the stretch of highly polished oak.

More wall flambeaux lit our way up the winding stairs. It was nice not to have to carry a candle and carefully guard its frail light. When we reached the landing, I turned to gaze down at the Old Hall. It was a relic of another age, filled with rich dark shadows, mysteries embedded in its walls, and perhaps even other sorts of things mixed in as well. Were I a very old spectral phenomenon, I would enjoy living here a great deal. This place had atmosphere.

"Our uncle's marriage to you—it has come as a great shock to all of us."

"I see that it has. I wonder why Lawrence kept it from you?"

Amelia seemed suddenly to make up her mind about something. She cleared her throat, obviously girding her loins, and said with appalling candor, "I do hope that it doesn't have to do with your antecedents?"

Not a very nice thing to say to your step-auntie, I thought, but given Lawrence hadn't said a word about me, I suppose it was understandable. Had he feared they would mount arguments because I was so much younger? And Amelia was worried. Still, it wasn't exactly smoothly and subtly done, and so I said, my voice a bit on the officious side, "I really don't know. I shall ask my husband."

Amelia persevered. "Your nickname— Andy—it was bestowed on you by perhaps a gentleman?" Her voice was both wary and defiant. Did she really believe me some sort of opera girl, a traveling mistress? Who could tell these days, what with old Lord Pontly bringing them home in droves?

I very nearly ruined my effect by laughing as I said, "How clever of you, Amelia. As a matter of fact, it was a gentleman. An older gentleman. I quite like it. Yes, I am thoroughly an Andy. Andrea sounds to me like a hateful biddy who should keep her bad manners to herself. What do you think?"

There, I thought, maybe she would remember that I was innocent until proven otherwise. She started to smile, then drew it back. I didn't want to deal with any more of this. I was tired, and a headache was beginning just over my left ear. I hated headaches.

"This corridor is endless. Thank God there are so many flambeaux on the walls."

"Yes," she said, her tone normal again, thank the heavens. "Devbridge Manor is a sprawling old house, so many small rooms that have no use as far as I can see, and there are even two sets of stairs that lead into blank walls. Perhaps it is very different from what you're used to?"

She was fishing again and not doing it with an ounce of finesse. I said, goading her, "I'll admit that there certainly weren't any *cul de sac* stairs in the house in London."

"Come, Andy, how did Uncle Lawrence meet you? At a ball? Some *soirée*? Or at the opera? At Drury Lane? I wish you would stop dancing around things and just answer me honestly."

Now this could be interesting, I thought, and gave her a sunny smile. There was doubt in her voice, and she was prodding me but good. She wanted honesty, did she?

"Ask your uncle," I said.

"No, I am asking you."

I pursed my lips and cocked my head to the side, as if trying to remember. Finally, I said, "You know, perhaps it was at Drury

Lane. It is difficult to remember. I have been to so many plays over the years."

"You don't have that many damned years."

Since she looked ready to burst her seams, I sighed and said, "Actually, he came to my home to present his condolences. And that, Amelia, is all I have to say about it tonight. Trust that I am not some sort of adventuress here to steal all your jewelry."

"I'm sorry," she said, but she didn't sound sorry at all. She sounded relieved. "Thomas and I just didn't know, and Uncle Lawrence didn't clarify a single thing tonight."

"No. However, I cannot imagine Lawrence standing before the three of you this evening and reciting my family names, my yearly income, and whether or not I am addicted to gambling."

"No, I don't suppose he could have. Actually, after about ten minutes, particularly after George bounded into the drawing room, I didn't think you seemed like a mistress sort." She sighed. "It is just that there is so much wickedness about. I'm glad you are not part of it."

"What wickedness?"

"Oh, nothing here, specifically. But wickedness does abound. I was just speaking in general. We live in very liberal times. I wonder what will happen to our world when so many of the children are raised with no closely held values, no sense of justice, little religious affiliation, or morality."

"I had not really thought of it that way, but now I shall." I stopped and put my hand on her arm. "Amelia, you are worrying about everything at once. Now, this corridor surely extends into the next century. Where is this infamous Blue Room?"

"Here we are. Your Miss Crislock is just beyond."

She threw open the door. There were at least six branches of candles set all about the room, filling every corner with light. A lazy fire burned in the fireplace. The room was welcoming, warm.

Actually, it was the most beautiful bedchamber I had ever seen in my life. I must have drawn in my breath, because after just an infinitesimal pause. Amelia said carefully, as if probing for a splinter, "If one isn't used to such splendor as this, one can be overcome, don't you think?"

She was jesting with me now, and I was

charmed by her. I nodded solemnly. "I would certainly agree. It is lovely. Of course, in the evening, with all the blunt-tattered edges muted, so to speak, it looks vastly romantic."

"Just so. Now, since you did not bring a maid, I will have my own Stella tend to you tonight. Stella was told to unpack all your trunks. See, she left a nightgown for you on the bed. I imagine she thinks that the stitching on it is really quite magnificent."

"That is Miss Crislock's doing." Although I really didn't need a maid, at least I could send this Stella for a dollop of brandy to ease my headache.

"Good night, Andy. I will show you the small black-painted room tomorrow morning. The best story I've heard about its history is that a butler was murdered by a long-ago countess in that room when he threatened to tell her husband that he was her lover."

"Oh, goodness, that makes me shudder just thinking about it. I really want to see the Black Chamber. Now you finally managed to say my name. Thank you. I promise you will get used to it. Everyone else seems to, even your uncle by marriage."

"I will see you in the morning."

"I look forward to it. And stop worrying about everything. You have nothing to fear from me. I am the most benign of creatures."

"I'll try," she said, looking at her quite lovely white hands. Then she blurted out, "Why aren't you sleeping in Uncle Lawrence's bedchamber or in the countess's bedchamber that adjoins it?"

I patted her arm. "Let it go, Amelia. It is really none of your affair. I know you have questions, but please, just leave off for tonight."

"I'm worried about Uncle Lawrence. He is not a young man. It's possible, isn't it, that you drew him in, and made him marry you?"

"You think Uncle Lawrence is a doddering foolish old man?"

"Naturally not, but he has been alone a number of years. I am worried that you could hurt him. None of us want Uncle Lawrence hurt. There, I have finally come out and said what really worries me."

"Ah, then that's all right," I said. "By all means, let's always indulge in full honesty, no matter how dreadful it is. Good night, Amelia. Believe me, I'm the very least of any problem you will ever have."

But once she had started, she couldn't let

it go. "I hope so. But don't you see? You are very young and very pretty. If you are honest and well-intentioned, then why did you marry him?"

"He is quite to my liking."

"Why would he marry you? A girl who is so young and so eccentrically brought up that she actually whistled when she wished to leave the table?"

"He is a man of infinite good taste? Good night, Amelia. No, no more honesty, at least for tonight. I promise I'll never whistle at the table again. You're right, whistling at the dinner table wasn't well-done of me."

"Then—"

I literally shoved her toward the door.

Amelia the worrier, I thought, as I firmly closed the door. I guessed there had to be one in every family. Actually, I was pleased that she felt such affection and concern for her uncle-in-law.

I didn't even have time to take three steps when Stella, her lady's maid, a woman I wouldn't want to meet on a dark night in an alley, suddenly appeared and gave me a niggardly curtsy and a stingy smile. She was of middle years, her dark hair, threaded with gray, pulled back in a harsh bun. She was taller than I—nearly everyone was—and so skinny I swear I could nearly see the shape of her bones in the candlelight. She had a dark mustache above her upper lip.

She didn't want to be here. I wasn't her mistress, Amelia was. I said, "Thank you for your assistance, Stella. Please fetch me a small glass of brandy for my headache, then you may remove yourself for the night."

A thick black eyebrow hoisted itself halfway up her forehead. She gave me the barest of nods and took herself off.

Oh, dear, I thought as Stella disappeared through the doorway. Would Stella now rush to the kitchens and announce to everyone that the new countess was a tippler? Probably so. Well, it would give them some nice gossip until they learned how truly innocuous their new mistress was.

Alone, I quickly walked to the long wall of drawn draperies and pulled them back. It was a dark night, with just a sliver of moon, and clouds were in constant shift over the stars. I tied back the gold curtain tassel. I couldn't see much, just thick dark shadows that I thought must be the home wood. There was no movement of any kind. Everything was calm and still.

I walked to the cherry wood armoire that had to be at least two hundred years old and pulled out a lovely crimson velvet cloak lined with ermine, and wrapped myself up. Dear George must be pacing by now. I didn't want any dog accidents our first night in our new home.

At that moment Stella reappeared with my brandy, a very full glass of brandy, and she handed it to me with a barely suppressed smirk. Once she was out of sight, I downed several sips, drew a deep breath, and told my headache to get a grip on itself.

A few minutes later I knocked lightly on Miss Chrislock's bedchamber door. I heard her call out, and opened the door to see that George was indeed pacing. When he saw me, he set up a din until I had him in my arms and was alternately kissing him and rubbing his ears. "You're ready for your before-bedtime stroll?" Once I was satisfied that Miss Chrislock was comfortably settled, I wished her a fond good night, kissed her cheek, then bore George away. Thankfully, he didn't bark at all until we were outside. Then he looked up at the dark sky, at the house and grounds he wasn't at all used to, and whimpered. He plastered himself against my leg.

"It's all right," I said, leaning down to pet him. "This is our new home. It is not all that different from Deerfield Hall. We can't explore tonight, it is too late, and my head feels like it wants to fall off my neck and go bouncing across the ground. I promise to take you all about tomorrow. Go find a suitable bush, George. I'll wait for you here."

The night was cold. Thank God there was only a slight breeze. I wrapped myself more tightly in my cloak and watched George pause at a bush, decide it was not to his liking, for whatever reason, then trot to the next, and the next.

"When will he come to a decision?"

It was John. I was quite alone with him. It didn't matter. He was my step-nephew. There was nothing more to fear from him.

"His record is eleven bushes and one skinny tree. As I recall, the weather was particularly warm and pleasant that evening. Since it's cold tonight, I doubt he'll dawdle."

George didn't dawdle at all. He appeared quite pleased with the fifth bush. When he came trotting back, he saw John and yipped wildly until John finally picked him up.

"I have never seen George toady up to anyone like he has to you."

"I told you that very first time I saw you that I had magic with animals."

"Yes," I said, "you did. Give me my dog now. Good night, John."

He didn't say another word, for which I was profoundly grateful. But I knew he was watching me cross the vast entrance space of the Old Hall, George in my arms, watching me climb the stairs. I never turned around. But George did and wuffed at him, and that's how I knew he was still there.

While I changed into my nightgown, George explored The Blue Room. He sniffed every corner, every piece of furniture, even sat in front of the fireplace for a moment, watching the orange embers twist and tumble and explode lazily into small bursts of flame. Then he stood in front of me and wuffed. "It's all strange, isn't it? However, you and I are young and flexible. We'll adapt."

It took me nearly ten minutes to snuff out all the candles that were arranged in beautiful candelabras all about the bedchamber, and climb into bed.

Once George was settled against my left side, his usual sleeping spot, I said, "I want you to be vigilant, George. If a wandering spirit comes for a visit, I expect you to alert me."

George was snoring.

We both slept throughout the night. I always hoped that I never snored as loudly as George did. If any spirits came to call, I didn't know it.

To my surprise, the early morning knock on the door wasn't Stella or my curious Amelia. It was Brantley. He averted his eyes, since I was wearing a dressing gown. He looked toward the armoire and said, "I am here to walk Mr. George."

George, who was sunk so deeply in the goose down that he had to bounce up and down on his short legs to see what was going on, glimpsed Brantley, jumped down from the very tall bed, and stretched. Then he trotted straight to Brantley, and lifted his paw. Brantley could have been charmed, I wasn't certain. He didn't say anything, just shook George's paw and picked him up. "We will return shortly, my lady." And he was gone.

Mr. George, I thought, had arrived.

However, I didn't have a clue about myself. I hoped that Lawrence would take care of all the questions that had bubbled out of Amelia the previous night.

Because I'd left the draperies open, early morning sunlight poured into the room. I visited the small bathing room just next to the dressing room, then walked about the very big bedchamber. There were three different seating arrangements, that wonderfully soft bed set up at least three feet on a dais, tall, very wide windows, with rich, pale blue draperies that I'd drawn to let in the dangerous night air.

I turned and looked about my new bedchamber. My first impression was that I had suddenly been immersed in the bluest of seas. Varying shades of blue wallpaper covered three of the walls. The fourth wall was painted the palest blue I'd ever seen, nearly cream. The carpet was a soft, pale blue, as light as a summer sky. Lawrence was right. The room was charming, large, airy, and filled with light.

It wasn't too fussy, either, which I appreciated. As I wandered over to the bell cord to ring for hot water, I wondered why anyone, no matter the age, wouldn't be thoroughly delighted with The Blue Room.

What the devil was wrong with it?

Chapter Nine

A very pretty young girl appeared not ten minutes later hauling a large can of hot water and panting hard.

"For your bath, my lady," she said, and tried to curtsy while holding that can of hot water that was nearly half her size.

"Goodness, where is a footman?"

"I don't need a footman," she said between pants. "This is my job, and I can do it. You'll see, my lady."

"I do see," I said, grinning at her show of independence. "Who are you?"

She set down the huge can and took a few moments to catch her breath. "I'm Belinda, formally a sometimes-maid to Mrs. Thomas when Stella is out of sorts, which she many times is, since she just stopped speaking to the butcher in Devbridge-on-Ashton, our village just a mile to the east."

I stared at her, fascinated. "Why did Stella stop speaking to the butcher?"

"Well, naturally I'm not one to gossip," she said, stepping closer, "but since you're the new lady of the house, you should know about this fellow, who, Stella heard, had been seeing Mrs. Graystock, a female of very loose repute who lives in a charming cottage just outside the village."

"Oh. That explains it very well. I am glad to meet you, Belinda. If you would pour the hot water, I would appreciate it."

"I'll do more than that, my lady. I'll scrub your back for you."

No one had ever scrubbed my back. Not even once in my life. "That sounds marvelous."

And it was. I didn't even think of dismissing Belinda after that. I had left all my black gowns in London. She helped me dress in a soft gray muslin gown, then sat me down at the dressing table and plaited my hair quite nicely atop my head. "If it were evening, I would thread ribbons in and out, but it's morning and we don't want to make Mrs. Thomas feel like a dowd compared to you."

When I rose, I felt my spirits also rise considerably when she said, all sincere and enthusiastic, "Oh, you're beautiful, my lady, just beautiful. Such glorious hair you've got—all red and brown and every shade in-between, and ever so nice and curly."

I would have kissed her for her splendid opinion if Brantley hadn't returned with George at that moment. "Mr. George," Brantley informed me, "walked all the way to the Devbridge stables with Jasper, a young footman of great energy and goodwill. Jasper reported a satisfactory conclusion to Mr. George's constitutional."

"Thank you," I said. Truth be told, I'd forgotten all about George once Belinda was rubbing a soft sponge over my back.

"It's only eight o'clock in the morning, my lady," Belinda said, eyeing the beautiful old clock on the mantel. "Mrs. Thomas won't be downstairs until at least ten o'clock. Just gentlemen, I fear, except for Mr. Thomas. Ah, that poor gentleman must be so terribly careful, you know. You will learn that Mr. Thomas's health isn't always steady. All of us want him to move slowly in the morning, to be certain that all his parts are operating well before he begins to partake fully of the day. We want to keep our beautiful young man as healthy as possible."

"He does look like a god."

"That is true. It is hard not to just stand and gawk at him." Belinda added with absolute conviction, "We won't let him get ill. All of us are vigilant."

George and I went to see Miss Crislock, who was still in bed, her lovely black hair, barely peppered with gray, plaited in a thick braid that fell over her shoulder. She was such a kind lady, about my mother's age had she lived. Miss Crislock had come to me when I had moved to Deerfield Hall to be with Grandfather. I was very fond of her. "You must let everyone in the family meet you today, Milly," I said, leaning down to kiss her smooth cheek. "I don't suppose you remember that man, John, whom I saw on three different occasions?"

"Of course, dear. You were afraid of him, although you didn't say so."

However had she come to think that? "Oh, no, I wasn't. Truly, Milly, it is just that he was very forward, perhaps even overly anxious, until he finally let me be." I drew a deep breath. "John is Lawrence's nephew and heir. It appears that he lives here."

Miss Crislock said thoughtfully, her brow furrowed, "The Lord works in mysterious ways, Andy. Very mysterious indeed."

I wasn't about to ask her what she meant by that.

"Regardless," I said, "he is now my step-nephew, surely somewhat odd, but we will doubtless learn to rub together well enough."

"It will prove interesting." She had never said anything either for or against my marriage to Lawrence. I suppose I had been afraid to ask her, and thus I hadn't.

I smiled at her and picked up George, who was now bored and wanted attention. "It's rather a strange household, but then again, I've never been in a house that wasn't strange, each in its own way. The house is large and complicated. So many different people building on over the years. You will want to go exploring. You have met Mrs. Redbreast, the housekeeper?"

"Yes, Andy, she is a very nice woman. A fount of information. I shall begin my explorations with her this afternoon."

"I will send my new maid, Belinda, to you. You will find her delightful. She is independent and brimming with tales about everyone who lives here."

"Be careful, Andy," she called after me.

Of what, I wondered.

I left her bedchamber, George trotting beside me. Because his legs were so short, he had to do little leaps from step to step down the staircase. I was laughing by the time he collapsed onto the ancient polished oak floor in the Old Hall. He immediately went to sniff out one of the suits of armor.

"I hope he won't pull one of them down on top of himself," John said.

To my absolute horror, George raised his leg and relieved himself on a suit of armor. "Oh, no. George, how could you?"

John was laughing behind me. The moment George heard his voice, the knight was forgotten. This time, however, John just smiled down at him and said firmly, "George, you will mind your manners. I know the armor was an overwhelming temptation. At least you relieved yourself on Flemish armor and not on English armor. But you will have to learn to contain yourself."

I was horribly embarrassed. I stared down at George, who was gazing up at John with naked adoration on his ugly little face, his topknot flopping up and down. "I can't believe you did that. You have never done anything like that before. You are a heathen, George."

"Has he ever been near so many old, smelly, and soon-to-be-rusted suits of armor?"

"No, he hasn't. But Jasper took him walking just an hour ago. He is fully housebroken. He shouldn't have done that. Oh, dear, what am I to do?"

"I will inform Brantley that the Flemish armor needs to be cleaned down. Don't worry. I imagine that Mrs. Redbreast will turn up a recipe to remove any odors." He ruffled his hand through George's hair. "If you wish, George, you may accompany us to the breakfast parlor."

"He loves bacon."

"Yes, I remember you telling me that. I believe my uncle just went in. You are an early riser."

"Yes."

"Somehow I am not surprised."

When we came into the small, quite

charming, circular breakfast room, with windows bowing around its entire perimeter, Lawrence immediately rose from his chair. "Good morning, my dear. I trust you slept well?"

"Immensely well. I instructed George to alert me if any otherworldly specters paid us a visit. If any did, we both slept right through their welcome."

"Don't listen to Amelia. She's her father's daughter, and that means that she must believe in ghosts and bizarre phenomena that naturally don't exist here at Devbridge Manor, or anywhere else for that matter."

He turned to John. "You are the first one about, John. I am pleased. I have alerted Swanson that we will be in the estate room promptly at nine o'clock. Your education will begin."

John only nodded then turned to the sideboard that held at least a half dozen silver-domed trays. I joined him, delighted that the plates stacked at the end of the sideboard were nice and large.

To Lawrence's evident surprise, no sooner had John and I sat down to eat than Amelia and Thomas came arm in arm into the room.

"I didn't cough a single time when I opened my eyes this morning," Thomas said, and beamed at us all. "Amelia pronounced me well enough to come down."

He looked so beautiful, his face so pure in its lines and planes, that I simply stared at him, a forkful of scrambled eggs halfway to my mouth.

"Do get hold of yourself," John said.

"It is difficult. Is there not anything ugly about him?"

"Not that I have ever seen," John said, and smiled toward his brother, who was dishing up an immense amount of food onto his plate, all the while telling Lawrence about the very brief bout of elevated breathing he'd awakened to at about two o'clock in the morning.

"I massaged his chest until his heart rate slowed," Amelia said, all seriousness and concern. "I must admit to being alarmed for a moment there."

John cocked a black eyebrow at his brother. "Whatever were you doing at two o'clock in the morning to increase the speed of your heart?"

Thomas blushed scarlet, from just above his cravat to his hairline.

"Oh," John said, and saluted his brother with his knife. "If your heart had not speeded up, Thomas, then it wasn't worth the effort. It's natural, trust me on this."

"That's what I told him," Amelia said, in a voice as cool as the two slices of toast she slipped onto her plate.

I fed bacon to George, who was thankfully minding his manners, sitting between me and John. I kept my head down, all my attention on George chomping down on that bacon. I knew what they were talking about. I wasn't stupid. I couldn't believe they'd talk about such things at the breakfast table.

Lawrence cleared his throat and lightly touched his hand to my shoulder. "Ah, here is Miss Crislock. Welcome, dear lady. May I serve you some eggs and kippers?"

I had not expected to see her until the afternoon. "Yes, Milly, do join us."

Once Miss Crislock was seated, a cup of tea placed gently in front of her, and everyone had been introduced to her, Lawrence said to the table at large, "Are you familiar with Oliver Wilton?"

"Yes," Amelia said. "He was the Duke of Broughton. My father knows him, said he was an old fossil with a splendid brain. I believe he died recently."

"Yes, that's right. Actually, he was Andy's grandfather. Her first cousin, Peter Wilton, has inherited the dukedom. He is the seventh Duke of Broughton. He is the former duke's grandson. Peter and Andy were raised together when they were young because Peter's parents were killed when he was a small child."

"Actually," I said, trying to smile at everyone, "Peter and I are more brother and sister than first cousins, and have treated each other as such since I was just a little girl."

"Then, what is your name, Andy?" Thomas asked as he carefully studied the crock of sweet butter at his elbow. Was there a bug of some sort in the butter? Finally, he pushed it away and began looking over the apricot jam, which was absolutely delicious.

I said, even as I fed George another bit of bacon, "When I went to live with my grandfather, he was going to adopt me and change my name to his, but my mother requested that he wouldn't, and so I still have my father's name. I'm Andrea Jameson."

"Andrea Jameson Lyndhurst," Lawrence said. "Regardless, she is Oliver Wilton's granddaughter, only offspring of his daughter, Olivia, who was named after him."

"Both you and your cousin orphaned at such early ages," Amelia said. "No, dearest, I think you would prefer the scrambled eggs from this platter. They're more firmly cooked, thus reducing the chance of inflaming your stomach."

Thomas nodded, smiled at his wife, and helped himself to a huge helping of the firmer scrambled eggs.

George barked.

John looked down at that precious little face with the hair hanging nearly to his jaws, and said, "George, you are so spoiled you will next demand to climb up on my lap and eat off my plate."

"I have never believed," Miss Crislock said in her sweet voice, "that an animal should be allowed in the same room where there is food. However, when I met George, I was so quickly besotted, I was willing to let him even drink my chocolate in the morning. He is a despot, that small fellow."

And my very tolerant husband of four days laughed.

Thirty minutes later I was back in The Blue Room replacing my soft kid slippers with some stouter walking boots. The morning was lovely, and Amelia was ready to explore the grounds with me.

I was whistling as I untied the ribbons around my ankles. A sudden glint of light made me blink. I turned my head at the same angle again, and there was another glint. It remained. I cocked my head in question and walked, one slipper on my foot and the other off, to the long bank of windows.

I faced east. The morning light was brilliant. I opened one of the wide windows and looked out. I could see the lads with their long wooden staffs driving the cows to pasture. I heard the gardeners talking about the roses in the lower garden just beneath my window. Then I heard a knock at my bedchamber door.

I turned only to feel a tug at the sleeve of my gown and then a tear. I looked down to see that my sleeve had caught on a jagged piece of metal attached to the outside of the window casement. Carefully I managed to lift the material from the jagged metal.

"Now, what is this?" I said aloud. George wuffed, but didn't get up from the soft rug in front of the fireplace. I looked more closely. It was a small, sharp piece of metal, and it seemed to be buried partially in a small circular hole. Holes—in the window casing? I looked more closely and realized quickly enough that there were several such holes placed at equal intervals along the outside casing.

There was another knock on the door.

"Come," I called out.

It was Amelia. "I am just changing my shoes," I said, smiling toward her. "I will meet you at the front door."

The moment she closed the door, I was back at the windows, studying that long row of holes.

I nearly fell over when I realized exactly what those neatly lined-up holes meant.

There had been bars in this window. I looked upward and saw matching holes in the window casing at the top of the windows.

"Oh, goodness," I said, and rubbed the gooseflesh on my arms. My heart began to pound, slow sharp beats. The Blue Room was the bedchamber none of them thought I should have. And I had wondered why.

There had been bars in these windows. Who had been imprisoned in here? How long ago had it been?

Maybe a mad uncle in the last century, I

thought, and looked over at George, who was still snoozing with his little head on his front paws.

I walked to all the other windows and flung them open, only to find that all the windows were just the same. At some point all of them had been barred.

I shivered, not from the cold of the fresh air pouring into the room, but from my discovery. It made no sense. Someone had imprisoned a mad relative in this beautiful room?

Naturally, there was an excellent explanation. It wasn't a question of otherworldly phenomena or errant specters, unless the specters had terrorized the inhabitant of this beautiful bedchamber into madness.

I flung my slipper across the room. I had turned very suddenly into a twit. This was nonsense, all of it. Who cared if there were bars? For heaven's sake, this house had been built nearly four hundred years ago. There were probably ancient bloodstains on many of the floors. Each room in this magnificent house had known death in all shapes and forms.

Those damned bars—they had to be from a long time ago. They had nothing to do with me. Still, I was intrigued. I would ask Lawrence as soon as I could find him alone. I slowly closed the windows, every one of them.

I found my boots in the bottom of the armoire and pulled them on. I laced them slowly, every few seconds looking back toward the windows, picturing those lines of holes, picturing black bars not more than six inches apart, picturing a vague image clutching desperate hands around those bars, screaming to the night air to be freed.

I left George to sleep off his bacon and went downstairs to meet Amelia.

Chapter Ten

Amelia was waiting for me just outside the great front doors of Devbridge Manor. It was a warm day, quite unexpected for November. A light breeze stirred the air, with only a lingering hint of chill. Yorkshire wasn't a thing like the counties to the south. It was ruggedly beautiful, and everything seemed oversized—huge clumps of trees, all densely clustered together in the midst of a barren plain, grand masses of rocks in the oddest places, as if strewn there by a god's whimsical hand. And, of course, there were the endless Yorkshire moors. The Grannard moor was just off to the east, so desolate with its stark and forlorn barrows and hillocks and its deep gullies that sliced haphazardly through the land like very old scars. I loved it, always had. During the past three years, though, Grandfather had preferred either the small manor house in Penzance at the end of rugged, mournful Cornwall, or the fifty-year-old Putnam Square town house in London that now belonged to Peter. Deerfield Hall was also now Peter's responsibility. Everything was now Peter's responsibility. I wondered if he would sell out and return to England to take over his duties as the seventh duke of Broughton. I hoped he would come to Deerfield Hall, his country seat now, and so very close to my new home. I felt a deep ache thinking of how we had parted in London just before my marriage to Lawrence. But Peter was fair. He would observe that I was happy, and he would come about.

I breathed in the richly scented country air, pulling it deeply into my body. I couldn't see the Grannard moor from here, but it was close, and just knowing that, made me want to take George there. I could see him staring at the strange landscape, wondering exactly what I expected him to do with it. George was used to London and all its noise and traffic. There wasn't a dray or a cart or the most elegant carriage he wouldn't chase until his short legs finally buckled under him.

But here, he would learn about an entirely different life. Perhaps I could take him to the Grannard moor this afternoon. I had left him sleeping soundly, after stuffing himself at breakfast.

Amelia said, as she carefully eased a pin into her hair, "It's lovely today, isn't it? I remember standing here just like you are, just looking around and taking everything in. It might take some getting used to. Many people hate Yorkshire."

"Do you?"

"I come from Somerset. Gentle valleys and hills and easy little streams crisscross the land through all the farms."

"Sort of like an innocent maiden mated to a violent warrior?"

She blinked, and I couldn't blame her for that. As a comparison, it was perhaps not all that accurate.

"If by that you mean that Somerset is the innocent maiden and Yorkshire is the warrior, then, exactly," Amelia said. "I've gotten used to it during the past year. Now I quite like it. Come with me to the stables. I want you to meet Buttercup, my sweet mare that my father brought over from Wexford. Also, has Uncle Lawrence yet offered you a mount?"

"No, not as yet."

The Devbridge stables were immaculate, the sun shining brightly down on the bright red tile roof. The paddocks were white, obviously kept freshly painted, and as I looked out into the nearest paddock, I fell in love.

He was an immense black-as-sin stallion, with a streak of white down the middle of his head and four white socks. His head had the proud tilt of an Arabian mare I once rode, but there was little else graceful and lithe about him. He was at least seventeen hands high, heavy strong legs, and thick powerful chest.

"What is it, Andy?"

"Just a moment, Amelia. I've lost my heart. I'll join you in a bit."

I walked toward the paddock, seeing only that magnificent animal. I called out to him. "Good day to you, Beauty."

To my astonishment and pleasure, he turned his great head toward me and whinnied. I reached the paddock and climbed the fence. I held out my hand to him, calling him beauty and angel and even an archangel, but I came back again and again to Beauty. I didn't have anything for him. I hoped he wouldn't take it amiss and bite my hand.

Again, to my delight, when I called to him, he trotted toward me, his tail swishing from side to side, his great head nodding up and down. He was perhaps four years old, in perfect health, his coat glistening beneath the bright morning sun.

He butted his big head against my hand and nearly pushed me backward off the fence. I laughed. "You are wonderful, you know that? Certainly you do. I should have asked Amelia who you were. I wonder what your name is. I can't keep calling you Beauty, not a handsome fellow like you."

"His name is Tempest."

I turned slowly, Tempest still butting my hand, to see John standing six feet behind me, dressed for riding.

"Why aren't you with your uncle and Swanson, the estate manager? You're supposed to be studying hard, readying yourself for the day when finally you may take over."

"Swanson's wife just birthed twins. My uncle decided to let him remain with her to-day."

"I should think so." I waved toward Tempest. Of course I knew the answer even as I asked. "He is yours?"

"Yes. You can forget snagging him for yourself. He is a soldier's horse, strong and intelligent, and meaner than the devil when he has to be. He is flirting with you right now, but were you to try to ride him, he would either ignore you entirely or toss you in the nearest river."

"Oh, no, he wouldn't." I turned back to Tempest. "Will you allow me to ride you?"

That grand animal eyed me with benevolence, I would swear that he did exactly that. "I ride well, it's just that I haven't been able to ride in a while. I'm really quite good. Anyone who is a good rider knows that a rider's physical strength has nothing to do with anything."

"Tempest is smart, but I doubt even he understood all of that. Besides, that last was meant for me. You might as well turn around and face me. Ask me if you may ride my horse."

I turned on the fence. "May I ride your horse, John?"

"No. Absolutely not. He gets impatient, he has his own ideas about where he wants to go, and when, and exactly what route he wants to take. He requires mastery, which he now accepts that I have. He can become vicious. What would I tell my uncle if I were to let you ride my horse and Tempest killed his blushing new bride?"

"I'm not blushing."

"The other two are true."

"All right, just what would you tell him?"

"Well, if you ever did ride Tempest, it would be without my permission, and you would deserve whatever he did to you. I would have to tell my uncle that his bride was an idiot."

"An idiot, am I? Now I will tell you what I think. You're being rude because I didn't flutter my hands and fall at your feet and whimper all over you in London. Admit it. It is not what you are used to from ladies. And now you have turned nasty. I will admit that I've been called things, but never an idiot."

He came up to stand beside me at the paddock. He put one foot up on a fence railing. He was wearing black Hessians, so perfectly polished I could see my frown in them, and something else. I could see that I was wary, very wary. Now that I saw the proof, I brought in the coldest thoughts I could to counteract what he made me feel. He was much too big, he knew it, he used it to dominate, but he couldn't hurt me, not here, not on his uncle's estate.

"A twit, then," he said.

"No, a twit is even worse than an idiot. I won't have either of them. It's true, isn't it? You are probably used to having to turn ladies away."

He cocked his head to one side and studied me a moment. I looked at my reflection in his boots again. I looked both cold and slightly arrogant. He said finally, his voice slow and thoughtful, "That is ridiculous. You don't know what you're talking about. You are just trying to rile me. When I first saw you in Hyde Park, I wanted to meet you." He shrugged and looked past me. "There was something about you that drew my interest. I recognized you were in deep mourning, but I promise you, there was never a wicked thought in my head. Then, to my surprise, you couldn't wait to get away from me. You were rude. I remember wanting to smack you, but I couldn't, not being a gentleman.

No, I bided my time until I saw you again. But it didn't matter, none of it."

He turned away to walk farther down the paddock, gave a light nearly soundless whistle, and Tempest raised his great head and snorted. He trotted up to John without hesitation and butted his shoulder. If he had done that to me, he would have knocked me into the dirt. John just laughed and continued to stroke Tempest's nose. He said over his shoulder, "It wasn't until the third time I spoke to you that I finally realized what was wrong. For some reason I still cannot fathom, you were and still are afraid of me."

It was like a blow to the middle. It wasn't true, it wasn't, and so I said, "That's utter nonsense."

"I believe it to be true, but who cares why now? None of it matters. You are my uncle's wife." He then turned to face me and said in a very deliberate voice, "If you rode my horse and he managed to kill you, then at least I wouldn't have to see you again."

"Once more. In my casket."

"I want to know why you married my uncle."

Amelia called out to me.

I walked over to pat Tempest's nose. He

leaned toward me, well aware that I was doting on him, and I hugged him as best I could with John in the way.

"I'm leaving," I said, and climbed down from the paddock fence.

"Why, damn you?"

I said over my shoulder, "Amelia asked me the same question last night when she took me to The Blue Room. It isn't any of your business. If you have such a consuming curiosity, ask your uncle."

I saw the surge of black violence in his eyes, then it was gone, once again well controlled. I wouldn't want to be his enemy in a battle. I saw the pulse in his throat, throbbing. He was angry. Well, it wasn't my fault. He said finally, his voice as hard as those bars would have been when they'd covered The Blue Room windows. "Evidently you're not afraid of men in general, since you married my uncle. Or is it just old men you don't fear?"

"Shut up, damn you."

"Ah, have I hit upon something here?"

"You could not hit that barn with a magnification glass."

"Riled you, have I? Hit you right between the eyes. Ah, yes, here you are three months later, my dear step-auntie, married to my damned uncle, a man certainly more than old enough to be your father. Why did you do it?"

"Go away. No, I will. Good-bye."

He said nothing more until I picked up my skirts and trotted toward Amelia, who was holding the reins of the sweetest-looking chestnut mare I had ever seen. I heard his laughter, the bastard. I patted her mare's nose, gave her a carrot that one of the stable lads passed to me, and never once considered looking back at John. I focused all my attention on that sweet mare. "You're a love, aren't you," I said. "What do you think of Tempest? Would you like to gallop with him?"

"No, Buttercup wants nothing to do with Tempest. I saw you patting him, Andy. You must be careful. Even though I have never seen him be nice before to anyone except John, you should take care. The stable lads are afraid of him. He's vicious."

I finally looked back over to the paddock. I watched John put a bridle on Tempest's tossing head, then swing up onto his bare back. I watched them sail as one over the far paddock fence. Soon they were gone from sight.

"Don't ride that horse, Andy. John makes riding him look very easy, but it isn't. John is amazing, but he's been a soldier for a very long time. He is used to taming savage sorts of things."

I could well believe that, but what savage sorts of things did Amelia mean, precisely? I wasn't afraid of him, curse his eyes.

"You seemed to be arguing with John. What about?"

"Nothing. You simply misunderstood."

Thank God Amelia didn't say any more about it.

Ten minutes into my tour of the stables, I found a sprightly little Arabian mare named Small Bess and promptly fell in love again. "His lordship jest fetched her here three months ago," Rucker, the head stable lad, said as he scratched her ears. That meant, I thought, that he had not bought Small Bess for me. What a pity.

"Why don't ye ask his lordship?" Rucker said even as he began brushing her long silver-gray mane.

"I will, thank you, Rucker. Good-bye, Small Bess."

"You may ask Uncle Lawrence at luncheon. He never said why he bought her, and no one really asked. The stable lads have been riding her, no one else."

"He didn't buy her for me," I said. "He didn't even know me then."

"We'll see. Now, Andy, let me take you to the Black Chamber, where some say that a long-ago Devbridge countess stabbed her lover."

I felt the unnatural cold in that small black room the moment Amelia unlocked the door and pushed it open. There was only a narrow cot in the room, nothing else, not even a rug to cover the wide-boarded floor. The walls were painted black. The single window was covered with a dark drapery. I couldn't tell what color, but close enough to black to make my flesh ripple. Amelia raised her candle branch high.

"It's a pit in here," I said, backing toward the door. "I don't want to stay in here. It is depressing. It invites premonition and nerves."

"Come along, don't be a coward. It's nothing. I wish there was something strange in here, for my father's sake, but I have never seen anything amiss with the room other than some loon painted the walls black. Did a former countess really stab her lover? I hate to admit it, but it does make an excellent story—but in person, in here? No, it's just a small black room. I suppose I could have it painted white and put a nice lacy curtain on the window. What do you think?"

"It's not right. Something is very wrong here. Don't you feel it, Amelia?"

I was standing well behind her, not two feet from the door now. She was standing in the center of the room, raising the candle branch high, sending the wispy candlelight into all the black corners. "Feel what?"

"The coldness. The unnatural coldness. Cold and clammy, and it makes your skin skitter and your heart jerk. It's not right."

She walked back to me, staring, her head cocked to one side. "What do you mean? Oh, yes, I know my father speaks about how in some rooms there will be a certain spot that makes one shiver because it is so suddenly and inexplicably cold. But I don't feel anything here."

"I do," I said, and quickly backed out of the room. "I don't know about any countess killing her lover, but there is something in there, Amelia, something that's malevolent and cold, and blacker than those walls."

She was shaking her head at me, even smiling, as she pulled the door closed and locked it. She didn't believe me, obviously, but that was all right. I didn't want to believe myself.

"Has your father ever visited that room?"

"No, Father hasn't visited me here as of yet. Thomas and I have been married a little under a year. Father would have probably come with me and Thomas and spent many hours examining each and every room in the Hall, but there's my mother, you see. She has been ill during the past year. She is fine now. I would very much like them to visit."

I was walking quickly away from that awful room, and Amelia had to skip to keep up with me. "What was your mother's illness?" I asked when we had walked halfway down the corridor. When she didn't answer, I turned to see that she had stopped, and was staring into a room whose door was open about six inches. A wildly bright splash of sunlight shot out into the dim corridor.

"How odd," she said, and walked into the room. "Just a moment, Andy." I stopped, then shook my head and prepared to follow her, when suddenly the door simply slammed shut in my face.

Why had she done that? "Amelia? Open the door. What are you doing in there? Amelia, answer me."

I heard her call out once. "Amelia!" I threw my shoulder against the door, but it didn't budge. I fought with the doorknob, but the door was locked. I felt utter terror, and for a moment, I was witless, locked into that terror. "Amelia, I have to get help."

The wide corridor of the west wing wasn't quite dark, but dark enough, since all the doors that gave onto the corridor were firmly closed and there wasn't a single window about. Shadows were everywhere, everyone of them coming at me, wanting to suck me inside them.

"Stop it, you idiot!" I yelled at myself, my breath lurching out hard and deep.

I finally reached the massive central staircase and went flying down the steps. I nearly tripped once, but grabbed the railing and righted myself.

"Lawrence, John! Help! Come here, quickly!"

There wasn't anyone anywhere. There were dozens of people in this huge house.

I called out again, as loud as I could. I wondered, though, how loud it really could be, since my heart was pounding louder than a clap of thunder.

I was nearly down the stairs when suddenly, someone flung open both of the great front doors so wide they banged back against the walls of the Old Hall. Dazzling, blinding light poured into the dim Old Hall, more light than I could imagine, overwhelming white light that filled even the shadowed corners, that touched the ancient suits of armor against the back wall, filled everything with such blank whiteness that it was painful. I screamed at that crushing white light, lost my footing, and tumbled down headfirst the remaining three or four steps.

I must have scrambled my brains, because everything was blurry and vague, and I really didn't care. I heard a man's voice, above me, saying my name over and over again.

I managed to get my eyes open to look up at him. He seemed to float above me, this creature who seemed all dark, yet he

was in the middle of all that blinding whiteness. And then I knew. I was dead.

Thank God I'd made it to Heaven.

"Are you an angel?"

Chapter Eleven

The angel blinked, I could see him that clearly. Those very dark eyes of his blinked yet again. He gathered me to him, so close that I felt his warm breath on my forehead, sweet and dark.

"Perhaps," said an equally dark voice.

"Maybe I was wrong about Heaven. Is this Hell instead? You're all dark, even your voice, like sins kept secret for a very long time. Are you one of the devil's angels? Grandfather always believed that the devil had his angels just like God had his. Is that what you are? Your eyes are nearly black. How can you bear all that white light?"

"It isn't all that strong. Hush now."

"It's like Heaven has split apart, and everything is gushing out of it. It's too much, really, it's just too much. I don't understand any of this."

And I closed my eyes again. My brain went blank, but deep down, I didn't want to be in Heaven or in Hell. I didn't want any angel at all to be with me, and if it turned out that he was one of the devil's angels, then I was in big trouble. I tried to remember major sins, but my mind only managed to dredge up the time I had stolen a shilling off the vicar's desk. Surely even the devil couldn't remember back to a sin that I'd committed when I was seven years old. No, surely not. "I don't want to be dead," I said to that dark face that seemed to fade in and out just beyond my nose. "I want to stay right here in Yorkshire and ride Tempest."

"You may only do the first, not the second."

Then he picked me up easily, and I realized this angel was very strong. He turned, and the incredible white light shown fully in my face.

Then the white light was gone again. "I want both," I said against his shoulder.

"I promise that you are still in Yorkshire. But you won't ride Tempest. If you try it, I'll thrash you. Now, just hold still." Everything fell suddenly into place. I knew then, all of a sudden, in that very instant, that it was John, and the fear pounded deep and steady. I hated it. I just didn't know what to do about it.

He said, his voice calm and deep, "That's it. Don't fight me. I know you're afraid of me. I don't know why, but perhaps soon you will tell me. Trust me, Andy. I'm not going to hurt you."

I could feel his heartbeat against my cheek. It was strong, steady, a bit fast. He was very much a man, never an angel. I opened my eyes to look up at his chin. My brain slipped a notch, whirling me back to uncertainty, and I said in a thin wispy voice, "Where are we going? Why aren't you simply flying me?"

"I am not a damned angel. I don't have any wings. I'm your damned step-nephew. Your cheek is against my heart. Can't you feel the human beat? No, don't say anything. Just be quiet, you're still half-witless."

"All right," I said, closed my eyes, and simply drifted away. The fear wafted away as well, and that was a good thing. I didn't think I was unconscious, but everyone who was suddenly around me did. There were so many voices, all of them speaking at once. Amelia, I thought. I had to tell them that Amelia was locked in a room on the second floor.

I forced my eyes open, felt a stabbing pain behind my right ear, and said, "John, please, I was running to get help. You must help Amelia."

Thomas nearly leaped on me. "Heh! What's this about Ameila?"

I focused on his suddenly pale face. "West wing," I whispered, "a room about halfway down the corridor on the right. It was open, and Amelia seemed surprised that it was. She went into it. I was following her, but the door slammed in my face. I couldn't get it open or break it down. Amelia cried out. I don't know why. I'm all right. Go to Amelia. Please, I don't know what's happening to her."

And then I just folded down. I knew now that I was very much still a part of this earth because the pain was building and building, and I just closed my eyes and let the pain take me deeper and deeper until finally I managed to ease away from it and slip into beautiful deep darkness.

I don't know how long I was away, but I woke up again, in that sort of twilight that was calm and soft, and there were no demands on me, no one talking loudly. I was just lying there, a nice cool damp cloth on my forehead. When I opened my eyes, my angel, who just happened to also be a man I was afraid of, wasn't there. It was Lawrence, no angel, but rather my husband, which meant I wasn't dead, but back here on earth.

"I hope I stay alive this time," I said.

"You're very much alive," he said, and smiled down at me. I felt him squeeze my hand. "How do you feel, Andy?"

"Amelia," I said. "Where is Amelia?"

He was silent a moment, turning away from me. I heard quiet voices. Then he was there again, so close to my face that I could feel his warm breath on my cheek.

"Amelia is sleeping. When Thomas and John found the room, the door was open just a bit and there was Amelia, lying on her side in an empty room, and she was sleeping."

"She was carrying a branch of candles," I

said, trying to find any sense at all in what he had said.

"Yes, the candles were there as well, no longer burning, just there, lying beside her."

"What happened to her?"

"Nothing happened, Andy," Lawrence said, squeezing my hand again, like I was some sort of brain-numbed invalid.

"She cried out." I tried to pull myself up. "The door slammed shut, and she cried out."

"No, don't move, it's too soon."

"Let me go," I said, and forced him to move away as I pulled myself up. I was lying on one of the sofas in the drawing room, a cream-colored throw covering me to my waist. I swung my feet off the sofa and sat up straight. There were a lot of people in the room, but only one of them a woman. I stared at her, and she said after a pained moment, "I'm Mrs. Redbreast, the house-keeper, my lady. We haven't met yet, well, now we're meeting, but it is rather strange this way."

Strange, indeed.

There were John, Lawrence, and Law-rence's valet Flynt, a man I detested with every ounce of dislike in me. He had the flattest eyes I've ever seen, black and opaque.

And another man, standing next to John. John said, "This is Boynton, my batman in the army and now my valet." This man looked hard and tough, his face darkly tanned, the texture of leather. He was nearly as short as I was. Then he smiled, and I saw the big space between his front two teeth, and despite what was happening here, I smiled back. He was old enough to be my father and a good ten years younger than my husband. The smile slid off my face.

I pulled the throw up closer and said, very slowly, very precisely, to the room at large, "I have told you what happened. I heard Amelia cry out. When I could not get the door open, I yelled to her that I was getting help. Even though I fell over my feet when John came through the front doors, I wasn't unconscious for very long."

"No, not long at all," John said. He frowned at me, and there was something in those nearly black eyes of his I didn't like. Maybe it was pity. Yes, pity. If I'd had a rock at hand, I would have thrown it at him.

He said, "The fact of the matter is, we got to that chamber very quickly. Uncle

Lawrence is telling you what happened. The door wasn't locked. Amelia was sleeping on the floor. She woke up and told us that she had seen the door open, was curious because that door was always closed, and had gone inside. She remembers you were in the corridor. Then she simply doesn't remember anything else. Nothing."

"She cried out," I said again. "And that door slammed in my face. It was locked. I pulled and pushed at it, but it just wouldn't open. I'm not insane or still addled." And I was tired of repeating the same thing over and over, particularly since no one appeared to believe me.

"I'm sure that's exactly what happened, my dear girl," Lawrence said. "Now, we're expecting our local physician at any time. He will ensure that you are all right."

I rose slowly. I felt only briefly dizzy, then it cleared. I was nearly back to being myself again. "I don't want a doctor. I want to see Amelia."

"Certainly," Lawrence said. "It is obvious you are very worried about her. However, she is asleep again. She was so tired, she said."

"Does any of this make sense to you?

Why would Amelia be tired? And say she was tired, why in heaven's name would she decide to take a nap on the floor in an empty room? Why would the candles all be out, like someone snuffed them out?"

No one said anything.

I didn't like this at all. I looked from one face to the next, from Lawrence, who looked faintly concerned, to John, who had the look of a dark angel who didn't know what was happening, to Flynt, Lawrence's valet with his flat black eyes, a bad man, I was sure of it. He looked at me like I was a liar, nothing more than that, a liar and of no account at all. As for Boynton, John's valet, there was a deep frown on that brown leather forehead of his. He didn't understand any of it, just like his master, and I didn't, either. I smiled at him again. This time he didn't smile back, his frown remaining firmly in place. As for Mrs. Redbreast, she looked mildly alarmed. Was she afraid that her new mistress was a loon?

"I'm going to my room now," I said. Dragging the beautiful cream throw behind me, I walked from the drawing room, in my stockinged feet, since someone had removed my shoes.

"Let her go," I heard my husband tell one of them. "I will see to her later."

I didn't do anything but keep walking until I heard George barking his head off through the closed door of The Blue Room.

Miss Crislock was walking down the corridor toward me, waving a delicate white hand. "My dear, what are you doing? I was just coming down to see you. I heard that you had fallen. What happened?"

"Just a small tumble down the stairs into the Old Hall. I'm quite all right now, Milly. Everything is just fine. I am just here to get George."

"I suppose George must have sensed that you were near—you know how acute his hearing is—and so he will raise the dead if you don't open that door quickly."

I opened the door to see George standing right in front of me, and in his mouth he held a small yellow mitten.

I went down on my knees in front of him, the beautiful cream throw falling to the floor around me, and began the game of "give it to Mama," to which George locked his little teeth firmly around the object. In this instance, I was afraid he would tear the glove, which looked quite well made and expensive. I cajoled and offered him more bacon for his breakfast tomorrow morning if only he would give me that glove. Finally, I managed to distract him, clicking my fingers together over his head, and he unlocked his jaws. I got the glove. It wasn't an adult glove. It belonged to a girl.

But who? There were no children here, were there?

I said over my shoulder to Miss Crislock, "Milly, I am truly all right. Why don't you find Mrs. Redbreast? Tell her that I am not mad. Yes, convince her that I am quite harmless. I have this feeling that she and Brantley run things around here."

"Certainly, dear. It's true, isn't it?" Miss Crislock patted my shoulder and left me, her lovely pale blue eyes narrowed. What else could I tell her? Reassure her? I couldn't even reassure myself.

Once in my bedchamber, I realized the last thing I wanted to do was leave it. I felt safe in here, even with all those bar holes in the window casements. I thought and thought about what had happened. I couldn't think of a single thing to explain it. When Amelia awoke, I would snag her. Surely she would recall something.

I stayed in my bedchamber for the next hour, until George jumped on the bed and sat himself right down on my chest, his nose an inch from mine. He wuffed.

"You need to go outside, don't you? Well, I feel more alive than otherwise, so let me put some shoes on and we'll be off."

Thankfully, I saw no member of the family as I let myself out of the drawing room French doors that gave on to a small back garden whose brick walls were covered with flowering roses, at least they would be in the spring.

I threw George's favorite stick across the garden, and he was off, yapping until he realized he needed all his breath to run after that stick.

I went over and sat down on a bench that was covered with a lovely white-painted arbor. Ivy threaded through the overhead wooden slats.

I closed my eyes and breathed in the clean chill air. The sun beat warmly down on my face. I began to feel a bit on the achy side, effects from my fall, no doubt. Aches I didn't mind, but the wretched mystery with Amelia was driving me mad. I would learn the truth. Surely Amelia had to remember more than she was telling. The thought that everyone believed that she had simply fallen to sleep on the floor of an empty room was ridiculous.

I opened my eyes when George hit his stick against my knee. Once he was off again, I closed my eyes, only to be startled down to my toes by a nearby rustling noise. After that strange experience with Amelia, I was actually ready to scream my head off. I opened my eyes, ready to take to my heels as fast as I could, but there was nothing mysterious or frightening there, just a pretty young girl of perhaps eleven or twelve standing a few feet away from me. She was small, dainty as a little princess, her hair a rich blond with just a hint of red in it. Her eyes were a lovely combination of a light blue and a dark gray.

"He's wonderful. Who is he?" She was pointing at George, who, with the stick clamped firmly between his jaws, was trotting back to me.

"His name is George. He's a Dandie Dinmont terrier. I agree with you. He's quite the most wonderful, most beautiful dog in all of England."

George stopped dead in his tracks about

three feet from the girl. He dropped the stick and began wagging his tail.

"I think he likes you. What is your name?"

"Oh, I'm Judith. Who are you?"

"Did you perchance lose a lemon-yellow glove?"

"Oh, yes. Miss Gillbank has scolded me for being so careless. I don't know where I dropped it, though."

"In The Blue Room. George found it and brought it to me. I'm Andy. I now live here."

"Why? Who are you? That is a rather odd name, isn't it?"

"Perhaps, but it quite suits me. I'm the Countess of Devbridge. The earl and I arrived just yesterday evening."

"How very odd," Judith said, fell to her knees, ignored me then, and held out a small white hand to George.

George obligingly sniffed her fingers then took a step closer. She turned to look at me. "May I throw his stick?"

"Certainly, if you wish."

I watched her hurl the stick as far as she could. She was strong. That stick nearly hit the far garden wall.

George danced on his back paws and hared off.

I watched Judith jump to her feet and applaud him. There was something vaguely familiar about her, but I couldn't pinpoint what it was.

"Do you visit Devbridge Manor very often?"

She turned to me. She looked puzzled. At the same time George crashed into her with the stick in his mouth. She went down, laughing, dirtying her gown, and not caring. She was having a fine time. I said nothing more until George had been petted to his heart's content and went off to find a bush.

I said again, "Have you ever visited London?"

"Oh, no. Papa said I would only go to London when I was ready to find a husband. I can't imagine traveling anywhere just to get a husband. Husbands are just boys who are grown up. And you know, boys are the very devil. Do you think that changes?"

"Probably not. Who are you visiting here?"

"I'm not visiting," she said, cocking her head at me. "I live here."

I had no clue what was going on here. "Who is your mama?"

The girl straightened up and then sat down next to me on the bench. She began brushing off the dirt stains and grass from her gown. She was no servant's child. Her voice was well-bred, free of the heavy Yorkshire burr, and her clothes were of excellent style and quality. Her gown was a soft yellow, the sleeves and neckline stitched with fine lace.

I said nothing more, just waited.

Finally, she said, "My mama went to Heaven when I was born."

"I'm sorry." I didn't look away from that beautiful little face, a very open face. What the devil was going on here?

"It's all right. I don't remember her. I was just born and don't have any memory of what she was like at all."

"Who is your papa?"

This time Judith looked at me like I was a complete half-wit. "He's the Earl of Devbridge."

I nearly fell off the bench.

Was she my husband's love child? His wife had been dead for many more years than Judith had been on this earth.

"I don't mean to be rude," she said now in a very precise soft voice, "but how can you be the Countess of Devbridge? You're nearly as young as I am. I heard Papa telling

Miss Gillbank last night that you were here, but I hadn't expected you to be so very young. I guess I thought you'd be more like Papa, but you're younger than my cousins, Thomas and John. You're younger than Amelia."

What to say to that? How to ask a little girl if she was a bastard? I gave it a diplomatic try. "Judith, who exactly was your mama?"

"She was Papa's wife, of course."

Well, that answered that. I was so stunned that I just sat there watching George as he went to sniff at his sixth bush. He still hadn't decided where to relieve himself. He was a very particular dog, was George.

Why hadn't my husband considered it important enough to tell me that I was his third wife, that there had been a second Countess of Devbridge? Two dead wives, I thought.

"Miss Gillbank says that my papa loved my mama more than he ever loved any other lady. I suppose that must include you, too, Andy, which is too bad. But you're very young, so it can't matter all that much, can it?"

I must have nodded or something, because she soon continued, "But I don't understand. Why would Papa marry you if he still loves my mama so much? You're even younger than Miss Gillbank."

"Your papa married me because I own George, and he adores George. Don't you? Just look at him, sniffing at every bush in the garden before making his selection. Shall we wager on which bush he finally picks?"

"He'll pick the rhododendron," Judith said, no hesitation at all. "I have a shilling. That's my wager."

I was thinking more along the line of wagering an apple or an orange. But there was her small hand, sticking out toward me.

"I'll take it," I said, and shook her hand. We sat there in rapt silence watching George sniff his way around the garden until he stopped at the only rhododendron bush, and raised his leg.

I sighed. "How did you ever guess he would pick that rhododendron? If there were a dozen of them, it would make sense because you would be playing what is called the odds. But there is only one rhododendron bush in this entire garden."

At that moment we heard a woman's

voice calling, "Judith? Where are you, child? It's time for your geography lesson. Oh, goodness, who is that ugly little dog wetting the rhododendron?"

Chapter Twelve

"He isn't ugly," I said, nearly going *en point* to defend George to the death. Facing me was a young woman, slender, quietly pretty with dark brown hair and rich deep brown eyes. She was dressed neatly in a pale blue wool gown. She was perhaps twenty-five, no older. She had a pointy chin that, surprisingly, was really quite attractive.

She gave me a charming curtsy. "My lady."

"Miss Gillbank, I just won a shilling from Andy."

It appeared that Miss Gillbank knew all about me. Unlike Judith, she wasn't at all surprised that I was just over the edge of my twenty-first year. She gave a quick nod toward George. "I am not used to dogs. I did not mean to insult him. Perhaps he looks more noble now that I think about it." Then Miss Gillbank said to Judith, "What is this about a shilling?"

"It was a wager," I said, and wondered if I had just assisted in the corruption of an innocent.

Instead of recriminations or looks of disapproval, Miss Gillbank just shook her head and sighed. "My lady, this child has won at least five pounds from me over the years. Don't wager against her if you wish to remain solvent. She's very lucky. Also I fancy she is something of a sharper, though you would never believe it looking at that lovely little face."

"I am beginning to believe it a talent, Miss Gillbank," Judith said. "I shall have to ask Papa if he is a gambler."

"He is, but he does not indulge very much in it," she said.

"And I was the one to suggest it," I said, for I myself had always to wager on just about anything that popped to mind. My grandfather had normally won our wagers, but not always. He was a gambler himself, but, he always said, "You wager more than you can afford to lose, you deserve to be shot." A no-nonsense man, my grandfather. Some had believed that he was perhaps too set in his opinions. He was, but since I shared just about all of his beliefs and opinions, I thought those who dared criticize him were fools.

I had never forgotten what he'd said about gambling. As I became older, there were always stories circulating about men who had gambled away their homes, their inheritances, even their horses and hounds, and most of them had shot themselves. I remember hearing about a woman who had killed herself because she had lost all her jewels and her husband refused to buy her more.

"What is a sharper, Miss Gillbank?"

"It is someone who gambles with such skill that everyone refuses to make wagers with him."

"I don't want to be a sharper just yet," Judith said. "If you refuse to wager with me, then my pile of five pounds would never grow."

"Then," I said, "you will have to lose a wager upon occasion, to draw people back into your net."

"Yes, that's it," Judith said. She turned to her governess. "Miss Gillbank, this is Papa's new wife, Andy. I think she is very young to be married to Papa, but she said that Papa adores George, so I guess that makes it all right."

"Hello," I said, and offered her my hand. She looked at my hand, perplexed, then finally shook it. Did she believe I would treat her like a servant?

"Welcome to Devbridge Manor, my lady. I hope Judith here hasn't shredded all our characters?"

"Oh, no. She has spent just about all her time playing with George."

"George isn't ugly, Miss Gillbank," Judith said. "Perhaps you need to put on your glasses to see him better."

Miss Gillbank eyed George, who, having finished his business with the rhododendron, was happily trotting back to three females he imagined to be here just for his pleasure. He picked up the stick in his mouth and waved it at us indiscriminately.

Judith immediately went to play with him. Miss Gillbank smiled as she said, "It is a great pleasure to meet you. His lordship spoke briefly to me last night. He appears to be very happy."

I sat back down on the bench and motioned for her to sit as well, which she did. I said without preamble, my voice quiet enough so Judith wouldn't hear me, "I had no idea my husband had a second wife and a little girl by that marriage."

One of her very pretty arched brows went up. "Oh, goodness, learning such a thing would come as quite a shock. I am so sorry."

"The fact that my husband chose not to tell me is hardly your fault, Miss Gillbank. I suppose I am merely thinking aloud. I simply do not understand why he wouldn't tell me."

"Perhaps you were so important to him that he feared losing you if he did tell you."

That sounded all sorts of romantic, but really rather silly, and it didn't ring true to my ears.

Lawrence had had a different reason, although I didn't have a single clue what it could be. I smiled at Miss Gillbank and asked, "Why weren't you at dinner last evening?"

"I don't eat dinner with the family," she said matter-of-factly, one eye on Judith.

"Actually, we had a fine time last evening. Perhaps you would enjoy yourself. I cannot imagine that it would be much fun for you to eat by yourself."

"No, it is not, but I have become accustomed to it." She gave me a crooked smile that showed her two front teeth overlapping just a bit. It was a charming effect. "A governess is a strange creature, neither fish nor fowl. I quite enjoy Brantley and Mrs. Redbreast, but they would be mortified at the notion of me dining in the kitchen with all the staff."

"Would you please be so kind as to join the family this evening, Miss Gillbank?"

"Thank you, my lady. I should be delighted." She paused a moment, looking toward Judith who was trying her best to pry the stick from between George's locked jaws. He was pulling and growling, his hind paws digging into the grass for more leverage. It did him no good. Judith simply pried his teeth open and grabbed the stick. I smiled as Miss Gillbank said, "I do have one lovely gown. It is simply five years out of style."

"It will be just fine. Perhaps soon we can visit York, and Amelia can take us to the best shops." I raised an eyebrow and said, without thinking, something my grandfather said would make me infamous if I weren't careful, "I presume my husband pays you sufficiently?"

She didn't take offense at that impertinence, just said, "Yes, certainly. I am a very well-qualified governess, my lady. I will have you know that my services are much sought after in these parts. I believe that just six months ago, his lordship was compelled to pay me even more because Mr. Bledsoe wanted me to come and instruct his six daughters." She laughed and shuddered at the same time. "I actually believe that he also wanted to marry me. Then he wouldn't have had to pay me any wages at all."

She clapped her hand over her mouth, those rich brown eyes of hers appalled at what had come out of her mouth.

I just laughed. "That is an excellent story. I imagine you are right about this Mr. Bledsoe. He sounds quite officious."

"Yes," she said, and rose. "Judith, come along, poppet. It's time we ventured into the Far East again."

Judith called back something that sounded vaguely like Chinese.

"Isn't she marvelous? That is 'good day' in Cantonese."

"I see that my husband believes in educating girls. That is rather forward-looking. My grandfather was the same way. The only thing is, he preferred to teach me himself, and depending on how you look at it, my education is very specialized or bizarre."

She laughed. "What makes it specialized?"

"I had a star named after me when I was eleven years old. Some night I will show it to you. It is a lovely star, brighter during the fall months here in England. It's a star in Orion's belt. I remember Grandfather hauling all his guests outside and bringing me to center stage to point out my star. It's called Andrea Major."

"What a wonderful man your grandfather must have been. He gave you your very own star. Just imagine."

After I left Judith and Miss Gillbank, I took George to The Blue Room, where he could nap—after, of course, I had fed him. Belinda brought him some bacon and some kippers left over from breakfast. George must have believed he'd gone to his rewards. He was snoring before he was even completely asleep.

I went downstairs to lunch. I hoped that everyone had dined at least an hour before. I still didn't want to see any of them, except Amelia. I rubbed my shoulder. It was beginning to ache, and my ribs as well. At least I hadn't broken anything. The bruises would go away soon enough.

I was very unlucky. Amelia wasn't in the small breakfast room, just John and Lawrence. I merely nodded to both of them and asked, turning to my husband, "I visited the stables this morning with Amelia. They are very fine. Rucker appears competent and enjoys the horses. May I please ride Small Bess?"

"Of course. I had already decided to give her to you. A wedding present."

I nearly leapt out of my chair to go hug him, just as I'd done so many times to Grandfather when he had given me a marvelous surprise. "Thank you," I said, as the Countess of Devbridge should, all calm and proper. "That is very kind of you, Lawrence."

He cocked his head to one side even as he said, "I am pleased that you like Small Bess so very well. Rucker believes, and I occasionally agree with him, that the horse breeding farms in Wexford consistently turn out excellent mounts. John told me that you were hanging all over Tempest when he arrived at the stables this morning."

"Yes," I said, nothing more. I speared several slices of thinly cut ham onto my plate and snagged a warm roll from under a napkin-covered basket.

"She knows she will regret it if she rides Tempest," John said. "Also do keep Small Bess away from Tempest. He wants that mare. He wants her badly."

"I shall keep her well distant from your horse, John."

"Andy, how do you feel?"

I didn't want to think about it, much less have to speak of it again. But here was my husband, looking all sorts of worried, and so I said, "Just a few aches here and there. Nothing to concern anyone."

John said to Lawrence, "When I first got to her, she believed I was an angel."

"It was a logical assumption, since it was you who caused me to fall."

A thick dark eyebrow went up. "I recall seeing you fall down those last three stairs from a good fifteen feet away."

"When you opened the front door, the sun was just at exactly the right spot to pour a sky's worth of white light into the Old Hall and all of it right in my face."

"So that's it," he said. "I couldn't understand everything you were mumbling."

"Still, my dear," Lawrence said easily, looking pointedly at my untouched plate, "you must take care for the next several days."

I took a big bite of my roll. "Where is Amelia?"

"I have this inescapable feeling, Uncle, that your bride likes to face things straight on, no shilly-shallying about with her."

"Amelia is still sleeping, Andy. She seems peaceful, just deeply asleep. Thomas is with her. He is very worried even though there is no reason for him to worry at all."

I looked both of them straight in the eye. "I believe we should wake her up. If we can't, then I hope there is an able physician in the area. This isn't natural, and both of you know it. Why are you pretending otherwise?"

The two men traded looks.

I gently laid my napkin beside my plate and rose. "I am going to see Amelia. Then I am riding Small Bess. I will take George with me. He needs to learn the grounds."

"I will accompany you," John said, and rose. I looked at my husband, but he was looking down at his plate. What was going on here?

Amelia was still asleep. I simply walked to Thomas and shoved him aside. I leaned over Amelia, clasped her shoulders, and began shaking her.

"What are you doing? Stop, you might hurt her."

I continued to shake Amelia, then lightly slapped her face. To my utter relief, she opened her eyes. I knew she was trying to focus on my face.

"Andy?"

"Yes, Amelia. Thomas and John are here as well. Wake up. It is past time."

Her eyes brightened. I helped her to sit up. "What happened? Why are you all here? What time is it?"

"You've been sleeping—if you wish to call it that—for well over three hours. It's nearly two o'clock in the afternoon."

Thomas slipped his hands under my arms and lifted me off Amelia's bed. He took my place, his palm against her forehead. "Does your head ache, dearest? I have the mixture that you gave to me that proved so very effective for my headache last Tuesday."

"No, Thomas, I feel quite well."

"Do you remember when we left the Black Chamber, Amelia?"

"Yes, certainly. What of it?"

"We were walking down the corridor of the west wing when suddenly you stopped and looked at a door that was open. You said something about that was odd and went in to look. Do you remember that?"

She was silent for at least a full minute. I felt a chill run up and down my arms even as I watched her. I was frightened. This just wasn't right. What had happened in that empty room?

She said finally, "What I remember, Andy, is that we were talking about my father and ghosts and otherworldly phenomena and then—" She looked down at her white hands. I watched Thomas caress her shoulders, bring her into his arms. He gave me a dirty look. Then she pulled away. "No, there is nothing else I remember, Andy. There is simply nothing else."

I said then, drawing a deep breath, "There is simply nothing to explain this. Amelia doesn't remember anything at all. I think we must have a ghost at work here."

"That is rubbish," said John, the first words out of him since we had come into Amelia's bedchamber.

"You don't know what you're talking about, John." I turned on him. "You weren't there."

"I have never seen or heard or experienced anything in this house since I was twelve years old that was remotely like some damned ghost. Forget it."

"Very well, then how do you explain what happened to Amelia?"

"I can't, but that doesn't mean there isn't a good explanation."

I turned back to Amelia, who was leaning against Thomas. He was lightly stroking his fingers through her hair. I said, "I believe, Amelia, that you should write your father. I think he should visit Devbridge Manor and search out the spirit that drew you into that room. Do you think he will come?"

"Oh, yes, if I write what happened, he will be here in a trice."

"Now, see here, Andy," Thomas said, "you don't know anything. Of course there are ghosts here, every old house has ghosts, dozens of them. However, our ghosts just do not seem to ever announce their presence. If there was a ghost in that room with Amelia, it didn't do anything bad or frightening, it just put Amelia to sleep. And she needed sleep after last night when she became so exhausted."

"Why was she exhausted last night?"

He flushed scarlet, and I remembered the comments at the breakfast table. I just shook my head. "Never mind. Amelia, have you had anything like that happen since you came to Devbridge Manor?"

"No," she said slowly, "this was the first time, but don't you see, Andy? I don't even know if anything happened. Perhaps I just had a sudden urge to nap and did."

"On the floor in the middle of an empty room? Listen to me, all of you. Who's to say that what happened to Amelia won't happen again? What if next time she doesn't just lie down and sleep? What if she goes to sleep but doesn't wake up? There must be some answers. We have to find them."

"I don't like this," John said. "I don't like what happened, and I don't like reducing all of it to a damned dead spirit."

I turned on him. "Then you come up with

something else, John. If all you can do is find fault, then you are not being very useful, are you?"

"I will think about it," he said to me, a wealth of dislike in his voice. "Oh, the devil." Then he held out his hand. "Come along, it's time for you to ride Small Bess. I'll take you around the property."

Before I went with him, I said, "Amelia, I don't want you to be alone. All right?"

"All right," she whispered, and I knew she was frightened. I was sorry about that, but she needed to be frightened. That way she would be careful. "Don't forget to write your father, immediately."

Thomas was sputtering when we left the bed-chamber.

"Don't mind Thomas," his brother said, his voice hard with irony. "He wants to be the center of Amelia's existence. He doesn't want anything to detract from her complete attention to him and him alone."

We were nearly to the stables when I said, "I forgot George. I forgot my riding clothes."

"I'll wait for you at the stables," he said. He raised his hand a moment, then looked off toward the home wood. He turned and left me.

In the end I didn't ride with John. Swanson, unable to bear the yelling of two newborn babes, took his own mother over to see to his new little boys, and brought himself to Devbridge Manor, to escape in the intricacies of estate management.

John was requested to join his uncle and Swanson.

George and I had a marvelous time. We didn't ride far because I didn't want to get lost. Small Bess suited me very well.

I was even singing at the top of my lungs at one point. We'd pulled up beside a small stream that bisected east to west near the Manor. George was drinking, and I was just looking around at the soft late afternoon light sifting through the willow trees that bordered the stream.

A beautiful place, I thought, a perfect place. I would be happy here. Once Amelia's father arrived to rid us of that strange spirit, then all would be well again.

But what about the bars? I would ask my husband about them. It would be nothing, I was sure of it.

I carried George back to the Manor in my arms. I was whistling.

Chapter Thirteen

Upon my return, George insisted on running up the staircase beside me, his little legs stretched and lunging. His tongue was lolling, and he was breathing hard by the time we reached the first landing. I slowed my step. We passed three servants—one footman and two maids. I stopped, nodded to both of them, and asked their names. I introduced them to George and asked that if they ever saw him alone to make certain he wasn't lost.

Belinda was in my bedchamber, smoothing out a lovely dinner gown of the palest green silk with small capped sleeves and a darker green velvet band beneath the breasts. There was the same darker green edging at the neckline and the hem. It was one of my favorite gowns—one I hadn't worn, of course, since Grandfather's death. I'd instructed Belinda to leave all my black gowns folded away in a big box in the dressing room. Grandfather had hated black, and I'd worn it only three months. It was enough. Lawrence had agreed when I had asked him what he'd thought. I remembered he'd said, "Your grandfather was a passionate man, overflowing with life and endless purpose. Somehow black seems indecent for such a man. Put the black gowns and veils away." And so I had, grateful for his belief.

"Ah, there you are, my lady," Belinda said. "I just finished doing for Miss Crislock—a lovely lady and ever so nice she is—and she's all fit and proper now, her hair all curled up in the most clever way. All the family is to be in the drawing room in thirty minutes. His lordship likes the family to meet there for an hour before dinner is served. I was beginning to worry that you wouldn't be back in time."

"I'm here," I said. As I walked near her, she sniffed. "Oh, dear, I'll order up water for a bath. We must hurry. This time I will allow a footman to bring the water."

With Belinda's help, I was walking to the drawing room door a half hour later, George at my side. She had even found time to twist and wind pale green ribbons through the braids atop my head. I looked quite fine, she'd told me.

As for my best friend, Brantley had sent Jasper, that very nice young footman whom George liked. George wasn't stupid, and he knew a besotted human when he saw one that would give him a good brushing. Now George looked quite pleased with himself and his appearance. Silky soft hair flopped over his eyes.

There were two things I wanted to ask my husband as soon as I could get him alone.

Brantley showed me into the drawing room, looking at me carefully, I thought, to see if there were no ill effects from my earlier fall. I saw my main question was right in front of me.

Miss Gillbank and Judith were seated side by side on a lovely blue-and-white-striped settee, facing my husband. Thomas stood behind Amelia, his left hand on her shoulder. John was leaning against the mantel,

his arms crossed over his chest. Miss Crislock was tatting something white and narrow. A low blaze burned in the fireplace. My
husband rose immediately when I came into
the room. I saw him look from me to Judith.
I would swear that he was girding his loins,
metaphorically speaking, to spit out the
truth. He was smart. He was doing it in pub-
lic, not in private. I would not forget his strategy. I found this fascinating. My husband
was nervous. Did he believe I would blast
him in front of his family?

He cleared his throat as he took my hand
in his. "Andy, I would like you to meet my
daughter, Judith, and her governess, Miss
Gillbank."

I looked him straight in the eye and said,
"I don't want to meet either of them, sir.
They don't look at all like nice people." I
turned to give Judith a quick wink. She giggled, then smacked her hand over her
mouth as she saw her father's face. He had
paled. He looked horrified. He was without
words.

I heard Amelia gasp.

Then I laughed. "Sir," I said, "I was jesting
with you. Please forgive me."

I gave him a fat smile, for I suppose I had

already forgiven him for not telling me about Judith or about a second wife. After all, whatever his reasons, they couldn't be that bad. "Actually," I said, still grinning shamelessly up at him, "I have already had the honor, my lord. In the small east garden earlier this afternoon. Not only have we become acquainted, we have also discovered we can bear each other's company."

George, who had been sitting very quietly beside me, now wuffed lightly. Judith leapt up from the settee, only to have Miss Gillbank gently pull her back.

I said, "I'm sorry, Judith, but George isn't speaking to you. He's calling out to John. He adores John. He worships him. It is unaccountable, but there is nothing any of us can do about it." I leaned down to pat his little head. I could hear the surprise in my own voice as I said, "You may be enthusiastic now, George. Thank you for this magnificent show of restraint and good manners. You may go leap on John."

George licked my hand, then dashed across the drawing room, yipping with every step, to be picked up by John. He raised an eyebrow toward me. "However did you manage to keep him so polite? He sat there quietly and didn't demand a bit of attention until you gave him permission."

"Brantley gave him instructions this morning when Amelia and I were at the stables. Whatever he did, it is an amazing result. We shall have to ask about his specific methods. I think he has shown more magic than you have, John.

"It is a relief," said Amelia. "He doesn't look quite so ill kempt as he did last night."

"No, Jasper brushed him a hundred strokes."

Amelia touched her fingers to her own glorious black hair, and I wondered how many strokes she pulled through her hair every night. She said, "So, Judith, you have already met your new stepmama and George?"

"Oh, yes," Judith said, her eyes still fastened on George, who had his eyes closed in bliss, since John's long fingers were rubbing in exactly the right place at the base of his left ear. "I did win a shilling off Andy. She hasn't paid me yet."

"However did you do that?" Lawrence asked.

"Oh, dear," I said. "Perhaps the wager itself isn't properly spoken of here."

"Nonsense," said Amelia. "What is it? The color of a certain flower? The scent of Judith's soap? What was your wager?"

Judith just blurted it out. "We bet on which bush George would use in the garden."

"Which bush for what?" Amelia looked blank.

John was laughing so hard I thought he would drop my dog. George thought so to, because he twisted about in John's arms and licked his jaw to remind him he was still there.

Lawrence looked from me to John, but he spoke to his daughter. "Judith, what is this all about?"

"Sir," she said, and immediately broke off, her innocent face flooding with color. "Oh, dear," she added in a whisper, her eyes, now pleading, on Miss Gillbank's face. Miss Gillbank cleared her throat, stoking up her nerve, I thought.

John said, before Miss Gillbank could embark on what promised to be a delightful recital, his voice still shaking with laughter, "George, Uncle Lawrence, is a very selective animal. He needs to examine many bushes and plants and trees, even low-hanging ivy, before he makes the choice of which to use to relieve himself. It is nothing more than that. Judith, which tree or plant did you wager on?"

"I said he would use the rhododendron bush, and he did. Andy couldn't believe it, since it's the only one in the garden, and it wasn't all that noticeable, but he went right to it after sniffing, then passing by, ever so many others."

Miss Crislock looked up from her tatting, and nodded as she said, "The next time I walk George, I will make a wager with myself. Just maybe I will win."

"Well," my husband said, first eyeing Miss Crislock with a good deal of fascination, then eyeing the rest of us, his own eyes alight with humor now, "it appears that there will be no uncomfortable silences, no overly polite conversations in order to get through the evening. Andy, do you have a shilling to pay my daughter?"

"I shall present your shilling to you tomorrow, Judith." I smiled around at all the assembled family, remembered that Lawrence had said in passing that Amelia was a snob, and said with a good deal of enthusiasm, "Sir, we are very fortunate. Miss Gillbank agreed to dine with us tonight."

I looked at Amelia as I spoke, but she wasn't paying any attention to me. She was kissing Thomas's hand. I found this show of affection between the two of them disconcerting. It made me uncomfortable, since this sort of thing between married people simply wasn't in my experience.

I added, turning back to my husband, "I believe I should also enjoy having my new stepdaughter dine with us as well."

At that addition, I thought Miss Gillbank would leap up from her seat and throw her arms around me. As for Judith, she was so excited she couldn't keep still. She jumped up, let out a little squeak, then hurriedly sat down again.

"An excellent idea," said my husband. Of course he knew blackmail when it smacked him in the face. He was a gentleman, I'll say that for him, and accepted what the cards dealt him.

And so it was that Brantley sent George back to The Blue Room in the devoted company of Jasper, but only after Judith had been allowed to pat his wet nose, and hug him until there was a colorful selection of dog hairs on her lovely gown.

In the vast dining room, I was pleased to

see that my husband had had several sections of the table removed so we wouldn't all be shouting at each other over platters of food and a very ugly epergne made up of giant porcelain fruits.

I don't know how Brantley managed it, but the two additional dinner settings were in place when we came into the room.

To no one's particular surprise, everyone rubbed along quite nicely. Judith was very quiet, understandably, since she was crowded in among adults. But she smiled a lot. Miss Gillbank didn't have to worry about being condescended to. Perhaps Amelia would have been a bit cool to her if she herself hadn't been found napping on the floor of an empty room that very morning, with no logical explanation to be given. She was quieter than usual, but she was perfectly pleasant. I prayed she had written to her father.

Perhaps Lawrence was mistaken. If there was a snobbish bone in Amelia's body, I had yet to see it. As for Thomas, he told Miss Crislock about the exciting climb he and his friends had accomplished just three months before up Ben Nevis in Scotland.

Amelia said, "I was concerned, naturally, that he would become light-headed with the increase in altitude, but he did marvelously well, only spraining his little finger when he grasped a rock and it came loose too quickly. It didn't impede his ascent at all."

"It was very cold on top of Ben Nevis," Thomas said to Judith. "You could see your breath, and here it was the middle of August. I'll tell you we were all wrapped up to our noses. When we reached the top, one of the lads broke out a bottle of champagne and we toasted each other. Of course, with my sprained little finger, it was difficult to hold the glass, but I managed."

"Did the champagne freeze?" Miss Crislock asked.

"We drank it far too fast for that to happen," Thomas said. "I choked only once, but the champagne was very cold, naturally, perhaps too cold for a throat such as mine." Thomas then gave us all the most beautiful smile. "Amelia insists that she always sip the champagne first to see that it isn't overly chilled."

I happened to look over at John, who was staring at his brother, his jaw nearly dropped to his chin. I suppose the brothers really didn't know each other all that well since John hadn't been about much in the past years. "Thomas," I said, "I believe Amelia has played a jest on you. She is simply using your throat as an excuse to drink more than her share of champagne."

"Is that true, dearest? Are you a tippler?"

"Not yet," Amelia said.

"Ah," said Miss Crislock, "I shall never forget the first time Andy had an after-dinner glass of port with her grandfather. The dear man was so very pleased."

There was just a small silence before I laughed and took another bite of the delicious chicken breast roasted in cream and curry sauce.

After dinner, Miss Gillbank took Judith away. Thomas and Amelia were speaking quietly in the corner, probably about her unexpected nap in that empty room and what it could possibly mean. John picked up a book on the exploits of some Frenchman called de Sade. I don't know why he was reading it, as he certainly didn't seem to be getting any pleasure from it. Every time I looked at him, he seemed to be perfectly appalled.

My husband said, "Andy, would you please join me in the library for a moment?"

I kissed Miss Crislock good night and walked to my husband.

Now was the time he would make his confession, bless him. I couldn't wait to hear his excuse about keeping mum about a second wife and a female offspring only six years removed from her Season in London. I was coming to realize that there wasn't all that much difference between younger people and older people. Lawrence had kept something from me, and now he had to clear the slate and offer an abject apology. How many times had I done the same thing from the age of three onward?

There was only one branch of candles lit in the vast library. It was dark and shadowy and strangely cozy with a healthy fire burning in the fireplace. I watched him take a turn about the room, walking in and out of the shadows. He seemed inordinately worried, or perhaps, he was reticent. Did he think I would rip up at him? I started to relieve his mind when he came back to me, took both my hands in his, and said, "I suppose you must see me as a miserable man."

That was a different approach and really quite disarming. "I don't believe so," I said.

"I kept something very important from you."

"Yes, but I imagine that you will now tell me why, and it will make sense to me, and I will allow you to pay me off and relieve your own guilt by offering me Small Bess."

He stared down at me, no hint of a smile in evidence. Oh, dear, I wasn't treating this with the appropriate gravitas.

"I am perfectly serious now, Lawrence. Forgive me for making light of things."

He waved away my apology and paced again. "Sit down," he said over his shoulder.

I went to the large, dark brown leather wing chair close to the fireplace, and sat.

He leaned against the edge of his desk, his arms crossed over his chest. "I was married, Andy. Thirteen years ago, I married Caroline."

Caroline, I thought, a lovely name. "Tell me about her," I said.

He closed his eyes a moment over a pain that was still greatly felt even after all these many years had passed. He cleared his throat. "It was such a long time ago. Caroline Farraday was the daughter of Wilson Farraday, Viscount Clarence. She was so lovely, so spirited and gay. She saw the world and all in it there to be at her command, and most people were quite willing to do anything at all for her." Another look of pain crossed his face, and he raised his hand as if to brush it away. I held my tongue. This was highly personal, these memories that had deeply scored his heart.

"Even though I was a good deal older than she, she wanted me and informed her father that she would wed no one else. And so we were wed in London. I took her to Cornwall on our wedding trip, a place she believed vastly romantic.

"It was only after I brought her back to Devbridge Manor that I began to understand her true nature. That is to say, Caroline was inclined to be vivacious one day, nearly giddy, she laughed so very much, and the very next day, she would be silent and sad, withdrawn, as if she'd lost her best friend. I never knew which woman would appear across from me at the breakfast table.

"When she became pregnant not long after we married, I rather hoped that the child would steady her. And it was true that during the months of her pregnancy she seemed more stable, her outlook more normal, if you will.

"In those days, neither Thomas nor John were here much, both of them at Eton. I'll never forget though that when they did visit, she became worse. She neither spoke nor ate. She resented them, I realized quickly enough. Obviously it was because she wanted her child, a boy child, to follow in my footsteps; and indeed, if she had birthed a boy, he would be my heir. I told her this, but it made no difference. She didn't want to have anything to do with either of the boys. I asked Thomas and John to stay away, to visit friends on their vacations. They both felt very sorry for me, I believe, and I felt immensely guilty.

"But nothing I did seemed to matter. Toward the end of her pregnancy, Caroline became more unpredictable by the day. I never knew what to expect, none of us did, including her physician. She would simply disappear, only to be found up in the old north tower, huddled in a corner, her eyes wide, staring, no explanation of why she had even gone up there. She insisted on riding her mare even though she was large with child. She never fell, thank God. I found her trying to chase down rats in the hay barn one afternoon. One night Brantley found her dancing in a heavy downpour. Once a servant found her wading in the stream, discussing with an invisible person how fine it would be to drown.

"I had no choice but to order a woman to be with her all the time. I was terrified that if she didn't try to harm herself, she would harm her unborn babe."

"The bars in The Blue Room," I said. "They were for Caroline."

"You noticed the holes, then? Yes, of course you did. I didn't believe them that obvious." He paused yet again, and drew a very deep breath. "One time I came into her room to find her outside on the narrow ledge, singing to a buck that was staring back at her from the edge of the home wood. I was never so frightened in my life. It seemed as if normal, predictable life no longer existed here. Everyone in the house tiptoed around, so afraid that something would set her off.

"Then Judith was born. When the doctor put her into Caroline's arms, I remember clearly that Caroline began laughing. She laughed and laughed and said, 'After all this, I still could not produce a boy child.' I assured her that it didn't matter. There would be other children if she wished. I will never forget how she smiled at me, smiled with such hope. I remember how she caressed my face, how she told me she was so very happy.

"To my infinite relief, after Judith's birth, Caroline became once again the same girl I had met nearly two years before. I remember thanking God for the blessed cure. The whole house seemed to breathe a huge sigh of relief. There was even some laughter to be heard once again at Devbridge Manor. To be honest, until I heard laughter, I simply had not realized how very grim everyone had become. Caroline appeared to adore Judith. She spent a lot of time with her, singing to her, rocking her, playing with her."

I continued to be so quiet I could have blended with the shadows.

Lawrence plowed his hands through his hair. "Damnation, there is no other way to say it—it was all a ruse. Caroline was fooling all of us, and very cleverly." He fell silent again. His hands were clenched at his sides. I could feel the great strain in him. "More time passed. But then it all ended abruptly. In her madness, she threw herself from the north tower. As it happened, I had Judith with me. She was all of two months old then. If she had been with Caroline, I am certain that Caroline would have taken her child over the tower balcony with her."

He drew a deep hard breath. He smashed his fist against his open palm. "There is just no way around it. I am responsible for her death."

Chapter Fourteen

It was difficult, but I held my tongue. I did not blurt out things like "what an idiotic thing to say" or "don't be ridiculous." Finally, I said in a lovely calm voice, "Please tell me why you believe that."

"Only the day before she had begged me to remove the bars from her bedchamber windows. I had them removed immediately, and I felt guilt that I had not thought to do it sooner. She had recovered; she was once again the lovely girl I had married. I remember how she was smiling when she handed me Judith, down in the drawing room, and left me, just for a moment. She told me she was chilly and wished to fetch her favorite shawl. Of course a servant followed her discreetly, and obviously she knew it. She went in The Blue Room, closed the door, and climbed out the window. She made her way along that narrow ledge between The Blue Room and the chamber next to it. From there she went to the north tower. If only I had been less ready to believe her normal again, if only I had waited, just a few more days, to have the bars removed from the windows, she would not have been able to hurl herself off the tower balcony."

It had all happened twelve years ago, and still he was carrying this mindless guilt he didn't deserve. I said, "If you had waited, well, then, it seems logical that she would simply have waited, then done the same thing once she was able."

"Perhaps, perhaps."

"It is a very tragic thing, Lawrence. I am very sorry."

"I couldn't bring myself to tell you, Andy, and I'm sorry I was such a coward. But I could not be certain that you wouldn't want me because I had a child who might carry her mother's madness. Or perhaps you would believe that the madness might have come from me."

And I said, "Do Caroline's parents visit Judith?"

He looked very surprised at that question, and I suppose that it was unexpected. "No, they have never seen her. They never wanted to see me again, if you would know the truth. John and Thomas know all about what they did."

"And that was?"

"They claimed that their daughter Caroline was perfectly normal, that nothing at all had ever been wrong with her, that it was I who ruined her, destroyed her somehow. They did not understand what possible reason I had for doing it, but there was no doubt in their minds that I had murdered their daughter. I was responsible for their beloved daughter's death. They said they never wished to see any child that was mine."

"They continue to deny their own granddaughter?"

He nodded.

"That is extraordinary, but hardly your fault. Incidentally, Lawrence, I think you've done a magnificent job raising Judith. She is a sweet child, very enthusiastic, bright as the sun itself, and utterly normal. You selected a fine woman to instruct her. I am very sorry for Caroline, but please believe me when I say that it was a very long time ago. None of it will touch Judith, nor should it."

And because it was all so grim, and there was so much long-ago misery still sifting through this room, I said, "I am twenty-one years old and have come to grips with the fact that I am now a stepmama. Judith and I will become great friends, I promise you. Forgive yourself, Lawrence, for I forgive you for not telling me."

"I may come eventually to forgive myself, but never can I forget it. I have already said it, Andy. Judith carries her mother's seed. Is there madness in her that will emerge when she gains years?"

I said, "The king is mad. Was his father, George II, mad as well?"

"Some Tories would quickly say that he was," Lawrence said. "But no, certainly he was not mad."

It was an attempt at a jest, and so I smiled. "You know as well as I do that madness is not something that is automatically visited by the father or the mother on the child. There is no madness in Caroline's parents, is there?"

He shook his head. "No," he said slowly, "there is not, only hatred toward me." I swear he wanted to believe that his young daughter would be just fine. "But I will tell you that before Miss Gillbank came, I feared for Judith."

"How old was she when Miss Gillbank arrived?"

"Perhaps three years old."

To me that was madness to even say that, much less think it, but again, I was the voice of calm and reason. "Judith was a toddler. I imagine that when a parent sees all the havoc a young child can create, they are ready to believe that the child is the spawn of Satan. That is how my grandfather viewed me upon occasion, and I didn't turn to madness. Yes, I remember now. He called me an ill-begotten imp of Satan."

He laughed at that, really laughed, just as I had hoped he would. Was I so pleased with myself and my handling of this situation that only I looked inordinately relieved? No, I swear he looked younger, his shoulders more square, as if a weight had been lifted off.

When he left me at my door awhile later, he lightly touched his fingers to my chin. "You are everything that I could possibly have expected. Perhaps even a bit more. I will think about what you have said tonight. Goodnight, my dear Andy."

When I finally got back to The Blue Room from walking George, who wasn't all that picky about his selection this time, and finally managed to dismiss Belinda, who wanted to remain and gossip, I eased myself into bed. I snuggled under my warm covers. George, too, decided to sleep beneath the covers and burrowed down to press his warm little body behind my knees. I had to admit that today was very probably the busiest, the most unexpected, the most frightening, and with that blow on the head, one of the most painful days I'd ever spent in my life.

I had felt something cold and malignant in the Black Chamber, known that something had drawn Amelia into that other empty room, and had fallen down stairs—oh, dear, even I was too tired to recite the rest of it in my mind. But everything had ended well, all except what had happened to Amelia, and everyone's refusal to deal with it.

I would go to that small empty room tomorrow and stand there awhile and see if anything happened to me. My flesh crawled at the thought, but then I decided that it was better to face the unknown than cower and deny it all like the rest of them were doing.

I fell asleep with George's nose on the back of my knee, a touch of wet through my light muslin nightgown.

I don't know why I awoke, for there was no sound, no shifting of light, no hint of a whisper. But one moment I was asleep, dreaming of riding over the Yorkshire moors, and in the very next instant I was wide awake, my eyes staring, adjusting to the moonlit room.

And then I saw it. I started shaking my head, not wanting to believe it, but the thing didn't fade away, didn't move. It just stood there, stiff and silent like a frozen statue from Hell itself, dead and still not more than two feet from the foot of my bed.

I remember hearing George's snore even as I felt everything freeze and curdle inside me. Slowly, ever so slowly, I eased my arms out from under the covers.

More slowly yet, I began pushing myself upright. George stirred but slept on.

That dead still figure began to move slowly around the end of the bed, toward me. In that moment when it crossed in front of the moonlit window, I saw it clearly. It was an old woman, terribly misformed, older than death itself. Tangled white hair hung about her hideous distorted face. I wanted to scream my head off, but to my consternation, when I opened my mouth, only a pathetic moan came out. I felt literally locked in place, nailed down, so scared I simply couldn't move.

In a cracked voice I heard myself say, "Who are you? What do you want with me?"

That old woman, who surely could not be real, said in a thin, papery voice, "You are an abomination. You are the evil that revisits this house. You are vile, and what you came from is even more vile. You will pay for all of it."

I was gasping I was so afraid. I felt George moving about now, and for the first time since I had jerked awake to see that thing at the end of the bed, I knew fear for something other than just myself.

I jerked back the covers, grabbed George, and rolled toward the far side of the bed, away from that ghastly apparition.

But I didn't move fast enough or that old grotesque creature moved more quickly than someone alive would have moved, but she was coming quickly now, leaning toward me across the bed, and in her twisted fingers she held a knife, not silver, but gold, the blade curved at the end, like one of those blades from the Arabian Nights. She held it high above her head, ready to bring it down.

I rolled off the far side of the bed, George barking wildly, trying to pull free of me to attack that creature. I yelled, "Who are you? What do you want from me?"

Stupid questions, I knew, but they just poured out of my mouth. Suddenly that creature was coming around the side of the bed, to cut me off, to trap me.

I didn't even think about taking my chances here with her. Even as she moved toward me, that strange golden knife was held high again, and I could see it coming down toward my chest. I grabbed up a pillow in my free hand and hurled it at her. It hit that knife and made her pause a moment, and in that same moment, with George barking his head off, I ran as fast as I could to the bedchamber door.

The knob wouldn't turn. Oh, Jesus, I thought, jerking on it, twisting it, my fingers trembling and white with the strain. I didn't remember locking the door, but I could have. I just didn't remember. I jerked on the knob, then turned the key that was in the lock. George was barking madly, and I turned to see the old woman running now toward me, her gait jerky, awkward, but she was coming fast. The key turned, and the knob finally twisted beneath my fingers. I jerked the door open and nearly fell into the corridor.

So I had locked the door. How had the creature gotten into my room?

I didn't look back, just ran as fast as I could, George pinned to my side. I wasn't about to let him go after that creature.

I managed to keep my balance. I ran as fast as I had ever run in my life, down that long corridor, not thinking, just finally coming to a panicked stop in front of a bedchamber door. I knew who was behind that door, knew that I had run specifically to this bedchamber. I pounded my fists against the aged oak.

I heard a man's muffled voice from inside. I kept pounding, pounding, and George kept barking his head off. I was grateful that he was making all that noise. It had to give that creature second thoughts about coming after me.

Even as I pounded on that door, I looked back. I didn't see anything, but it didn't make my heart slow at all.

Finally, it seemed at least a century had passed, the door flew open and there was John, a pair of breeches pulled quickly on, and wearing nothing else.

It wouldn't have mattered if he was in his bathtub. I threw myself at him. George realized who it was and went berserk.

John managed to keep his balance at the shock of my weight hurled against him. "Andy, for God's sake, what's going on? What's wrong? George, be quiet!" There was only one way to quiet George, and that was to pick him up. So John did, just jerked him away from my nearly locked-down right arm. He had George in one arm and the other around me.

I was breathing so hard and so fast I couldn't speak. I just stood there, leaning against a man I feared all the way to my bones, and I didn't want to move, just feel him there, warm and hard and strong, holding George and holding me and knowing we were both safe.

"It's all right," he said, his voice soft and deep now, warm against my hair. "Everything will be fine. George, that's right, just lick my arm and my shoulder, lick as far as that little tongue of yours will reach. Andy, do you have your breath yet? Can you tell me what happened?"

"Almost," I said, my breath hot against his shoulder. "Not yet, but almost."

"Just keep breathing, calm deep breaths . . . that's it." He just held me and George, standing calm and steady. I had never in my life been so grateful as I was in that moment that this man was here and he was so close I could feel his heart beating against me.

"Now, when you're able, tell me what happened. Did something happen to George?"

I felt his big hand splayed over my back. He covered a lot of me. I felt the heat of his hand through my linen nightgown. I felt the heat of him through the front of my nightgown as well. It felt wonderful. I felt alive. I felt safe.

I was counting his heartbeats, feeling them deep inside myself. Solid and warm and ever so steady, those heartbeats of his.

I could breathe now. I didn't want to, but I pulled back, just a bit. I didn't want to lose the heat of him, or I simply knew I'd just freeze up and shatter onto the floor.

"I'm all right, yes, really, I am now all right."

"There is no fire in your bedchamber?"

"No fire."

"The armoire didn't fall over?"

"The armoire didn't move."

"No bats came flying through the windows?"

"No bats."

He cursed then. I was so surprised I nearly fell over.

"It's that damned Blue Room," he said, and cursed some more. "You saw what you believed to be a ghost, didn't you? You fancied you saw something, and it scared you witless."

"I did see something. It was horrible, and it was real. It tried to kill me with a knife that had a wicked curved blade. I grabbed George and ran. Here. To you."

If he thought that was strange, if he wondered why I wouldn't run instead to my husband, who was only one bedchamber beyond his at the end of the corridor, he didn't say anything, just pulled me back against him again. I wrapped my arms tightly around his back. His flesh was so warm, so smooth, and he was a man—a dangerous man. Here I was all plastered against him, and I had almost nothing on at all. A simple nightgown.

"Oh, damn," I said, and very slowly I began to pull away from him.

There was a measure of amusement and something else I could not identify in his voice. "I wondered how long it would take for you to realize that you were up close against the beast, and he just might be more dangerous than whatever it was you saw in The Blue Room." Then he sighed, a very deep sigh. "You know, Andy, the beast isn't dangerous at all, but you just can't bring yourself to believe that, can you?"

I couldn't deal with this now, I just couldn't. "You are speaking nonsense, and it simply isn't appropriate now."

He laughed. "Come with me. Let's get some light in here, and you can tell me more about this creature who attacked you with a knife. George, be quiet, I'll pick you up again, just give me another minute to light the candles."

George and I trailed after him, because I wasn't about to let more than a foot get between us. But first, I closed his bedchamber door and locked it.

"I don't think the creature followed me, but I don't want to take any chances. If the creature were to come in, just perhaps you would swoon with fright, and I would once again find myself in a very bad fix."

He just shook his head at me. "You were so frightened you couldn't even talk as of two minutes ago, but now you can jest about it. You are really quite amazing." He was still laughing when he managed to get the candles lit.

He held up the branch of candles and looked me up and down. "You're probably getting cold," he said, and fetched me his dressing gown. He dressed me in it as if I were a child. Then he tied the sash at my waist.

George whimpered. John leaned down and picked him up.

"Thank you for coming to the door so quickly. Another three seconds, and I would have tried to kick it in."

He looked down at my bare feet. "You say the most outlandish things. It is a gift you've got." He set George on the floor again, and moved the candle branch to a small table beside the door. Then he walked right up to me, pulled me against him, and began stroking my hair. It was curling wildly down my back, my night hair ribbon that secured it was long gone.

"Are you all right now?"

"Yes," I said slowly, and now I knew fear from another quarter.

"Perhaps," he said, pulling away from me and picking up George again, "it's time for you to fetch your husband. You know, that old man right down the corridor just on the left? Surely he is the one, not your step-nephew, to help you in this matter, don't you think?"

"You bastard," I said, turned on my bare heel, and walked to the door. I unlocked it. I was pleased that my hands were steady.

When I pulled the door open, I saw Lawrence and Thomas running from opposite directions toward me.

Lawrence reached me first. He took in John's dressing gown, my bare feet, my wild hair, and said, "Something happened. Are you all right?"

I stood there, apart from him, because I

had my balance again, and I didn't want to be pressed against another man, regardless of who he was. "Yes," I said. "George and I are both fine."

Thomas came to a panting stop. Even with his dressing gown flapping around his bare feet and ankles, his hair tousled all over his head, he looked beautiful.

"What is going on here?" he said, but Lawrence just shook his head.

"I don't know as yet. But something has happened. Andy?"

We were all standing there in the middle of John's bedchamber, the candlelight flickering slightly because there was an open window beside John's bed. I hugged myself, but that wasn't enough. I leaned down and picked up George. I wasn't about to let him go. He seemed to realize that something was going on here and that I needed him. He settled himself comfortably in my arms.

"Tell them what happened," John said, and he walked away to the fireplace to set a fire.

Then Amelia was standing in the open doorway staring at all of us, that lovely black hair of hers streaking down her back, like a long silk swatch.

"I woke up suddenly," I said, and swallowed because I heard a tremor in my voice. "I don't know why, but I did. And I saw something very ugly, not really human, and it was standing like a dead thing at the foot of my bed, still as a statue, like it wasn't really there. I realized soon enough that it was an old woman, hideous, with tangled white hair, and when I asked her what she wanted, she said I was an abomination, and other things along that line, and that I would pay for it all. Then she raised this knife and came toward me. I threw a pillow at her, grabbed George, and we managed to get out of the bedchamber."

There was silence.

John said, "Do you remember exactly what the old woman said to you?"

I shook my head. "Perhaps it will straighten itself out tomorrow. Right now, it's just a blur except for the abomination part. One doesn't easily forget being called an abomination."

And the silence continued with four sets of eyes just staring at me.

"Listen to me, I know you don't want to believe me, not after what I felt in the Black Chamber and what I said happened to Amelia, but it is all true. I would not make this up. Actually, I don't think I would even be able to conjure this up. It was terrifying. It was very real. The old woman tried to kill me."

There was more silence, then my husband said in a very low, gentle voice, "Certainly something happened, Andy. Would you like a cup of tea?"

"Excuse me," John said. "I'm going to The Blue Room and see what I can find."

"I'll come with you," Thomas said.

I knew, of course, that the room would be perfectly empty. The old woman wouldn't be there. Why would she remain?

"You have had quite a fright," Amelia said. "No matter what happened, dream or something else, you are still shaking. Come and sit down, Andy."

"No," I said. "I want to go back to The Blue Room." I ignored my husband, whose hand was stretched out toward me. George trotted after me. We walked down that corridor together, and I felt the curdling fear grow stronger and stronger with each step nearer.

By the time I reached the open door, I felt numb with fear. It was a horrible way to feel. I felt helpless, and my brain just didn't want me to move in any direction. I just wanted to shut myself down.

George barked.

"It's all right," John called out. "Both of you can come in."

"There is nothing here," Thomas said, and I saw that he was gingerly moving his left hand. What the devil could possibly be wrong with his damned left hand?

"I didn't expect the old woman would remain to greet you after she failed to kill me. Or perhaps she meant to frighten me, if that is what she meant by me paying for all of it. I don't know, but that knife with its curved blade was sharp. It glittered when she raised it over her head."

"A curved blade?" John said, and grew very still.

"Yes. It wasn't silver, either. It looked like burnished gold. Why?"

He cursed under his breath, then said, "Just a moment." And he was gone.

Chapter Fifteen

I sat down on the edge of a delicate winged chair, George thankfully content to remain settled in my lap. I stroked his ears while I sat there, saying nothing, just looking into the cold fireplace.

Lawrence and Amelia came into the room. "Andy," Lawrence said, and came to where I sat. He kneeled beside me and took my hand. "You are in a new house. So much happened today, frightening things, unexpected things, things that could easily give the most phlegmatic of individuals violent nightmares. My God, you even fell and hit your head. Who knows what that blow to the head could produce in the dark of the night?"

I smiled at him. Everything he said was quite true. "I did not make it up. I did not dream it. It all happened just as I told you."

Amelia said, "Andy, nothing like this has ever happened before here at Devbridge Manor. Has it, Uncle Lawrence?"

He shook his head. "There have been stories, of course, of spirits in this bedchamber, of strange noises, and shadows that should not have been here, but none of us have ever seen anything unusual. It has always been servants' tales, nothing more."

"No," Thomas said slowly. "That is not quite true. I remember I was in here once, not long after Caroline died, and I was just sitting there, in front of the fire, reading, and I must have fallen asleep. Something touched my cheek, and it felt warm and yet somehow like a touch of ice at the same time. When I opened my eyes, I saw her, but just for an instant, and then she was gone, simply vanished."

I stared at him. I didn't want to believe him. It sounded like a fanciful boy's imagination at work. But then, what was I? I was a girl with a very vivid imagination.

But I hadn't dreamed it, I hadn't.

I looked up when John came back into the room. George raised his head and wuffed. I began patting him again, slowly, slowly.

"My knife is in its place, the cabinet locked."

I stared at him.

"I collect knives," he said to me. "One of my most valuable is a royal Moorish ceremonial knife, more than three hundred years old. It has a sharp curved blade, a fine silk red tassel attached to its handle. There are two large rubies set in the handle. Most importantly, its blade is gold, not silver. It is there, safely locked beneath its glass cover."

"I want to see the knife," I said, then rose and walked toward the door before my husband could hem and haw and demand to know if I was as mad as his second wife.

John perforce had to come with me since I had no idea where he kept his knife collection. It was in his bedchamber, of course.

He lit more candles. All of us trailed after him, even Amelia, who was yawning and saying that it was just too much for my mind, that it was a strange dream that any of us could have had, given all that had happened today, this my first full day at Devbridge Manor.

I said nothing, just marched after John. I nearly swallowed my tongue when I saw that knife lying there on a bed of crimson velvet. I did take a quick step back.

"That's the knife the old woman was holding," I said. "I remember the tassel now. It swayed and fell back when she raised the knife. And the two big rubies, one at each end of the handle. All I remember is bright flashes of red."

I turned to look at all of them. "How could the knife have gotten back here so quickly?"

"It couldn't have," Lawrence said matter-of-factly. "You must have seen it earlier when you came in here and it became the knife in your nightmare."

"No, I did not," I said.

"Andy," Amelia said, coming to pat my shoulder, "You must let this go. It's over. You are all right. George is all right. It has been a difficult day. You will forget all about it in the morning."

In that moment, for the first time, I wondered if perhaps I didn't imagine the old woman, if it had been a violent nightmare, brought on by the blow to my head or the dreadful cold menace I'd felt in the Black Chamber. And there had been the slamming door in my face, Amelia trapped, calling out to me.

I no longer knew. I felt a huge wave of sheer exhaustion wash through me. I had nothing else to say. I turned away from all of them and walked back to The Blue Room, George trotting just behind me.

I heard Thomas say, "This was only her first day here. I dread to see what will happen on her second."

I dreaded it more than he did.

I shut my bedchamber door, paused just a moment, then turned the key in the lock. If the old woman came back, then she was either a violent aftershock from my mind or she was a spirit. Either way, I knew it would not be a very good thing.

I surprised myself. I fell asleep almost instantly. However, George managed to beat me. I closed my eyes with the sound of his snoring in my ears.

In the morning, my first thought was no, I did not imagine anything. If I had to do it myself, I would search every inch of Devbridge Manor. I would find a clue to that miserable old woman who had frightened me witless.

When I saw how everyone was looking at me the following morning when I came down to the breakfast room, I decided to change my tactics. I gave everyone a big smile and said, all modest humility, "You have all been so very kind. Goodness, you even treated me well in the middle of the night when my imagination went berserk and I conjured up a vision to terrify myself. I apologize to all of you. It is forgotten. Thank you for being so very kind. I should love some scrambled eggs."

I picked up my plate and went to the sideboard. I fetched George three slices of very crispy bacon and one small kipper. It was no surprise that conversation was on the stiff side. However, I just continued to beam good humor, smiles, and speak of nothing more weighty than the lovely weather, so unusual for November, and it did not take long for everyone to breathe metaphorical sighs of relief and resume their normal thoughts and actions.

Toward the middle of the morning, I changed into my riding clothes and walked to the stables, George trotting beside me. It was overcast now, a bit on the chilly side, the lovely weather only a memory. But Brantley had assured me that it would not rain until late afternoon.

Since I was convinced that he was Moses, I believed him implicitly.

Rucker saddled Small Bess for me and gave me a hand up. I petted Small Bess's glossy bay neck. "You are lovely, you know that?" George was barking, and so I asked Rucker to hand him up to me. "He can run later. Right now, he can ride."

I did give Tempest one wistful look before I lightly tapped my heels into Small Bess's sides. I called back to Rucker, who was standing there, watching me, "If anyone wonders where I am, just tell them that I'm going to the village to meet our merchants."

I didn't ride to the village. George, Small Bess, and I went to the narrow stream that ribboned east to west on Devbridge land. I left Small Bess free to eat whatever grass pleased her. I carried George to the edge of the stream and sat down beneath a billowing willow tree. George sat beside me, tall and straight.

"George," I said. "I could have imagined

that hideous old woman. I don't think I did, but we have to consider it a possibility."

George turned to look at me. He cocked his head to one side.

"On the other hand, there is simply no way you would have imagined her as well. I saw you looking at her, barking your head off. You were as scared as I was, but you were ready to leap for her throat, weren't you, my brave lad?"

He gave me a light wuff.

I began to pet George's head, and he stood there, staring out over the stream, trembling slightly because he loved me to pet him, to scratch here and there, in places he had trouble reaching.

"Wouldn't you say that it was also rather impossible for a violent spirit to return the knife so very carefully to John's collection that just so happens to be in his bedchamber?"

George wuffed again, probably at the sound of John's name.

"But you know, George, we are considering two very different things that are happening here. There was something awful in that wretched Black Chamber, and it scares me to my toes because I can't imagine what it is. But that old woman—she was very human. Even if I lost my wits and dreamed her up, you couldn't have. No, she was real, she exists, she is here.

"And then there is what happened to Amelia in that other room. Well, you and I will look into that when we go back to the Manor, although I am not all that certain I wish to go back there. Someone either tried to kill me or scare me into leaving. I am to pay for all of it. What does that mean? And who said it and why, George?"

George remained silent.

I picked him up and held him tightly against me. He allowed it for a few seconds, then pulled free and ran to chase a pheasant that had just burst from a thicket of brush.

I eventually collected George and remounted Small Bess. I did not ride to the small village of Devbridge-on-Ashton. It frankly seemed a silly thing to do when someone had come at me with a Moorish dagger in the middle of the night. I returned to Devbridge Manor. I now knew what I was going to do.

I stood in the middle of the empty room Amelia had entered the previous day. There were two long, narrow windows, no draperies to soften them, that gave onto the front of the house. If you looked off to the right, you could see the stables, the left, the home wood.

The room, which had a nicely polished wooden floor, was completely empty. I went into each and every chamber around it. They were either bedchambers, charmingly furnished, or they were small sitting rooms, likewise nicely furnished.

Only the small room Amelia had entered was stark and empty. I felt nothing as I stood there, nothing at all. But there had been something there the day before, something that had slammed the door in my face. Yet it wasn't the solid, very real, old woman who'd come at me with John's Moorish ceremonial knife the night before.

I had brought George with me. He sniffed about, but he didn't feel any more in that small room than I did. No hair stood up on either of our necks.

I returned to The Blue Room with George, shut and locked the door. This had been Caroline's room. She had climbed out through one of the large windows in this room and made her way along the ledge until she could get back inside the Manor. Then she had walked to the north tower and thrown herself off.

The old woman of last night—could she not have also climbed out those windows and walked along the ledge until she could climb back into the house, into another room?

Thomas had told about the woman he had seen here very briefly when he'd been younger. Had it been Caroline's ghost? Why would she come back here? Why would she want to come back here, to this particular room? Was Caroline the reason the servants believed this chamber was haunted? Or was Caroline in that other room, the small one that was very empty?

I searched out Mrs. Redbreast, the Lyndhurst housekeeper for certainly more years than I'd been on this earth. I found her in her charming suite of rooms in the east wing. If she was surprised or discomfited in any way to see me, she didn't let on. She invited me into her lovely sitting room, furnished with very old pieces from two centuries ago. A softly warm fire glowed in the fireplace. All the draperies were drawn against the deepening autumn chill. It looked like it would begin raining any minute, but when I mentioned it, Mrs. Redbreast shook her head, smiled, and said, no, Brantley said not before three o'clock in the afternoon.

"My lady, a cup of tea?"

I accepted. I complimented her on the delicious India tea, told her in all seriousness that I was counting on her to guide me, since Devbridge Manor was such a very large house. When it was necessary, I could lie better than one of those damned weasel-tongued Whigs, as Grandfather had told me more than once. In truth, I had managed Grandfather's various houses since I had turned fifteen, including Deerfield Hall, larger than Devbridge Manor by a good dozen bedchambers and a ballroom the size of a London block. I had made a hash of many things in those early years. However, by the time I was eighteen, I was as at ease discussing the mending of an old washtub with copper bands with a butler and the blacksmith as I was deciding upon baking a buttock of beef in the French fashion with the cook.

I asked her about her family and was told that she was one of the Hildon Dale Red-

breasts, and her family had been in Yorkshire since the Vikings came from the sea,
to rape, pillage, and settle. Yes, she said, it
was likely her ancestors had some of that
raping and pillaging blood in their veins.

I moved ever so slowly, planning to steer
her eventually to what I wanted to talk about.
When I handed her my teacup for a refill, I
said, "Have you ever experienced any unpleasantness in The Blue Room, Mrs.
Redbreast? Recognized, perhaps, that
something was different in that room?"

She dropped her cup she was so startled.
Fast as a snake, I managed to snag it in the
air just before it hit her shiny oak floor.
Thank God it was empty. I set the cup down
and said calmly, "Do tell me about it, Mrs.
Redbreast. I am the mistress here now, not
Lady Caroline or her ghost. Tell me what
you have seen or heard or experienced in
that room or in other rooms, like the one
where Mrs. Thomas was found napping on
the floor."

Mrs. Redbreast was a very large woman,
on the shadowy side of middle age, but still
handsome. Her black hair was streaked with
white, but it was thick and well styled. It was
her face, though, that held me, her eyes.

They were as dark as her hair and, at the moment, frightened.

Of all things, she began wringing her hands. I was swimming into very deep waters here.

I merely smiled at her. "Mrs. Redbreast, I am new here. My husband has given me something of a history of the family, but not nearly enough. I ask you to help me understand."

"My lady," she said slowly, "what happened yesterday was a shock to all of us."

"A greater shock to Mrs. Thomas."

"Oh, yes, the poor lady. But she fell asleep, that was all there was to it, just a nap, in the middle of the day, and the door wasn't locked."

"I'm very sure it wasn't by the time the gentlemen of the house were there to try it. But that isn't the point, is it? I am now the Countess of Devbridge, Mrs. Redbreast. There's no going back from that. This is now my home. Doubtless you've also heard all about what I reported happening to me last night."

Oh, yes, she had heard, and I could imagine all the speculation going on below stairs. Very possibly all the servants were beginning to wonder if the earl hadn't married another Caroline. Well, I had changed my tack with the family. I would not, however, change with the servants. Servants knew everything, and they loved to talk. They were a part of the family, and everything that happened concerned them. They were my best bet at finding things out. Goodness, there was much wariness, or was it fear? in those dark eyes of hers.

Push her, I thought, and so I leaned toward her and clasped one of her large hands between mine. I looked her right in the eye. "There is a malignant presence in the Black Chamber. There was something altogether different in that small empty room Mrs. Thomas went into. However, I simply don't know about the old woman who was in The Blue Room last night. Help me, Mrs. Redbreast. I don't wish to die in this house or perhaps lose my mind, as did Lady Caroline."

Mrs. Redbreast pulled her hand away and rose very quickly for one of her size. She walked to the windows, and whipped back the dark blue draperies as if she were angry at them. Then she slowly turned back to me.

"Lady Caroline brought her madness with

her, inside her. You are very sane, my lady. Now that you have admitted to the family that what happened last night must have been some sort of a nightmare, then no one could think otherwise."

True enough, I thought. I smiled at her. "No, indeed not. Tell me about Lady Caroline."

"After she killed herself, the poor lady, stories began to pop up, always spoken in whispers, about her returning to The Blue Room. I didn't want to believe them. Who wants to live in a house where there are spirits roaming about?"

"I don't want to," I said, then nothing more, just waited.

"I finally went there myself, slept in that large bed, and I swear to you nothing happened. I slept very well, better than usual. And when I awoke I felt calm, perhaps even unusually calm."

"Perhaps as if someone had watched over you that night, someone who liked you and had no wish to hurt you or frighten you?"

She nodded slowly. "Yes, that's exactly how I felt. There have been so many stories, and perhaps I believe some of them, but I would never admit that to his lordship. If the poor lady returns occasionally to that bed-chamber, it is because she spent most of her time there and it is familiar to her."

"Did Caroline spend a lot of time in that other small room that now stands completely empty?"

"Yes," Mrs. Redbreast said. "It was her own private music room. She played her harp there, so beautifully she played, and the sweet sounds drifted from those windows. Everyone would smile and look up when they heard her playing her harp. Some have heard the harp over the years."

"Why is the room empty?"

"His lordship had all the furnishings removed. I believe Lady Caroline's lovely harp is in one of the attics. No one goes in there anymore."

"Because the door is kept locked?"

"Yes, that's exactly why. I open it once a week so that one of the maids can dust. But there is nothing more, my lady, I swear it to you. As to what happened last night, I don't know, I simply don't know. There are spirits, every great house has them, but it is something else when a spirit actually threatens you. No one would appreciate that happening."

"Then it will remain a bad dream, Mrs. Redbreast, because anything else isn't acceptable." I stood then. "I want to thank you. You have greatly eased my mind. That horrible misshapen old woman who came at me last night with Master John's knife, I will forget about it soon enough. Yes, that is the wisest course to follow."

"But consider what happened to you yesterday, my lady, so many dreadful things, and this is a new home. Something like that must of course seem utterly real, for you are there, trapped in the middle of it, so frightened it nearly swamps you."

She'd hit that on the head. "Yes, all that," I said, and walked to her door. I turned. "I hope that nothing more enters my dreams." And, I thought, as I left her standing there, her hands clasped over her ample bosom, that more than likely she would doubtless tell the servants at dinner that who knew what had really happened to the new Countess of Devbridge in the middle of the previous night? Ah, who knew? A dream, an aberration, perhaps a vision? Who knew? The servants would talk and speculate, and perhaps one of them would know something and I would hear it.

I had never felt so alone in my life.

Chapter Sixteen

It was John who found me standing yet again in the middle of the small, empty room—Caroline's music room. I was thinking that Mrs. Redbreast had forgotten to lock the door again after all the commotion yesterday.

He came into the room. I didn't have to see or hear to know that it was him. There was a new spark in the air itself.

"I was told that you have changed your tale. Now you are agreeing with everyone that the old woman in your room last night was all a nightmare."

"That's right," I said easily as I turned to

face him. I didn't move from the window. I wanted to keep my distance from him, particularly after last night.

"Well, then, if you truly believe it was some sort of dream, then there doesn't seem to be any reason for you to hie yourself back to London and to safety."

"No, a knife in a dream can't stab you."

"Not to my knowledge."

I smiled at him then. "If one were to wonder, however, why it took you so very long to open your bedchamber door, I wonder what you would say?"

"I was naked."

I looked down at his body. I simply couldn't help myself. And he knew, damn him, he knew what he had evoked in my mind.

"Yes, you do know of naked men, don't you, Andy? And it distresses you." Then he shrugged. "It doesn't matter. As I said, when you pounded on my door, I was naked and thus had to get my britches on."

My eyes were strictly on his face now, and they would stay there.

I said, "Lawrence told me that Caroline resented you and Thomas. She wanted to bear the heir, you see."

He accepted my shift and said readily enough, "I just don't remember. Caroline was—" He paused and looked toward the long windows, perhaps seeing something that was no longer there.

"Was what?"

"She was like a fairy princess. I was a boy, all of twelve years old. Thomas and I had only lived here for about six months before Uncle Lawrence married her. Neither of us minded in the least. Caroline was kind, it seemed, and her laughter was the sweetest sound I had ever heard in my young boy's life. There was something else, of course. She was all of eight years my senior. Even then Uncle Lawrence wanted a very young wife."

"You saw nothing at all wrong with her?"

"You're speaking of her madness. That came later, after she and my uncle had been married awhile, perhaps a year or so. I remember the servants wondering aloud at some of the strange things they had been told she had done. I remember Uncle Lawrence telling me that my stepmother wasn't feeling well. And I can remember telling him that she was breeding and that was obviously why she wasn't feeling well. I told him that ladies occasionally vomited when they were breeding."

"You, a twelve-year-old boy, knew that? Actually said that to your uncle?"

"Oh, I was thirteen then, perhaps fourteen. Yes, I told him that, and I got clouted for it. To be honest, I remember Caroline as laughing, as carefree, nothing more, nothing less. But I was rarely here during their marriage or afterward. Are you jealous of my uncle's second wife?"

I didn't say anything. I stared at him hard now, and said, "If one were to imagine, just for a moment, mind you, that the old woman really happened last night, it occurs to me that you are the only person in Devbridge Manor who would like to see me long gone from here."

"Yes, that's quite true. You don't belong here, not as my uncle Lawrence's nubile young wife, who sleeps alone in her own bedchamber while he sleeps alone in the master's suite."

"It is none of your affair what either of us does."

There was that flash of anger or violence in his dark eyes. I couldn't miss it this time, it was dark and intense and deep as a well, and I felt it like a blow. "If I could," he said, his voice low and savage as he turned to leave, "I would throw you in a carriage and drive you to London right now. But you know, Andy, I would never call you an abomination. Isn't that what the old woman said?"

And then he was gone before I could say anything.

I turned back to the window. I don't know how long I stood there, not really thinking, just being there to absorb anything that might be in this strange room when she called out to me from the doorway. For one instant, I believed it was Caroline, come here now to find me in her room.

"I hope you are feeling well today, Andy."

Naturally it wasn't Caroline.

"Judith," I said as I turned around. I was pleased to see her. There was no guile, nothing at all hidden beneath her sweet girl's face. "I am fine, thank you."

"I was worried about you, Andy. So was Miss Gillbank. She said what happened to you was perfectly dreadful. She said she didn't think she would have had the courage to dash to the bedchamber door like you did."

"I think all of us find we can do just about anything when we are forced into it."

"What are you doing in here?"

"This was your mother's music room, wasn't it?"

Judith nodded and began walking around the empty room, touching her fingertips to the wall here and there. "That's what Mrs. Redbreast told me. She said my mother played the harp so very beautifully. I don't appear to have any of her talent. Miss Gillbank says I should just keep practicing, but I know she believes it's hopeless. Andy, what happened last night, do you really believe now that it was a nightmare?"

"Well, that's what everyone else believes, so perhaps it is what really happened."

"That was well said, but you didn't say anything."

It was not as easy to lie to her as I had to everyone else. "You will keep this to yourself, Judith, all right?"

Her eyes grew larger, and she stepped right up to me. "What? I swear I'll not tell a soul."

"The old woman last night was very real."

"How can you be so sure?"

"Because George saw her. He saw her

clearly because he barked his head off, nearly leapt out of my arms to attack her. A dog doesn't bark at someone else's night-mare."

"Oh, goodness, you're right. There is no doubt then. Did you tell Father that?"

"No, I didn't. Listen to me, Judith. Adults don't like to believe in things that cannot be readily explained. It makes them nervous, uncertain. Even if I told them about George, they wouldn't like it. They would prefer to believe that I made that up, too."

"But you didn't. Have you decided what you are going to do?"

I smiled at her and managed to speak the truth at the same time. It was difficult. "You mean, am I going to leave Devbridge Manor before I'm made to pay for all of it?"

"That's what the old woman said to you?"

"Yes, and a lot more besides."

"What is it you are supposed to pay for?"

"I don't know. But I remember that I am also the evil that revisits this house. Does that make any sense at all to you?"

She shook her head. Perhaps I was speaking too frankly to her, but I felt she de-served the truth. "I wish I could think of something," she said then, and walked to join me by the window. "I used to stand here and watch the gardeners scythe the front lawn. The sweet grass smells came right up through the open window. It was summer then, of course. I don't want you to leave, Andy, but I know that you must be frightened by all this."

"I don't want to leave, either. I am the mistress here now. Most would say that I belong here."

"Then, what are we going to do?"

It was we now, not just me and George. She stuck out her hand, and I took it. "Would you like to come with me to The Blue Room? Perhaps we can find out who scared me so badly last night. It was John's knife the old woman had. Then later, the knife was back in its place, in John's collection, sitting in its velvet case. How did that happen do you think?"

"Oh, no, you don't believe it was John who disguised himself as that horrid old woman and came into your bedchamber?"

"It was his knife. When I ran down the hall and pounded on his bedchamber door, it took him time to open the door. I wonder why."

"Oh, dear, you're wondering if it took him

awhile to shuck off that tangled gray wig and that old woman's gown?"

"And replace that Moorish knife of his back in its glass case."

"But, Andy, if he was in your room and he didn't chase you down the hall, then how could he have gotten back to his bedchamber to answer your knock?"

"That's an excellent question, isn't it? There's more, Judith. I locked my bedchamber door before I went to bed."

She cocked her head at me, a thick tress of blond hair falling like a curtain down her cheek. "I don't understand. No, wait." Then Judith, that very proper little girl who made wagers, whistled. "Another way into The Blue Room? A secret passage? That's what you are thinking, isn't it? Oh, goodness, Andy, a dark narrow passage that winds throughout the house. Oh, my."

"There is another possibility. The ledge outside the windows. It's wide enough so someone could make their way along it and then climb back into another room." I wasn't about to tell her that this was how her mother had escaped to make her way to the north tower and kill herself.

"I would rather have a secret passageway," Judith said, and bounded out of the room with me following more slowly behind her. Actually, I thought, I would prefer a secret passageway myself. Was it a mistake to take her into my confidence? I didn't think so, but nothing made sense here at Devbridge Manor. At least since I had arrived here.

"You've never heard anyone speak of any passageways? Your father? Brantley? Anyone?"

"No," she said, clearly disappointed. "But if there is one that opens into The Blue Room, we will find it. But you know, Andy, Father is the one to ask. Surely he would know, would he not?"

"Very probably." But I couldn't very well ask Lawrence about secret passageways and such. Of course he would know, but if I asked, then he would know that I hadn't changed my tale at all. He would know that I firmly believed the old woman was as real as he was.

"Don't you ask him, Judith. Let's just keep this between ourselves for the time being. Now, you and I can spend some time hunting up that passageway. All right?" She agreed, very quickly. I couldn't remember if a twelve-year-old girl could be counted on to keep mum about anything.

I opened the door and walked into The Blue Room. George was sleeping in front of the fireplace. He cracked open an eye, saw Judith, obviously remembered that she adored him, and got lazily to his paws, taking his time to stretch out each leg. But he didn't bark.

"Evidently Brantley has been giving him more lessons," I said, still amazed. "That is why he isn't barking his head off now." I watched Judith walk to George, go down on her knees, and say in the most worshipful voice, "Have you missed me, George? Should you like to come and sleep with me one night? I'll sneak down to the kitchen and bring you anything you would like." She raised her face to me. "Can he be bribed, Andy?"

"In an instant," I said. "He adores crispy bacon. You feed him that, and he is yours."

George licked Judith's hand, and allowed his acolyte to pick him up in her arms. He had no shame.

Judith laughed, and George licked her face until his tongue must be dry. She said then, "Why were you standing alone in Mother's music room, Andy?"

"Like you, I enjoy the prospect from the front window. I'm also considering making use of it myself. Perhaps I can make it a study, where I can write letters and such."

She nodded. She didn't care one way or the other. To be expected, since her mother had died shortly after birthing her.

"This is a large room," I said. "I believe I'll start on the wall with the fireplace."

Judith gently set George back onto the rug that lay in front of the fireplace. He went back to sleep, and I'd swear that mutt had a grin on his ugly little face.

Judith took the far wall.

"You're looking for a hollow sound," I said as I tapped.

We both began knocking on the walls.

We hadn't been at it all that long when there was a knock on the door.

I immediately climbed down from the chair I'd been standing on. It was Amelia; she stepped into my bedchamber and placed her hand on my arm. "Listen, Andy, I remember more now about what happened yesterday. I was lying on my bed just a little while ago, taking a nap just as Thomas begged me to do. When I closed my eyes, I remembered that door slamming shut in your face. I remember you shouting at me." She came to an abrupt halt. "Oh, goodness, it's you, Judith. Whatever are you doing here? Why are you standing on that chair?"

Judith looked scared. "I'm sorry, Amelia, I found Andy and she—"

"I wanted to hang a painting," I said easily. "Judith was checking the height I wanted." I didn't want Amelia to know we were sounding the walls for a hollow space. My new tale would certainly be hoisted on a petard, then.

Judith said nothing, smart girl.

"Judith also wanted to see George. She is second only to John in George's affections," I added. "He just went to sleep again. Judith, don't you have to go back to your lessons now?"

"Yes, Andy. May I come back perhaps early this evening? To play with George and to help hang your painting?"

"Certainly, I would like that very much."

Amelia didn't say another word until Judith had quietly closed the bedchamber door after her.

"Yes, what else do you remember, Amelia?" I led her to a chair in front of the fireplace. George cocked open an eye, looked at her for a moment, then went back to a sleep.

She sat down, fretting all the while with a loose thread on her sleeve. "I remember you calling to me. I remember standing there, just looking at that closed door, and doing absolutely nothing. I didn't want to do anything. Then I set the candle branch on the floor and lay down on my side, my cheek pillowed against my hands.

"I remember that I felt so very tired, just all of a sudden, I couldn't keep my eyes open. Then—"

"For God's sake, Amelia, spit it out."

"I'm not mad. I know I'm not mad."

"Tell me."

"I felt something very warm, something thickening the air above my head. But it wasn't scary, Andy. Then there was this very soft voice, not really a voice, but I felt her voice deep inside my head, and she said something about how she was sorry, but I wasn't the right one. Then I woke up a bit to see Thomas and John over me."

I didn't say a word. I'd never been so afraid in my entire life, even last night and that dreadful old woman with that knife coming at me, wasn't as scary as this.

Because the old woman had been flesh and blood, and this wasn't. Whatever this was, it wanted me, not Amelia. I had no doubt of that at all.

"I didn't want anyone to think me mad, but when Thomas admitted seeing a young lady here in The Blue Room, I knew it would be all right to tell you. You won't tell anyone else, will you? Promise me, Andy. Thomas worries so. I don't want him to become ill because he is distressed about me."

"All right." I thought a moment, then said very slowly, very precisely, "Amelia, did you know that the empty room was Caroline's music room?"

"I suppose so. She died so long ago, there was no reason for me to remember. You believe she wanted you in that room, don't you? Not me. You believe her ghost was there yesterday."

"It makes sense, does it not?"

Amelia rose, that very soft jaw of hers set in hard lines. "I don't care that Thomas doesn't want me to, I am going to write my father now, Andy, right now."

"Good."

She marched out of my bedchamber before I could say another word. George raised his head and wuffed.

I spent the next hour knocking on the walls, but there was no hollow sound. Then I heard something. I quickly turned to look at the door. I saw the doorknob slowly turn. I nearly fell off my stool.

Then there came a quiet knock.

I had to get hold of myself. I had locked the damned door. I went to open it.

It wasn't Caroline or that old woman. It was Belinda.

She gave me a bright smile. "His lordship said you were napping, a good thing, I say. Did it clean all the ghostly webs out of your mind, my lady?"

"There's not a single web left."

"Good. Wicked dreams are like some men, my ma used to tell me. Sometimes they can just burrow in, and it takes the devil himself to yank them out." She continued talking while she pulled out the gown she deemed appropriate for me to wear to dinner. She didn't ask me, simply nodded when she smoothed out the lovely skirt of a pale peach silk gown, with a crepe overskirt of a darker shade.

"Now, ribbons," Belinda continued to herself. "Yes, here they are, all tangled up. Now, how did that happen?"

She turned to see me still standing there, staring at nothing at all.

"It is being in a new house as well," she said, sounding like a comforting nanny with a new charge. "New houses can make a body as nervous as a canary drinking a cat's milk. Now, a bath will help you."

And so it was that an hour later, my hair finally dry, I knocked on Miss Crislock's bedchamber door and let her worry herself over me for a good five minutes. When she'd finally exhausted all of her concerns, given me all her advice, patted my arm at least six times, she said, "Now, don't you fret, Andy, about me. I am just fine. Everyone is quite helpful, Mrs. Redbreast especially. I do not believe I will join the family this evening. I am a bit on the bilious side, not a charming thing for a new family to see. You enjoy yourself, my dear, and try to forget the strange things that have happened, or that haven't happened, as the case may be." And I kissed her, hugged her tightly, wishing she weren't bilious, then walked down the main staircase, my shoulders back.

Belinda had assured me that I looked such a sweet lovely lady. I would rather have looked ill-tempered, ugly, and had a gun in my pocket. A gun, I thought. Now, where would I get a gun? Just the thought of being able to protect myself made me slough off a good portion of the grinding fear.

"My lady," Brantley said. "May I say that you are looking no worse for all your adventures?"

"You certainly may, Brantley. Thank you."

He came closer, and to my astonishment, he appeared confiding. He said in a lowered voice, "It is a very fortunate thing that Lord and Lady Appleby just left and you were spared their onerous company."

"Are they so very dreadful, Brantley?"

"They are more dreadful than that Cockly boy in the village, who painted all the ducks that swim in the pond in the middle of the green."

"Painted them? Goodness, what color?"

Brantley actually shuddered. "Pink. The little booby painted them pink."

"However," my husband said, coming out of the drawing room to join us, "her ladyship will be pleased to hear that we are going to have a ball in her honor, three weeks from now, on Friday night."

"That will be two weeks before Christmas, Uncle Lawrence."

"Indeed, it will, Amelia. Ours will be the first party of the season, and with Andy arranging for it, it will also be the finest. What do you think of that, Andy?"

"A Christmas party. I should love that. Grandfather always held a huge affair at Deerfield Hall every Christmas. It is very nice of you, Lawrence. I hope that everyone involves themselves." Actually, I wasn't at all certain what I felt about a Christmas party at all. So much had happened so quickly, and now I was to arrange a ball?

Amelia said, "Oh, yes, you are not to worry, Andy. Unfortunately, I fear that we are now in for it. Lord and Lady Appleby were just here. Their daughter, Lucinda, was gushing all over John. Her predatory mama has set her eyes on John. He should be prepared to go to ground, for she's got him in her sights." Then she giggled.

I smiled as well when John and Thomas came into the Old Hall. Both of them were frowning, but for very different reasons.

"You have already attached a local girl, John?"

"What? Oh, you mean Miss Appleby." I do believe he shuddered, just like Brantley had when he spoke of the Cockly boy painting the ducks. "She's a child."

"What is this, John?" Amelia said. "She is only two years younger than Andy. Ah, the soulful looks she was casting in your direction. I thought one of her lesser efforts looked like a painful squint. I was just telling Uncle Lawrence that Mama Appleby wants to snag you for her little darling."

Amelia stopped cold. She was by her husband's side in the next instant, touching her white fingers to his cheeks, his forehead. "Oh, Thomas, my dearest, whatever is the matter? Are you ill? What pains you? Tell me what isn't right so that I may fix it."

"It is nothing," Thomas said, and shook his head at something that only he knew about. Without another word, he marched back into the drawing room. Amelia stared after him, her mouth gaped open.

"I don't believe this," Lawrence said slowly, staring after his retreating nephew. "He had a chance to establish a new illness or injury or pain, and he didn't. What is going on with your husband, Amelia?"

She said quietly, staring after Thomas, "I don't know. It worries me."

Miss Gillbank again joined us for dinner. She was wearing one of my gowns that Belinda had altered for her, a charming pale blue muslin confection that was simple and elegant, perfectly suited to her classic features. She asked about Miss Crislock, whom she and Judith had met this afternoon in the east garden.

No one mentioned the old woman. No one mentioned anything else that had happened the day before.

As for Thomas and John, they were both distracted, very bad company, as a matter of fact.

When Lawrence left me at my bedchamber door, I didn't want to go inside. I just didn't. It wasn't the middle of the day now, and I wasn't knocking on the walls in the clear light of day. It was dark, very dark, with scarce a sliver of moon to shine in the windows. Jasper was walking George. I wanted to be walking with Jasper myself.

I waited in the corridor until I heard Jasper coming. He was speaking to George. "A fine selection you made, Mr. George. That old yew bush needed some attention even though it was a rather noxious sort of liquid attention you bestowed on it. Yes, you did well."

I still didn't want to go inside my bedchamber. I thanked Jasper, took George in my arms, and forced myself to open the door.

Chapter Seventeen

There were three branches of candles lit against the darkness. A healthy fire burned in the fireplace. The room was warm. I stood there, holding George too tightly, feeling as if my blood had frozen in my veins. I stared at the shadowed corners, unable to see clearly, knowing that there could be things in those shadows, hiding from me.

George wuffed and strained to get away from me. He didn't see anything amiss. Still, I just stood there, looking now toward the windows. Belinda had pulled the draperies closed. I'd told her to leave them open. She had forgotten, or perhaps she was trying to break me of what she considered a very un-healthy habit.

I locked the door, turned the knob one way, then the other, did everything I could think of to pry it open, but it held. Yes, it was well locked. I walked to the windows and jerked back the draperies. I opened the windows. Cold dry air washed over me. I breathed in deeply.

There was nothing and no one here. It was very possible, if I had indeed locked my door last night, that the person had come through my open windows. I shut and locked them. I looked down at the empty bar holes on the casement and wondered if Caroline was still here, if the violence of her death was somehow holding her here. Poor, poor girl. I couldn't imagine such an illness, but I knew it existed. One of grandfather's oldest friends had even forgotten his own wife and his children. The day he no longer recognized Grandfather, I saw my grandfather cry. He would die alone, my grandfather had said, alone, because there was no one he knew and loved to be there with him.

I took off my clothes and pulled my night-gown over my head. I tied the pale blue satin ribbons into pretty bows. I suppose it had been my mother who taught me that. So long ago. I couldn't call up her face anymore. I picked up George, and together we settled ourselves under the mountain of warm covers. I didn't wake up once.

The next morning I rode Small Bess into Devbridge-on-Ashton, a small village clustered around a central square that held an old church, a vast graveyard whose oldest stone was dated 1311, and a meandering stream. I looked closely at all the now-white ducks swimming in the stream, at the clumps of skinny oak and lime trees. Stone houses lined up on either side of a very old inn called The Queen's Arms. There was an almshouse, a blacksmith, his hammer ringing loud in the morning air, and a good half dozen other small shops that carried everything from tobacco to leather to barrels. Many villagers were out and about, and I smiled and met a good thirty of them. Everyone was friendly, which I certainly appreciated. It had been a long time since there had been a mistress at Devbridge Manor. I began memorizing names, something, I knew, that would hold me in good stead. I also spent money at every store I visited. My last stop was the gunsmith, housed in a ground-floor narrow little room just off High Street. The owner was Mr. Forrester, a very short smiling individual, with freckles covering his face and his bald head, who looked to be about my husband's age. His grandchildren were playing in a corner. Near the guns. That surprised me, but didn't seem to faze him at all. He knew who I was, and was voluble in welcoming me to Devbridge-on-Ashton. I was from the Big House, the new mistress, and I knew that every word I spoke, every look that could possibly convey any opinion at all, would be remembered and then shared with everyone in the village. If Grandfather had seen me going through the village, he would have just patted my cheek and told me that I was behaving exactly as I should. I was treating people with the respect that some of them might even deserve. Everyone would believe me a nice proper young lady, just so long as they didn't notice the wickedness in my eyes. Then Grandfather would laugh.

"Ashton is the name of that stingy little meandering stream that used to be much larger," Mr. Forrester told me, "back when Cromwell wandered the land. Cromwell had a lot of hair, you know. Unfortunately, even the small rapids disappeared during my grandfather's time. I have read that many of the Roundheads had more hair than they deserved."

"That is a pity," I told him. "Not about all that hair given out unjustly. No, I am very fond of rapids."

After ten more minutes of observations on my part, I simply couldn't help myself, I said, "Whatever happened to the Cockly boy, Mr. Forrester, the one who painted the ducks pink?"

I must say that the question took him aback. Then he gave me the biggest grin. Mr. Forrester was missing quite a few of his back teeth. "He was whipped by the vicar himself, a dozen times with the vicar's cane, then forced to clean the paint off the poor ducks. They bit him hard, many times, the little devil."

Then, and only then, after he was laughing and distracted by the duck story did I tell Mr. Forrester that I wanted him to find me the very smallest gun he could. It was a Christmas present for my cousin, I told him, who traveled a lot and needed something very small that would go everywhere with him. Mr. Forrester told me that would be a derringer, small enough for a lady's reticule, but naturally, no lady would ever want to touch one of the nasty little things. He didn't carry something like that in his small shop. He beamed at me when I ordered the most expensive derringer he described to me, and assured me he would have it here in under a week. I paid him for the derringer, and as a result received three very deep bows from Mr. Forrester, and little bobs from all four of his grandchildren, all lined up to see me safely out of their territory.

I visited the butcher's shop, ordered the pork the butcher specifically recommended, purchased some crockery from the small dry goods store, and finally searched out the local seamstress from whom I immediately ordered three chemises in the very finest lawn she had on the premises. My last stop was the ancient stone church in the square. I met the curate, Mr. Bourne. The vicar, I was told, was visiting his bishop in York.

When I returned to Devbridge Manor, I rode into the stable yard to see Tempest trying his best to trample one of the stable lads.

I didn't really think about it, just climbed off Small Bess's back and ran to the lad.

"Give me the reins," I said, and he was so surprised that he obeyed me instantly.

I didn't pull or jerk on the reins, just held them loosely, giving Tempest even more slack. He reared and snorted and kicked out with his front hooves. He was very angry. I stayed as far out of his way as I could. I spoke to him as I'd been taught by Grandfather, softly, my voice pitched low, nonsense, most of it, just repeating over and over that everything would be all right, that I thought he was magnificent, and I would be angry if someone was jerking me around like the stable lad had been doing to him. But everything was fine now, I would get him an apple, and so he could calm himself down.

Slowly, ever so slowly, he began to ease. As he did, I tightened my hold on the reins, coming closer and closer to him until he was blowing hard against my palm. His great body shuddered. "It's all right, boy." I let him punch his nose against my shoulder. He very nearly knocked me over. I spoke to him for another five minutes before he simply dropped his head and blew softly. I called out to the stable lad, who was standing there, pale, sweaty, wringing his hands, "It's all right now. Bring me an apple, and hurry."

I fed that beautiful animal a huge apple, felt him lip my fingers, then chew some carrots that Rucker, the head stable lad, handed me silently.

I said nothing to any of them, simply wrapped my hands in Tempest's thick mane and pulled myself onto his bare back, something I could never do in London. But this was Yorkshire, and I was mistress here. He twisted his head about to look at me.

"Just you and me, Tempest. Let's just walk about for a while, until you're all calm and happy again."

And so we did. Tempest walked until he was bored, then cantered a bit. I didn't let him gallop all out. If there was still anger in him, I didn't know if I could control him. I guided him down to the stream and slid off his back. "I'll teach that lad what's what, Tempest. He won't ever jerk and pull on your reins again. If he tries it, I'll smash him into the ground. Then you can kick him. No, you won't have to get yourself upset anymore."

I heard a laugh. Of course it was John. When I turned, he was standing not six feet away, just walking around one of the huge willow trees that hung over the stream. He was dressed in riding clothes, a riding crop in his right hand. He looked big and dangerous, and instinctively, without thought, I stepped back, bumping into Tempest, who merely butted me gently with his big head.

The laugh fell off his face. He was wearing Hessians, polished to a mirror finish, buckskin britches, a tan riding coat. I wouldn't want to have him coming up to me like this on a battlefield. I could easily see a sword in his hand. He was very angry indeed. Well, what could I expect? I had taken his horse.

"What the hell have you done?"

Of course his anger at me wasn't entirely because of Tempest. He was furious because I had stepped away from him.

"Didn't Rucker tell you that I merely took Tempest for a walk to calm him down?"

"I told you never to ride him. He could crush you under those hooves of his." Then he looked at Tempest and slapped his forehead with his palm. "Evidently Rucker did not believe it important enough to tell me that you rode him bareback. Are you mad, woman?"

"I don't think so," I said, "particularly since I changed my story about the old woman so no one will believe I am another Caroline. I didn't hurt your bloody horse, and I didn't hurt my bloody self, either. Now, how is your knife, John? Safe and snug on its red velvet cushion?"

"Don't," he said, and walked to me. I wanted to swing up on Tempest's back, but I knew I wouldn't make it. He couldn't very well hurt me with Tempest playfully hitting the back of my head every so often with his nose. "Damn you, don't goad me. It isn't to your benefit."

"Stop acting like a soldier in a battle facing an enemy. Listen to me. I don't deserve your anger. He would have crushed the stable lad if I had not taken the reins from him. He is perfectly fine. He hasn't a thought to hurt me."

At that point Tempest began chewing on my hair.

John looked from his horse to me, and laughed again, something I knew he didn't want to do. "You deserve to be beaten," he said, and began to detach a long curly hunk of hair from his horse's mouth.

And because I didn't have a brain in my

head, I said without hesitation, "Just who do you think would be stupid enough to try that?"

He said slowly, looking down at me, "You barely come to my chin. It's true you're strong, since you evidently pulled yourself up onto Tempest's back—no mean feat for a female. But that makes no difference at all. I could do anything I pleased to you. Lower your arrogance, madam." He stopped then, looking away from me, out over the stream. He didn't look back at me, just said low, violence in his voice, "Damn you for being here. Oh, yes, I would be stupid enough to thrash you," and he grabbed me. Tempest whinnied, I dropped the reins and tried to pull free, swamped with complete and utter terror. I must have looked suddenly different, because John let me go. I saw white, all blank nothingness, then red, violent, and flowing, and I simply cried out and fell to my knees.

I heard someone screaming, agony screams, death screams. I saw my mother's face, so clearly, right in front of me. She was pale, tears oozing out of her eyes, and she looked utterly bereft. Then there was a man there amid the screaming. He looked around, and then he just shrugged and walked away. The screaming didn't stop, just went on and on until once again, there was the blessed empty whiteness.

Suddenly, John was on his knees, facing me. His hands were on me, and he pulled me against him. I felt the hardness of him, the strength, and for just a moment, I wanted every ounce of strength he had, but I knew I couldn't have it. His hands were stroking up and down my back. He was saying things in my ear. What, I don't know. My riding hat was on the ground beside me. Then I felt his hands in my hair, pulling the braids free, pulling out the pins Belinda had so carefully placed. His hands were in my hair then, his fingers touching my scalp, then suddenly, he stopped. He pulled back. I didn't want to, but I looked up at him. We were on our knees, facing each other. It was odd, but I knew this was wrong, since I was married to his uncle, and I felt that more than I felt the fear of being near him, a man who could hurt me so easily, humiliate me, make me scream and scream until I died. I drew a deep breath and slowly, so very slowly, I began to pull away from him. He dropped his hands to his sides and quickly got to his feet. He walked away from me, to his horse. He swung up on Tempest's back.

He said from his great height, "I have told you that I would never hurt you. This fear of yours, it is something very dark and very deep inside you. Whatever it is, it's bad, it is corrosive. It is directing your life, not you. You have married an old man because of it.

"And me, madam? Just look what you do when you are around me. Jesus, it unmans me." He shook his head. There was such pain on his face that I couldn't bear it. "This will stop, it must." Then he kicked his boots into Tempest's sides, and rode away.

I didn't move for a very long time. It took me even a longer time to get my hair plaited and pinned, and the riding hat perched back on top.

It was a twenty-minute walk back to the Manor. I supposed the horse John had ridden to the stream had made its way back to the stables. I met with Mrs. Redbreast and discussed replacing linens that had been too many times mended. Then I met with Cook to plan the following week's menu. George and I played with Judith, then we shared her geography lesson with her and I learned how to say good day in Mandarin Chinese.

For dinner that night, Miss Crislock joined the family, and I was so very pleased to see her. She was the only one there for me, only me. She'd known me forever. She loved me.

John wasn't there.

After my husband had lightly kissed my cheek, and left me at the door to my bedchamber, I fetched George, walked him for an hour until the dreadful cold finally drove us back into the house.

I slept horribly. George snored the night through.

Chapter Eighteen

The days passed swiftly. John was rarely at the Manor. I heard stories of Lady Appleby chasing him down and chaining him to their dining table so her daughter could bat her eyes at him. I hope he suffered. I wanted him to.

As for Thomas, he seemed back to himself. I found out that he'd fancied e had caught chicken pox from the children in the village. However, there was no chicken pox reported, and it turned out to be a small rash brought on, Amelia decided, by a particularly rough bit of wool that had scratched against his chest. She was now feeling, with her own hands, any material that would come into contact with her beloved's body.

I heard Lawrence speak of how John was learning everything he could, and he was learning it quickly. And that was why, he said one evening at dinner, that we saw him so rarely. He was busy. And I knew that was good that he wasn't often around, and I hated it, which made me an idiot.

Days would pass without my seeing him, and that was good, too. I knew that. The other things that were also true that I didn't want to know, didn't want to explore, I locked firmly away.

The elegant little derringer that Mr. Forrester had fetched me himself from York was safe under my pillow, wrapped in one of my handkerchiefs. Grandfather had taught me to shoot. I went out only one afternoon to practice with my new gun.

A week later, Lawrence suggested that I invite Peter home for Christmas. I immediately wrote a letter, and Lawrence franked it. He was a splendid man, my husband. So very thoughtful. And I could never forget that. What John had said to me that day by the stream—that my fear of men had directed my life, had resulted in my marriage to his uncle. I knew it was true, but I didn't want to change anything, except in moments when I was lying in my bed at night, trying to sleep and John would slip into my mind and I felt a deep hard stroke of pain and regret that left emptiness. And, in the light of day, I remembered who and what he was. He was big and dangerous. If there was darkness deep inside me, as he had said there was, it was because of what he was, because of what every man was, that had put it there.

I myself was very busy, planning for the big ball. All of us were involved. The guest list was made up and refined, argued over, added to, and finally the invitations were sent out, many of them delivered by messenger. Lawrence was pleased about the preparations. The menu was selected. I asked if we could have the orchestra that had played for my coming-out ball two years previously. Lawrence, my very kind husband, had Swanson, the estate manager, see to it.

So much to do, thank God. The Black Chamber and its malignant presence faded from my mind. I never went back there. As for the empty room that had once been Caroline's music room, I never went close to that, either. And I locked the door to The Blue Room, religiously, every night.

Three days before the ball, Amelia's parents arrived. Her father, Hobson Borland, Viscount Waverleigh, a man so preoccupied with his own thoughts and ideas and internal discussions on otherworldly phenomena, was so distracted, that within five minutes of meeting the family, he walked into a door, poured his tea in a lovely big potted plant just beside the settee where he was sitting beside his wife, Julia, and stared fixedly at the far corner of the drawing room.

Strangely enough, or perhaps not, Amelia's father was every bit as beautiful as Thomas. The viscount was utterly immersed with the spirit world, and Thomas, his equal in male beauty, was absorbed with his health—as mysterious as the spirit world, some could argue.

It was also interesting that Amelia appeared to treat her father's eccentricities just as she did Thomas's, with love and tolerance and endless patience.

Viscountess Waverleigh said, after she managed to pull her husband's attention back to her, "Hobson, my dear, there are mysteries here for you to solve. Do you remember? Your daughter, Amelia, wrote to you about them. She said she needed you to solve otherworldly problems."

"Amelia? Yes, yes, a lovely daughter that I managed to bring into this magical world myself when the damned physician got himself thrown into a ditch and finally brought himself to see to you after three days, his arm broken."

"Yes, and you did splendidly."

"Am I not here because Amelia asked me to be?"

"Yes, Father. There are mysteries to solve, just as Mother said. There is also the Christmas ball." She said to Lawrence, "My father is a splendid dancer as well. Like Thomas, he is so very graceful."

"I like to dance," the viscount said. "It passes the time between hauntings." Then he pointed. "I am glad I do not have to dance at this moment because there is something over there, something interesting happened right over there in that corner. Do you feel it?"

This was said to me. I shook my head and said quickly while I still had his attention on me, "There are two chambers, however, that we would much appreciate you investigating for us, my lord."

He immediately rose, stared around at all of us, and said, "Well? Where are these rooms? Are we to sit here all day doing nothing at all? But that corner, it is of interest to me as well. Julia, do write that down in your book to be investigated later."

"Yes, my dear Hobson," said Viscountess Waverleigh.

I didn't want to go back to the Black Chamber, but I did. John, whom I hadn't seen for a day and a half, showed himself when Amelia's parents had arrived. He accompanied Amelia and me and his lordship to the west wing. Lawrence excused himself, saying he himself had no liking for anything not of this world.

As for Thomas, he had just laughed, lightly patted his wife's cheek, and said, "No falling asleep in any more rooms, my dear."

She turned instantly pale, then managed to pull herself together enough to smile at him.

"Does anyone know what happened in this room?" the viscount asked. "Something violent?"

"Nothing," I said. "No one even remembers why it was painted black. Amelia showed me the room, said one of the best stories was that a former countess had stabbed a lover, but there is nothing to prove it. It was only I who felt a malignancy, a dreadful sense that something evil is in there. I don't believe anyone else has felt anything out of the ordinary. Just me."

"Hmmmm, we will see. Sensitive to this sort of thing, are you?"

"Not that I ever knew of."

I couldn't bear to go back into that room. Amelia, since it was simply another room to her, went in first with John, then stepped aside for her father to enter, which he did very slowly, one short step at a time, sniffing, listening, so intent, that he nearly fell over a stool near the door.

Then he stopped cold. He stared in the exact corner that had felt so dreadfully cold to me. Lord Waverleigh, however, wasn't a coward. He walked right into the middle of where that dreadful cold had been. I took another step backward, into the corridor now.

"Can you feel it, sir?" I called to him. "It is just that one spot. It feels cold, the sort of cold that seeps right into your bones and soul, and there is menace to it, as if something evil happened right there."

He said nothing at all. He simply stood there, and closed his eyes. No one said a word, just watched. He opened his eyes, nodded to his daughter, and came back out into the corridor. He took my hands in his. "Listen to me, that is no spirit hanging about in that room, locked in there by some long-ago violence. I felt everything you felt, and more. Something violent did happen in that room, but the evil that is in there, that permeates the very air and space, it is not from the spirit world. It is from our world; it exists right here, with us now, in this house." And then Amelia's father, closed his eyes and slid down the wall to the corridor floor.

Terrified, I dropped to my knees immediately.

"No, Andy, it's all right. Father always does this. I believe that what he feels, what he sees, exhausts him. John, could you carry him to his bedchamber? He will sleep for an hour or so and then be all right."

"Just as you slept, Amelia?"

"Yes, just as I slept. I do have my father's

blood, after all. But there is nothing in that room for me, except the ridiculous black paint. John?"

I watched John hoist Lord Waverleigh over his shoulder and carry him off down the corridor.

Lady Waverleigh merely nodded when told that her husband was sound asleep in his own bed. "My dearest Hobson will be just fine in a little while. Then he will drink three cups of very strong tea." She sighed and smiled at me. "It is his way. I hope he was of help to you, Lady Devbridge?"

"Yes, ma'am." I could think of nothing else to say besides that. Or should I say, evil was in this house, not a long-dead evil, but an evil that lives right here, in our midst, and what, pray tell, does that mean? But I knew it was here, I knew it was just waiting.

But for what?

The next morning at breakfast, I was listening to Lord Waverleigh speak of a castle in Cornwall, in ruins now, very close to Penzance, in which he had personally located twelve different spirits, all of them long dead and alert and in lively spirits, so to speak. "None of them wanted to leave, even though it was now a ruin and no one lived there. It suited them, they felt it clearly to me. They never bothered the local Cornish. But they very much enjoyed terrorizing any visiting Englishman who chanced upon the castle."

I didn't want to believe him, but I did. He planned to visit the small room where Amelia had fallen asleep, Caroline's music room, just after breakfast. Lawrence had told me he wished to be a part of this visit when he had seen me to my room the previous night. He smiled down at me, gently laid his palm along my cheek. "You are doing so well here, Andy. I am very proud of you. I heard your praises loudly sung when I was in the village today. You also very wisely put some money in every shopkeeper's pocket. Well-done." He kissed my cheek then, something I was used to now. I no longer pulled away, even in my mind. Progress, I thought, trust. He was a good man, and I promised myself yet one more time that I would never forget what he had done for me.

And what had he done for me?

He had made me the mistress of a beautiful home. He had given me the protection of his name. He had made no demands on me whatsoever. And I thought, what have I done for him?

I wasn't a clingy milksop, but how important was that? I wasn't evil or malicious or ignorant. I amused him, so he told me often. I got along well with the family and the servants. I liked his daughter, and she seemed to like me. Surely that was to everyone's benefit.

But what I was, I knew now, and recognized it for the first time, was supremely arrogant. I had set everything up and assumed it would remain exactly as I wished it to.

One thing I was as well, I now freely admitted to myself—was stupid. I was a blockhead. I had made a huge mistake marrying Lawrence. But it was done. Never, never, would Lawrence know anything from me but all the affection I could muster, all the kindness that was in me, all the loyalty that I felt to my very bones.

That morning, just Lord and Lady Waverleigh were with me at the breakfast table— and George, of course. Lady Waverleigh had taken quite a fancy to George, and he was exploiting her shamelessly.

I had just buttered a piece of toast, fed George a piece of crispy bacon—which, if he weren't such a glutton, he would have refused, since Lady Waverleigh had already stuffed at least three slices down his gullet—when Brantley came into the dining room and brought me a silver salver. "A letter for you, my lady," he said, and left the room as quietly as he had entered it.

"I know he was Moses in the Bible," I said to my guests, smiling. In the next minute I was so excited I nearly ripped the paper. "It is from my cousin," I said, then lowered my head to spread out the page. It was too soon to hear from him about coming for Christmas. Ah, but maybe he wished to make peace with me and my marriage to Lawrence. There were two pages. I smoothed out the first.

November 25, 1817
Brussels, Belgium

My dearest Andy:

I will be with you as soon as I can leave Brussels. I ask you to read the enclosed letter from your father. He sent it to me because he feared you wouldn't read it if he posted it directly to you himself. Actually, I also believe he is afraid that it would be intercepted and not reach you at all. Although he doesn't state his reasons, I know he is nearly frantic to get to you.

Read it, Andy, for me, if not for any other reason. I will see you by Christmas. Please take care—

My love,
Peter

I looked up, aware of voices, but the owners' faces were a blur. *My father.* No, not him, not that horrible man. I suppose I had assumed he was dead. He should have been dead for a very long time now. He didn't deserve to live, yet here he was writing to me, and my mother had been dead for more than ten years.

My fingers shook as I slowly smoothed out the single page. I didn't recognize his handwriting. It was large and dark and bold, sloping slightly.

November 22, 1817
Antwerp, Belgium

My dearest daughter:

I pray you are reading this letter. I won't waste time telling you of my sorrow at our separation for so many years. Perhaps soon, you will agree to give me a chance, and I may come to know the woman you have become.

I read of your marriage to the Earl of Devbridge. This cannot be, Andrea. You are in danger, extreme danger. I know this is difficult for you to believe, but you must do as I say. Leave Devbridge now, or as soon as you can without detection. Return to London, to your grandfather's house. I will be with you as soon as possible and explain everything. Peter is waiting for me to finish, so I will close by saying that I have always loved you.

Your father,
Edward Kent Jameson

I rose from the breakfast table, smiled at Lord and Lady Waverleigh, and excused myself. George barked, then fell in beside me. I walked to the ballroom at the back of the manor. No one was there. Just the week before, a half dozen servants had descended on the ballroom and scrubbed and polished everything to a rich shine. The chandeliers were lovingly cleaned until the glass sparkled like hundreds of twinkling jewels. The heavy brocade draperies covering the tall windows had been taken down and beaten until all accumulated dust of at least five years floated to the ground.

I opened the letter again and walked to the far windows, so clean it looked like I could walk directly outside. I reread his letter.

He wanted me to leave Devbridge Manor immediately? But why? What was his reason? Why didn't he simply write his reason? Ah, because he was in such a hurry, he didn't have time. That was ridiculous. There was no reason. He simply wanted to insinuate himself back with me. But why? Surely he had enough wealth, didn't he? Did he want me to give him money when all was said and done? Perhaps he had feared that someone else would read the letter and would be alerted to—what?

So he had read of my marriage. Because of my marriage I was in extreme danger?

Bosh. Then, of course, I saw the old woman, John's knife raised high, ready to send it into my heart.

I looked up to see gardeners scything the grass on the east lawn. Two peacocks preened, their tail feathers spread wide as they strolled lazily toward the small rock garden. The scene before my eyes was so normal, so calm, so real.

But there was something and someone in this house that wasn't normal or real. There was someone evil.

But did that mean I was the target?

I folded the two letters and walked upstairs to my bedchamber. Belinda was straightening my brushes and creams in the dressing table. I went to my desk and pulled out my Italianate letter box. It was empty. I put the two letters in the box and locked it. I looked at the small gold key. I started to simply drop it in the drawer, then stopped. I found a gold chain, looped it around the key, and hung it around my neck.

I picked up my derringer from beneath my pillow and put it in my pocket. I wasn't about to leave my home; on the other hand, I wasn't an idiot. Whatever my father was talking about, whatever it was that he believed was wrong, I would be prepared. If that old woman came into my room again, I would shoot her. If anyone at all threatened me, I would shoot them. Let him come here, I thought. Let my precious father come here and face me.

But no one came that night.

Chapter Nineteen

The following morning, all of us accompanied Lord Waverleigh to Caroline's empty music room. Amelia declined to come into the room. I didn't blame her. Lawrence beside me, we followed Lord Waverleigh inside.

I didn't move, simply watched Lord Waverleigh walk around the small room. He said nothing at all. Finally, he raised his head and said, "There was no violence in this room. This was a young lady's room. She perhaps wrote letters here, or read here, or any number of things that she could do in private. She felt safe here, calm. It was her haven.

I can feel her unhappiness, but nothing more than that. Is this where Amelia fell asleep, on the floor of this room?"

"Yes, Father," Amelia said from the doorway. "And I felt this young lady—this chamber was Caroline's music room—she was Uncle Lawrence's second wife, and she apologized to me, I swear it to you. Not in words, of course, it was rather like she felt to me that she was sorry, that I was the wrong one."

"You say she was your second wife, Lawrence?"

"Yes. Poor Caroline killed herself after she birthed her daughter. It was all very tragic, very sad. Unfortunately, she was mad. She was only Andy's age when she died. Her death affected us all profoundly."

Lord Waverleigh started to say something, then he just shook his head. He looked at his daughter who had taken one step into the room. "If you were the wrong one, Amelia, then who is the right one?"

"I suppose it was me," I said. "But I have felt absolutely nothing in this room, sir, nothing at all. If Caroline wanted me specifically, I have given her many opportunities to speak to me, or feel her thoughts to me. There has been nothing."

"Hmmm," said Lord Waverleigh, stroking his chin. "You are the third wife. Caroline was the second wife. I wonder what she wants? I also wonder why she hasn't come to you, since you have given her the opportunity?"

"I don't know," I said.

He said then, "I should like to visit the spot where she killed herself." I thought Lawrence would refuse. He was pale, his hands fisted at his sides. Of course this would upset him. Even though it had all happened many years before, Caroline had been his wife, he had loved her, he had grieved for her when she hurled herself from the north tower. Finally, he nodded. "Very well," he said. "It is this way."

John, Lawrence, and I accompanied Lord Waverleigh to the north tower. At the end of the west wing, there were narrow stairs that twisted sharply, going up and up, until finally there was a narrow door that grated like a shrieking ghost when my husband opened it. There was an ancient bed in the circular room, with tattered bed hangings. A chest stood at the end of the bed. Nothing else.

"I have never had the tower room cleared," Lawrence said. "Everything is older than the oak trees all clustered together in the eastern forest, and they are very old indeed. I don't know who slept in that bed, but if they are continuing to sleep there, I see no reason to disturb them."

He walked to a tall narrow door and pulled it open. It moaned each inch it moved. There was a narrow balcony outside the door, in the form of a half-circle, a three-foot-high stone balustrade enclosing it. I walked to the balustrade and looked down. It was a very long way down, much farther than I would have thought. And directly below was a stone walkway. I felt gooseflesh rise on my arms. She had climbed up upon the balustrade and jumped. I closed my eyes. Ah, Caroline, I thought, I am so very sorry.

"I found her." I turned quickly. John was at my elbow. He was pointing. "There, on that second stone, that was where she landed. There is still blood in that stone. It simply will not be scrubbed out. I remember when I found her that I at first thought she was asleep. Then I turned her over. There was so much blood, so very much."

"I'm sorry," I said. "You were a young boy. It must have been very difficult."

"More so for Caroline," he said, and turned away.

I turned to Lord Waverleigh, who was simply staring around that circular room. He was frowning. "I would have expected to feel the violence of her passing, but I do not. In my experience a man or woman who chooses to take his life is confronting an excruciating decision. There is doubt, pain, anguish, terror. It is not easy to convince yourself that death is preferable, yet I feel nothing of what she should have felt here. Nothing at all. It is strange. Usually I feel these things very strongly."

"Sir," I said. "Caroline wasn't well. Perhaps her mind simply did not react the way yours would or mine. Perhaps there was no great decision for her to make. To end her life was a compulsion."

"Certainly that is possible," he said, but he continued to frown. Then suddenly, he turned to my husband, and he laughed. "I believe, Lawrence, that this lovely old bed was used by one of your distant ancestors to entertain his neighbor ladies. Perhaps he even kept a mistress here in this tower, hidden from his wife. That is speculation, of course."

"It could have been Leyland Lyndhurst," Lawrence said, "my great-grandfather. His reputation doesn't bear much examination. He lived a very long life and was said to pass to the hereafter with a smile on his lips."

He turned to me. "I'll show you a portrait of him, Andy. You will tell me if he has the look of the scourge of the neighborhood."

Lord Waverleigh turned and walked out of the tower room. I heard his footsteps retreating down those narrow steep stairs. I looked down once more to where Caroline had struck against the stone. I shuddered.

"Come, Andy," Lawrence said from just behind me. "This is a place that makes my soul wither, despite all the amusing and very wicked theories about that damned bed."

I knew exactly what he meant. "I'm so very sorry, sir," I said, and took his arm. "About Caroline." Any opinions I had about a former earl and his use of the tower for illicit *affaires* I kept behind my teeth.

John followed us down the tower stairs.

After luncheon, George and I went to the stables. Rucker saddled Small Bess even as John strode up, and blinked when he saw me. "I thought you were with Judith and Miss Gillbank. Or with Miss Crislock. She was looking for you, I believe."

"I will see all of them later. First, I want to clear my head."

He gave me a crooked smile. "What is in your head that needs to be cleared out?"

I thought of the damnable letters, of that seed of fear that had a firm hold on me now. I shook my head.

We left Small Bess standing there in the stable yard while I went with John to fetch Tempest from the paddock.

He saw his master, then he saw me. I would swear that he didn't know what to do. He stood there, looking from one of us to the other, shaking his great head.

John called out, "Enough, you big lout. I am your master, not this young chit here who cannot even manage to keep her dog's loyalty."

"Unkind," I said. "It appears I am getting my revenge on you."

George came trotting over, tail up high, barking with each step. On the way he picked up a stick.

Tempest snorted and trotted to where we stood at the fence.

"Throw the stick for George," John said as he went through the gate to put the bridle over Tempest's head. "A good long way. He needs to run off some of the mountains of food he's eating."

I did, hurling it a good twenty feet away. "It will help," I said, shading my eyes against the sun's glare. "I fear Lady Waverleigh is feeding him whenever he happens to trot into her vicinity. She dotes on him as much as she does her husband."

I watched John saddle Tempest, threw George's stick again, fought with him when he brought it back to me, and forgot for at least five minutes that something was very wrong here at Devbridge Manor. As much as I wanted to discount everything my father had written, which wasn't hardly a thing, truth be told, something wasn't right.

When finally we were both mounted, George had decided to remain. He was thoroughly enjoying himself playing with Jasper. Jasper could throw the stick much farther, and thus George could leap and trot and sniff flowers and bushes, and have a great time before he had to carry the stick back, as the rules of the game dictated. The exercise would also keep him from dropping onto his fat stomach and dying from gluttony.

Small Bess reared and twisted her head about when I settled myself on her back. I immediately leaned forward and stroked her neck. "It's all right, my pretty girl. What's wrong?"

"She wants to play. I have seen her do that occasionally since she arrived."

"Do you know why your uncle bought her, John?"

"No. Perhaps he had made up his mind to go to London and find himself a wife. He bought Small Bess on speculation."

"I must remember to ask him. Do you think perhaps she is a racing horse in disguise?"

"That I doubt very much."

Lawrence had never given me the impression that he had come to London in search of a wife. He had made me believe that his feelings for me had hit him immediately and strongly. He had not expected such feelings, particularly at his age. But still it felt to me as though he had brought Small

Bess here specifically for me. I shook my head. None of it made any sense.

I looked over at John astride Tempest. He was a magnificent rider, at one with that huge stallion. He was looking off into the distance. I wished he would look over at me, but he didn't. No, I thought, no. I had to stop this. I didn't want John anywhere near me. At the same time I wanted to weep because he was near me. I didn't want to let him out of my sight. It just wouldn't do. I thought of my husband. I owed him my complete loyalty. I thought of my fear of men, buried so deep, that I knew it would be a part of me my entire life. I knew I would never escape from it, nor did I want to. Young men like John, who was big and strong, were dangerous, they would hurt and destroy and humiliate. No matter what John made me feel, I would never forget that. If I ever did, I was a fool, just as my mother had been. No, what was there, so very deep inside me, was the truth, and a warning, and I would always heed both of them.

When we were walking through a rather densely wooded glade, side by side, John said, "Why do you think Caroline would want to speak to you?"

"I don't know," I said, realizing that here we were discussing the spirit of my husband's long-dead second wife. But oddly enough, it didn't seem strange. "What I don't understand is why she hasn't spoken to me. I have certainly given her many opportunities to communicate with me. I have gone in and out of that room many times now."

"Are you really certain you want to hear what she has to say?"

"Oh, yes. It must be something important, at least to her. Possibly, she wants me to assure her that I will take care of Judith, that I am not a mean and petty stepmother. I have even said that out loud whenever I go into her music room, but there is nothing there. Perhaps she has come to the belief that I won't hurt her daughter. Perhaps she even trusts me now."

"Judith has always been a happy child. My uncle pays her little attention, but she doesn't seem to suffer from it. She has Miss Gillbank, and that lady seems to love her very much. I predict she will be a beauty in about five years. What do you think?"

"She will break hearts at a fine clip," I said.

He leaned forward to pat Tempest's neck. Small Bess nickered and took a step sideways. I shifted my weight, and she calmed. "What Lord Waverleigh said about the Black Chamber. What do you think that means?"

"I don't want to think about it. It scares me to my toes."

He said, musing aloud, "That the evil in the room lives now, lives right here at Devbridge Manor, lives right here under our noses." He shook his head. "I think his lordship is being fanciful."

"If he isn't, then it would mean that the evil that lives here with us committed a horrible crime in that room. What crime could it be?"

He looked away from me, toward a distant copse of maple trees. "I've thought about it. There are no recorded foul deeds in the recent past. Ah, there are some excellent jumps over this field." He arched a black brow at me.

I laughed, and dug my heels into Small Bess's sides. She snorted, pulling violently on my reins. I patted her again, but now I was frowning. "What's wrong, my girl?"

John was riding ahead of me. I saw Tempest sail through the air, clearing the wooden fence with a good three feet to spare. The ground was muddy, covered with debris, but Tempest had had no problem clearing all of it. He looked magnificent. "Let's outdo him, Bess."

I leaned forward, pressing myself against her neck. She trembled beneath me, then ran faster than I could imagine. Closer and closer we came to the fence. I sat up, readying Bess and myself, and locked my legs around her belly.

She screamed and jumped, both at the same time.

I flattened myself against Bess's neck and grabbed the reins close to her mouth, but she was maddened, out of control, and I was nothing but something she wanted off her back.

In midair, I could feel Bess twist under me, trying her best to throw me. I knew, too, in that second that she would never be able to keep her balance. She cleared the fence, barely, but just before her hooves touched the slippery mud on the other side of the fence, she gave a great cry of anger and pain, and tore the reins from my hands. As she fell toward the fallen trees just beyond the mud, I kicked free and jumped, landing on my back on a slight incline. I rolled over and over, grabbing at grass, trying to stop.

I hit my head on something, felt a searing pain lash all the way to my skull.

Before everything went black, I heard Small Bess's cry of pain as she fell. Then I didn't hear anything at all.

Chapter Twenty

I didn't want to open my eyes. I didn't want to come back because I knew I wouldn't like it. I felt arms around me, John's arms. I knew the feel of him. I felt his heartbeat against my cheek, fast, pounding, and I opened my eyes because I knew he must be afraid for me. He was blurred, and I blinked several times.

I tried to raise my hand, but I couldn't. "You're there, aren't you?"

He took my hand and gently pressed it back to my side. "Yes, I'm here, and I'm not going anywhere. How do you feel?"

I felt his arms tighten around me. I felt no

instant shudder of fear. I felt rather safe, cherished. It was a nice feeling. "Oh, dear," I whispered, "let me up—now. Quickly."

He let go of me instantly. I jerked up, twisted about, and retched into the daffodils beside me.

When my head was hanging down, and I wanted to die my head hurt so badly, I felt his arms come around me again. He wiped his handkerchief over my mouth, then gently eased me back into his arms.

"Is that better now?"

"Yes, but my head is going to fall off next, that or split open. That would be a mess. I wish you could make it all stop. I don't like this at all."

"I don't blame you. Just lie still and listen to me. You don't have to think or anything else, just listen and don't move. That's right. Just breathe slowly, lightly. Good. Now, when I brought Tempest down, I turned to see Small Bess corkscrew in midair, then you flying over her head. What happened? Did she slip? How did she manage to throw you? If you wish, if you feel like it, you can talk now."

My eyes flew open as memory flooded back. I tried to sit up, but he held me down.

"No, don't move. What's the matter?"

"Oh, God, there is something very wrong, John. Small Bess was maddened, frantic, and I couldn't calm her. Please, go see to her."

"In a moment. First, can you move your legs?"

I could. I didn't want to, but I could and I did, because I knew he'd keep after me until I proved that I could.

He was running his hands over my ribs, then my arms. I allowed it. I had no choice. Also, to my surprise, I still wasn't terrified to my toes, and he was the same as he'd always been—too big, too strong, and too dangerous. You could just look at him and know he was dangerous. And he had held me close and safe against him.

"All right, I'll check her now," he said. He eased me down on the ground and pulled off his riding jacket. He folded it and gently eased it under my head. "If you move, I won't be pleased with you."

"Prepare to be pleased with me, then," I whispered, and he smiled.

Some minutes later, he pulled me again gently into his arms. He began rocking me very slowly, very gently.

"How is she?"

"I don't think we will have to put her down. Rucker is very good with injuries, as is my valet, Boynton. Her right foreleg appears badly sprained. And there are some bad cuts on her back. We'll see."

"I can help," I said. "I spent many hours in the stable at Deerfield Hall learning how to care for the horses. Oh, God, I can't allow her to be put down. It must have been my fault. I must have done something—"

He spoke slowly, his voice measured. "It wasn't your fault. Be quiet now."

I tried to focus on his face until it was clear to me. He looked grim. He also looked furious.

"No," I said. "I didn't cram her, did I, John?"

"No, of course not. You're much too good a rider." He drew a deep breath, and when he spoke, his voice was utterly emotionless. "I told you there are some bad cuts on her back. Well, I discovered this under her saddle."

In his hand he held a large, circular band of wire. Attached to the wire were long barbs, bent downward. The barbs were covered with blood, Small Bess's blood.

I just lay there and gaped at that horrible thing he carefully held in his hand. "No, that isn't possible, it just isn't. Who would do such a thing?"

"Someone placed this beneath her saddle. That someone knew it would madden her. Every time you shifted in the saddle, every time you tightened your legs, the barbs dug into her back. When you readied for her to jump, Small Bess had to be in great pain, and that's why she tried as hard as she could to get you off her back. I would like to know who this someone was. I want to kill him."

"I get to kill him first, the damnable bastard. Trying to hurt me is one thing, but doing this to my horse, my God, I will shoot the person who did this."

His arms tightened, as if in surprise. Then he grinned down at me. "We will have to see about that," he said, then grew quiet for a moment. "You know, Andy, if I had been the one riding her, the barbs would have gone in very deeply, probably all the way. Since you are much smaller, it took longer and it took more movement from you. But it happened. She was enraged, maddened by the time you jumped. The pain must have been very bad indeed."

I swallowed. "If I hadn't gone over her head, she would have fallen on me."

"Very probably."

My father's letter was clear in my mind. I said, turning my face into his shirt, breathing in his warm scent, "A warning, yet another warning to me. That someone who did this could never be certain that it would end up with me dead. The same thing with the old woman and that damned knife of yours telling me that I would pay for all of it, whatever that means. Warnings, both of them. But why?"

"I don't know. But now I'm really mad, and I fully intend to find out. The first thing is for you to go back to London, to your grandfather's house."

It sounded like a fine plan to me. It sounded smart, logical. It sounded safe. It sounded like entering a nunnery and locking big iron doors behind me. Nothing could hurt me there. But, there would never be any answers. Worse, perhaps I would never be safe, even hidden in my nunnery. I said, my voice miserable, "No, I can't leave. Don't you see? If I leave, then we will never know who is doing this and why. Perhaps even if I did leave, this unknown person would still want to hurt me and would come after me. John, no, don't argue with me. You know I'm right. I won't be safe until I find out who is doing this to me. Listen, I'm not unprotected. I bought a derringer from Mr. Forrester. I know how to shoot it. I'm not a complete idiot. It's fastened to a strap around my thigh."

His arms tensed, then slowly eased again. I hadn't convinced him. But that made sense, he was a man. "Everything you said is true, but there is still a very big problem. We won't know where the next threat will come from."

"I will try not to be alone anymore. I have my derringer. I know how to shoot. Give me a villain, and I'll put a hole through him. Normally George is with me. George makes a lot of noise. He is good protection."

He didn't say anything to that, but I knew that, like Grandfather, he was probably just holding silent until he came up with arguments. "Do you feel well enough to return home now?"

"Yes."

I watched him shrug back into his riding

jacket and place the barbed circle of wire into his pocket.

"Try to hold on to me." He lifted me in his arms and held me high. I was clutching his shirt, my face pressed against his neck. He carried me to Tempest, who was eating some lovely goose grass some fifteen feet away.

"Hang on, Andy. Once we get on his back, I'm going to seat you in front of me."

"I can do it."

"Good girl." I don't know how he managed it, but he got both of us up on Tempest's back. He eased me in front of him. The pain was so ghastly that I couldn't keep still even with my fist stuffed into my mouth.

"All right," he said close to my cheek. "It's all right. Just breathe slowly, lightly. That's it. I'll hold you, and we'll go very slowly." He simply eased me crossways on the saddle, pulled me close to his chest, and managed Tempest's reins with one hand. "Hold on to me as best you can. Keep your eyes shut. It should help with any dizziness. If you need to vomit again, tell me. Try not to worry about Small Bess. I'll send Rucker out to get her as soon as we return."

"I'm glad I was with you," I said into his

neck. "I fear my derringer wouldn't have been much help this time. I would have just expired there by the daffodils."

"I know you, Andy. You would have managed something."

"Do you really mean that or are you just trying to make me feel better?"

He leaned down and kissed my forehead, then he cursed. "I'm sorry about that. It won't happen again. Forget I did that, all right?"

But I wouldn't. His mouth felt nice and warm against my skin.

"Yes, I meant what I said. You have grit, Andy, and a brain. You would have managed something. Now, what do you want to tell my uncle?"

I thought of my father's letter, safely locked away in my Italianate letter box. I had said nothing to Lawrence about that. I hadn't said anything to anyone. Why? Because anyone could be the someone who was doing this. The only thing was, I couldn't think of a single reason for anyone, particularly my husband, to want to harm me. I had never done anything to him or to anyone else living in this house. Lawrence hadn't even known me. He hadn't had to marry me once he had met me. He had not been forced to return to Grandfather's house after that first condolence visit. It made no sense. I said, "No, I don't want anyone to know anything. Let the person who is responsible just wonder what we know or don't know about any of this."

"I agree. What then? A rabbit hole?"

"It will be obvious to Rucker and anyone else who bothers to look that those deep cuts on Small Bess's back had nothing to do with stumbling into any damned rabbit hole."

"I will tell Rucker the truth. He will take care of her himself. I will also tell him to keep it all mum. Rucker is a good man. This is going to make him very angry. I know he will keep quiet. The only person who will know the truth is the one who placed the barbed wire beneath the saddle."

"I don't like it," I said, and pressed my face into his shoulder.

"Your vanity is showing. I won't let anyone believe you're incompetent. No, I will tell everyone it was a very deep, utterly unavoidable rabbit hole that yawned right up in front of you, no possibility to avoid it. Even if everyone believes you bungled things, I will continue to defend you."

I wanted to punch him, but I couldn't even make a decent fist.

I heard him chuckle, felt his arms tighten around me.

He had to stop Tempest one time for me to be sick again, something he handled well, I suppose. I felt so rotten I really didn't care.

There were too many people, all of them hovering over me, all of them talking, all of them with an opinion, and if I'd had the will, I would have told them to all to go to the devil. As it was, John eased me down on a very soft settee. I kept my eyes closed and weaved in and out of the ether.

It was Thomas's beautiful soothing voice that I finally recognized, and I didn't want to kill him, which meant I just might be feeling a bit better.

"Here, Uncle Lawrence, place this wet cloth on her forehead. Amelia always places a wet cloth on my forehead when I have one of my headaches."

The wet cloth felt wonderful. "Thank you," I managed to get out.

"Just lie still, Andy," my husband said. I felt his warm breath against my ear. I smelled something else, brandy, and it was soothing and familiar and I breathed in deeply.

"I am all right, Lawrence, truly, just give me a moment longer."

Then Amelia had to stick her oar in. "Uncle Lawrence, I think you should fetch Dr. Boulder."

"I don't want a bloody doctor anywhere near me, Amelia," I said. "Mind your own business." I heard John laugh.

"Just let her lie there in peace for a while," he said.

"All right," I heard my husband say, "but I don't like it. I would feel better if Cuthbert looked her over."

"Not until I'm dead," I said. I managed to open my eyes and look up into Lawrence's face. "You are my husband. You are supposed to care about me. Don't torture me. Don't let this Cuthbert fellow near me."

"Very well," he said, and I heard the amusement in his voice as I floated into the ether once again. It was warm there, the voices all vague and blurred, the pain tamped down.

I don't know who carried me to my bedchamber, but it was Belinda's face I saw before I fell into a very nice deep sleep with the help of some laudanum from Mrs. Redbreast, that wonderful woman.

When I woke up, it was late afternoon. I lay there, waiting for my body to hurt or not to hurt. To my relief, all I felt was a nagging headache. I slowly got out of my bed. Belinda had undressed me and put me in a nightgown.

I heard a squawk. There was Belinda, seated in a chair near the bed, ready to leap up.

"No, no, my lady, don't move. Your parts, they're not ready to move yet, surely."

"My parts are just fine," I said, and set my feet on the floor. I rose slowly. I was stiff, felt bruised and achy, but otherwise I was all right. "It wasn't a deep rabbit hole," I said, thought of John, and smiled. Despite everything, I smiled.

She was at my side in the next instant. I held up my hand to ward her off. "No, Belinda, I am just fine. I think I should like a very hot bath. It will soak out all my aches and pains." And it would also get rid of her, I thought, then felt guilty. She was worried about me. But I didn't want anyone around me. I watched her walk from the room, looking back at me several times, frowning.

I was afraid. My derringer. I panicked, then reached under my pillow. It was there. Who had put it there? John, I hoped. If it had been Belinda, she would have said something, probably to Lawrence. No, it had to be John. Had he allowed Belinda or anyone else to see it, or had he managed to come into my bedchamber and pull it from under my riding skirt? The thought of him doing that was enough to send me back onto my bed. I sat there holding my derringer, just looking across the room at the windows with the bar holes in the casements. The bars for Caroline because she had been mad.

I don't think I did anything but breathe until Belinda returned with enough buckets of hot water to drown me.

An hour later, with her following on my heels, clucking over me, wringing her hands, I left The Blue Room, dressed in a sturdy old gray gown that was faded from so many washings and some walking boots. I'd worn both a lot at Deerfield Hall, trudging on the moors. I pulled on an equally old velvet cloak and gloves. The derringer wasn't strapped back against my thigh this time. It was right in my cloak pocket. I could pull it out and fire it in but a moment of time. I could protect myself, and I most assuredly would. My head ached, but I was more angry than hurt now.

Brantley was by the front door. He saw me and became as still as the plaster statue of the naked Greek god that stood in a recessed corner just outside the drawing room.

"I am going for a walk," I said, and my voice was as cold as the air seeping in beneath the great front doors. "I will be fine, Brantley. You are not to worry about me. It was just a rabbit hole, a very big one, but I am not a milksop. I will be just fine. I am just going down by the stream. I like it there." And I waited for him to open the door for me. I wondered if he would immediately find Lawrence and tell him that his idiot wife had gone for a stroll around the grounds.

As I walked across the wide front lawn, I wondered about my decision to remain here, and my future with this house.

It didn't look promising. I shuddered, but not from the cold, although the air was chilly, very still, the late afternoon sky a lead gray. I hadn't particularly noticed before, but the trees now had nothing but naked branches, no more bursts of colorful autumn leaves at all now. Winter had finally come to Yorkshire. I began to shake off the final effects of the laudanum, and my bone-deep fear was ridding me very quickly of my lethargy.

I walked toward the stream, some distance away from the manor, my head down, thinking, thinking. I had told Brantley where I was going. No one would try anything, it would be too risky. Besides, I couldn't think clearly if someone was hanging around me, clucking and carrying on, and driving me mad. And that brought up the best question. Who could I possibly trust?

John, I thought. I had to trust him. There was simply no choice.

I kept thinking, sorting through things, trying to pick things apart, but there was just nothing. Simply nothing.

Except Caroline wanting perhaps to talk to me, however a spirit managed to do that.

And the malignancy in the Black Chamber that was still here, still alive, waiting, waiting. For what?

I reached the stream bank. I pulled my cloak very tightly around me and sat down beneath one of the huge willow trees. I stared out over the narrow ribbon of gray water. The surface was very still, like a smooth gray slate. I didn't know where the ducks were.

I realized now that I had forgotten all about George. He had not been in The Blue Room. I hoped Miss Crislock or Judith had him well in hand. If something were to happen to George, I didn't know what I would do. If I'd had the energy, I would have gone back and fetched him, but I didn't. I felt the willow bark dig into my back.

I was becoming hysterical. Nothing would happen to George. But I knew if it did, I would tear down Devbridge Manor with my bare hands.

I don't know how long I sat there before I heard him say from behind me, "Belinda stopped me in the corridor and wailed about you tottering out of bed, nearly drowning yourself in your bath, and actually leaving. I asked Brantley if he had seen you, and he told me you looked nearly dead and had planned to come down here." He paused a moment, then shrugged. "I came after you." He shrugged again, but I knew him. He was just revving himself up to blast me. It wasn't long in coming. He actually pointed his gloved finger at me and shook it.

"I did not even come close to drowning in my bath."

"Damn you, Andy, you promised me that you would never be alone. What the hell is wrong with you? Did the blow to your head render you an idiot? No, probably not. You come by that quite naturally, don't you? Answer me, damn you."

Chapter Twenty-one

He was right, I suppose, if one chose to look at things in just that particular sort of very harsh light. I just shook my head, saying nothing, and that certainly enraged him even more.

He walked quickly over to me and positioned himself right in front of me, legs spread, hands on his hips. He didn't block the sun, since there wasn't any, but he did fill up too much space. He's too big, I thought, staring up at him, much too big and too strong. But I knew he wasn't dangerous to me, even though it was obvious that he would very much like to throw me into the stream.

And I smiled up at this man, who had once made me feel drilled into the ground with fear. "I have my derringer." I lifted my hand out of my cloak pocket and pointed the small gun at him. "I'm perfectly safe."

He cursed. It was colorful. I'd never heard such a fluid and creative description of both people and animals put together. Grandfather would have been impressed. He probably would have slapped John on the back— and maybe even timed him to see how long he could go without repeating any curses.

"Goodness, can you do that again?"

"Yes, but first I'm going to strangle you. Don't try to weasel out of this, Andy. No trying to distract me. You do it very well, but not this time, not now. What the hell are you doing out here alone? Dammit, you don't even have that famous watchdog George with you."

"He would protect me with his life if he had the sense to realize that my life was in danger. Oh, dear, I hope no one is out searching for me. Tell me you didn't announce my temporary defection and raise an alarm?"

"No, no, I told Brantley not to worry. I told him I would keep an eye on you. I believe Uncle Lawrence, Miss Gillbank, your step-daughter, and Miss Crislock are being en-tertained by Lord Waverleigh or 'Hobson dear,' as Lady Waverleigh calls him. She adds even more alarming details while he relates ghostly manifestations he has ex-perienced. As for Thomas, he is lying down upstairs, Amelia lightly stroking her fingers over his brow. At least that's what he told me they were going to do. I don't think I be-lieve him. Amelia's cheeks were flushed, and her eyes were very bright. I do believe they were—no, forget I said that. Are you not cold?"

I shook my head, then said, "Did you un-strap the derringer from my leg?"

"Yes, certainly, when I carried you up-stairs. I didn't want anyone to know about it. I had a moment when Belinda was pulling back your bedcovers, moaning and clucking over you, dashing about your room for what-ever reasons I don't know. I put it back un-der your pillow."

"Yes, I found it. Thank you. That doesn't sound at all like Belinda. She is a very in-dependent girl, she told me when I first arrived. She has her own ideas about things. She is strong."

"All that's possible, but she acted like a mother chicken whose chick came too close to the kitchen ax. She calmed after we got the laudanum down your gullet. Why did you come out here alone?"

I wished he would just let it go, but knew well enough that he wouldn't. I said, "You are just like my grandfather. He never let anything go until he was satisfied. He would just continue to push and prod until I spilled my innards to him. If it turned out then to be something he really didn't want to know about, he would just stare at me, shake his head, and go for the brandy bottle.

"Oh, all right. Perhaps the fall did scramble my brains. I just wanted to come here and think, to try to figure out who is doing this and why."

"And what have you decided? Have you managed to deduce our villain and his motive, since you have had all this time alone with no interruptions until I had the gall to come along?"

"Your sarcasm is too blunt. You have no subtlety." I sighed again. "I'm sorry, you're right to want to yell your splendid curses in my face." I gently shoved my derringer back into my cloak pocket. I gave him a crooked smile. "But you know, John, with this, I can even protect you."

I thought he would explode, but he managed to hold himself in check. My grandfather usually hadn't had that great an amount of self-control.

I said, "Thank you for not shouting at me anymore. My head still aches and throbs a bit. Now, I haven't decided anything, truth be told. I cannot seem to find anything to latch onto so that I could think of something to decide."

"It bothers me that I understand exactly what you said."

I smiled, impossible not to.

He walked away from me, down to the edge of the stream. He bent down and picked up a pebble. He sent it skipping over the water. Four skips. It wasn't bad.

I called out, "My record is six skips."

He tried with three more pebbles, but he only got five skips on one of them. As he walked back to me, he tossed a pebble from one hand to the other. "You could be lying, of course. Six jumps? You will have to prove that."

"Certainly," I said.

He didn't sit. He just stood over me and stared down at me, tossing that damned pebble. He was quiet for a very long time. Finally, he said, and it seemed to me that he still didn't want to talk, that his words were being dragged out of him against his will, "You want to know the truth of things? That first evening when you walked into the drawing room, my uncle at your side, his wedding ring on your finger, I just stared at you, refusing to believe that it was you. How could it be? I had left you, a very young woman, back in London. What the hell would you be doing with my uncle? Then George heard me and tore across the drawing room to jump on me. No, I didn't want to believe it was you, but since it was, then I didn't want to believe that you had actually married my damned uncle. I still wake up sometimes during the night, and I will think for a couple of seconds that it isn't true, that you did not marry him, that you are still in London, waiting for me to come back. But of course you're here, and you're his damned wife.

"I was shot once, in those dry scrubby hills just outside of Lisbon during a fight with a band of guerrillas. I will tell you that the pain I felt seeing you here as my uncle's wife, was greater than the pain from that bullet in my leg.

"I knew I couldn't remain here and keep my hands off you. Oh, yes, I know you're terrified of me, of any man, I suspect, and perhaps you'll tell me one day why this is so. But it didn't matter. I wanted to touch you, kiss you, teach you that you didn't have to be afraid of me, ever. I would never hurt you, you see, and whatever happened to you in the past, I would make you forget it. But, of course, I couldn't do that. You are my uncle's wife.

"I knew I had to leave. I simply couldn't remain here and be near you, but not have you. I would know, day after day, that you were my uncle's wife, not mine. But then the old woman attacked you with one of my knives, taken right out of my own damned collection. Everything changed. I couldn't leave, not with you in danger."

He was big and dark, and he looked more dangerous in this moment than a raging dark storm gathering speed as it roiled over the horizon. He never looked away from me. What I hated most was the pain I felt in him.

"God, how I wish you'd never come here."

I wasn't afraid, not at all. I was something else, something I now realized that I had felt with him that very first time I had seen him with George and he'd laughed and teased me, but then I'd been me and whipped it all up and made it a part of the deadening fear. But fear had nothing to do with it, and I knew it. I just didn't know if I could accept it, if I could even bring myself to come to understand it.

"You wanted me?" And I knew exactly what that meant, I felt it deep inside me, and I savored it and held it close and waited for him to answer.

"You sound incredulous. Are you so very blind to what you are? Oh, yes, from the moment you came after George that first time I saw you in Hyde Park, I wanted you. The look on your face, the outrage, the utter betrayal, that George wanted me more than he wanted you. I knew in that instant that you were the only woman for me. I hadn't laughed in a long time, too long a time, but the look on your face, it pulled laughter out of me until I was shaking with it. I wanted more. I wanted you. But then, of course, you would have nothing to do with me. It was the first time in my life that I have ever gone out of my way to attract a woman. But I couldn't have attracted you if my life had depended on it. By God, you wouldn't even tell me your name. It was an immense failure. I hated it, but there was nothing I could do about it except retreat. I came back to Devbridge Manor, planning to return to London after you were out of mourning."

He laughed, an ugly mocking laugh, a laugh that was aimed at himself. "That was a rather remarkably disastrous decision on my part, wasn't it?"

I rose to stand in front of him. I felt as though I was standing in a deep hole, black earth all around me, the gray heavy sky so far above me, and the hole was sinking and I was sinking deeper and deeper with it. I felt tears sting my eyes, felt them begin to slide slowly down my cheeks.

I watched him take off his glove. I watched his hand. He touched his fingers to my face, wiping away the tears.

"There has been so little between us," he said, and now he cupped my cheek with his palm, "and there can never be anything more. I probably shouldn't have told you any of this. To be honest, it just fell out of my mouth without my permission, obviously without any sensible thought on my part. But none of it matters now, Andy. I can't leave until I find out what's going on here. I can't allow you to be hurt. I would rather cut my heart out than have you hurt. When you fell from Small Bess, I nearly expired with the fear of it. Do you understand, even a little bit?"

His palm was very warm. The ache inside me was very deep. "Yes," I said. "I understand." For the first time in my life, I raised my hand and lightly touched my fingers to a man's face, and it wasn't my grandfather. He was so very warm, so very vibrant, passion and life pulsing through him. I wanted to cry because I was a fool, because I had made a huge blunder, destroyed my own life, but it wouldn't matter. What was done would remain done. Nothing could be changed.

I dropped my hand.

"What do you think we should do?"

He looked away from me. He was tense. I confess I felt much the same. "The ball is the day after tomorrow. Guests will begin arriving tomorrow morning. There is no way to cancel it now. Uncle Lawrence wondered about that when you were in your room resting, but he knew that guests were already on their way, some of them coming even from London. No, the ball will go on, and there will be guests remaining here for up to four days before they leave for other Christmas parties. What to do? Well, we will have to be on our guard. Please, you mustn't simply decide again that you want to think alone. I won't let you off so easily if you try it again."

"Just what will you do?"

He smiled before he lightly closed his hands around my neck. He dipped his face down and touched his mouth to mine. I didn't move. I didn't do anything, just stood there, waiting for my brain to explode in fear, but when it exploded, it wasn't fear at all, it was quite something else. I didn't know what to do. Well, yes, I did. I wanted to throw my arms around him and hold on forever. But I didn't, of course.

Loyalty, I thought, I had promised my loyalty. Slowly, so much pain flowing through me I knew that he must see it, recognize it, I stepped back.

"We will get through this," he said. "Come along, now, we'll go back to the Manor."

I fell into step beside him. "I should enjoy hearing some of Lord Waverleigh's ghost stories."

"Yes, just as long as they don't involve any of the restless spirits here at Devbridge Manor."

I didn't agree. I wanted to know everything about anyone who had died here.

Everyone was in the drawing room. George was sitting beside Judith, his head on his paws, as calm as could be. Everyone was still listening to Lord Waverleigh. He looked up at us a moment, and waved us forward. "You are looking well again, my lady," Lord Waverleigh said. "Come and listen to this strange tale of the laird near Fort Williams who buried his wife alive behind his bedchamber wall."

Judith shuddered. I admit that I couldn't see any reason not to shudder with that introduction. But I smiled and let John lead me to a chair. "Please, sir, tell us now if the dreadful laird came to a bad end."

"The very worst. The wife didn't die. One of the laird's men dug her out and nursed her back to health. I suspect they were lovers all along and that was the reason the laird had bricked her up, but there is no one to say one way or another. Anyway, the laird's man and the laird's supposedly dead wife made plans.

"The wife haunted the laird. I don't know the tricks they pulled on him, but they scared the fellow so badly that he ended up hurling himself from a cliff into Loch Ness, and many claimed to have seen the Loch Ness monster gobble him up."

Judith gasped. Miss Gillbank squeezed her shoulder, then clapped. "A splendid end to the wretched man," she said.

Miss Crislock said after a thoughtful moment, "That is the sort of tale that should curb wickedness. It fair makes the hair stand on end, Hobson. What do you think, Lawrence?"

My husband rose and crossed his arms over his chest. "My dear Miss Crislock, any wife who is unfaithful to her husband deserves to be bricked up."

"Ah," said Lord Waverleigh, "I don't know that unfaithfulness was the case at all. Perhaps the laird was just a bully and abused her and perhaps tired of her. Perhaps he didn't like the way she managed his household, and thus he decided to do away with her, or he found another lady he preferred to her. Regardless, it wasn't well-done of him. Don't you believe he got his just desserts?"

Lawrence just smiled. "Now that you explain away any unfaithfulness on the lady's part, I suppose I must agree that a fall into the Loch Ness monster's maw was exactly what the laird deserved. Now, Andy, your cheeks look rosy. You're feeling just the thing now?"

"Certainly. I cannot wait for all our guests to arrive. The ball is very kind of you, Lawrence. I will meet all our neighbors." I smiled at him, and felt the very real tug of affection that was inside me.

I turned. "Now, George, you have given Judith enough attention. It is time to come for a nice walk with me. Judith, I still haven't paid off my wager to you. Why don't you come with us, and we can wager again. Perhaps this time I will beat you, and we will be even."

George, the traitor, selected the far yew bush that Judith had pointed to. I groaned, and went back to the house to fetch the shillings I now owed my stepdaughter, that laughing girl who now twitted me mercilessly. Lawrence was standing right there in the entrance hall, two shillings in his hand. He laughed as he handed them to his daughter.

And that night, when I pulled my derringer out of the deep pocket in my beautiful lavender gown to shove it beneath my pillow, I saw John's Moorish ceremonial knife, with its lovely red tassel. Its burnished gold edge gleamed in the dull light. It was quite beautiful. It could slice into a heart so easily.

I nearly lost my dinner at that moment the shock was so great. I leapt back, slapped my hands over my mouth so I wouldn't shriek. George wuffed and jumped up onto the bed, his head cocked to one side. I just stood there, staring down at the dreadful thing.

Then I forced myself to pick it up. I didn't wait.

Both George and I walked down the long corridor to John's room.

Chapter Twenty-two

He opened the door, wearing a dressing gown. He held a book in one hand. George went berserk.

He picked up George, said nothing at all, and stepped back for me to come into his bedchamber.

I knew it wasn't proper, but that didn't matter.

"What the hell has happened to you? You're pale as death."

I said nothing, merely held out the knife.

He sucked in his breath as he took the thing. He turned away from me and walked to the far corner of his room, where he kept his knife collection. I saw that his feet were bare. He had big feet, like the rest of him. Good feet, I supposed, steady, solid feet, I continued to suppose, my brain happy to focus on him for the moment, away from the deadening fear.

He returned, George still tucked under his right arm. "It wasn't there, naturally. Where was it?"

"Beneath my pillow. I was putting my derringer away. I lifted the pillow, and there it was."

He pointed to the big winged chair set in front of the blazing fire. "Sit," he said, and carried George over to his desk, where a bottle of brandy sat. He poured me a good amount in a lovely crystal snifter.

"Drink it."

I drank. The savage warmth of that brandy hit my stomach like a stone, then exploded. I gasped and coughed. "Goodness," I said.

"Excellent, you've got your color back." He walked to the fireplace and leaned his shoulders against the mantel. He was still rubbing George's ears. That idiot animal was trying to lick his hand as he rubbed.

"The someone who placed that circle of

barbed wire beneath Small Bess's saddle wasn't pleased that there was no hysterical result, or no injury. And so it continues. It is like upping the ante in a card game."

"Yes. The someone is succeeding. I am scared silly. I nearly collapsed on the floor, I was so afraid when I saw the thing."

"Well, you didn't. You got yourself together and you immediately came to me to see if it was indeed the same knife. It is, of course."

That wasn't entirely the reason I had come immediately to him, but I didn't say so. "Do you believe this someone could honestly think I would believe you the guilty party?"

"Good question. The fact is that someone came in here and removed the knife. Then the someone had to wait until your bedchamber was empty, then go in, with no one seeing him or her, and place the knife under your pillow."

"Yes," I said, and slowly rose. "I shouldn't be here. I must go back to The Blue Room."

He walked me back. I said at the door, "I have knocked against all the walls. I didn't find any sort of opening that gave onto a passageway."

"I didn't know you had done that. It was a good idea. Keep your derringer close, Andy."

He handed me George, who whined at his hero's rejection, patted my cheek, and strode back down the long corridor to his bedchamber, his dark blue velvet dressing gown flapping around his ankles. Strong, solid feet, I thought, staring after him.

Yet another night that I lay in my bed, staring up at the dark ceiling, with George snuggled next to me, wide-eyed, waiting for the sun to rise.

By noon the following day, thirty guests had flowed into the house bringing servants, laughter and holly and presents, and more trunks than I could count. Carriages swamped the stable yard.

"How will Rucker manage?" I asked Lawrence as we finished greeting Lord and Lady Maugham, longtime friends of the Lyndhurst family.

"I believe everyone coming to stay is here now. Rucker will manage. We have enough room for all the horses. How is Small Bess doing?"

"You don't miss a single thing, do you?" I

smiled up at him, and for the first time I was wondering if he was the someone who wanted me dead or scared to my toes or perhaps even both. No, I thought, it made no sense at all.

But then again, nothing did.

"Yes, I was out seeing to her this morning. Her hock is much better, thank God. If we'd had to put her down, I would have been—"

He lightly touched his fingers to my cheek. "I know, my dear. It would have hurt you dreadfully. Small Bess will be just fine. I also checked on her."

And again, as I looked up at him I had to wonder: did you stick that horrid barbed circle of wire beneath her saddle? And I wondered if he had noticed the horrible deep cuts on her back. Evidently he hadn't. I supposed that Rucker had kept the blanket over the soft white cloths on Small Bess's back. And Lawrence hadn't noticed anything amiss, thank God. But then again, perhaps he already knew everything about all of it.

Miss Crislock came to my room when Belinda was helping me change gowns. I needed at least three gowns a day, and it required a great deal of time to get oneself looking just so with each change of garb. "It is the strangest thing," Miss Crislock said after flitting about The Blue Room, looking through my armoire, and straightening bottles on my dressing table.

"What is, Milly?"

"Oh. I saw Amelia coming out of John's bedchamber yesterday. Isn't that odd?"

I felt my heart plummet to my knees. Amelia? No, I thought, no.

"Perhaps she needed to borrow something," I said. "For Thomas."

"Well, evidently she did. When I saw her a few minutes later come out of his bedchamber, she was carrying something wrapped in a cloth."

I couldn't deal with this, I just couldn't. I kissed Milly's soft cheek, and together we went back downstairs.

The house was decorated with masses of holly from our home wood and the bags of it brought by our guests. There was a huge Yule log burning in the cavernous fireplace in the Old Hall.

Gifts were beginning to pile up on every available surface. Just after lunch, a messenger from York arrived with a huge box for me. I nearly skipped up to the nursery, I was so pleased that it had finally come, and just in time, too. I had been preparing myself for the disappointment.

"Andy, goodness," said Miss Gillbank, smiling at me, "you're visiting during an Italian lesson." She turned to Judith. "Well, my very bright girl, what do you have to say?"

"Come sta? Favorisca sedersi." And she swept her hand toward a chair.

"Sto molto bene, e Lei?"

"Oh, goodness, Andy, I'm doing very well, too. Now, sit down. What is in that huge box? Is it my Christmas present?"

"Sorry, Judith, but you will have to wait. You see, I made this wager with Miss Gillbank. I lost, just as I am always losing to you. However, Miss Gillbank is a much more seasoned gambler than you are, and she insisted that the wager be something extraordinary."

"Miss Gillbank, I didn't know you ever gambled. Is it true? What did you wager on?"

"Do you remember, dear Miss Gillbank?"

She stared from me to that box and then back to my face. "Funny thing, that wager of ours has completely slipped my mind."

"Ah. Well, Judith, Miss Gillbank and I made this wager just after all of us had met in the garden. You had already dined once with the adults, and she wagered that you would be allowed to dine with us yet again, very soon. I didn't believe it, after all, who would want to dine with a girl who is so very beautiful and sweet to George? And so I wagered nearly all I had that you would never again be allowed at the dinner table. And I lost.

"Just after all our guests leave, you, Miss Lyndhurst, are cordially invited to dine with all the adults, for a full week. Your father insisted." That was a lie, of course, but who cared? "So, Miss Gillbank, here is your prize for your brilliant wager."

And giving her no chance at all, I swept over to Judith's writing table, moved aside some books, and set down the huge box. I opened it, then stood back. "It is just as you ordered it, Miss Gillbank. I trust you won't be disappointed."

Miss Gillbank was beyond mystified. She lifted the lovely silver paper and just stood there, staring, not saying a single word.

"What is it, Miss Gillbank?"

I said, "It is her gown to wear to the ball tomorrow night, Judith. What do you think?"

With Judith shrieking for her to hold up the

gown, Miss Gillbank, still wordless, lifted out the beautiful gown I had ordered for her. I'd filched one of her gowns so Belinda could measure it. It was glorious, a golden velvet ball gown with an inch-wide band of golden satin beneath the breasts, the neck was very, very low indeed, and the sleeves were long and fitted. There were no bows or flounces or rows of lace. It was simple and elegant, its lines classical. She would look magnificent.

She held the gown in front of her. Judith touched the soft velvet and shouted, "Oh, goodness, you must try it on for us to see. Now, please, Miss Gillbank."

And Miss Gillbank, that very steady and composed governess, carefully laid the gown back into the box and burst into tears.

"Oh, dear," Judith said to me. "Do you think she doesn't like it? Didn't you get exact instructions for what she wanted, Andy? Perhaps you misunderstood what color she wanted? Perhaps the neckline is too low? It rather looks like it would come only to her waist."

Miss Gillbank laughed through her tears. She refused to try on the gown for us, mumbling something about she wanted to look just perfect before she put it on, which would be tomorrow evening.

I was whistling when I left the nursery. I had forgotten for a good fifteen minutes that someone wasn't happy with me being here at Devbridge Manor. What had Amelia carried out of John's bedchamber yesterday? Surely not the knife, surely.

I looked up to see a man duck around the corridor ahead of me. "Wait!" I shouted. "Who are you? Wait!"

But of course the man was gone when I rounded the corner. "Well, damn," I said. My fingers were closed around my derringer. I was ready. I hadn't frozen.

That evening, garbed in yet another beautiful gown, I stood by my husband as thirty-six guests sat down at the dining table. I had overheard Brantley instructing Jasper and the rest of the footmen to fetch every table leaf from the storage room behind the pantry.

The table looked magnificent. The crystal shone, the silver and the dishes were perfectly arranged. Brantley had hired on an additional ten footmen so that they were each responsible for only three guests each.

The menu, something everyone had advised me on, would have delighted even that fatuous gourmand, the Prince Regent. There were sixteen different dishes, I'd counted them as they were brought so elegantly and formally into the dining room.

I looked down the table at Miss Gillbank, simply beautiful in one of my gowns, lengthened for her, a soft Nile green silk with an overskirt of darker green silk. Belinda had dressed her hair. I had placed her next to the son of a local baronet I'd heard her mention once. She was laughing. I looked at Amelia and Thomas, seated next to each other, in the middle of the immensely long table. They were speaking softly to each other. About what? Then they turned, as if they'd planned it beforehand, to speak to their neighbors.

My dear Miss Crislock was seated at Lawrence's left hand. She was smiling at something he said.

Everyone seemed in good spirits. I couldn't begin to count how many bottles of wine were poured down guests' throats during that two-hour dinner.

I looked down at John, even though I didn't want to, even though I knew it would just make me hurt and question myself and call myself a hundred times a fool. He was seated next to one of the most beautiful women I've ever seen in my life. Her name was Lady Elizabeth Palmer. She was a very rich widow and couldn't have been more than twenty-five years old. I suppose that Lawrence was trying to marry off his heir and thus had invited her. To be honest, he had excellent taste. I didn't like her, but then again, she hadn't been particularly pleasant to me when she had arrived with friends. She had looked through me, and that made me want to slap her, on both cheeks. But she was flawless, damn her. She had lots of thick blond hair all plaited up on top of her head, with at least a dozen tendrils falling haphazardly over those white shoulders of hers and surely too much white bosom on display. My grandfather would have looked at that face and bosom and not said a single word. He once told me he preferred to admire perfection in silence. And he would have remained silent for a very long time, curse him.

Evidently John was different from Grandfather, at least in this. He was laughing and talking and hanging on to her every word. It was nauseating.

It didn't hit me until I was chewing on a particularly delicious lobster patty that I was jealous. I nearly dropped my fork I was so horrified at myself. I simply stopped eating and stared down the table. They were speaking to each other, their heads close, hers so blond and fair and his so dark, damn him.

But I couldn't be jealous. It was madness to be jealous. I was married. John could be nothing to me, nothing at all. He was my step-nephew. He would always be my step-nephew. Eventually he would bring his wife to live in this house. Maybe that wife would be Lady Elizabeth Palmer.

He had lied to me, like every man in this world, he had lied. And I was surprised by it, I'll admit it, more fool I. He was showering Lady Elizabeth with all his attention, absolutely deluging her with his humor, his damned wit, his observations, and he was doing this after he had poured out his innards to me but the day before.

He had lied.

On the other hand, I didn't want him to simply hang about, sullen and silent, being unhappy because he couldn't be with me. Besides, I didn't want to be with him. He was too big and too strong—and I nearly laughed my head off at my ridiculous litany.

No, it wasn't ridiculous. He had lied. Like my father. And I thought of his letter just then and realized I hadn't told John about it. Well, there was no need to.

There was nothing for it. I spoke to my neighbors, a duke from Manchester who was as desiccated as old bones and had a wit equally as dry as his bones, and a marchioness who had the biggest bosom I had ever seen in my life, most of it uncovered. I tried desperately not to stare at that bosom, unlike most of the gentlemen nearby.

I was vivacious. I dredged up some wit, and laughed at theirs. The marchioness with the bosom turned out to be rather amusing, what with her tales of all her little Pekingese dogs, of which she had a hearty dozen, all of them sweethearts. The desiccated duke loved to gossip about folk in London I'd never heard of, but I laughed and carried on just as I was supposed to. I had to make Lawrence proud of me.

As for how I looked, my own gown was glittery silver, and I knew I looked very fine indeed. Perhaps I didn't have as much white bosom as Lady Elizabeth, and my hair was curly and red, brown, blond, and rust, all blended together like a bunch of fallen autumn leaves; and perhaps it was not as stylish as hers, but—I had to stop this. I didn't own John. I couldn't ever have him.

I was an idiot.

How could I have changed so much? He was still a man, actually a man I had seen on three different occasions in London and managed to dismiss all three times. Only I hadn't, not really.

I had made a huge mess of things.

But most importantly, right now, I was the hostess. I wasn't a provincial miss. I was a countess, and even though I was young, I knew what I was about. I knew what to do when. And when I rose to lead the ladies away, I looked only at my husband and smiled at him. He nodded.

"Gentlemen," I said, my voice pitched to the exact volume to gain their collective attention, "the ladies will leave you to your port." They barely paid any attention to my announcement at all. Most of them were happily drunk. They were looking forward to port and brandy and God knows what else. I turned at the doorway, and called out, more loudly this time, "Ladies, we will have our brandy in the drawing room. We will discuss the news about Napoleon, if there is any news worthy enough to speak about. We will discuss which of the gentlemen present at dinner is the most handsome, the most literate, the most charming."

Several of the women laughed, several even patted me on the arm. Some disapproved, but who cared? I didn't dare look back to see what my husband thought of that parting shot.

The men had heard every word I had said. Now they were all talking at once. I heard outrage, laughter, yells.

Lawrence would probably blast me later.

I was all the talk in the drawing room. A good half of the ladies had a snifter of brandy. We did speak of Napoleon for a bit, but soon turned to his poor wife, the Austrian princess, Marie-Louise, and how Napoleon, so desperate for an heir, that he no sooner had her on French soil, than he dragged her to his tent and consummated the marriage before it had even happened.

"Absolutely shocking what men do to women," said Lady Elizabeth Palmer, too beautiful for her own good, and now she was actually showing interest in something other than fashion and gossip. "Now, who is ready to vote for the most charming gentleman at the dinner table?"

Most of the ladies laughed at that.

Lady Caldecote, waving her fan vigorously even as she sat very close to the fireplace, said to me, "That was very clever of you, my dear young lady. You certainly got their attention. I do wonder what they're talking about now?"

"Naturally, they are discussing which of them will be elected the most charming by us," Lady Elizabeth said. Then she laughed and nodded to me, as if seeing me with new eyes. "That was clever of you."

The marchioness with the immense bosom said, "I heard it said that Napoleon had many mistresses and that it infuriated Josephine. She began to tell anyone who would listen that Napoleon wasn't all that much of a man, if you know what I mean."

It was obvious that I didn't know what she meant, because when I said brightly, "Well, if he continues with mistresses now that he is married to Marie-Louise, then he surely isn't much of a man at all." Every one of the sixteen ladies in the drawing room stared at me like I was an idiot.

Elizabeth Palmer laughed. "My dear countess, you are a married lady. I can't imagine that Lawrence hasn't showed you exactly how much of a man he is."

I just looked at her.

My precious Miss Crislock said comfortably, "Lord Devbridge is very solicitous of his precious young wife. He is patient. He is understanding. Do give me a snifter of brandy, my dear."

With those well-intentioned words, the ladies didn't desist, rather, they crowded around me. There were raised eyebrows. There were snickers. There were smiles barely hidden behind hands. Amelia stayed back. Miss Gillbank looked frantic.

"You mean that you are still a virgin, my lady?" Mrs. Birkenhead said, leaning so close I nearly gagged on her heavy perfume. Attar of roses, I thought, splashed on much too liberally.

Amelia cleared her throat, loudly. "I suggest that Andrea play a Mozart sonata for us. She is very talented. She can also sing, only not as well as she plays. Come along, Andy, perform, now."

"I doubt her performance could top the one she gave to the gentlemen when we all left the dining room." This was from a motherly lady whose name I couldn't remember.

I walked to the pianoforte and began to play. I played the sonata well enough. When I looked up, it was to see my husband standing very close to me.

I said quickly, just as soon as the applause died down, "I'm sorry, Lawrence. The devil made me do it."

He laughed, turned to the gentleman at his elbow, cleared his throat, and announced to the room at large, "My wife informed me that the devil made her do it."

My reputation, for whatever that was worth, was made.

I had been pronounced an original, Miss Crislock told me much later. When next I was in London, I would be at the very center of things.

"What things?" I asked her.

"Parties and such, I imagine," she told me, patted my cheek, then gave me a very long look. "You don't look happy, Andy. What's wrong, dear?"

I nearly swallowed my teeth. "Nothing, Milly. I am quite the perfect young lady."

It was nearly two o'clock in the morning

when Lawrence escorted me to The Blue Room.

He looked down at me, a thoughtful expression in his eyes. "You continually surprise me, Andy."

"I hope most of the surprises are good ones."

"At least half. Don't worry, this one was delightful. The gentlemen could speak of nothing else but who was the most charming, the most literate, the most amusing of us all."

"That's what Lady Elizabeth Palmer said the gentlemen would do. Actually, I surprised myself. Most of our guests are very good sports, sir."

"Yes, they are. They like you. I hadn't expected it, truth be told, you are so very young. You were charming."

"Now you sound as if you're no longer certain you liked what I did."

"Do I? How silly of you to think that. Good night, my child." And he walked away.

Did he really think of me as a child?

Chapter Twenty-three

Early the next morning I was spreading a rather noxious smelling potion, one of my grandfather's recipes, on the healing cuts in Small Bess's back. There were seven deep cuts forming a nearly perfect circle, about a quarter of an inch between them, and looking at them, seeing those ghastly sharp barbs digging into her back, made me see red. The monster who had done this deserved to be shot between the eyes, by me, with my new derringer.

"I see she is better."

It was John. I turned slowly. I didn't want to see him. On the other hand, I wanted more than anything to just stand here and stare at him until Small Bess kicked me out of her stall.

I shook my head free of those futile thoughts. "Yes, she is better, much better, thanks to Rucker, but it still makes me so angry, I want to explode. It is very early. I am surprised that you are awake."

He looked me up and down, and I knew what he saw. I was wearing a very old dark brown wool cloak and stout boots that were so scuffed they could have been used for goat food at least a year past. My hair was plastered to my head and pulled back into a knot at the nape of my neck. Already corky curls were escaping. Then he smiled. "You're awake. Why shouldn't I be?"

"You were still all cozy with Lady Elizabeth Palmer when I finally went upstairs well toward the middle of the night."

I know he heard the acrimony in my voice. The man wasn't a dolt. Then he had the gall to smirk at me. "Actually, you don't have to say her entire name. Lady Elizabeth is quite enough. There is no other guest here quite like her, don't you agree?"

I did agree, but I wasn't about to tell him

that, which didn't stop him, not for even half a second.

"It is interesting that you noticed. I can see that it would bother you to speak of it further—your lips are just a thin seam of a line—so I will move smartly on to something more benign. Actually, many of the gentlemen are already up, and if they're not yet talking, they are drinking coffee and reading the newspapers. Ah, there was a bit of conversation about you, since Uncle Lawrence wasn't present. You have caused quite a stir, Andy. I can't imagine that my uncle will be very pleased."

"For your information, I already apologized to him. I am not a complete dunce. I apologized immediately. Surely that would make him realize that I was very serious and contrite."

"No, I'm not talking about your brazen little performance at the dining room door with all the ladies flocked around you. No, it was the other."

He had my attention now. "What other? I didn't say anything else, I swear it. I listened a lot. I laughed. I played Mozart, not badly if I say so myself, but I swear, I didn't say anything else to embarrass him."

John began to laugh. "My, my, you really don't know, do you?"

I just stared at him. I began to lay the soft white cloths back on Small Bess's back and gently smooth them down. Small Bess twisted her head about to see what I was doing. I petted her and lightly stroked her neck, then looked back at him. "No. I don't know what you're talking about."

"I guess that you don't," he said slowly, his head cocked to one side, a habit of his that I was getting accustomed to. He did it whenever he was puzzled or undecided about something.

"Obviously you want to tell me, so get on with it. You have all the subtlety of a fanatic vicar. What did I say that was so embarrassing to Lawrence?"

"Everyone now knows that you are still a virgin."

I jumped so high Small Bess kicked out with her back legs. It took me several moments to calm her, then I said, furious and appalled, "That's impossible. I mean it's true, but I didn't say anything about that. It would have been absurd to say that, and disloyal, and above all, surely stupid. Can you imagine me turning to the marchioness and saying, "Well, my lady, here I am married to this very nice man, and I'm a virgin, you know."

His hands were fists at his sides, I saw them, then they eased again. He flexed his fingers, and said, "No, you didn't do that. I believe the ladies were discussing the fact that Napoleon isn't reputed to have much in the way of, well, endowment, or size."

"What endowment? What size? You mean that he isn't very tall? I have heard that said often. There's nothing in that, surely. What does that have to do with virginity?"

He rolled his eyes. Then he looked remorseful, and that surprised me, because I knew that he meant it. He was embarrassed. He was sorry he had brought it up. "I want you to forget it. I meant to tease you about your damned naïveté, but I cannot. Andy, just forget all about it, all right? You're innocent, and it is just fine. Don't let anyone tell you differently. There is nothing for you to apologize about to my uncle, nothing at all."

"But—"

He lightly touched his fingertips to my lips. His damned voice was tender, with just a touch of humor. "No, Andy, just forget it. If you hear anything more about this, any little jabs or comments, just ignore them, all right?"

I nodded uncertainly.

"Let me be even more clear. Anytime in the next three days that you hear pointed little comments specifically about Napoleon, you simply keep your mouth shut, you promise?"

"All right. But I don't—"

He said, "Small Bess is much better. However, you cannot ride her for weeks to come. And no, forget about riding Tempest. He wouldn't need to throw you into a rabbit hole. He would just pound one into the ground and toss you in. He would eat you along with his oats for breakfast. He would—"

"That's really quite enough. These flights of fancy merely reflect what you would like to happen if ever I have the gall to ride your horse."

"Possibly. Now, you should ask Uncle Lawrence if he has another mount suitable for you. You will not even feed Tempest. He would gnaw off your hand. Oh, yes, one other matter. Don't try to get rid of Boynton, my valet, who will now be following you everywhere." He turned then and left the stable.

I stared after him. Boynton would be following me?

What the devil was that all about? The warning about Tempest was nothing new, but this size thing that had to do with Napoleon, this was very strange indeed. Well, I would forget it, all of it. Boynton following me. I felt safer already.

As it turned out, I didn't have much free time that day to fret about anything except the ball.

The only time I had ever seen servants more excited than right here and right now, had been at my own coming-out ball. Even Brantley unbent enough to yell at one of the footmen for dropping a potted palm in the entrance hall. It rolled into a suit of armor and sent it crashing to the floor. Brantley never yelled. It was seen by all the servants as a good omen.

I laughed and laughed, I just couldn't help it. Brantley stopped yelling and looked so chagrined that I wanted to console him, something I knew he wouldn't ever accept, and so I said nothing, just grinned shamelessly at him.

I came downstairs that evening wearing my beautiful new pale blue silk gown, the exact shade of my eyes, Belinda had assured me. It was cut low to show off my bosom, something my modiste had told me was simply imperative to do or I would look like a dowd, and thus reflect on her. Then, she assured me, no one would come to her shop ever again, and she would starve in a ditch and it would be my fault. I thought that was a bit dramatic on her part. After all, how could my bosom be the reason for her possible demise? But I allowed her to cut the gown as low as she wanted. I still thought there was too much white flesh showing and said so to Belinda. At that point, Belinda gasped with outrage. When I suggested wearing a nice shawl over it, I thought she would swoon she was so distraught.

So, with my bosom on full display, I walked down the wide staircase and immediately ran into Lady Elizabeth Palmer.

We eyed each other like two fighting cocks, not that I'd ever actually seen cocks do this, but I could imagine it, once I stood eye to eye with her. I was the hostess, I was charming. I had no choice, curse it. "Good evening, Lady Elizabeth. May I say that your gown is lovely?"

"Of course you may," she said, then looked at me full on. "Somehow I hadn't expected to see you show off this much of yourself. You seem so very young. But you are quite adequate, Andrea—"

"Ah, do call me Andy."

"Very well. Yes, all the gentlemen are sure to agree with me, particularly your dear husband who has you on the longest leash I've ever heard about for a new husband."

"I don't know what you mean, but let me assure you that I am not a dog. I don't even use a leash on George. Would you like to meet George?"

"I have met your dog. He would not leave John alone. We were forced to bring him with us on our lovely stroll in the east gardens or he would have barked down the house. He is the strangest color—it is mustard, a particular vile shade of mustard. In any case, what I meant about a very long leash is that your husband is treating you like a young schoolgirl who needs to be cosseted and protected—which is the last thing you need—what with his waiting to bed you.

Until when? When you have gained your twenty-first year?"

"I have reached it."

"Ah, then you have this religious vow to remain chaste? And Lawrence is actually giving you your way? Everyone agrees that it is extraordinary.

"Now, your gown is quite lovely as well. The pale blue is unusual, a delicious shade. How odd that you are dazzling every gentleman who happens by with this display of flesh, but you refuse your husband."

I couldn't let all of that just go by. There was simply just too much to ignore. My charm slipped. I was ready to do battle. "I like to dazzle gentlemen. I rather thought, though, that my hair would be the focal point of my presentation this evening, not my bosom. My husband says that my hair combines more colors than all the autumn leaves he has ever seen, all of them mixed together. He admires my hair. All the gentlemen are sure to admire my hair as well." I paused a moment, then sighed. "Although, to be perfectly honest, which is sometimes difficult, I must say that I think you have the most beautiful hair I have ever seen. It has given me some very uncomfortable moments, what with realizing that I am jealous of you. Well, there you have it. I do hope you enjoy yourself this evening. Are you coming to the drawing room?"

"In a while," she said, those beautiful eyes of hers gleaming at me.

"Oh, yes, Lady Elizabeth. I was meaning to ask you, what do you think about Napoleon's size? His endowment?"

I thought she would burst her seams she sucked in so much air. She stared at me as if I had just told her that there was lint in her eyebrows, then she started laughing. Laughing until she was crying and hiccuping as she turned away and walked gracefully up the stairs. I could still hear her laughter when she gained the landing and turned into the west wing.

I only wished I knew exactly how and why I had managed to fell her.

It was perhaps the twentieth ball I had attended since my coming out, but it was the very first ball where I had been in charge, from assembling the invitation list, to checking that all the sheets were in prime shape for fifteen sets of guests, to the cleaning of the huge ballroom. In many cases, I was cleaning alongside the servants, something

I had grown up doing at Deerfield Hall. The servants were beaming on the day of the ball. They were pleased with themselves, and they were pleased with me. Brantley never beamed, but he did nod to me, in approval, several times during the evening.

I knew I would never remember all the courses served at dinner, even though I had spent hours on the menu, several times actually arguing with Mrs. Redbreast and Cook with a good deal of passion, which seemed to please both of them no end. As I watched the endless stream of platters laid with great care along the huge long table, I was nonetheless counting. There were to be forty-two dishes in all. There were forty-three. Goodness, how had that happened?

There were platters of baked sole, oyster patties, game pies, garnished tongue, crimped cod, pork cutlets, it just went on and on. Between the soufflé of rice and the Nesselrode pudding, there was something to please the most fickle palate. I was too excited to eat, nearly floating two inches off my chair.

Everyone seemed to be having a fine time. The gentlemen did not remain in the dining room because all our other guests were arriving for the ball. Lawrence efficiently removed them from the brandy bottles and led them to the ballroom.

By ten o'clock that night, the ballroom held at least one hundred and twenty persons, all of them talking, laughing, drinking more champagne punch than was good for them, flirting and gossiping. The chandeliers glittered overhead, and the scents of the winter flowers were sweet and seductive. There were so many jewels clasped around throats and wrists and earlobes, a thief would have believed he had died and gone to Heaven if he could have gotten his hands on them. So many beautiful people, and they were here because I had invited them. Well, I suppose I must also give Lawrence some credit.

The orchestra was in fine fettle. I was tapping my foot when John lightly touched his hand to my arm. "A waltz, Andy. I particularly like the waltz. Will you dance with me?"

I said nothing at all, just drew a deep breath and turned into his arms. He was a marvelous dancer, smooth and graceful. He was still too big and too tall, but he did lead very well, and I felt safe, which was surely a strange thing, given he was a man, but it was true nonetheless. I was now getting used to it.

He dipped and whirled me about in big circles, and I laughed and enjoyed myself so much that I never wanted it to end. But it did, of course, and then I waltzed with my husband.

He was graceful and smooth and held me at exactly the right distance, and I did smile a good deal. He told me he was proud of me. He also mentioned that I was the most beautiful woman present, and he was very pleased that I was his wife. He never once looked overlong at my bosom. Did he even want to look overlong? I sincerely hoped not.

"Thank you," I said. "You are very kind."

He kissed my cheek when the waltz was over and told me he particularly liked the way I had arranged my hair. And I said, "Didn't you once tell me that you very much liked all the mix of different colors?"

"I'm sure that I must have," he said, all smooth as honey, "for I have never before witnessed such harmony on a woman's head." He flicked a fingertip over my cheek. I grinned. My husband always knew when to say exactly the right thing. He left me smiling to attend the marchioness, whom, he said to me, had told him that I was an audacious chit—ignorant as dirt—but audacious. I did not think this could be much of a compliment what with the dirt thrown in.

There was a portly gentleman waiting to take his place on the dance floor with me. He was on the tipsy side, but no matter. By the end of the evening, I had no doubt that I would be adept at avoiding trodding feet. I was pleased to see that there were gentlemen littered everywhere, all of them thankfully disposed to dance. I suppose they were so amiable because it was, after all, the holiday season and they were on their best behavior, also I knew that Lawrence had told all the gentlemen that there would be no cards or gambling tonight. And so, no lady went without a partner. My bosom got ogled more than was proper, but I didn't have to say anything nasty. There was one skinny gentleman, though, who looked at me and actually licked his chops. I simply laughed, he was so ridiculous, which didn't please him at all. I think he would have preferred for me to act affronted by his behavior. When I mentioned this to Lawrence, he laughed. The skinny gentleman, he told me, wore quite a bit of padding. He was relieved that I hadn't hit him. The padding just might have slipped.

As for poor Lady Elizabeth Palmer, I feared she would surely wear holes in her slippers she danced so exuberantly, with such an inexhaustible supply of grace, the wretched too beautiful woman. Three times she waltzed with John. That was scandalous, at least that is what I told both Miss Gillbank and Miss Crislock, both of whom were doing a great deal of laughing. Miss Gillbank danced at least twice with the young baronet, Christopher Wilkins, whom I had seated next to her at dinner both evenings.

I drank more champagne punch than I should have, and finally, at nearly three o'clock in the morning, the guests began to take their leave.

I fell, literally, into my bed, making George growl because I landed on him, at four o'clock.

Chapter Twenty-four

The next four days were an education for me. I learned how to gossip. I learned how to keep my face perfectly blank when I didn't understand something scandalous. I learned how to flirt with men without being perfectly terrified, and I fancy that by the fourth evening, I wasn't bad at it. Still, I knew not to trust any of them. I made certain that I was never alone with one of them.

Except John.

He came upon me in the stables seeing to Small Bess two mornings after the ball. He came on me actually not an hour after

Lady Elizabeth Palmer had finally cornered me and told me about Napoleon.

She had caught me just outside a small back parlor where I'd fled to just after the marchioness had informed me, in front of at least twenty other ladies, that I should strive to be taller, since my bosom was too large for my torso. That really wasn't at all true, it was just one of those little jabs that occasionally popped out of a guest's mouth.

"I can't bear it any longer," Lady Elizabeth said, coming to within two inches of my face.

"What's wrong? Are you wearing a corset that pinches your ribs? Was your toast burned at breakfast? Did your maid have the gall to refuse to bring you hot water?"

"Shut your mouth," she said, obviously irritated. "You cannot make me laugh, so stop trying. Someone has to tell you, and I suppose it will have to be me. It's about Napoleon."

"You mean his blasted size?"

"Yes," she said, staring at me as if I had grown another nose.

"John told me I was to disregard anything anyone said about Napoleon's size. He said I was simply to forget it. I was to continue blissful in my ignorance."

"A man's size or his endowment simply refers to his manhood," Lady Elizabeth said, staying her course. "Surely you know how gentlemen are fashioned?"

I stared at her blank-faced. "Yes, certainly. Do I look like an idiot?"

She managed to roll her eyes and nod her head both at the same time. "Yes."

Then, of all things, my husband rounded the corner and nearly plowed right into Lady Elizabeth.

"Goodness, forgive me, my dear. What are you two ladies doing? Talking about the latest fashions?"

"Exactly," I said. "I dislike ruffles, and Lady Elizabeth informs me that ruffles will be the newest thing this spring. It is disappointing."

And my husband said, "You make me laugh even when you are lying to my face," and he went on his way.

And that was the end of our conversation.

And now I was spreading more ointment on Small Bess's back, and John strolled in.

He grinned like a sinner who had just slipped by St. Peter through the Pearly Gates. "I just spoke to Lady Elizabeth. She told me of your aborted conversation."

"I tried to ignore all talk of Napoleon, just as you suggested, but she was adamant."

"Then my uncle came along, and you never learned the end to the tale, hmmm?"

"That's right." I looked beyond his shoulder. "She did ask me if I knew how men were fashioned, but nothing more than that." I sighed. "She is so very beautiful. I feel like a pathetic dowd. I see her, and I want to smack her because I'm jealous."

He threw back his head and laughed. Small Bess whinnied. I heard Tempest trumpet in his stall.

"Well, she thinks you're an original," he said.

"So is she."

"And an ignorant twit."

"She would, curse her."

"Yes, but that doesn't matter, does it?"

I looked at him then, really looked, and said slowly, "I don't know. Does it matter?"

He just ignored that, and began petting Small Bess's neck. "You are taking care?"

"Yes."

"No, you aren't. I followed you here to the stable to make sure no villain would try to do away with you. Don't let down your guard, Andy. Whoever wants to make you pay for it all, whatever that means, is still here. Boynton simply cannot be your shadow every moment. Take care."

He was right, and on the final morning after all our guests had taken their leave, I walked back upstairs to my bedchamber. The truth of things hit me in the face as I walked down that long corridor. I didn't see a single servant. The house was very empty now. Hollow, yet filled with menace I didn't understand, like the Black Chamber, with that horrible cold that bespoke, Viscount Waverleigh had said, of an evil that was here, right now, hidden among all of us.

There was even no sign of Belinda. I fetched George and took him for a very long walk. Boynton walked some ten feet behind me. I was grateful to John. Boynton made me feel safe.

Dinner that evening was a subdued affair. Thomas sighed a lot, Amelia's parents had evidently exhausted their supply of other-worldly phenomena stories, because most of their attention was on their plates. Lawrence was quiet, even thoughtful, as he picked at his food. As for Miss Gillbank, she smiled a lot, but it wasn't meant for us, it was for someone she was thinking about. I wondered if it was her baronet, Christopher Wilkins. As for Miss Crislock, she talked about the Christmas gifts she had sewn and needed to send back to her friends in London. She told me that she had quite a surprise planned for me. Bless her heart, for as long as she had been with me, nearly ten years, she'd always had the very best surprises. Last Christmas, she'd had ice skates made for me and had hired someone to teach me how to perform tricks on the ice. I had nearly broken my neck when I skated backward into a huge barrel set at the edge of the ice, but that was neither here nor there. If she'd been sitting next to me, I might have cried on her neck and blessed her for always being here for me.

John asked her what she had made for him. She just shook her head at him and said he had to wait, like all the rest of us.

I thought about Napoleon, but kept my mouth shut. Everyone went to bed early. Belinda wasn't there. Where was she? My room was empty. I didn't like it. I held George until he pulled away from me.

I awoke at ten o'clock the next morning, stretched, and petted George's topknot because he'd stuck his face into mine and licked my nose until I laughed and ducked away. I swung my legs over the side of the bed. The tiny golden key to my Italianate letter box fell forward outside my nightgown. I had forgotten about it, and my father's wretched letter that hadn't really told me much of anything except that I should leave Devbridge Manor right away.

Well, I supposed that I should consider it. I wanted to see that letter again. I carried George over to my writing desk and opened the top drawer. I lifted out the letter box, lifted the golden chain over my head, and stuck the key in the box. The lock was broken. I stared at it, unwilling to believe it. Slowly I opened the box. It was quite empty.

My father's letter was gone.

George didn't realize the significance of the empty letter box. He wanted to go out and relieve himself.

I was shaking even as I dressed quickly to take him for his morning walk. Boynton weaved in and out of the shadows some twenty feet behind us. I wanted to ask Boynton to bring two friends the next time.

Amelia's parents left that day, after Lord Waverleigh had once again paced about Caroline's music room. Nothing, he said, there wasn't anything at all. And I had to agree with him. No vestiges of Caroline. Had it indeed been Caroline who had locked Amelia in the music room so long ago? Or maybe I had imagined the door slamming shut in my face. Maybe all of it was just madness.

He also visited the Black Chamber once again, and reported to all of us that the evil was still here and it was quite real. And he had shaken his head when his dear wife had said, "Now, Hobson, there's no reason to scare everyone."

"Yes," he had said, and he looked over at me, a puzzled look on his face. "Yes, there is, but you're quite right, my dear, since I do not begin to understand it, then I shouldn't terrify the household." And he thought that erased what he had said? I wanted to hit him. He had terrified me and given me no explanation.

His words also killed any hope of conversation. It also hurled me into a well of fear. I was frankly relieved when they finally took their leave. We all stood in the front of the Manor, waving when their carriage rolled down the long driveway.

Thomas said to Amelia, "Your father told

me that I was to cease complaining about my health, or else when I died, my ghost would not give forth a strong aura. I would never be able to see you again, even from that metaphysical distance. I would, he told me, be doomed."

It took all the strength I had not to burst out laughing.

John had no reticence at all. He clapped his brother's shoulder and said, "I don't want you to be doomed, Thomas, no matter what sorts of distances we're talking about. Do consider what your father-in-law told you."

Amelia was staring down at the toes of her slippers. What was she thinking about this, I wondered? Or was she thinking about the evil in the Black Chamber? She didn't say a word, merely offered to prepare Thomas a very nice tisane if he would accompany her to their bedchamber. I stared at them, walking so very close together, speaking in low voices. About what?

When John and I were alone. When I was certain that there was no one hanging about, I said, "There is something I suppose I should tell you. I should probably have mentioned it before, but I didn't, so perhaps now is a good time to do it."

One of those dark eyebrows of his shot up. He eyed me. "Well? Come on, out with it."

"All right. Two weeks ago I received a letter from my cousin Peter. He enclosed a letter from my father, a man I had hoped was long dead and in Hell, where he so richly deserves to be."

"Your father? I believed he was dead. You lived with your grandfather, did you not?"

"Yes. I do not wish to discuss it. I despise him. He murdered my mother."

"How?"

"I don't wish to discuss it. Just believe me. In any case, in this letter he wrote me, he said that he had read of my marriage to your uncle. It unnerved him. He told me to leave Devbridge Manor at once, that he was coming as soon as he could."

I saw that flash of violence in his dark eyes, then it was gone, and I knew he was angry. "May I ask," he said very pleasantly, "why the hell you did not tell me of this damned letter before?"

"I did not feel that it was anyone's business. Actually, that isn't quite all of the truth."

"And the truth is what, exactly?"

"I didn't want you to know about the man who is my father."

"Why?"

"I don't want to discuss it. The main reason I'm telling you now is that his letter has been stolen from my letter box." I pulled the gold chain with the gold key attached to it from my bodice. "I kept the box locked. I have worn the key. Now that everyone is gone, there are no more distractions. I wanted to reread the letter. It is gone. Someone stole it. I searched all over my bedchamber, which turned up a pair of stockings that George had pulled out of a drawer, but nothing else."

He cursed, very fluently, and for a good length of time.

"When you keep me in ignorance, you unman me," he said, looking at me like he wanted to strangle me, and I immediately started shaking my head.

"No, if that is what you feel, then I am sorry. I believed my father's letter to be ridiculous. No, not really, since all these things have happened to me. No, what's important now is that I leave. I don't want to stay here and let someone kill me or make me pay for all of it. I will return to Grandfather's house in London."

"Yes," he said, "I believe you must leave. And while you are gone, I will get to the bottom of all this."

"How?"

"It's time I did a bit of searching about," he said. "No, it won't work. For example, just what would you tell Uncle Lawrence? There is no good reason. You cannot leave, dammit."

"I have no choice."

"All right. Just what reason will you give him? Give everyone?"

"Oh, God, I don't know. Let me think. There must be some good reason that calls me back. I know—Peter. He's now the Duke of Broughton. I will tell everyone that he has written me and asks me to come assist him in redecorating the London house. What do you think?"

"It sounds ridiculous."

"Just because you didn't think of it—"

"No, Andy. Think. Next week is Christmas. Families stay together for Christmas. You are newly married to my uncle. No one would ever accept that you would leave him during the Christmas holidays. Moreover, as the new countess, you will attend services in the village, lend your presence to many parties given by the local gentry. There are gifts to be bought and wrapped and given out. You will be expected to have a Christmas ball for the servants and to present them money. No, it has to be something else. Damnation, I can't think of a blessed thing at the moment, but I will." He rubbed his chin, turned, and left me standing there. I saw Boynton lolling next to one of the ancient sessile oak trees.

I went to visit Judith and Miss Gillbank, and learned to say good day in Turkish. I spent an hour with Miss Crislock, who couldn't stop talking about all the guests. I swear that each and every one of them had flaws that she had to detail at great length.

Finally, I picked up George and carried him outside. I waited patiently for him to sniff at a good dozen trees, bushes, hedges, plants, before giving his custom to a lone skinny maple tree. I hoped the tree survived. It was getting colder.

Someone broke into the letter box and stole the letter. I tried to remember who all knew that I had received it. Brantley had brought it in. That meant any and everybody in the house could have known. Shadows were lengthening over the horizon. It was colder now than it had been just five minutes before.

I hurried to the stables to visit Small Bess, George at my side. He tried to bite her hock. The other horses looked at George and raised a ruckus. I picked him up, apologized to the animals, then walked slowly back to the house. It was then that I happened to look up at the north tower, where Caroline had hurled herself off that small balcony to the flagstone below. In that instant, I saw a light move in the narrow-slitted windows. Then nothing. My eyes were deceiving me. No, wait, there it was again, a brief light, like a single candle, with someone holding it.

But why would anyone be in the north tower? That made no sense at all.

Then I realized that I very much wanted to know why someone was walking about up there. I dashed back into the house, George barking madly, tucked under my right arm. I ran past Brantley, who said nothing, just stared at me as I ran up the stairs, holding my skirts up to my knees. I shut George into my bedchamber, lit a candle, then headed for the north tower.

I felt the blood pounding through my body. I passed servants and footmen and nodded pleasantly to them, not pausing to speak at all. I was filled with a heady combination of utter fear and excitement. I had my derringer. I wanted very much to see the person who was doing this to me.

It took me nearly fifteen minutes to make my way to the north tower. Only when I pulled open the very old door at the base of the winding tower stairs, did I pause. I pulled my derringer out of my pocket, lifted my candle high, and walked up the uneven wooden steps.

No one was in the circular room at the top of the stairs. The air was still and icy cold. There was no candle in evidence. Someone had brought the candle and then taken it away.

There was still only the bed and the chest at the end of it. I carefully set the candle down on the floor, my derringer beside it. I opened the lid to that ancient wooden chest. On the very top lay a gold brocade gown of the last century. It was yards and yards of very heavy material, so much of it. I couldn't imagine being able to stand upright it weighed so much. I lifted the gown out and carefully laid it on the wooden floor.

Beneath it was a very old-fashioned night-gown of fine lawn sewn with the most beautiful lace I'd ever seen. The lace was yellowed with age.

There were riding boots and slippers with the soles nearly worn through.

And on the very bottom of that wooden chest was a long tangled mass of white hair.

Chapter Twenty-five

I jerked back. I stared at that horrible mess of tangled gray hair. I didn't shriek, but I wanted to. My heart nearly leapt into my throat. I recognized that hair. The old woman had worn that hideous wig when she had come to my bedchamber with John's knife. I didn't want to, but I reached out my hand and touched the hair. It was coarse and thick. It was ancient, that wig. I shuddered as I lifted it out of the chest.

Beneath it was the ugly white shapeless robe the old woman had worn. When I lifted it out, I did cry out. A mask fell from between the folds of that ancient robe, a hideous mask with holes for the eyes, and aged, crinkled skin. I had wondered, but now I knew. Someone had worn this disguise to terrify me.

That person had certainly succeeded.

So, this was where the monster had hidden his props. In the room where Caroline had come, then walked out on the stone balcony, climbed over the railing, and thrown herself to her death.

Everyone had access to the tower room. It wasn't locked. Anyone could have stashed the disguise in the bottom of this chest.

I lifted everything except the disguise back into the chest and closed the lid. I carefully laid the old woman's clothes, the wig, and the mask over my arm, and walked downstairs.

John wasn't in his bedchamber. I went in and walked immediately over to where he kept his knife collection in the corner of the room.

The knife was gone.

No, I thought, no. John had nothing to do with any of this. He couldn't, just couldn't. Why? I asked myself. No one had a reason to harm me. The fact that John didn't have a reason, either, didn't mean he was innocent of this. But I simply wouldn't accept that damning thought into my brain. I couldn't, I didn't want to discuss with myself why I felt so strongly. No, John had simply put the wretched knife elsewhere, to keep it from being taken again.

I carefully laid that dreadful wig, the old wrinkled robe, and the mask on the counterpane. I turned to leave when he walked in. His head was down, and he was rubbing the back of his neck. I must have made a noise because his head jerked up. He stared at me, just stood there and stared at me. He cleared his throat. "May I ask what you're doing in my bedchamber?"

I saw the heat in his eyes from twenty paces. I took a quick step back. My legs hit the side of the bed, and I sat down. I jumped up immediately.

I splayed my hands in front of me and felt like a fool. "I knocked, but you weren't here. The knife is gone again, John."

"Boynton has it."

"I found these things in that chest in the north tower room. I brought them here to show you."

"Why did you go up there?" he asked as he walked toward me and the bed.

"I was walking back from the stables, and I saw a candlelight coming from that room. Someone was up there, walking about."

He said nothing more, just stared down at the items I'd laid out on his bed.

He picked up the mask and pulled it tight over his fist. "Jesus, it's terrifying. I'm surprised you didn't fall over with heart failure."

"I am, too."

"Anyone could have hidden these things in that chest."

"I know."

"I'm going to return them to the chest. I don't want the person who is behind this reign of terror to know that you found them."

I didn't want to go back there. I told him how they were layered with the other clothes. Then I went back to my bedchamber. Belinda was there laying out a gown, a rich dark blue velvet, for the evening. So normal. Everything seemed so completely normal. Even to the velvet matching ribbons she planned to thread through my hair.

I took a very long bath, singing to George as I rubbed the soapy sponge over myself. He was playing with Belinda by the fireplace, tugging on a belt she was holding, shaking his head wildly about, growling all the while. He'd managed to make Belinda a devoted slave within twenty-four hours of his arrival in The Blue Room.

And that evening, over the course of vermicelli soup and fried eels and savory rissoles, Lawrence said, "My dear, I must leave for London early tomorrow morning. There is business I must see to. I promise I will be back before Christmas. Is there anything you would like me to purchase for you?"

"How can you possibly be back in time for Christmas?" John said. His spoon was halted in midair, and he had become very quiet. "Christmas is only eight days from tomorrow."

"My business won't require all that much time," Lawrence said. "I trust all of you will rub along well together in my absence."

I said not a thing. What I was thinking was that while he was gone, I would search his study and his bedchamber. I looked down the length of the table at him, and smiled. "There is nothing I need you to bring to me, thank you. Do you like the soup, sir?"

"Indeed, it is delicious."

And that was that.

That evening Lawrence asked if I would

enjoy playing a game of chess with him. We had never played before. I was pleased he assumed that I knew how to play. I did indeed. My grandfather called me a killer. I beat him nearly half our games by the age of fifteen.

Lawrence must have seen my eyes glitter, because he laughed. "So you are good at it, are you?"

I lowered my eyes modestly. "I know all the moves."

He lightly touched his fingertips to my cheek. I didn't move. We settled down in front of the fireplace, the chessboard on a marquetry table between us. He offered me white. I insisted that I put a black and a white piece behind my back and that he pick the hand he wanted. He got the black pieces anyway.

I always played the Ruy Lopez as white. I knew the first dozen best moves better than any other opening and could counter most defenses played against me. I moved my pawn to king four. Lawrence answered with the standard move, his own pawn to king four, and I was pleased. I quickly played my knight to king bishop three, and he answered with knight to queen bishop three. And so it continued, classic plays and classic responses, and that gave me the edge.

He was a good player. He knew what he was doing. He played some moves I hadn't seen before, which set me to thinking hard. This was our first game. Regardless of the outcome, I wanted to prove to him that I was a good player. I wasn't about to be swept under the carpet. On the eighteenth move, he tried to fork my queen and my rook with his king's knight, but I caught the trap easily, and pulled him short before he could ever make the move. Ten moves later I knew I would checkmate him soon, six moves, perhaps, no more. And as I looked over the small table at him in the soft firelight, concentrating, his chin on his hand, I wondered yet again if he was the one who was terrorizing me. And always I came back to the conclusion that he had no reason. No reason at all. It was driving me mad.

And then it was done, coming to pass just as I had seen that it would. I had won. I sat back, steepled my fingers, and said, "My grandfather was one of the best chess players in all of England. He taught me. He was a very stern taskmaster."

"I see," he said, nothing more.

When he left me at the door of The Blue Room, he said, "You are accomplished for one so young. I am proud of you for that, and perhaps that is a pity." Then he patted my cheek, as was his habit, and left me. I stood there wondering what he had meant.

He was gone near dawn the following day. At seven o'clock in the morning, I was still wondering what he had meant with those strange words when I let myself into his study. I had been in this room before, but just to look at it for a moment, nothing more. It was dark, that was my first impression. It was dark and very somber. I didn't like it. It was also frigidly cold. This was where he worked with Swanson, his estate manager, a man I had only met twice now.

I pushed back the draperies. The morning was a leaden gray, snow was threatening. But there was enough light for me to search. I went through every drawer in the massive mahogany desk. Tradesmen's bills, letters from his man of business in London, the man I assumed he was going to see. Why wouldn't a man of business come to the patron and not the other way around? I didn't know the answer to that, since I knew next to nothing about anything to do with business dealings.

I kept looking. So many papers, so many neat piles, but nothing to give a hint of anything at all nefarious or secret or in any way suggestive of wrongdoing. It was frustrating. I heard someone clear their throat.

I jerked around to see Brantley standing in the doorway.

"Oh, it's you, Brantley." Never, never, back down in front of a servant or try to explain yourself, Grandfather told me upon several occasions. If you do, you'll be buried. I gave Brantley a sunny smile. "What do you want?"

"Does your ladyship require a fire built?"

"No, I don't think so. I haven't found what I'm looking for, and I don't think that they're here. Perhaps my papers are back in my bedchamber."

I gave him a fat smile and waltzed out of that dark, depressing room.

I walked directly upstairs, turned right, and walked to the very end of that long corridor. Thank God, Lawrence had taken his miserable valet Flynt with him. I didn't relish running into him while I was searching through Lawrence's dressing table drawers.

I had never before been in my husband's suite of rooms. The door wasn't locked. I looked down the corridor. No one was about. I opened the door and quickly stepped inside, pulling the door closed behind me. It was also frigidly cold in the bedchamber. I could easily see my breath. Well, why should the servants bother with a fire when no one was here? I shivered, slapped my arms, and forced myself to get to work.

It was a huge room, long and narrow, and it was beautifully furnished with exquisite chairs and tables and a magnificent bed with golden draperies looped at the four corner posters, all the opulent gold and white of Louis XV. I was seeing another side of my husband, the man whose belongings I was searching to see if he was the monster who wanted to kill me.

There was irony in this, I thought, but I couldn't think about that now. I went through every drawer in that huge room. I found nothing at all. I went into his dressing room, another chamber beautifully furnished, soft carpets on the floor. There were several dressers, all of them gilded and exquisitely fashioned. I found nail files, handkerchiefs, drawer after drawer of cravats beautifully pressed. There were brushes, combs, shaving things. I opened every drawer. I found nothing at all.

I walked back into the large bedchamber. I stood then in the middle of the room, shivering. I don't know why I happened to be looking at the armoire—I had searched it thoroughly—but I did, and there was this slight seam in the beautiful ivory Chinese wallpaper just beside it. If your eye didn't land directly on it, you wouldn't see it.

Once I did look directly at it, I realized quickly enough that it was a narrow door, built into the wall. There was only a small curved spring just behind the armoire. I could reach it. I fiddled with it until it snapped down suddenly. The door opened smoothly inward.

I stepped into a very small room that had only one narrow window. There was no fireplace. It was perfectly square, so small, so very small. It looked like a monk's cell, stark, nearly empty, the desk very old and simple, not a single ornamental swag or carving on it. The chair behind it was stiff and looked very uncomfortable. There was nothing else in the room. Even the wooden floor was bare. My shoes click-clicked as I walked toward that desk. I realized that at this point I was invading his privacy past the point of no return. I also realized that I had no choice.

This was indeed a private place, a place where I should not be. I wondered what Lawrence was like when he was in this room. Surely he would resemble more the fanatic grand inquisitor Torquemada of Spain rather than a peer of our modern Regency. I walked to the desk and sat down in the stiff hard chair. There were three small drawers in the desk, and I hesitated only a moment, knowing well that this was the ultimate invasion. I opened the top drawer. It slid out easily. It was filled with neat stacks of letters, each stack tied separately. All the letters seemed to be personal correspondence, many of them yellowing with age. I picked up each stack and thumbed quickly through the letters. There were letters from Lady Pontefract, Lord Holliston, Lady Smithson-Blake—all people whose names I had heard, but had never known. They were names my grandfather would mention, prominent figures of my grandfather's time— and of my husband's.

It was at that moment, sitting in that austere, narrow room, holding letters of love, of intrigue, of politics, that I finally saw clearly, deeply inside myself. Those fading, yellowing letters were symbols of the mistake I had made. I had married a man who belonged to the century before—to the French Revolution, to the rise of Napoleon, to the great naval victories of Lord Nelson. I adored that world, for it held limitless fascination, but it was not real; it was not a part of my world.

Peter had been right. I had tried to escape my time, my world, by marrying a man who was too old to touch my heart, or my fears. I had chosen a man I believed would keep me free of fear, a man who would protect me just as my grandfather had protected me. Freedom and protection—now those were two things that hadn't applied since my first night in this house. I thought again of the irony of all this, but I couldn't accept it. I was a fool. All I could feel was despair at my own folly. I had seen John, but I had not seen beyond him, until now.

I looked down at my hands. I had crumpled the edges of some of the letters from gripping them so tightly. Not good. I tried to smooth them back out. They looked well enough, I thought, then placed them neatly and carefully back into the drawer. I gently closed it.

The second drawer contained only writing materials and elegant stationery. I tugged at the third drawer. It was locked. I felt my heart begin to pound. Perhaps, just perhaps, at last I would find some answers. I pulled a pin from my hair, carefully inserted it into the lock, and twisted the pin gently. I slowly worked it back and forth. Nothing happened. I moved it more vigorously. The next instant the lock sprang loose, and a long narrow drawer slid open.

I'd done it. I sat there a moment just staring at that drawer. The drawer was empty save for one envelope. It was addressed to his lordship, the Earl of Devbridge, and it had been sent from London. I pulled out one piece of foolscap and smoothed it out on the desktop. I read:

8 December, 1817

My lord:

Edward Jameson has just arrived in London.
I await your instructions.

Your obedient servant,
Charles Grafton

I just sat there staring down at those words. My father was in London, as of the eighth of this month. It was now the seventeenth of December. Where was he? What was he doing? And most importantly, why did Lawrence care?

What bloody instructions? Why would Lawrence give instructions about my father to this man named Grafton? I read and re-read the two lines, trying to make some sense out of them. It was no use. I had so urgently sought to find some clue, to discover the answer to this deadly game I was trapped in. Now the clue I had searched for was in my hand, and still I did not understand. Then I realized the date of the letter was only three days before someone had put that horrible barbed circle of wire under Small Bess's saddle.

I put the letter down and pressed my fingers against my temples. At least now I knew, knew that my father's warning was against Lawrence, my husband. That was why he was so shocked and dismayed at my marriage. But what had my father to do with all this?

I felt as though I were trapped in that marvelous maze at Richmond, only in this maze I didn't know if I would be able to find a way out.

I slowly placed the sheet of foolscap back into the envelope, and put it exactly in the same place it had been when I opened the drawer. There was just no away around it, my husband was the one who wanted to make me pay for all of it. But why? Why then did he marry me? What had I done to deserve his hate?

Was he also the evil that Lord Waverleigh had said still lived here? In the Black Chamber?

I stared about me. I had been here all too long. Someone might come in. I closed the drawer only to realize that I had to use the hairpin again to move the inside little lever. I moved the pin back and forth until, finally, mercifully, the lock clicked back into place.

I quietly closed the small narrow door, and walked quickly out of his bedchamber. I had taken only three steps when I saw someone, the shadow of another person, and then they were gone, around the corner that led to a servant's staircase. I sincerely hoped it was Boynton, John's valet, keeping an eye on me. But if it was Boynton, why had he run? I heard a noise from just behind me. I whirled around so fast I nearly stumbled on my skirt and went down. Another shadow, a face, looking at me from around that corner, and now it was gone. I raced to the corner, around it, and dashed up another back staircase, calling out, "Who is there? Come back here. Damn you, who are you?"

Chapter Twenty-six

No one answered. I stood there, heart pounding, wondering what the devil I was going to do now.

I quickly entered my room, and locked the door behind me. The Blue Room had never seemed so welcome. George looked up and wagged his tail for a bit before he took two drinks out of his water bowl and went back to his nap. I sat down in the winged chair close to the fire. It felt wonderful. I hadn't realized I was so cold, both on the inside and the outside. I stared into the flames. I wondered why Lawrence had married me and brought me here, to his home, only to terrorize me, to tell me that I would pay for all of it. I knew it involved my father, but how and what, I still had no idea. I had to see John. Perhaps he had learned something.

He wasn't in his bedchamber. He wasn't downstairs, either. No one had seen him. I could not find Boynton.

I didn't like this at all. I went slowly back to my bedchamber. Belinda was humming as she carefully folded some of my chemises. She smiled when she looked up to see me. "Jasper took Mr. George for a walk, my lady," she said. "Now, it is time for luncheon and aren't you just a sight? What have you been doing?"

"Just exploring," I said, and closed the door behind me. I leaned against it a moment, closing my eyes. John, I thought, where are you?

I did what Belinda told me to do, and I thought and thought. I would go down to lunch. Why not? I would talk to everyone, and I would wait for John.

And then I would leave this place.

Belinda cleaned me up within the hour, and I walked downstairs to the dining room. Amelia and Thomas were there, and Miss Crislock. No one knew a thing about John.

Thomas said after he'd carefully chewed a bite of pork cutlet with tomato sauce, "I have decided that Amelia's father is right. I do not wish my aura to be weak and insubstantial, my shade to be indistinct, my otherworldly spirit to hover about powerless. I have decided that I will ignore my pains and illnesses. Even though at this very moment I can feel a very strange itch in the vicinity of my right armpit, I will pay it no heed. I know Amelia will worry, but I am determined."

He leaned over and kissed her, right on the mouth, in front of all of us. Miss Crislock gave me one of her delightful crooked grins, and a wink.

I took a bite of my oyster patty.

Where was John?

Amelia said, "My love, tell me about this strange itch so I can know whether or not I should concern myself."

Instead he kissed her again.

We laughed. I don't know where that laugh came from, but it came, full blown and charmed at the two of them.

Lawrence wouldn't be home until Christmas. I had more than enough time to make plans and execute them.

The afternoon passed quickly. I met with Mrs. Redbreast and discussed the servants, the state of the linens in the servants' rooms and the replacement of dishes in the kitchen. I planned menus with Cook. I complimented Brantley on George's training, although I wanted my old dog back. This new George who sat obediently until told otherwise just wasn't as much fun. I looked in on Small Bess. Her back and her hock were healing nicely.

It was late that afternoon when I visited Miss Gillbank and Judith in the nursery. I learned how to say good day in Greek.

It was then that Judith reminded me that I had promised her that she was supposed to dine with the adults for a full week. I had forgotten. My brain was weighted down with fear. Ah, this would be a diversion, one that I sorely needed. I smiled at this beautiful girl and told her I would speak to Mrs. Redbreast immediately so that Cook would make some Iced Charlotte for her dessert.

Actually, it was Brantley who agreed to see to the Iced Charlotte for Judith's dessert. I changed my clothes while Belinda fussed. I enjoyed her fussing. It made me feel safe, a feeling I knew well was an illusion.

I walked quickly down the main staircase, across the Old Hall and into the main drawing room. I hoped John would be here.

I was smiling.

Then I froze.

There was my husband, his head bent as he listened to something Miss Crislock was saying. She was seated gracefully in a winged chair, Judith and Miss Gillbank sat opposite. Amelia was standing behind a high-back chair, twirling her glass between long graceful fingers, looking somewhat distracted. Neither John nor Thomas was there.

"Good evening, my dear."

I didn't know what to do. Should I scream that my husband wanted to hurt me? Perhaps slice my throat? I just didn't know what to do, so I wiped the fear off my face and smiled.

"What a wonderful surprise, sir. So very unexpected." It was well-done, I thought. I knew I had managed to overlay any fear with lots of fresh excitement and pleasure at seeing him. What the devil was he doing here? He had just left early this very morning. I couldn't believe this.

Where the devil was John?

I stretched my hands toward him as he quickly placed his sherry glass on a table and walked over to me. He grasped my hands and leaned over to kiss my cheek, his warm breath fanning against my cheek. "Ah, my dear Andy, only a man who was an utter fool would not come home as quickly as possible with such a beautiful and very charming lady waiting for him."

What did I do to you? I wanted to ask him that so badly that I nearly had to bite my lip. Instead, what came out was "Lawrence, you just left. What happened? Is there some sort of problem? Oh, yes you are also a dreadful deceiver, sir, all that flattery." And I laughed, I truly managed to laugh.

He leaned over and kissed my cheek again. I didn't jerk away, but it was close. As he straightened, I looked directly up into his face. His eyes, I saw for the very first time, held no warmth at all. At least there was none directed at me. They were a cold gray, like hard steel. He was smiling as he looked back at me, and I shivered. What was he thinking? Planning?

I looked away and said my good evenings to everyone. Judith was so excited she could barely sit still. Miss Gillbank looked particularly lovely in a dark gold muslin gown of mine that Belinda had made over for her. It flattered her. As for Miss Crislock, she was tatting a scarf, by the looks of it, in her own special chair by the fireplace. A beautiful screen protected her from the heat. A book lay open in her lap, a gift, she had told me, from my dear husband.

"What are you reading, Miss Crislock?"

"Ah, my dearest Andy, it is a novel Lawrence thought I would enjoy. It is about a girl who is very bad indeed, but her parents are resolute and teach her the path of righteousness."

"Oh, dear," I said, and turned to Amelia. Lawrence believed she would enjoy that? "Where is Thomas? Don't tell me he has succumbed and is ill?"

"No, he walked up and down three flights of stairs ten times. He wants to make himself even more fit. I left him in his bathing tub, soaking away his sweat."

I laughed, a healthy laugh, one that just came out, despite the fact that my husband was standing not ten feet from me and I didn't have a clue what he was thinking.

"Lawrence," I called down the table to him once we were all seated in the dining room, "you have not yet told us what happened to your trip. You left this morning, and now here you are back for dinner."

"There was a simple misunderstanding. The men I was to meet with were coming here to see me. We conducted our business in Leeds. It is wonderful to be home. I even had time to do some shopping for Christmas gifts." He was speaking toward Judith as he said this.

She immediately sat forward. "Would you perhaps like to tell us something of your shopping, Father?"

"Oh, no, you must wait, just like everyone else, including your lovely stepmother."

"Has anyone seen John?" I asked after Brantley offered me some braised goose with celery sauce. I knew I would gag if I ate any of that goose.

"Didn't you know, Andy?"

I blinked at my husband. "Know what, sir?"

"John has gone to the Cockburns' weekend Christmas party over near Harrowgate.

He wished to spend more time with Lady Elizabeth Palmer."

I didn't say a single thing.

Amelia laughed. "Well, it is about time. John must needs consider marrying soon and setting up his nursery. Lady Elizabeth certainly charmed him."

But he was only twenty-six, I wanted to say. Not at all old for a man. Naturally a woman of twenty-six—unmarried—was quite a different matter, an embarrassment, to say the least. Had Lady Elizabeth really charmed him?

"I like Lady Elizabeth," said Miss Crislock. "She is ever so lovely, and so very tall. John won't have to get a crick in his neck when he is speaking to her. What do you think, Lawrence?"

He shrugged then took a sip of his wine. "I trust that she will not take a lover until after she has bred him an heir."

There was a heavy bit of silence until I cleared my throat. "I think Lady Elizabeth is charming. She is perhaps a bit imperious, but she is so beautiful, it would be difficult not to be. I do not believe she would be unfaithful were she to wed. After all, why marry in the first place if you planned to be unfaithful? It makes no sense. It is a disgusting thought."

I had been too passionate, the age-old bitterness showing through, I knew it. Judith was staring at me across the table, and she was frowning. I tried to smile at her, to soften what I had said, but I couldn't. I sat there, saying nothing, waiting.

"We will see" was all my husband said. "Perhaps John will have better luck than most men."

Amelia immediately went on to talk of Thomas's new exercise regimen.

"If he becomes as strong as John," Miss Crislock said, "he will be formidable indeed. Thomas is already so beautiful, he sometimes makes even my ancient pulses flutter a bit."

Amelia loved that.

"Yes," I said, "Thomas is glorious."

Amelia loved that even more. She turned to Miss Gillbank, ready to have more husband-praises heaped upon her head, and that lovely young woman said easily, "I have never in my life seen a more handsome gentleman nor one who was so very kind."

I thought Amelia would begin to purr, she was so very pleased.

Dinner went on until finally Miss Crislock said, "Andy, my dear, don't you wish the ladies to go to the drawing room now?"

"An excellent idea," said my husband, rising with me. "I wish to have Andy to myself this evening. I have to regain my self-respect. She trounced me at chess last evening. It is my turn for retribution."

Amelia just stared at me. "I have seen Uncle Lawrence play. He has never been beaten."

"Yes," I said, looking at him straight on, "he has. I beat him."

We would be in the study. He couldn't very well do anything to me in the study. After everyone went to bed, then I would act. I would be gone from here.

I realized, as I walked beside him to the study, after bidding everyone good night, that I wanted to play another chess game with him. I wanted to grind him into the dirt. Poor Judith. She, naturally, had not wanted the evening to end so quickly, but there was nothing I could do about that. The chances were that I would never see her again after tonight.

This time Lawrence pointed to my right hand. It held a white knight. I enjoyed playing black. I played the French Defense well.

He began with a king pawn opening, and I smiled as I moved my king pawn to king three.

"Ah," he said, "the French Defense. I wonder just how well you will play it."

"Very well indeed. It was my grandfather's favorite defense. As you realized last night, my grandfather taught me well," I said, never looking up from the board. When it was his move, I looked at his bent head, his dark hair streaked so gracefully with white. I wanted desperately to ask him about my father, but I kept my mouth shut. I just didn't know enough yet to do anything. Besides, I was alone here. All the servants were loyal to Lawrence. I had no idea about his wretched valet Flynt or if he had other villains hanging about the house.

No, I would keep my mouth shut, and then much later this night, I would leave. Besides, he did not know that I had searched his bedchamber and that small little monk's cell of his, or that I had found that letter about my father.

Our play continued. I prayed I was safe

for the moment, in my seeming ignorance. But what would happen if—I was lightly tapping my fingertips against my chair arm. Lawrence cleared his throat. It was my move. It was time to castle. No reason to wait. I reached out to pick up my king. Then I looked down again at the board, really looked and dropped the king. Oh, dear God, I'd very nearly handed him the game, and all because I was so bloody scared I could scarcely keep my wits together.

I looked with my full attention, and quickly saw that if I had castled my king, my queen would have been lost a move later by a fork by his knight. It was a deceptively simple trap, one that would not pass unnoticed to a chess player of any merit. I realized then that he was smiling at me. It wasn't a nice smile at all. It was patronizing, as if I weren't worth much of anything at all. Perhaps, something warned me deep inside, perhaps I should let him win. Let him feel smug and superior. Let him think I wasn't worth anything at all.

But no, I just couldn't. There was too much anger in me—at him—at this man who had so deceived me, who appeared to hate me for no reason that I could discover.

I would show him that I was indeed an opponent to be reckoned with. I would wipe that self-satisfied look right off his face. He had seen my abstraction, possibly wondered at it, and knew he would win because I was naught but a female and I couldn't think logically, couldn't analyze, not like a man.

At that moment, the game of chess symbolized my own victory or defeat in this house.

He saw the difference in me immediately, of course. Soon his own concentration equaled mine. If he wondered what I was thinking now, if he wondered at all at my new absorption in the game, I didn't know. And he didn't say anything.

Brantley entered with the tea tray, and seeing us totally engrossed in the game, departed as silently as he had entered, pausing only long enough to add three more logs to the fire.

After about ten more moves, I managed to gain the advantage. I mounted a very strong king side attack that I knew would crush him. I moved my knight to the crucial king bishop five square. There was no challenge from him. Within a few moves my queen and her bishop were bearing down upon his king. A final move by my knight, and I had him boxed in.

A queer smile played over my lips as I looked up at him, straight into his eyes, and said ever so softly, "Checkmate, sir."

I felt I could conquer the world in that moment. I felt strong and whole and indomitable. My eyes glittered. I knew I was smirking.

After a few moments of silence, Lawrence gently lifted his conquered king, held it aloft for a moment in long, slender fingers, then gently laid the piece on its side. He sat back in his chair, his fingers lightly touching his pursed lips.

The firelight danced about us, casting fanciful shadows and shifts of light over his face. Finally he said in a slow, thoughtful voice, "A well-played game, my dear. Victory tastes sweet, does it not?"

I turned my head slightly, so that my face was in the shadows. I felt tense, afraid, and excited. "Of a certainty it does, my lord. Could victory ever taste otherwise?"

The oddest smile flitted across his face as he said, "No, there is nothing like it—to see, to feel, to deal the final blow to one's enemy. But do you not agree that the most important of victories, the sweetest by far, is the final and ultimate victory, the total devastation of the adversary?"

What was he talking about? What did he mean? I could not ask. I could not risk exposing what I knew. Ah, but I had just beat him.

I had beat him, I had beat him.

I was brilliant, I was strong, and so I said in a clear, overloud voice. "Yes, and that is exactly what I just did to you, sir. However, tomorrow is another day, perhaps even another game of chess, and then it begins all over again. In chess there is no ultimate victory. It is a good thing, but perhaps it is also a very disappointing thing."

Lawrence began to gather the chess pieces into the center of the table. He righted his fallen king and placed it in front of the white pieces, on the square directly opposite my black queen. He looked up into my face, his eyes narrowed and grim, the blue so dark as to be nearly black. I forced myself to look back at him steadily. It was he who looked away first, into the fire, and then down at his shapely white hands. I sat perfectly still, and waited. I had no choice at all. When he finally spoke, his voice was soft, almost pensive. "You played with intelligence, finesse, and yes, courage, Andrea. Most unusual characteristics for a woman. As to your intemperance just now, perhaps in the glow of your small victory, I should let you revel in it, even if it will only last for a very short time."

He was a different man now. Perhaps he was finally the man he truly was. "I was not aware, my lord, that men were the sole proprietors of intelligence and courage."

He kept playing with his damned white king, turning it between his long fingers. I wanted to throw the board at him. Then he sighed. "Ah, my dear, there you are wrong, and I think that you must perforce bow to my superior years of experience in the matter."

"I don't see why."

He stiffened. He was focused directly on me now. His eyes were cold, hard, utterly without feeling or compassion. His voice was as cold as his eyes now, and cutting, like a rapier through the silent air, "Oh, yes, your sex is weak, vain, and totally lacking in moral character. You are no different."

Still I could not see through this morass of anger in him, but I did realize that it had to do with a woman. I stood and leaned over the table toward him, my palms flat on the chessboard. My own voice matched his now, and I felt the harshness of my voice to my very soul. "Those are words of a bitter man, my lord, words that lack both measure and a balanced judgment. No, my lord, even your immense number of years, all your endless supply of experiences, none of it can justify such an unbalanced, even an unstable opinion."

He jerked forward in one swift movement, grabbed my wrist, and pulled me toward him across the table, so that my face was very close to his. I heard chess pieces roll on the wooden floor. "Brave words, my girl, but words without substance, without meaning. Ah, yes, you silly creature, you can taste fleeting victory at a game of chess, for you were well taught. But in life, Andrea, in life you have been but an insignificant pawn in a game of my own making. And now I have what I want, my girl. I no longer need you. I no longer need to pander to your foolish whims and laugh at your outlandish attempts at humor."

"I do not understand you. What are you talking about? What do you mean?"

His grip tightened. Pain shot up my arm, but I made no sound.

"You are mad."

"Mad, am I? We shall see."

I looked into his eyes then. I saw no madness there. He looked as cold as my grandfather's flesh had felt when I had given him a final good-bye. He looked deadly and calmly furious. I wondered if he was going to kill me, right here, right now.

Chapter Twenty-seven

Abruptly he released my wrist, and in one swift motion, closed his long fingers around my throat. I instinctively grabbed at his hands to free myself, but his hold tightened inexorably. "You shall see, my dear, that you are quite helpless. And never forget, will you, that you belong to me. You are my new, my very pretty young wife. And what does that mean? It means you are naught but my chattel—to do with as I choose."

His fingers tightened. I was scratching at his hands, pulling at his hands with all my strength. I was becoming light-headed. Was he going to kill me, right here in his library?

Would he simply shove my body beneath his desk?

Suddenly, he jerked his hands away from my neck. He quickly moved around to my side of the small table, and in the next instant, while I was still trying to suck in air, he pulled me against him. I felt his hot breath upon my face. "My beautiful young wife," he said, and kissed me so hard, so roughly, that I tasted blood in my mouth. I felt more rage than fear, at least for the moment, and I kicked him in the shin even as I struggled. He wrapped his arms more tightly around me, pinning my own arms to my sides, and continued to grind his mouth against mine. I felt his teeth, felt his hot breath in my mouth. Then my mouth was open, and I felt his tongue against my teeth, and I tasted that hot breath of his and nearly gagged. I knew he must have tasted my blood.

Abruptly he flung me back, away from him. I would have gone sprawling to the floor had my chair not been directly behind me. He knocked away the chess table with his fist. Chess pieces went flying. One pawn rolled into the fireplace. He stood over me with his legs spread and his hands on his hips.

"Can you breathe again?"

"Yes, no thanks to you. Don't touch me again. You swore you would not, ever."

"I can do exactly what I wish to do with you, my dear wife. Anything at all."

And I said, unwisely, "You are really quite mad, are you not? You are also repellent, my lord. If you touch me again, I will probably vomit on you."

I thought that he would strike me, his rage so great his face turned scarlet. But he kept his control. He just stood there, staring down at me for the longest time. Then he said in a soft meditative voice, "Of course you have no notion of how to kiss a man. You are completely innocent and have a young girl's natural apprehension. But I liked the taste of you. It was the taste of fear, I know that, but perhaps within moments it would have changed, and you would have opened your mouth to me, and welcomed me."

"No."

"How strange that I have never before noticed that you are really a remarkably lovely girl. I noticed, but not in the way a man usually notices a woman. But now I do." And he reached out his hand toward me.

"No," I whispered, and pressed myself as far back into the chair cushions as I could. "No."

He stood straight now, his arms crossed over his chest. He was directly in front of me. I didn't know how I could get around him. I couldn't very well knock him over, he was twice my size. He said, "I have decided to take you, Andrea, as a man takes a woman. You are a virgin. I have not enjoyed a virgin in a great number of years. It will be exciting. I won't mind you fighting me, but not all that much. Just a bit to give excitement to the taming. Since you are my wife, you must obey me. Ah, to have your virgin's blood on me, to feel my seed deep inside you. I will enjoy that. I will be the only man ever to have you."

"No." I felt nausea stirring deep in my belly. But why? I was afraid and very angry, but this debilitating nausea? It didn't make sense. Then I heard myself say in a pathetic, shaking voice I knew had to be mine, "You cannot mean that. You promised. You signed your promise in the marriage contract. You are my husband in name only.

You won't touch me. You won't, or I will kill you." I felt the acrid taste of hysteria in my mouth, in my throat, and I hated it.

"You kill me? Now, that is one of the most amusing things you have said to me since I met you." He shrugged. "As to the marriage contract-—what nonsense, all those silly promises to you. What can that possibly have to do with my wishes now? It is just a worthless piece of paper, designed merely to calm your anxieties, so that, my dear, you would consent to this marriage. And of course you did consent. You were quite willing to have a supposedly harmless older man take care of you after your grandfather died.

"Just look at you, white, trembling, your eyes so afraid they're showing black in the candlelight. Listen to me, Andrea. All women are whores at heart. You cannot be that unlike the rest of your sex. You just need a bit of practice, some experience, which I will give you, to learn about your true nature."

"No, not all women are whores, that is ridiculous. My mother wasn't a whore. No, it was my father." The instant the words were out of my mouth, I no longer saw Lawrence's face staring down at me, so close really, but I no longer saw him. He simply faded into nothingness.

I was shaking my head, violently, and the words just erupted from my mouth. "No, I don't want to go back there." But I didn't have any choice. I was warding all the blackness away with my hands, but it didn't stop the images that were now alive in my mind, a child's mind. It was like yesterday, so very close to me, beside me, at last finally inside me, and I couldn't escape it. I had tried to forget, but of course I hadn't. I was there once again, and it was perfectly clear. I saw myself as a child of eight, curled up on a window seat behind heavy curtains in my father's study. I was dozing over the book I had pulled down from one of the shelves. I was awakened suddenly by low hearty laughter followed by some very odd sounds. I looked out around the curtains. There stood my father and a parlor maid, and they were tightly pressed against each other. They were kissing each other frantically, wildly, he pulling at the cap that sat atop her hair, his fingers streaking through the thick curls, and he was moaning and so was she, and arching up against him, strange keening sounds coming from her throat.

I didn't know what to do, and so I stayed quiet and just stared at them. He lifted her and tossed her down to the soft Turkey carpet, lowering himself over her. I saw him pulling at her gown, tossing her petticoats up until they frothed around her face. Her hands were on his shoulders, kneading him and pulling at his clothes. She was moaning as his hands slid up under her petticoats. Her legs came apart, her knees spread wide, and I watched my father pull back. He pulled apart the buttons of his britches and pulled out this immense hard shaft of flesh that was attached to him. And then he shoved it between her legs. I saw her legs go up and clasp him around his hips. They were kissing and rocking back and forth and crying and moaning, like animals, like animals, and they didn't stop, stop, stop.

My mother's pale face appeared before my eyes. She was strangely silent, dark shadows scored the delicate flesh beneath her eyes. She was staring at my father, and I heard her scream at him of his lechery, his unfaithfulness, and it shamed her to her soul. I felt her hatred of him and of Molly, the maid who had let him throw her skirts around her face and stick himself inside her.

And she was screaming of other women and what he had done, and her humiliation and pain. But he didn't care. He just looked at her, then turned and walked away.

Suddenly, my mother's face faded away, and I saw Molly's face, heard her dreadful screams. I knew then that I was in the servants' quarters on the third floor, and it was hot up there, the heat of mid-summer rising to blanket these attic rooms. She was screaming, and she simply didn't stop. Scream upon scream, and then, suddenly, she was silent. I heard people talking. She screamed again, but not as loud this time, and I knew she was exhausted. I saw her gross belly, naked now, saw her back arch up and her face distort with agony. They pulled a small, limp, bloody object from between her legs. Then there was blood, fountains of gushing, spurting blood, covering Molly's legs, flowing onto the bed, dripping onto the wooden floor. My fingers were sticky red, the blood all over me, covering my clothing. Now they were screaming, rushing frantically, stuffing sheets between Molly's legs.

But Molly wasn't screaming anymore. Her head lolled to the side. Her eyes were wide and blue, and there was no life at all in them now.

The blood, so much blood, and it was dripping silently to the floor, a red pool that was now turning black. There was my mother, my beautiful mother, just standing there, her hands at her sides. She was so stiff, so cold to the touch, so white.

And I heard her whisper, "He killed her. He killed Molly as well. How many other women has he killed with his lust? He is an animal. I had hoped he would die, but he didn't. He won't ever die, ever."

Lawrence jerked me upright and shook me, nearly shouting in my face, "For God's sake, get a grip on yourself. You're damned hysterical. Snap out of it."

I opened my eyes, and I was back here, alone with this man in the library, and he was shaking me. I looked up into my husband's face. I felt battered, ripped apart inside, and terribly, terribly alone. But he was here, and he was going to hurt me, perhaps kill me, as my father had killed Molly.

His eyes were intent as he looked down at me. I was trembling, I knew that, but I couldn't stop it. "How I wish I had never seen any of it, never known any of it," I said.

He let me go. I stepped away from him. I rubbed the palm of my hand across my forehead. Was I trying to rub away those dreadful memories? Memories that I hadn't seen or felt so clearly in more years than I could count.

The silence was deep, endless, but it did not really matter, for I was trying to vanquish my own personal nightmare, and the coldness of the silence, the menace of it, didn't really touch me.

I heard his voice over the snapping and soft explosions of the burning logs in the fireplace. "Perhaps now I understand why you married me, Andrea. You thought I would take your grandfather's place, did you not? That I would protect you and keep you safe from your own fears, those horrible nightmares and visions from the past that still come to you as they did just now? No, there is no place for a lusty young husband in your plans, is there?"

I saw John laughing, stroking his large hand over Small Bess's mane. John, holding George, again laughing at something I had said, and I had loved his laugh, felt it to my very soul. John, angry now, that surge of violence stark in his dark eyes, angry because

I was his uncle's wife and couldn't ever be his. A knife turned in my heart.

Slowly, I shook my head.

"Would you like to tell me what your father did? What you saw him do? What you heard about him?"

"My father," I said slowly. "My father. What do you know of him? What has he to do with this madness?"

"It is really of no importance, not now. You will learn that I know more of your past than you realize."

He leaned down over me, his face close to mine. He must have seen the soul-shattering fear in me, because he straightened and laughed. It wasn't a nice laugh; it made my heart shrink. "Ah, don't worry that I will rape you. I haven't the time, truth be told. I would like to take your virginity, but it isn't meant to be. It is a pity."

"Why did you marry me?"

He pulled his chair close to mine and sat down, his arms folded across his chest. I had no clue what he was thinking, what he was planning, but I knew it wasn't good. I needed him to talk. I needed time. John would come, surely. No, he was with Lady Elizabeth. He had left me. I knew I shouldn't be surprised, for men were never honest with women, but I was still devastated that he was gone. Knowing what he knew of my danger, he had still left.

"You really were quite stupid in your search of my rooms."

Searching his room? Well, damn. How could he have known? Still, down deep, I wasn't surprised that he knew. I watched as he reached into the pocket of his waistcoat and pulled out a letter, its edges crumpled. He held it up for me to see. "What happened? You read all my letters, and this particular one really annoyed you, and so you nearly destroyed it? You were not very accomplished in your searching methods. You couldn't even manage to smooth out the envelope well enough for me not to notice. Also, I smelled your scent, light and soft and really quite distinctive. I breathed in, and I knew you had come into my very private room."

I gave him a shrug. "That envelope you're waving at me—it looks like a very old letter, my lord, a letter that one would have written a very long time ago, perhaps a time when even you were young."

I thought he would strike me, but he didn't.

"Your endless impertinence—you are arrogant, my girl, but in the end, you proved yourself quite an unworthy opponent—stupid really. Do you want me to hit you? No, probably not." He began folding and refolding that old letter between his long fingers.

I said, "You stole the letter from my father."

"Oh, yes. Actually it was Flynt. That damned miserable dog of yours nearly took his leg off. He wanted to kill the little beast, but he couldn't. I had been told that you had received a letter. It wasn't difficult to find. And you, my dear, know that your father was in London on the eighth of this month."

"Tell me why you have done this. Tell me what my father has done. Damn you, what have I done? Is it not my right to know?"

"You have no rights. But, you will find out everything in good time."

He stood up. "Now, enough of this. I really have no more time to waste on you." He paused a moment and looked at the strewn chess pieces on the floor. "I cannot believe that you managed to win a second game from me."

"It wasn't difficult. You play well enough, but your level of play cannot match mine.

Take your attempts at strategy—they are as commonplace as the time-worn strategies the old men use who play in Hyde Park. As for your attempts at logic and planning, I had but to invite you, and every time you leapt to take my bait. It is you who are the un-worthy opponent."

He struck me then, hard, his palm flat against my cheek. I didn't make a sound. I leapt up at him, brought my knee up, and got him squarely in the groin. He howled and stumbled back away from me, holding him-self, moaning, bent nearly double. I picked up my skirts and ran. But he was on me, still bent over like an old man, which he was. He was strong, and he held my arm, twisting it until I was moaning with the pain of it. I tried to jerk away from him, but each time I moved, he just twisted my arm higher be-hind my back. Finally, he was able to straighten.

"You damned bitch." He slapped me again, hard, on the other cheek. I would have slammed against the wall if he hadn't been holding me up. He jerked me against him. "Listen to me, you try to hurt me again, and I'll strangle you, right here, right now. It won't make all that much difference. Now,

you and I are going to walk up to your bedchamber. You will say nothing. You won't try
to get away from me. If you do, I will simply
tell everyone you have succumbed to the illness that destroyed my poor Caroline. Keep
your mouth shut. Think of that dog of yours,
think of Flynt picking him up by his neck and
wringing it off."

"Bastard."

"Yes, now you understand."

There were no servants in evidence. I had
prayed to see Brantley, at least, but the Old
Hall was empty. As we neared The Blue
Room, Lawrence said, "I have dismissed
Belinda. She should be at her mother's
house in the village by now. However,
George is in your bedchamber. You and he
will wait for me. I will come to you later,
never fear."

He opened the door, shoved me in, then
slammed the door in my face. I heard the
key grate in the lock.

Chapter Twenty-eight

The bitter winter wind burned my face and tore at my woolen cap. I leaned close to Tempest's neck to suck in the warmth of his steaming mane. His breathing was becoming labored, his flanks lathered. I slowed him. I didn't want him to collapse. John wouldn't be happy if I rode his prized stallion into the ground. John. No, I wouldn't think about him. I felt George moving about inside my cloak, his little head right beneath my heart. Every once in a while, he licked me, and my shirt was wet in that spot. I prayed he wasn't too cold.

I guided Tempest off the road, into a

copse of pine and maple trees, slid from his back, and pulled the reins over his head. He tossed his head, flecks of foam whirling from his mouth onto my gloves. The trees provided some protection from the vicious wind. I had no choice but to put George on the ground, telling him to stay close. He whimpered and pressed himself against my leg. "It will be all right," I told him. "Just give me a minute." I rubbed down Tempest with his own saddle blanket, then I spread it over him again to protect him as best I could from the wind that sliced through the naked tree branches. I petted his neck and pressed myself against his head. "Thank you, Tempest. John was wrong. You wouldn't throw me and George into a ditch. You are going to save our lives. My only question is, though, why didn't John take you with him to his damned Christmas party with Lady Elizabeth? I nearly fell over my feet when I saw you in the stables."

He nickered softly, butted his head against my shoulder.

The wind billowed my cloak as I walked slowly back to the main road and peered intently in the direction we had come. The pale slice of winter moon glittered down on the empty expanse of road. A lone owl hooted on an oak limb now ten feet away from me as I sank down to my knees in the bushes near Tempest and pressed against the naked branches for warmth. A pain shot through my ankle. I sat back quickly, pulled my legs from beneath me, and began to massage my ankle as best I could through my boot. If only I had been luckier it wouldn't have happened. But I was carrying George belted against my middle and couldn't very well use my dog to break my fall.

I looked up at that small bit of a moon, so stark and white overhead. I patted George's silky topknot, and I remembered how such a short time before I had stood in the middle of my bedchamber, staring at the locked door, listening to Lawrence's retreating foot-steps.

George had bounded to his feet and run toward me. I caught him up and hugged him tight. "We have a problem, my sweet Georgie. A very big problem, but at least that madman has left us alone for a while, and that means, George, that you and I are going to leave this place, somehow."

Of course I knew what I had to do. I didn't waste time pulling at the doorknob or pounding on the door of my bedchamber. I was sure that no one was anywhere close enough to hear me. No, it was going to have to be the window for George and me, and a nice scary climb down to the frozen ground. Then I had to steal a horse. Well, not Small Bess, her back and hock weren't well enough yet. I would see what horses remained in the stables.

"Come, George, let's see what we've got here." I carried him to the windows. I pulled back the heavy curtains, and looked out into the darkness. It looked very very cold out there, a small sliver of hard white moon shining brightly. The drop to the ground was too great a distance, and the outer walls seemed sheer. The bitter wind stung my eyes as my fingers probed along the casement. I knew there was a ledge. Caroline had climbed out on it, walking along it until she had managed to get into another chamber. It had to be wide enough. But I would be carrying George. It would be tricky.

I jerked up. Tempest was snorting, pawing the ground. I got to my feet, trying to ignore the sprain in my ankle, and crept to the road, George held beneath my cloak. I stood listening, but I didn't hear anything.

I waited for five minutes, then went back to Tempest. He seemed rested, his breathing even, his body tense and ready. As I quickly smoothed the blanket and hauled the saddle back onto his back, I wondered whether Lawrence had discovered my escape and was now, even at this very moment, riding hard after me, that wretched valet of his on his heels. Tempest must have felt my urgency because he twisted his great head around and whinnied softly. Finally, saddle in place, I grasped the pommel and pulled myself up on his back. We regained the main road, and Tempest, with no encouragement from me, broke into a steady, long-strided gallop. I leaned down again and rubbed my ankle, thankful that I had escaped with such a slight injury. It could have been much worse. I had certainly believed it would be.

The ledge was narrow, dangerously narrow. I had pulled back into the room and looked down at my heavy velvet gown. A dress would never do. If I had to walk on that narrow ledge carrying George and keeping my balance, I had to get rid of the ridiculous skirts. I found my boy's britches tucked away in the bottom drawer of the huge armoire. I had last worn them two years before, in Yorkshire, at Grandfather's country estate, Deerfield Hall. What better disguise than to travel as a boy, safe from curious eyes. Deerfield Hall was my destination tonight. I figured it would only take me three or four hours to ride there, perhaps longer if I had to hide. No matter, I could manage it. I quickly changed. I was fastening my cloak when I realized that I didn't have any money. I found only a few odd shillings in my drawer. I grabbed a handful of jewelry and stuffed it all into one of the pockets of my cloak. I pulled my derringer from beneath my pillow and carefully slipped it inside my britches. "Well, George, are you ready to hold tight to me while I try to keep my balance?" And with those words, George wuffed and jumped up on his hind feet, waving his front paws at me, ready for me to pick him up. I looked at the lovely ormolu clock on the mantel before I opened the window. It was nearly three o'clock in the morning. No wonder there hadn't been any servants about when Lawrence had forced me up here. They had been in bed for hours. I just hadn't realized how very late it was.

I swear that stepping out on that ledge required more guts than anything else in my life. I had this feeling that there were a lot more bad things out there, waiting for me. I looked at that ledge. I didn't want to set a single foot on it. I was afraid for both myself and for George, but there was simply no choice. I wasn't about to just sit in that bed-chamber and wait for Lawrence to come and strangle me at his leisure. The thought of Flynt strangling George made me hurry. I would make my way to the ground. There was simply no other choice. I stepped onto the ledge and steadied myself, gripping the open window frame. I took a deep breath, pressed hard against the stone, and focused my eyes on the narrow ledge in front of me. "Don't let yourself get excited by anything, George. What you hear is just the wind, no banshees or demons from the Black Chamber. It's just you and me, and we're going to get away from here. You just keep yourself very quiet, all right?"

I heard a soft wuff.

My gloved hands clung tightly to the rough edges of the stone as, inch by inch, I slid my feet toward the corner. Strange thing was that I was sweating, in this blistering cold weather, I was sweating.

Where had Caroline climbed back into the Manor?

I gained the corner and pulled myself around it slowly, only to discover that the ledge ended abruptly. In its place stood the jutting outline of a massive chimney. To my unbounded relief, the stones were set at angles, and staggered, protruding so I could fit my hands and feet on them. I didn't have big hands or feet; surely I could get a firm grip on the stones so I could climb down. "George," I said as I eased him out of my cloak. "I need both hands. You will have to keep yourself very still. I'm going to stick you inside my breeches and belt you in." And that's what I did. I probably looked like a pregnant woman.

"Hang on, George. We're off."

I swung my legs off the ledge, and for one long moment I dangled in midair until my feet found furrowed edges for support. I felt George stiffen against me. I hope he was praying as hard as I was.

My climb down was painfully slow. Several times I hung by my hands as I felt around the stones to find a foothold. Suddenly, as I loosed my grip to find another hold, the stone crumbled beneath my feet and I went down hard, all the way to the ground. Thank God it wasn't all that far, only about six feet. My legs twisted under me as I fell sprawling on my side. I lay still for a moment as a stabbing pain shot up my leg. I prayed that my leg wasn't broken. I rose slowly, flexed the leg, and discovered that it was fine but that I had wrenched my ankle. Thank God I hadn't landed on George. I quickly unbelted George and pulled him out. I told him he was the most splendid dog in the western world. As I stood there, sending thanks heavenward that I was still alive, I realized that Caroline hadn't climbed from the ledge back through a window into another room. There weren't any more chambers between The Blue Room and the chimney. I wasn't wrong. Lawrence had told me that Caroline had climbed out the window, walked along the ledge, and let herself into another room. He had lied. Well, why should I be so surprised? He had lied about everything else.

"I'm an idiot, George." And I thought: what really happened to you, Caroline?

I looked up. I had climbed down a good twenty feet. Not badly done.

Tempest snorted, snapped up his hind

legs to get my attention. I realized quickly that I was cold and my ankle hurt, but I was alive, and that was just fine indeed for the moment. I saw pinpoints of light in the distance. It was a village. I wondered if I dared risk riding into the village to trade Tempest for another mount. He was blowing hard again. I didn't want to kill him. No, I couldn't stop. I was still not far enough away from Devbridge Manor, and the Lyndhurst family was well-known in these parts. Would people recognize John's horse? If someone did recognize Tempest, then I could be taken for a thief. It would not take long for anyone with half an eye to realize I was a woman, that I was more than just a woman who was a thief, that I was the damned Countess of Devbridge. "Ah, you stole your step-nephew's horse because you are escaping from your husband who wants to strangle you? Perhaps you are just like the former poor countess who was stark-raving mad?"

I shuddered at that thought. No, it was not worth the risk to stop at this village. I would simply have to ride Tempest to the next village or a farmhouse.

I slowed Tempest, looking about for the best route to skirt the village. There was an open field just to my right. Tempest sailed over the low fence. George barked all the while we were in midair. He liked to fly.

Once beyond the village, I brought Tempest back onto the main road. The long ride continued, the silence broken only by an occasional muffled wuff from George and by the steady pounding of Tempest's hooves. I slowed him to a walk. I wasn't about to kill this wonderful animal. Time dragged on. The cold settled into my bones. My face was so cold I simply couldn't feel it anymore. Think about something else. And so I thought about what I was going to do and decided I would remain at Deerfield Hall until Peter came. The servants would hide me, lie for me, if Lawrence came to see if I was there. Once Peter was with me, he would know what to do. He would protect me from the madman I had married.

"I know, I know, to make a mistake as colossal as the one I made, requires a good deal of blindness and self-deception," I said to George, and petted his head through my cloak. He wuffed back. I knew he was probably agreeing with me.

Of course there had been no one to protect that poor stable lad, Billy, from me.

Thankfully, Rucker was asleep in his own bed and nowhere around. I would not have liked to tangle with Rucker. Billy was another matter entirely. He was young and slight, and I knew he would have a headache from the blow I gave him to the head, but he would be all right. I had tied him up and hidden him beneath a mound of hay. Taking Tempest had been easy, which was a good thing, because I was getting so scared I was beginning to stutter even when I spoke to George.

Suddenly, Tempest raised his head and stilled. Had a bird or an animal frightened him? He whinnied.

I jumped off his back, nearly fell to my knees because my legs were so stiff and cold, and pulled him to the side of the road. I clamped my fingers down on his nostrils. I could not let him whinny again. The two of us remained motionless in tense silence, waiting. I could feel George's cold nose, now wet through my shirt.

I felt the ground shake beneath my feet. Horses were coming. I felt them even before I heard them. There were several riders, perhaps three, and they were coming closer. I pulled Tempest farther into the line of trees. They were mostly maple trees, and all bare and thinned here, which wasn't fair, but it couldn't be helped. I clutched Tempest's nostrils more firmly.

The horses slowed not thirty feet away from me. I could hear the men's voices. Oh, no, they must have heard Tempest's first whinny. I clung to him, feeling him shudder, but he held still, bless him.

"I tell you," a man shouted into that cold still air, "I know that bloody horse can't be far. He's fast, and he's got endurance—he's a war-horse. But even he must be flagging by now."

No, you're utterly wrong, I thought. Tempest is beyond any horse you know about. He could fly all the way to London without slowing or tiring. Why don't you just keep hunting, tracking. Go, go, go. I said it over and over to myself, a litany, a prayer. Yes, just keep going. We're not here. There's nothing for you here, keep going.

"You're right. She can't have gotten farther than this. John's horse is fast, but even he must tire, and by now, he must be nearly dead." It was Lawrence, my dear husband. Oh, God, it wasn't fair. Too close, he and his men were too close. What to do?

"She is close by, I feel it." Again, it was my husband. "I would swear that I heard a horse whinny. It was close by, I know it." I heard another man grunt, but he didn't add his opinion. They were coming ever closer. Any minute now one of them would see us and then it would be all over.

It wasn't Tempest who gave us away. It was George. He didn't know what was happening, and so he scratched at my chest and wuffed loudly. Not that it would have mattered. They would have found us, impossible not to.

No choice, I thought, tightened my belt more firmly around George, grabbed the saddle horn, and climbed up into the saddle. We shot from the trees onto the road like a cannonball.

It was a desperate chase, but I knew that I had no chance. Tempest was heaving beneath me. It was too much for him, he was slowing. Tears of sheer frustration slid down my face, nearly freezing by the time they dripped off my chin. I looked over my shoulder once and could make out my husband's grim face in the pale predawn light. I was fairly choking with fear.

But a moment later a horse was beside

me. A man leaned over and grabbed me around my waist. George howled, and the man fell back in his surprise.

"It's a damned dog," the man shouted. "She's got him inside her cloak."

I heard the men shouting to each other. Soon, too soon, the man was back, and this time, he grabbed Tempest's reins, jerking them out of my hands. Slowly, the man pulled him up. Then Lawrence was on the other side of me. He backhanded me, knocking me off Tempest's back. I grabbed George and managed to pull him free before I hit the frozen ground. I didn't land on him, thank God.

The breath was knocked out of me. I lay there, looking up in that cold gray light of dawn, trying to suck in some air. George was barking wildly, flying around me in circles, trying to protect me. Then he whimpered and climbed on top of me. I saw Flynt's face above me.

"She's alive, my lord," Flynt said to Lawrence, who was standing right there beside him and could plainly see for himself that I was alive. "Just knocked herself silly, that's all. The dog is all right, finally shut his yap. Just look at it—sitting on her chest and licking her face. You want me to kill it? I hoped when you knocked her off the horse, she'd land on the cur and kill it."

If I could have drawn a breath at that instant, I would have told him what I thought of him. But I couldn't do anything, just lie there, wondering if air would ever come into my body again.

"No, leave her something," Lawrence said, "although she doesn't deserve any kindness from me. I believe she turned into more of an annoyance than she was worth. Yes, leave her that miserable little cur. The good Lord knows she loves the animal more than she loves any human being."

"Ain't right to love a mutt that much," Flynt said and spat, missing my face by perhaps two inches.

"She has nothing else," Lawrence said, and I hated him more in that moment than I had ever hated another human being in my life, because he was right.

Lawrence stood over me now, the wind whipping the cloak about him. He was smiling as he said in such a lovely kind voice, "Don't fight me, now, madam, or I will simply let Flynt kill the dog. Do you understand me?"

"Yes," I said, sucking in great mouthfuls of air. "I understand." His smooth voice had scared me more than being knocked off Tempest's back.

"You have been a nuisance," he said. "You have caused me difficulties. You have wasted my time. No more. Get up now. We have a distance to go."

No one helped me. I managed to turn over and come up on my hands and knees, then slowly, I managed to stand. I hugged George against me. My derringer, I thought, was tucked still snug against my waist, but I had to wait to use it. It held only one bullet, just one.

It had taken them hours to track me down. They had caught me because their horses were fresh. They must have changed them in the village. If only I had dared the risk, I might still be free.

My husband looked as dark as the devil, standing there in front of me, wrapped in a black cloak, black gloves on his hands. "I underestimated you, Andrea. No, I won't call you Andy anymore—a ridiculous name. I had to pretend to enjoy that affectation to keep you trusting and content. You might even have escaped had I not decided to drug you. Perhaps a servant would have walked past your bedchamber and heard you yelling or perhaps hitting a chair against the door. Yes, I realized that you wouldn't just stay quiet in there, waiting for me to come back for you. I was bringing a nice drug to pour down your throat. I was quite surprised to walk in to a very cold, very empty, room. It was frigid, really, since you had left the window wide open. I would have killed you had I caught you then. But I didn't, lucky for you. I am calm now, and I have you again, and now it is all over."

I stood there, breathing easily again, staring up at the man I had trusted, the man whose affection for me I had believed was deep and abiding, at least at first, at least before that old woman had appeared in my bedchamber with a knife raised. Lies, all of it lies, a ruse. But to gain him what?

"What happens now, my lord—will you take me back and lock me in The Blue Room? Will you bar the windows again as you barred them for Caroline?"

The wind swirled his cloak around his boots. "Do be quiet, you stupid girl. You don't know what you're talking about."

"Don't I? I know that you lied to me. Caroline did not walk that ledge into another room that was unlocked so she could make her way to the north tower. There is no other room before the ledge stops at the chimney. What did you do to Caroline?" But of course I knew. He had killed her. He had thrown her from that balcony so high above the flagstone walkway below. He knew exactly what I was thinking. I could see it on his face. And so, because it didn't matter, I said, "You forced her to the north tower, and you hurled her from the balcony, didn't you?"

He drew back his arm. I saw his black-gloved fist. I saw the rage on his face, the venom in his eyes, and knew I should have kept quiet. I knew he would hit me hard, perhaps break my jaw.

No time, no time to save myself.

Chapter Twenty-nine

Flynt's shout cut through the air. "My lord. Best not to hit her. You just might kill her by accident. It's too soon. Not yet."

Lawrence slowly drew back his fist. Instead of striking me, he took my arm and twisted it up behind me until I couldn't suppress the hiss of pain in my throat.

"Do not provoke me again, madam."

He released my arm and gave me a shove. I was off balance. I fell, landing at Flynt's feet.

"Just look at what she has done to John's horse," Lawrence said. "She's ridden him into the ground, the bitch."

I was on my feet again, not to try to run because I knew I wouldn't get far, what with Flynt right at my elbow. I hated him with every fiber of my being. "Listen to me, old man. You would have ridden him into the ground as well, were you trying to escape a madman."

Again, he looked like he wanted to kill me right there, but he didn't. Why was I baiting him? Why couldn't I simply keep my mouth shut? But I knew why. This man had drawn me in so very smoothly, had gained my trust so quickly, had made an utter fool of me. I hated myself as much as I hated him for doing that to me, so easily, so very easily. He had guessed what I needed and provided it. He had realized that I wanted no husband in my bed, and thus, he had simply sworn it would be a marriage in name only. He was courtly and glib, this man, and he'd had me eating out of his hand within a week of our meeting. God, I hated him, hated him.

But what did he want?

A sudden wave of dizziness struck hard. One too many blows, I thought as I went down on my knees. I kept my head down, panting hard, trying to get my balance back. The third man, who hadn't said a word until now, stepped over to me. I stayed there, rubbing my forearm. George was pressed against my side.

The man knelt down next to me. "Are you all right? Can you stand?"

I recognized his voice. It was the man who had been at the inn when Lawrence and I had stayed on our trip from London to Yorkshire. He was simply another of Lawrence's henchmen. I managed to nod. He helped me stand. Then he picked up George and silently handed him to me. Thank God the dizziness had lessened.

Lawrence stepped back to me.

I looked him straight in the eyes. "Where are we going now?"

"That you will find out soon enough. Keep quiet. Freeson, toss her up on Tempest's back. You don't have to tie her hands to the pommel. You will take her dog up with you. If she does anything ill-advised, you will kill the damned dog."

"I have never done anything to harm you, Lawrence," I said, wondering who this man really was that I had married. He was so filled with rage, with contempt for me. It made no sense.

"You have thwarted me, madam, and you

have meddled. You found out things you shouldn't have. I will tolerate no more from you. You have done things that I did not believe anyone would do, much less a supposedly innocent young lady."

I had no idea what he was talking about. Surely thwarting didn't include looking through the desk in his monk's cell. "Why did you place the barbed circle of wire beneath Small Bess's saddle?"

He said with sublime indifference, "It served its purpose. You knew someone there wanted you dead—"

"Wanted me to pay for all of it."

"Yes, that is what I wanted. A nice ambiguous threat, wasn't it? I also wanted you terrified, helpless, and you were. That pleased me enormously, watching the fear grow day by day in you. Had you been killed, it really wouldn't have mattered, but I will admit, I prefer having you with me right now, here, at the ending, the final victory, my sweet revenge." He didn't care that he could have killed Small Bess and that infuriated me more than anything. The fury filled me to overflowing. "I don't even know what you're talking about. You hurt Small Bess. You are really quite contemptible, you miserable old man." I knew it was a mistake, and yet I had still opened my damned mouth.

Freeson had wound rope around my hands. There was no way I could protect myself when the blow fell. Lawrence hit me with his fist against my head. The force of the blow sent me staggering against Freeson's chest. White lights exploded in my head. It was the strangest thing, all those white points of light that just burst one after another until, finally, the lights winked out and everything went mercifully black. I heard George barking wildly. Then I didn't hear anything at all.

I was aware of the horse's rhythmic motion before I fully regained consciousness. When I finally managed to force my eyes open, the world was spinning. Nausea flooded me. I was so dizzy that if Freeson hadn't been holding me, I would have fallen off the horse. I swallowed and closed my eyes tightly. I must have moved, for I heard Freeson's voice right behind my ear. "Please do not move, my lady. I will keep you steady."

I became aware that his arm was about me and that I sagged against his chest. "Where is George?"

"Flynt is carrying him. No, don't worry. He isn't abusing him."

"Who are you? What is happening here?"

"I cannot tell you. Hush, now."

I said nothing more. Words were beyond me. I concentrated on not vomiting on his horse. My head ached so badly from that madman's blow to my temple, I prayed my brains were still intact.

"Can you not tell me where we are going?"

"I cannot." He hesitated, then he leaned closer to me. "I tried to convince his lordship that his quarrel was not with you, but to no avail."

"Then, who is his quarrel with?"

He looked over at Lawrence, then ducked his head down. "It does not matter. I cannot tell you."

There was simply no one else, and so I said flatly, "With my father."

He took a sharp intake of breath. "Please, my lady, I cannot speak of this matter further. I cannot." So he was afraid of Lawrence, then? I didn't blame him. I was afraid of him, too.

We rode on in silence, Flynt and my husband some little distance ahead of us. There was no sun this morning. The sky was leaden, snow threatened. I thought dully that we must soon be nearing Devbridge Manor. My grand escape had gained me nothing. If he did take me back to the Manor, what would he tell the servants? Miss Crislock? What would he say to John, for God's sake? No, whatever he planned to do with me, he would not take me back to his own home to do it. It would be too great a risk for him.

I wasn't particularly surprised when our small cavalcade turned off the main road onto a rutted, narrow path not two miles west of the manor. I turned my head and looked at Freeson. He shook his head and looked resolutely ahead. Soon we came to a small cottage set in a clearing and surrounded by a forest of maple trees. Smoke gushed from the disreputable chimney. There was a single horse tethered to a tree beside the door.

Lawrence pulled back, then reined in beside us. "Ah, madam, I see that you are awake. It is good of you to oblige me in such good time." He sounded happy, so pleased with himself that I wouldn't have been surprised had he burst into song at any moment. He sounded, I thought, like he had just won a huge victory.

We pulled up in front of the cottage. Lawrence lifted me down and untied my hands. He had a firm hold on my left arm. I couldn't get free of him, he was just too strong.

"Steady, now, my dear, I would not want you to faint now, when I have such a surprise for you." He was so excited that his eyes glittered.

I said nothing, but I knew, oh, yes, I knew very well what his damned surprise was.

He gave me a puzzled look. "You are not stupid, I will say that for you. You read the letter in my desk. You know, do you not?"

I just shook my head, and kept quiet. He laughed, and waved Flynt to open the cottage door. Flynt dropped George to the ground. George wasted no time flying to me. I picked him up and held him close. Lawrence pushed me through the cottage door. It was very dim in there. There was one scarred table, that didn't look all that steady on its legs, several old chairs set around it, a poorly burning fire against the far wall, that was only about six feet distant from the door. Then I saw the single bed shoved against the far side of the cottage, nothing else, save a cracked chamber pot halfway under that ragged bed. There was a man lying on that bed. I could just make out his outline.

I had no doubt who it was.

My father.

I hadn't seen him for ten years. I had hoped he was dead. He deserved to be dead for what he had done, for what he was. But he wasn't dead. He was here. And I knew why he was here, why he had traveled here from Belgium. He had come to save me. From Lawrence.

I accepted this, but still, it made no sense. Why?

A rough-looking man I hadn't seen, stepped out of the dark shadows in the corner, and nodded to Lawrence. He was dressed in rugged wool homespuns. Dark stubble covered his cheeks.

"Has he given you any trouble?"

"Nay, my lord. Quiet he's been. His shoulder is still bleeding, but he's alive."

"Good," said my husband, and he smiled down at me.

I took a step toward that bed. I saw the man was half-covered with a filthy blanket.

Lawrence said, such pleasure, such antic-ipation in his voice, "Surely you don't want to be shy, now, do you? Go and greet him. Tell him how very much you have missed him. Hold him to you. Ask him why he left you so many years ago and never came back. Ah, you have so many things to say to him, do you not, madam?"

Lawrence pressed his hand against the small of my back and shoved me toward that bed.

My father stirred, moaned softly, and then pulled himself up painfully on one elbow. He stared at me. There was no recognition in his blue eyes—my blue eyes—just the dull glaze of pain.

I couldn't look away from him. My heart began to pound, strong deep strokes. I wanted to scream, to yell, and so I stuffed my fist in my mouth. Ten years faded away in but an instant of time, like a veil lifting from a familiar face. It was my father. I rec-ognized him immediately. He looked exactly the same as he had the last time I had seen him. Perhaps there was a bit of gray hair at his temples, but the rest of his hair was the thick reddish-brown I remembered. And the vivid blue of his eyes, the upward slant of his dark eyebrows that made him look curious and immensely interested, both at the same time. Nothing had changed. It was all the same. I would have thought after ten more years of living the way he had, that he would have looked depraved, utterly dissipated, but he didn't. He was very handsome. I saw that so clearly now as I hadn't when I was a little girl. Women would be drawn to him. He was propped up on his elbow now. He was also staring at me with still no recognition at all in his eyes. He had no idea who I was.

"Well, Jameson, see what I have brought you." Lawrence shoved me even closer to the man who lay there on the bed, just looking at me, his eyes vague, unknowing.

He frowned, but said nothing.

Lawrence shouted, "You damned fool, don't you recognize her?"

I suppose it was at that moment that Lawrence realized that my father was looking at a skinny boy in a long black cloak and tight-fitting cap, holding a terrier against his chest.

Lawrence tore the cap from my head, and my wildly curling hair spilled out over my shoulders and down my back.

My father gave a hoarse cry. "Andrea. Oh, no. Damn you to hell, Lyndhurst, you have brought her here. You bastard, you unspeakable bastard. I'll kill you for this." My father leapt at Lawrence, but Flynt and the man who had been here guarding my father, both jumped at him. They shoved him back down on the bed. His whole body seemed to hitch on the pain as he fell onto his back on the bed.

When he could speak over the pain, he said, "My poor child, you did not escape. I told you to leave him immediately, to return to London. Why did you stay? Did he keep you a prisoner?" His voice was hoarse and low. He was in pain, bad pain. It really didn't touch me as I just stood there looking at the man who was my father, the man I had hated for so very long, the man who had made my life a nightmare of bitter, emptying fear, and had made me a coward. John had been right. I had blanked out life, and it was all because of this man. I saw him reach out a hand to me. A strong hand, well shaped, steady. I didn't move.

I thought how very much alike we were. It was like looking in a mirror, seeing myself in another thirty or so years. My poor mother,

I looked not a bit like her. I heard myself say in a calm, very distant voice, "You wrote me a letter that made no sense at all. You wrote nothing of any real substance, just melodramatic drivel about being in danger. No, I am lying, and it is too late for deception of any kind now. I planned to leave very soon, but it wasn't just because of your warning letter. This monster terrorized me, and that is why I was going to leave. I just didn't realize that he was the one responsible for all of it until yesterday."

Lawrence tightened his grip on my arm. It hurt, but I kept quiet. "I, a monster? Look at him, my dear wife, that is the monster, and well you know it."

And then I really looked at the man who lay on that mean narrow bed, the man whose blood I carried, the man who had given me his features, the man who had come to England to rescue me, the man who, I realized finally, was in dreadful pain only because he had come to save me, and I whispered, "Father. You are hurt."

I saw the horrible stain-caked blood on his right shoulder, saw the raggedness of his clothes, the mud and the filth.

I made a move toward him, but my husband once again tightened his grip on my arm and held me still.

"Does this mean that you wish to forgive him for all he did to your mother? All that he did to you? Oh, I see the pity in your eyes for him. Don't worry, I placed the bullet well. He won't die just yet."

I began rhythmically petting George, who had pressed himself hard against my chest. I said to my husband, "What did he do to you that you have hurt him? That you lured him to England and shot him and made him a prisoner?"

Lawrence laughed. "Well, Jameson, do you want to tell her of your despicable lechery or shall I?"

My father said, "It does not concern her, Lyndhurst. Leave it between us, where it belongs."

"I don't think so, Jameson. After all, it was only through using her as delicious bait that I could get to you. Even then I wondered if you would come, if you had any feeling at all for her. How I prayed that you did. I decided the best way to get you back, probably the only sure way, was to marry her. Then you would accept that she was completely in my power. But I tell you, when I sent the announcements to every newspaper I could think of, I was praying that you would discover what I had done soon. If you had not, then I would have been stuck with her until I could think of something else. Ah, but you did read my beautifully phrased wedding announcement. You wrote her that letter to warn her, and then you came, her white knight to rescue her. But, of course, it didn't matter. I controlled everything. Yes, everything I planned has worked out perfectly. You, her, even my miserable nephew.

"Ah, my dear nephew John. Now, that was a treat. I watched him fall in love with her. Indeed, I believe my poor nephew fell in love with her even before I had arrived in London to woo her. But she was so damaged by you, made so wary of men by the example of your blatant lechery, that she saw my nephew as nothing more than a danger to her. When he smiled at her, even spoke to her, I'll wager she was terrified of him.

"I hadn't realized just how badly you had scarred her until I saw that my nephew did love her, that he had probably tried to attach her when he'd been in London. He is a soldier, well made, a handsome young man, and I, I had to admit, was older. Yet she chose me over him. He had failed with her. And I wondered why. Of course it was obvious to anyone who simply asked a few discreet questions. Of course, I knew exactly who to ask. And I knew for certain then that she was afraid of a young man because of what she had seen you do."

I turned slowly to look at him. All his words flowed over me and again, I saw fully my own blindness, my own inability to deal with what was real in my life and what wasn't real, what had haunted me, twisted me. He had known that John loved me? Ah, but what had he done to John? I said, "What do you mean you controlled John?"

He smiled down at me. He looked ready to rub his hands together, he was so pleased with himself. "I took care of John."

"He isn't at a Christmas house party with Lady Elizabeth, is he? That is why Tempest was in the stable. You have done something to him. My God, you killed him, didn't you? You murdered your own flesh and blood."

Chapter Thirty

That monster actually laughed. "Not yet. But soon, my dear, soon."

Something broke deep inside me, broke completely, irrevocably. I dropped George to the floor and lunged at my husband. I ripped off my gloves and went for his eyes, but he was simply too tall and I couldn't reach that far. I dug my fingernails into his cheeks. I felt his flesh shred, felt the wetness of his blood on my fingers. "Where is John, damn you? Where?"

He grabbed my wrists even as he yelled in pain. I had hurt him badly. It felt very good. I was panting hard, kicking at him, but my cloak wouldn't allow me to get in the vicious blows I wanted. Lawrence said to Flynt, "For God's sake, go get Major Lyndhurst from the shed. Leave Boynton there. Let the little bitch see that I haven't yet killed him. Also, why should he miss this wonderful exhibition? It is, after all, the conclusion to all my well-executed plans.

"Now, you will hold still, madam, or I will kill him and then I will kill that damned dog."

He released me and touched a handkerchief to his cheeks. "You will pay for that."

"Yes," I said. "You already told me that I would pay for all of it."

I leaned down and picked up George. I didn't say another word, just stood there, shaking with bone-deep rage, with frustration, looking at my father. There was only the deep harsh breathing of the men in the small cottage. I didn't think I was breathing. I was just standing there, frozen, Lawrence's blood on my hands, beneath my fingernails. My father lay still, making no sound at all. The fire hissed, sparks flying upward.

The cottage door opened again. I whirled around to see Flynt shove John into the room. His hands were tied behind his back. He was wearing only a white shirt, breeches, and his boots. He had to be freezing. The bastards. There were bruises on his face. He looked thinner, haggard. Black whiskers covered his cheeks. How long had they kept him here? But I knew. They had held him and Boynton for two days.

I wanted to run to him, but I knew better. I said very calmly, very slowly, holding myself perfectly still, "Are you all right, John?"

Amazingly, he smiled at me, his teeth very white in the dim light of the cottage. "I'm just fine, Andy. Just a bit on the cold side, but I'll survive. Boynton will survive, too. I wondered how long it would take for him to bring you here. I knew he would. I'm sorry I could not stop him. I tried, but I was just too late. He was waiting for me, his bully boys with him. Now, I believe that is your father lying on that bed?"

"Yes." George began to bark wildly. "No," I said, "John cannot hold you now. Remember Brantley's training. Just be patient, George."

Lawrence said, "If it makes your life mean a bit more, John, let me tell you that the little bitch here loves you. As much as you love her? That I don't know. But she tried to kill me when she heard I had taken you. Just look at what she did to my face."

"I wish she had managed to do more than just scratch you," John said. He looked at me, smiling very widely now. "Do you love me more than I love you, Andy? Do you think that is possible?"

I just stood there, frantically petting George's topknot.

"No," I said. "It is not possible."

He gave me a blazing smile then, but said nothing.

"She is only a small girl," Lawrence said, frowning at me, sounding a bit bewildered. "She managed to tear my skin with her fingernails. Ah, you can be certain that she will pay fully for that."

And I thought yet again of my derringer, pressed against my stomach. I wanted to shoot him so badly, I was shaking with it. I said to my husband, "You have gathered all your players. You used me as bait to get to my father. You now have both of us. You have even brought your own flesh and blood here. Don't John and I have a right to know what this is all about now?" Surely Lawrence wouldn't kill his own nephew, his heir?

Would he? No, it was too monstrous. That left my father and me.

"Well? Won't one of you tell me? Tell John?"

My father winced at the pain in his shoulder, then looked down at his hands. When he finally lifted his head, he looked directly at me, and I would have had to be blind not to see the absolute despair in his eyes.

He looked just beyond me, into the past, I thought. He said, "It was such a long time ago—" He broke off, shaken by a spasm of coughing. The room was still except for his racking cough.

He wiped his sleeve across his mouth, and then, slowly, he said, "I met Lady Caroline in Paris. She was at the time Lyndhurst's second wife."

Of course. Caroline. I suppose that I should have figured it out, but I hadn't. So obvious, really. My father liked women, they probably flocked to him, and he used them. Why not Caroline? My mouth was dry, so dry that I could hardly breathe. I petted George and felt John standing not three feet behind me, silent, but I knew he was thinking, trying to assess what he could do to save us.

"We became lovers. Andrea, listen to me. I loved her, and she loved me. Never have I loved a woman as I loved Caroline. You must try to understand that I could not help myself, nor could she. You must try to forgive me."

"Continue, Jameson," Lawrence said. "It is time she knew the whole truth about her father."

"I already know the whole truth," I said, but they both ignored me.

"Very well," my father said. "You shall hear it all. Lady Caroline became with child. I, of course, was married to your mother. Finally, both of us realized there was no choice. She would simply have to pass the child off as Lyndhurst's. It was then that she told me she had been traveling—without her husband—for nearly a month. She wasn't certain she could pass the child off as his, but she knew she had to try. What was a month, after all? Babes were born before their times quite often. But, still, we had to part. Both of us felt great despair."

I said, "Ah, yes, that sounds vastly romantic, Father. You killed Lady Caroline, just as you killed my mother, just as you killed Molly, the maid. Your excuses are pathetic, sir. Your lust is unspeakable."

"Who is Molly?"

I closed my eyes. "Dear God, you don't even remember her, do you? She was a maid in our household. She was the downstairs maid. You got her pregnant, and she died birthing your child, and you just walked away, damn you. You just left, probably whistling, probably on the hunt for your next conquest. She meant nothing to you. And my mother knew, she knew about Molly, all about your other women. There were so many, how could she not know? I remember her pleading with you, tears streaming down her face, her sobs that should have stopped you, yet there was nothing but your indifference."

"Andrea, for God's sake, you were only a child. You could not possibly have understood. You saw everything through a child's eyes. That is never what is real, what is true. Listen to me. Your mother—she tended toward hysteria, surely you realize that now. She saw everything as a slight to her, even the smallest word would make her cry and scream and lose her head completely. Beyond that, she was a cold woman. Oh, yes, she was beautiful, but she was cold. She didn't want me as a man needs to have a woman want him. She didn't want me to touch her, but more than that, she didn't want me to have any other woman.

"I was not a monk. I had to have companionship, share desire and passion with someone who cared about me. Your mother didn't. I was nothing more than a possession to her. I tell you, I had no choice but to find a small moment of pleasure, of peace, with other women. She gave me no other choice. She drove me away from her."

I said very calmly, looking directly at him, directly at his beautiful mouth that had just spouted so many lies about my mother, "All of what you said, it is nothing more than your weak excuses to justify what you did, and you know it. My mother loved you with all her heart. You hurt her, continually, without caring that you did. She told me. I was only a child, yet I actually held her while she cried whenever you went off to be with another woman. She was destroyed by your blatant disregard of her. You ended up killing her with your indifference. You were her life, yet she was nothing at all to you. You are as much of a monster as this ridiculous old man here."

To my surprise, he nodded. "You are right about a lot of it. I am trying to excuse myself."

Lawrence said, "You wondered, did you not, why he did not write you exactly why he was warning you to leave Devbridge Manor? Can you imagine him actually writing to you that he had taken another man's wife, gotten her with child, and then returned her to her husband? Can you ever think he would condemn himself like that? He didn't have the guts to write you the truth. Surely you see that now."

Yes, I did see it now. I heard John behind me. What was he thinking? There was dead silence in the room. I looked at my father, saw the red blood staining his once-white shirt. I saw the nearly uncontrollable pain in him, from the wound in his shoulder to the wounds I was inflicting on him. Damn him to hell, he deserved nothing from me, nothing but my contempt, my hatred. I stood rigid, lost for a long moment in the past, my mother's wan, tearful face passing before my eyes. Ten years ago—my mother was dead, buried, gone. Then, quite suddenly, a door closed in my mind. The past lay behind that door. There were no shadows, no bitter images or memories to slither through. No, there was nothing but clarity now. I felt as if I had just been lifted out of a pit. I felt light engulf me. I felt free. I felt whole. I looked into those brilliant blue eyes of his, the color, the shape, just like mine, and said, "Why did you leave me? Mother died, and I never saw you again. Why did you leave me alone?"

"Your grandfather gave me no choice. He had power, enough power to ensure that I could not come near you." He added in a voice full of bitterness and regret, "I was forced to leave, my child. Your grandfather would not allow me near you. I would have tried to see you after your grandfather's death, but a dear friend of mine was dying, and I could not leave her."

"Did you kill her, too, Jameson?"

"No, you bastard, I did not." He looked directly at me again. "You believe I wanted never to see you again, my only child? Oh, no, Andrea, I loved you. Not seeing you left emptiness in my heart."

I looked at this man who was my father, not all that good and honorable a man perhaps, not all that steady and reliable a man, but he was still my father, and he had tried to save me. He had stayed with a dying friend. I stretched out my hand toward him. I wanted to cry and hug him so tightly I would feel the essence of him deep inside me. I whispered, "Did you come to save me, Father?"

"Oh, yes," he said. "Oh, yes." He rose slowly to his feet. None of the men stopped him. He walked to me and took my hand in both of his. He petted George. George licked his hand. He smiled down at me. "You are still small. I wondered how tall you would grow." He lightly touched his fingers to my hair. "The color is incredible—so many different brilliant shades, not just the red or brown of mine. You are beautiful, Andrea. And I imagine that you are brave as well. You have become an admirable woman."

Lawrence did nothing at all, just stood there, watching us.

I saw my father weave where he stood. I walked with him back to that narrow bed and helped him sit down. "Tell me the rest now, Father. It seems that all three of us are in this situation together. You owe it to me, to John. I must know the rest."

"There is not much more, Andrea. Caroline left Paris to return to Lyndhurst. She didn't want to leave me, but there was simply no other choice for either of us. Her family wouldn't have helped her, she knew that. She was so beside herself at one point that she tried to abort the child, but it didn't work.

"She wrote to tell me that Lyndhurst had taken her back immediately. I received one more letter from her that said he did not seem to suspect at all that the child wasn't his. I was terribly sad, but relieved. I wanted Caroline to be safe, to find happiness, and I knew she wanted the child, our child.

"Then I heard that Lyndhurst was spreading the story that his wife was mad. There is no doubt in my mind that he knew she was pregnant with another man's child. Perhaps he even knew it was me. It is my belief that after the child was born, he murdered Caroline."

"Yes, I guessed that he had," I said. I heard John suck in his breath behind me.

Lawrence said, "I dislike John having to hear these accusations, and that is all they are, base accusations. As to your tawdry *affaire* with my wife, once she told me she was with child, I knew what had happened. It didn't take me long to find out the name of her lover.

"Her attempts at concealment, at perfidy, amused me. Actually, there was never any question at all in my mind. You see, I was unable to impregnate a woman. My seed was lifeless. Thus, it was obvious that Caroline had betrayed me. I did nothing wrong. You are the dishonorable one here, Jameson, not I."

"No, sir," John said. "I don't believe they are simply accusations at all." He sounded so calm, so in control that in the deepest part of me, a bit of hope sprang to life. "I had already come to the conclusion that only you could be behind all the incidents at the Manor—the old woman wearing that marvelous disguise, wielding my Moorish knife, that barbed wire beneath Small Bess's saddle. They were clumsy, yet very effective. You scared both Andy and me witless. There was really no one else to be responsible, but I couldn't bring myself to believe it.

"You are my uncle, after all. You took both Thomas and me into your home after our parents were killed. Despite our differences,

I believed I was important to you, to our line. But you changed, didn't you?

"You did kill poor Caroline, didn't you? She was unfaithful to you, and so you killed her."

"All my surprises," Lawrence said, and there was petulance in his voice. "I believed that you were fooled, for the most part, John. I saw you take her side, saw the way you looked at her, saw the way she looked at you. I laughed to myself, John. I owned her, she was my life, my chattel, and you would never have her, never. Would you have tried to seduce her? Would you have eventually succeeded? Would she, like Caroline, have tried to foist her bastard off on me?"

He was shaking his head and laughing a little. "Ah, but she is so very afraid of men and what men and women do together. I honestly don't believe it ever would have happened, more's the pity. You would have failed.

"Yes, naturally I murdered the faithless bitch. Caroline was a whore, she betrayed me, she deserved to die. It was simple justice."

And there it was, all of it, the betrayal, the

lies, and Caroline's death. No, I thought, her murder, after she had birthed her child.

"Father," I said. "You have a daughter. Her name is Judith. I remember now that when I first saw her, I realized there was something familiar about her. It was myself that I was seeing in her. It was you. She is lovely. She is bright and kind. She will become a beautiful fine woman."

John said from behind me, "I, too, realize that Judith does resemble Andy. I felt a tug of familiarity after you came, Andy, and it is there, of course. All these years, Uncle, you have watched and seen the father in the child, only it was Jameson here, and not you."

I saw the rage in Lawrence's eyes, but with John, with his nephew, he controlled himself. He said nothing at all.

John said, "You did well, Andy. My uncle will wear those scars on his face until he dies."

"She will not be around to see the scars," Lawrence said. "So, did you know of your daughter, Jameson? Or is this a lovely surprise for you?"

My father said, "Yes, I knew of her, I have always known. Caroline managed to sneak a letter out to me before you murdered her. I came to Devbridge Manor. I tried to save her, but I was too late. The story was that she had jumped to her death from a tower at the Manor. Did I believe that she had killed herself? Perhaps in odd moments I did. But I always wondered, and now I know that you destroyed poor Caroline. As for my daughter, there was nothing I could do save pray that you would not hurt her."

Lawrence laughed. He was happy now, his face alight with it. "Do you not wonder, my dear, why I let the child live? The fruit of a whore and your dissolute father? Well, I will tell all of you. Every time I looked at the child, I thought of your miserable father, and how I savored thoughts of my revenge. I knew it would probably take me years to have you in my power. But I knew the day would come, and it has. Caroline's death was but half of my vengeance."

He moved quickly forward and grabbed my arm to pull me from my father. In that second my wounded father, with strength I would have never guessed he still had, lunged toward him and grabbed his throat between his two hands. Freeson and Flynt were on him in an instant, jerking him back,

Flynt striking his face, his wounded shoulder. Now was my chance. I dropped George, jerked the derringer from my belt. I said very precisely, "I will kill the earl if you do not release my father now."

Lawrence didn't hesitate. I saw the fury on his face as he lunged for me. I jumped back out of his reach. He stood there, panting, staring at that small gun I was aiming at him. I said, my voice low and vicious, "Come at me again, old man, and I will put this bullet right between your eyes." I waved my hand at him. "Yes, do come on. Do you wonder if I have the guts to shoot you? Do you think that as a female I cannot do it? That I will perhaps whimper and start to weep? Well, come on, take the gamble."

He didn't move, just stared from my face down to the gun in my hand. "That gun," he said slowly. "Where did you get that gun?"

"I bought it in the village, from dear Mr. Forrester. I believe he traveled to York to fetch it for me. I am not a complete idiot. I knew I had to protect myself. Father, are you all right?"

He had sagged back down onto the bed, breathing hard. "I am all right, Andrea."

Lawrence still stared at that gun, disbelieving. "You shouldn't have a gun. It never occurred to me that you would have a gun. You're only a woman."

I laughed. I actually laughed. "That makes you a fool, then, doesn't it? No, the three of you, don't move, or the old man here is dead. In an instant—that's all it will take. Don't even think about twitching, or he is dead.

"John, come here and let me untie you." The man who was behind him shifted to the side. "Hold still, you fool, or I will kill the man who had paid you. I am a good shot. My grandfather taught me well."

I thought Lawrence would howl. He was flushed nearly scarlet in his rage, in his frustration, but he had no choice. For the first time I had the power and the means to hold him in check. John stepped away from the men and ordered them onto the floor. "Lie on your bellies and put your hands behind your heads." Once they were down, John moved closer and I began to work at his tied wrists.

"Well-done, sweetheart," he said, never taking his eyes off those three men. "In war, a man likes to have someone he trusts guard his back. I am very proud of you."

I think I grew three inches taller at his words. I nearly had the knots unfastened, nearly. I looked away, down at those blasted knots, not longer than a split second—but that was all it took. Lawrence pulled a knife from his cloak, and in a single fluid movement, he hurled it at my father. It struck him cleanly through his wounded shoulder. My father yelled.

The three men jumped to their feet. They looked determined, ready to kill us.

"Stop, damn you all, or I'll shoot the earl."

They didn't stop.

I pulled the trigger.

Chapter Thirty-one

I didn't shoot him between the eyes. My rage, the urgency of the moment, both made my hand jerk. I got him through the thigh. He howled, grabbed his leg, fell to his knees, then toppled to his side.

John was free. The three men were scrambling, but John was faster. He grabbed up two of their guns, and I saw the soldier in action. He was so very calm, so steady, and his voice was deadly. "I have two bullets, gentlemen. One of you will escape death, but which one? Who wants to take the chance? Come on, don't be cowards, do something. Look at the man who paid you to kill innocent people. He isn't going to help you. He will lie there until his leg rots off and he screams his way to Hell. Come on. Don't you want to bring me down?"

The three men looked among themselves, then, very slowly, they lowered themselves back down to the floor.

"Lace your fingers behind your heads."

They did.

I ran to my father. He was unconscious, the knife sticking obscenely out of his shoulder. There was so much blood. I closed my eyes an instant, getting a hold on myself. "You will not die on me, damn you," I said. I jerked off my cloak and tore off my shirt. I ripped it apart, tearing it into wide strips. I made a thick bandage out of the strips. Then I drew a deep breath, and jerked the knife out of his flesh. I nearly retched at the ghastly feel of doing that, the easy slide of the metal through his flesh. I couldn't begin to imagine the pain my father would feel. "I'm sorry," I whispered. "It's out now. I'm sorry."

I pressed with all my strength down on the bleeding wound. He moaned, his eyes closed, but his hand came up over mine. I looked down at his hand. It was big and strong, brown. "You will live," I said. "I swear you will live."

"Yes," he said, and his blue eyes blazed up at me. "Yes, I must." He closed his eyes again, his hand fell away from mine. He was alive, and unconscious. I was grateful for that.

"Keep the pressure up, Andy. You've got to get the bleeding stopped." Then John was beside me, shoving me out of the way. "Kept both guns on our villains here. I'm stronger, I'll apply the pressure."

I stood some feet away from them. I looked at my husband, who was just lying on the floor, unconscious now it seemed, his wounded leg drawn up, blood pooling beneath him.

I had shot him. Would he die? I felt strangely dispassionate about it. He was a murderer. However, I did not want to be a murderess. But I made no move to staunch the flow of blood on his wound. I remained standing where I was, watching those three men.

One of the men moved. I walked over to him, bent down, and knocked him on the head with the butt of a gun. At that moment

I heard some movement, but I wasn't fast enough. Lawrence had come up on his knees. He had a gun in his hands. Another weapon? Was he a bloody arsenal? I suppose so, dammit.

It was George who saved me. He leapt at Lawrence, growling, his teeth bared. I jerked up one of the villain's guns.

Everything happened so quickly, it was a blur. Flynt grabbed my ankle, George attacked Lawrence, and John, without hesitation, picked up the knife his uncle had hurled at my father, and sent it straight through Lawrence's throat. I never even saw the knife, it flew so fast. There was utter surprise on Lawrence's face. He tried to say something, but could not. He dropped the gun and grabbed that knife, but he didn't try to pull it out. I heard an obscene gurgle. Blood gushed out of his mouth. He looked over at my father, and a terrible anger seemed to freeze his expression. He slumped backward onto the floor, George standing over him, barking his head off. He died with that expression on his face.

Flynt, with a cry of fury, jerked hard on my ankle and managed to pull my legs out from under me. I went down hard, but it didn't matter. I was calm now, focused, and I yelled, "Get away from me, Flynt, now, damn you."

But he didn't get away. He was stumbling at me, his hands outstretched, his fingers curved to strangle me. Flynt was beside himself, screaming, "You bloody bitch, I'll kill you. You killed my master. I'll wring your skinny neck off."

I heard John shout something, saw his quick movement, but knew that only I could save myself. I didn't falter. I got hold of myself, knew what I had to do, and I shot Flynt, a clean shot, right in his chest.

There was utter silence in that small room. The two men remained on their faces, glued to the floor. John ran to Flynt and stood looking down at him. "Jesus, I was terrified. You did it, Andy, you did it."

George looked at John and wuffed. His tail began to wag, then faster until it was a blur. Then he jumped at John, a good foot off the floor. John caught my dog up in his arms. "It's all right now, George, quite all right. No, calm yourself now. You did very well. You saved all of us. No, don't relieve yourself on me in your excitement. Good boy."

John carried George over to me. He came down on his knees beside me. "Are you all right, love?"

I slowly nodded. I had no words. We were surrounded by carnage. The smell of blood was thick in the air. I heard my father groan. "I'm all right," I finally managed to whisper.

He kissed me quickly, lightly, on the mouth, patted my cheek, and rose. "Let me bind up your father's shoulder. We need to get to the Manor and have Dr. Boulder fetched as soon as possible. I must also free Boynton from that shed." He paused and said over his shoulder, "I am very proud of you, Andy. You are brave. However, I don't think it's possible that you can love me more than I love you."

My father moaned again.

John immediately sat down and began to bind the wound tightly. "Don't worry," he said, not looking up. "I was a soldier for six years. I have had a lot of practice doing this."

I rose slowly, and picked up the other gun. There was only one bullet left. It was enough, I thought. Neither of these two men cared what had happened to their master, only Flynt, and he didn't care about anything now.

I took a deep breath. All of us were alive. I heard another groan of pain. No matter what my father had done, I didn't want him to die.

I prayed in those moments, prayed that he would survive, prayed with all my heart.

My father did survive.

He now lay between a drugged sleep and unconsciousness, Dr. Boulder remaining at the Manor to take care of him.

Rucker hauled the two men off to the local gaol, and he was none too gentle. I remember John holding me against him, I remember the touch of his mouth against my hair. I remember Boynton wringing John's hand in relief. I remember Thomas and Amelia holding each other, Amelia crying. I remember everyone, their horror at what had happened. And I remember eating in the study, by the fire, John beside me. Then suddenly, without reason really, things just seemed to fade into nothingness. I tried to open my eyes, tried to speak, but I couldn't. What was happening to me?

"It's just been too much," I heard John

say, and I knew he was carrying me. "She's just closed down."

I knew there were people about, I heard them speaking, very quietly, as one always speaks when around a person who is ill. Was I sick or something? I didn't know. I just knew that I was deep inside myself, and I couldn't escape it.

I slept and I dreamed.

I dreamed I heard Peter's voice, dreamed he was holding my hand, lightly running his fingers over my cheek, telling me to wake up, that it was only four days until Christmas and it was rude of me not to welcome him. Had I even bought him a present?

But I couldn't wake up. I floated on blackness, felt emptiness surround me, cocoon me.

And there was Miss Crislock holding up my head, telling me to drink, and so I did, and then I slept so very deeply. Mrs. Redbreast was feeding me, nice warm chicken broth, and I swallowed it. I heard her say that it was lucky that I would swallow it, otherwise I would just wither away and that would be the end of me. I wanted to tell her that I liked it very much, that it slid right to my stomach, and felt marvelously warm. I wanted to tell her that I didn't want to do any withering.

I heard Judith's voice, and she said good morning to me, in a Virginian accent, she told me. Her "morning" stretched to a good half minute. Miss Gillbank laughed, patted my hand, told me to wake up soon, she missed me. I wanted to tell her that I missed her, too. So many people around me, all of them whispering, all of them lightly touching me, patting me, and I wanted to open my eyes. But I couldn't, and I hated it. I wanted to open my mouth and tell them to do something else besides whisper and creep around. I wanted them to yell, to laugh. Yes, I wanted to hear laughter and perhaps some music. But there wasn't any, just whispers and endless, fathomless, deep silence.

It was in the deep of night. I don't know how I knew this, but I did. I felt warmth, supple warmth, and it touched me everywhere. And there was George's wuff, right near my ear. I wanted to smile, wanted to tell George not to drive John mad with his naked adoration.

The warmth covered me and seeped inside me, to my very bones. I realized it was John, and he was holding me against him. I felt his big hands rubbing up and down my back. I felt the hard warmth of him against me. I felt his warm breath against my temple. I liked it. I felt comforted and safe.

He was speaking, his voice warm against my temple. I loved the sound of his voice, the feel of it, how it rumbled deep in his chest. I knew he loved me, knew that he was frantic with worry, but there was just nothing I could do. Then he said, his voice impatient, no whispering now, "Listen to me, now, Andy. I have had quite enough of this. I have treated you kindly, gently, but you haven't come back to me. I have decided that you don't deserve my gentle touch anymore. You will obey me, damn you. You will be my wife, and a wife is supposed to obey her husband.

"Why are you refusing to wake up? You have been like this for six days now. The doctor doesn't know what is wrong with you. He babbles on about shock and female nerves and female brainstorms and such, but I told him that your nerves could stretch from here to France without breaking. As for female brainstorms, I told him you would stomp me to the ground if I ever said anything like that to you. He just shook his head, probably appalled.

"Then I told him that you shot a man and there had been so much death, so much pain and fear, that perhaps you had simply been unable to bear it, that you had retreated to where it was safe, and you would remain there until you could deal with it again. Yes, I suppose I believe that. Perhaps he did, too. He just grunted. I think he liked much more his pronouncement of female brainstorms.

"But it has been six days, damn you, Andy. It is time for you to deal with life again, deal with it, and marry me, and play the pianoforte for me and let me make you laugh. We could wager with Judith on which bush George would select to relieve himself.

"All right, you just listen to me. I love the feel of your breasts, very nice soft breasts you have. I love the feel of your mouth, but your lips are dry. I must remember to rub cream on your mouth. Your father is mending. Dr. Boulder has remained here since the beginning. I think it is because of the excellent meals Cook is preparing. He eats his weight in her thin ham slices.

"It is very cold now, we've had snow for

the past three days, and Small Bess is nearly well. She whinnies whenever someone comes to her stall. She misses you.

"All of us are waiting for you to open your beautiful eyes and make some sort of impertinent announcement, like perhaps demanding a glass of brandy with your chicken broth. And that includes Peter. He has been pacing about, sitting here for hours watching you. He is fast losing his grip, Andy. You must come back to everyone and have your brandy. What do you think?

"Open your eyes, Andy, smile at me. I want to kiss you and teach you how to kiss me. I want to make love to you and show you that a man and a woman can be magic together. We will be magic, you will see. And you will trust me and love me and perhaps even you will leap out at me from behind the occasional door, you will want me so much, and you will kiss me until I am mad with it. And we will be together.

"It's true. You will trust me, Andy. I will be faithful to you until I breathe my very last breath. Then my spirit will be faithful. No insubstantial aura for me. No, I will stick to you until you curse me and wish me to remove myself to the ether. Believe me, Andy. I would never lie to you, ever."

Kiss him until he was mad with it? I liked the sound of that. I felt his big hand on my bottom, pressing me against him. I wanted to be even closer. He was big, and he was strong, and I wasn't in the least afraid of that now. I wanted to laugh at that, laugh at how much I had changed and it was because of him, and I would love him forever. Beyond forever. My aura would be more substantial than his, I wanted to tell him.

He had given my life back to me. I wanted to tell him this, and I did, somewhere deep inside of me.

I don't know how long he spoke to me, how long he held me, and stroked me and kissed me, but it wasn't long enough. I never wanted him to leave. But he was gone then. I felt George lying pressed against my side. Everything was all right.

Then there was a light, I felt it hot against my eyelids. I didn't understand this. No one ever came close with a candle. What was this?

I heard a soft voice saying over and over, "I haven't gotten a chance to get to you alone, damn them all. Always someone close to you, particularly John, may God damn him forever for murdering my dearest Lawrence.

"I feared the drug would wear off and you would wake up, but you didn't. For two days now I had no chance to feed you more. But now I'm here, no one else, and thank God you are still asleep. Now, you wretched girl, let me raise your head so you can drink this lovely potion I mixed up especially for you. I gave it to you that very first night, when you brought Lawrence's dead body home, when you brought your miserable father home and had Dr. Boulder take such excellent care of him. And he will be well and my poor Lawrence is rotting in the cold earth. I gave you the drug and you just collapsed, and everyone saw how distraught I was, how I cried I was so worried about you.

"I gave you the drug one other time, watching it just slide down your throat and lock you deeper inside yourself. Finally, you're getting weaker, just lying here all the time, not moving. Can you even hear me? I wonder. No one really knows. This last drink will send you away, forever, and about time I say."

I was afraid. Miss Crislock was speaking

madness to me. She wanted me dead? She wanted to kill me? She loved Lawrence? I felt her hands on me. No, no, I must be dreaming, a nightmare, no more than a hideous nightmare. I frowned, wanting desperately to wake up. And then I did. I opened my eyes and looked up into Miss Crislock's face.

She had a small glass in her hand filled with a milky-looking liquid.

My mouth didn't want to work, but I knew that I said aloud, "Milly? Why? What are you doing to me? You have always loved me. Why?"

She laughed, but it wasn't the sort of laugh anyone would ever want to hear. It was an ugly laugh, a demented laugh, one filled with hatred. I realized that I was the object of that hatred.

"So you heard everything, did you? I'm killing you, you miserable whelp. Lawrence failed, but I won't. Jameson killed your mother, and I will have to kill him, but you must die first. That will distract everyone, and then I can get rid of him. When your eyes simply remain closed, no one will know what happened to you, just that you faded away, died. The doctor will have nothing at all to say. Nothing will happen to me. No one will ever suspect me. But I will know, and I will smile because I killed you.

"You thought Lawrence was the old woman who appeared in here with that knife, but it wasn't. I played that role. I wanted to scare you into madness, but you have no sensitivity in you, you are hard and tough, too much of this practical earth. Yes, I hoped you would simply fall into hysteria, but I should have known better. You are not your mother's daughter. Lawrence thought it would make you frantic. I hoped it would, but I wasn't as sure as he was. He didn't know you, and so he didn't listen to my concerns. Just look where it got him. It got him murdered by your damned lover, you little bitch."

She grabbed my head and jerked me up. I saw that glass coming closer. I had no strength. "No," I whispered, "no."

"You killed my dearest Lawrence. You deserve to die."

"He was evil," I said. "Evil."

"Oh, no, he was a man betrayed, both by Caroline and by your wretched father. He was a good man, a man who would have married me once you were buried deep in the frozen ground. I came to know him very well when he came to London. I did not want him to marry you, but he convinced me it was necessary. He told me he loved me, only me, and you were only a pawn, for him to gain his vengeance.

"I loved him, do you hear? I would have wedded him. But not now. Now I have nothing. As you fall back asleep this time, think of your father and how he will soon join you. He is weaker than you. He will be with you quickly. I believe I will kill him on Christmas Day. What do you think about that? Ah, and then there is John. Will I kill him? I haven't made up my mind yet."

"No, Milly. You mustn't kill John. He has done nothing wrong. Oh, please, no, don't hurt my father."

"He is pitiful in his weaknesses," she said, hovering over me, too close now, that glass nearly to my mouth. "Here, now, let's end this."

I felt such helpless fear, I was choking on it. Then I heard a man's sharp voice.

"Miss Crislock, let me take this." It was John. He grasped her wrist and pulled the glass from her hand. I saw him hand it to Peter, who stood directly behind him. Then he looked down at me. "Welcome back, Andy."

"You're here. Why are you here?"

"I wondered about the old woman. I wondered even more why you didn't wake up. Peter and I discussed it, decided we would wait in here, just to see if anyone came in. When Miss Crislock entered, we nearly welcomed her, but Peter held me back and we waited and listened to her. She is mad, Andy, her hatred has twisted her. But it's over now, all over, and you're back with me again, thank God."

Suddenly Miss Crislock screamed, a curdling scream that sounded like a demon just released through the gates of hell. She was striking out at both John and Peter, yelling, kicking, her hands flying. I saw Peter pull back his arm and strike her in the jaw with his fist. She collapsed. He simply let her fall to the floor.

George was out from under the covers, wuffing until John, laughing, picked him up. "Just look at your mistress, George. She's finally looking at me again. You know what I think? I think it will be quite some time before she once again believes she can best me, either with her wit or with her fists. What do you think?"

George wuffed.

I was so happy, but there were no more words in me. There didn't seem to be anything. I tried to smile at my beloved cousin Peter, and at the most precious man in the world to me, the man who had brought me from the darkness into blessed light, into freedom, but I felt that blankness drawing at me. I wanted to cry out against it, but I only managed to say, "I am so very sorry. It seems I'm not quite ready to come back."

"No, no, don't leave me again, Andy."

But I knew I had no choice. Everything just went away from me again, I couldn't stop it, and I sighed and closed my eyes.

I heard Peter say, "I will get Dr. Boulder. He is with her father."

John said slowly, "No, she doesn't need him. She will be all right. Look, she's breathing easily. I think she's just asleep." And I felt him kiss my mouth, and say, "I must rub some cream on her lips. They're dry."

And I laughed to myself. When, sometime later, I heard his beloved voice again, I knew my mouth was very soft now.

I opened my eyes. This time I kept them open.

Chapter Thirty-two

Deerfield Hall
Three Months Later

He came to me at Deerfield Hall in early March. It was still cold, more snow swirling on the horizon, ready to blanket the moors, and the Yorkshire winds howled at night.

I saw him standing in the doorway, his hair windblown, wearing riding clothes, and he looked healthy and brown and very big. Too young and strong, I thought, and smiled at him.

"It is time," he said, striding toward me.

And so it was.

Peter gave me away, and our local vicar married us. It was a quiet ceremony, with only our families in attendance and many of our people from both Deerfield Hall and Devbridge Manor.

It was a lovely time, that day. So much merriment and drinking a delicious champagne punch that Peter made himself. And everyone laughed and smiled and wished us well. My little sister even snagged a glass of champagne, thanks to Amelia.

We remained at Deerfield Hall that first night of our married lives.

I will never forget John's first words to me when he walked into my bedchamber to see me lying in the bed wearing a white nightgown with its ribbons tied under my chin, and George clutched to my chest. I was staring at his bare feet, knowing that he didn't have a stitch of clothing on beneath that nice blue velvet dressing gown he was wearing belted at his waist.

He stopped six feet from the bed and said, "I swear to you that I will always love you. You are my wife and will soon be my lover, and together we will share everything there is for a man and a woman to share together.

I pray we will have children, an equal number of each, I hope.

"I will never betray you. Now, George, come here to me. She doesn't need your protection."

And George bounded off the end of the bed and jumped up so John could pick him up.

I was scared, though, I couldn't help it, but John knew what I was feeling, and between very light kisses, he said into my mouth, "In no more than three minutes from now, you will want to sing you will feel so very nice and then you will laugh, and perhaps even yell. I am going to give you pleasure, Andy, and you are going to enjoy yourself immensely. Do you trust me?"

"Yes," I said. "I trust you." I believe I sang an army ditty within two minutes, not three. And when, at last, he came into me, I tensed a moment at the pain, then wept at the wondrous pleasure.

I did yell. As I recall, so did he.

One Month Later
Venice, Italy
Palazzo Dolfin Manin

John held me close, rocking me, as was his habit. I loved to be held by him. I also loved Venice, the dark rich feel of it, the romantic smiling gondoliers who came by each day to sing up to me and wave.

It was April, the weather so sublime even the locals could talk of little else, other than their endless rounds of parties, balls, masquerades, their gambling, their newest lovers, of course.

It was thankfully too early for the ripe summer smells that could send a man to his knees, John told me. I looked up at that incredible blue cloud-strewn sky, and wondered if it ever rained here, if it was ever damp and cold and miserable. Did they ever have a wind that was so strong it would nearly rip your hair from your head?

Not now, in April, they didn't. It was Venice, and I felt its magic to the depths of my soul. The sounds of the gently lapping water of the Grand Canal against the ancient pilings below us soothed me to my very bones.

George liked the sounds, too. He snored more loudly when he napped on the balcony and could hear the water.

It was perhaps a half hour before sunset, the most vivid time of day, when the sun shone gold on the water, and grew so large as it neared the horizon that it seemed to swallow the earth. I stared as the water glistened off that brilliant dying sun, spreading dazzling sharp points of white everywhere. A magic hand had strewn diamonds over the water. I heard a gondolier singing to the dying sun, and I wanted to weep with the wonder of it.

I stretched in my husband's arms, and he dropped a kiss on my forehead. George sat on a cushion beside us, sleeping, his ugly little head resting on his paws.

"We have been here for two weeks now," John said, and kissed my left ear.

"Yes, and the weather is so perfect, so absolutely, impossibly perfect, that I find myself pining for a nice stiff wind off the moors at home."

"When I was a young man, just arrived here, I decided that I wanted to come to Venice with my bride. And because I am a man who can manage just about anything, here we are, my bride and I, all cozied up in Venice. What is this? Are you bored with me already?"

His hand lightly cupped my breast. I leaned into him, wanting to feel his hand, his fingers, the warmth it sent all the way to my belly.

"Perhaps in fifty or so years," I said, and leaned forward to kiss his neck.

"I received a letter from your father today. All goes well with him. He feels fine now, and his diamond-cutting business continues to prosper despite his absence. He will visit us in June. Miss Crislock is being kept in a house near Leeds run by this woman Dr. Boulder knows. He said that she and her staff care for the insane. They are not maltreated. She is fine, Andy."

I nodded, not liking to even think about the woman I had regarded as my second mother. I lightly rubbed my palm over his chest, feeling the slow steady beat of his heart. The feel of him, so different from me. It was still a wonder to me. "I never thought a man could be so precious," I said, and kissed his heart through his jacket.

He laughed, I felt the rumble of it. "Does

this mean that you are thinking spiritual thoughts about me?"

"Probably not."

"Ah, then you want to have your way with me?"

"I rather like that thick carpet in front of the fireplace."

I thought he would swallow his tongue. I had changed so much, and it still occasionally floored him. Of course he was himself responsible for all the changes, and it pleased him enormously.

"Actually," he said, "I do, too. We're alone, and George isn't snoring for the moment."

"It's a miracle."

He laughed and hugged me close. "I will hear your laughter every day of my life. It is a wonderful thing. Now, there is another party for us this evening. The Contessa di Marco. Are you yet tired of all the fetes and *soirées* and balls?"

I shook my head against his shoulder. "I wish to wear that beautiful turquoise silk gown you selected for me. There is something else, too, John. I don't want to leave Venice until we finally see a bit of rain, perhaps a bit of wind, perhaps feel a chill to our bones."

"Then we might be here until next November."

George wuffed, and John added, "He nearly fell into the canal the other day, trying to search out the perfect bush. There wasn't much of a selection for him."

John leaned down and kissed me, not a light, friendly kiss this time, but one that was deep and made me hungry, so very hungry for him. I felt his hand slip inside my gown, touch me, make me want to howl with the glorious pleasure of it. I whispered into his mouth, "I think I would like to throw you down on the carpet, my lord, right now."

"I pray you will never lessen your demands, Andy. Never." He laughed as he rose, carried me in his arms back into our bedchamber, George on our heels, wuffing with every step, his tail high, wagging.

Epilogue

One Year Later
Devbridge Manor
Yorkshire, England

My husband and my dog became proud fathers within a week of each other. On the day after Easter, Miss Bennington, a Scottish terrier so cute that it was hard to stop squeezing her whenever she came near enough for you to grab her, delivered five small balls of fur in the immense basket that sat near the fireplace in our large suite. George stood watch the entire time, occasionally yelping right along with Miss Bennington as she struggled to birth yet another pup. When it was all over, I swear that Miss Bennington looked fit to kill poor George for his part in the matter.

"I fear there is a lesson in this," I said to John, and I wasn't wrong about that, more's the pity. Not even six days later, I was felled by the most ghastly pain I could have ever imagined. John, like George, stayed with me. I remember telling him if he left me, I would have George relieve himself on all of his new cravats that I had made him for his birthday. I cursed him, but it was paltry because I kept having to repeat myself—but I was loud.

I had nearly shouted myself hoarse when Jarrod Franklin Lyndhurst finally decided to make his entrance into the world. I heard him howl when Dr. Boulder smacked his small buttocks. I heard John's voice, so pleased he sounded ready to explode with the wonder of it all. He kissed me and thanked me for his son. "I'm the one who did all the work," I whispered. "Thus, he is *my* son." His kisses and his laughter washed over me, and I smiled even as I fell into a deep sleep.

All in all, holding my tiny son the next day,

I decided it hadn't been all that bad. I was perpetuating a lie, Mrs. Redbreast told me sadly, shaking her head. Yes, she said, all the little mites that were our sons and daughters would make us forget, and then we would do it again. Now, there was something to consider.

My father was here at Devbridge Manor on one of his long visits. It moved me unbearably to see him holding his grandson. When he called Judith in to see her nephew, she smiled at the baby, but immediately came to me.

"You are all right, Andy?"

"I am perfect," I said.

"I heard you, it was awful."

"Yes, but it's over now, and we have Jarrod. What do you think, Judith? Does he look like me or like John?"

"He looks just like his grandfather," my father called out. "Come here, sweetheart, and behold your papa when he was just a babe."

And Judith laughed, at ease now with her father. We had told her no lies, hadn't shaded the truth for Judith. No, she wanted to know everything, and so we told her. She was very quiet for a very long time. Finally, she walked up to her father, looked up at him thoughtfully and said, "You cannot be all bad, sir. You are also Andy's father, and she turned into a very fine sister to me."

And they progressed from that very strange beginning.

As for Thomas and Amelia, they had spent Easter with us as well, but had left the day before Jarrod decided it was time to present himself to his proud parents. The previous spring they had moved to Sussex, to Danvers Grange, the home of Amelia's parents, Lord and Lady Waverleigh. Thomas had taken over the management of the estate so that Lord Waverleigh could travel to Jamaica. Lady Waverleigh said he had become enthralled with voodoo and wanted to study it up close. She just shook her head, smiled at her very handsome, very distracted husband, and said she didn't mind. She was ready to have her bones heated, and she heard that the sun was so bright in the West Indies that she would surely get her wish.

Shortly thereafter, I once more went to Caroline's music room. I walked to the center of the room and just stood there. I walked to the window and looked out at my husband speaking to his valet Boynton. I heard the door close. I didn't turn. Then I heard something behind me, but it didn't frighten me, not in the least. I slowly turned, but naturally there was nothing there, at least nothing I could see. I felt a deep, consuming weariness. And suddenly there was great warmth, as if someone had lit a fire and it had caught very quickly. I was tired and warm, and I eased myself down on the floor. I felt the warmth flow through me. I felt an immense sense of peace, and then I fell asleep.

When John, his face white, leaned over me, I just smiled up at him and said, "Caroline is fine now. Everything is all right."

There was no menace now in the Black Chamber. Lawrence had been the evil, and he was dead. I had the small room painted white the following day, laid a lush white carpet on the floor, and white curtains at the single window. Judith liked to come to that room. She furnished it with a lovely Louis XV desk and small settee. She set her mother's harp in the corner. A pianoforte soon joined it. She announced, that the White Chamber was now her music room. Caroline, I thought, you would be so proud of her.

Before Amelia and Thomas had left after

Easter, she eyed my big belly and told me she was also pregnant. Even as she spoke to me, she couldn't take her eyes off Thomas. She now had everything, she said. She was mistress of her own home, she would have a child, and, oh, goodness, just look at Thomas—and I did, of course. He was beautiful, nothing new in that, but more than that, he hadn't been felled by a single cold, a single twitch, not even a single crisis of nerves. Actually, truth be told, he looked like a god now, completely fit, his face tanned from working with the farmers, another activity Lord Waverleigh recommended to keep him healthy. John just looked at his brother and grinned.

Miss Crislock died the preceding November, which, I suppose, was a blessing for her. It still brought me pain when I thought of her and what she had become.

As for my husband, the proud papa, in the days following Jarrod's birth, he whistled a great deal, and laughed, and caught me behind a dressing screen to kiss me and tell me that he would allow me to drink brandy with him at dinner that night.

Life, I thought, as I smiled at my sleeping small son, was very sweet. But having life,

I knew that I had to savor every blessed moment. I looked up when John came into our bedchamber. He had a bunch of beautiful blooming flowers in his hands. "From the Batherstoke's greenhouse, where our Miss Bennington used to live. The flowers are in appreciation for bringing George into her life and into theirs."

I heard George barking outside. John had inadvertently closed the door. I looked over at all of George's offspring nestled together in the big basket by the fireplace, Miss Bennington licking them.

John let George in, and he marched immediately to the basket. He took his post, standing tall, his topknot quivering, his tail waving gently to and fro, their protector.

I laughed and hugged my son and his proud papa to me.

COUNTY LIBRARY
TILLAMOOK, ORE.